The Witches of Claw and Fang

by

Zach Stivers

The Witches of Claw and Fang

Cover Art by *The Wild Rose Press, Inc.*

The Wild Rose Press, Inc.
PO Box 708
Adams Basin, NY 14410-0708
Visit us at www.thewildrosepress.com

Publishing History
First Edition, 2024
Trade Paperback ISBN 978-1-5092-5686-0
Digital ISBN 978-1-5092-5687-7

Published in the United States of America

Dedication

To Mom, for all the stories, from the very beginning.

Author's Note

The Blue Ridge Mountains are old.

As far as Earth's mountains go, they count themselves amongst some of the oldest. Most of their peaks have been smoothed and softened over the eons by the gentle but inevitable squeeze of time. Their forests are likewise ancient, the same woods have seen and suffered the progress of mankind, watched as tribes of early humans crossed into their shade from the north and the west and found the glens and valleys and meadows to be to their liking, watched as thousands of years later, different tribes arrived from the east, from the coast, more pale and more consumptive, greedier for wood and land.

Being surrounded by such ancient mountains, the prevailing scientific community believes Shenandoah valley in Virginia to be at near-zero risk of any seismic activities. Nevertheless, on October thirtieth, a magnitude six-point-five earthquake tore across the region. It devastated roadways and mountain passes and bridges, isolating the small region, cutting it off from the rest of the state.

Buildings shook almost to collapse in the valley, in small towns like Pineville, Luray, and Elkton, yet in cities just over the mountains, like Charlottesville to the east and Harrisonburg to the west, they barely trembled. Happening so late in the evening—*more accurately, early in the morning*—most people in those cities slept through the quake, waking to find barely a mention of it on their local news channels the next morning. This may be hard to believe, considering the extensive coverage that the aftermath of the earthquake received, but it is so.

It took nearly forty-eight hours for the horrors of the earthquake's devastation to be revealed to the press. In fact, only the most sensitive seismographs in Washington D.C. and Baltimore even registered that there had been any significant geological activity east of the Mississippi river, and it seemed so small that no follow-up was flagged necessary by the monitoring computers.

The other obvious factor, also now known to the public, which slowed the already delayed emergency response was the unusually high amount of rain that fell in the valley. Coinciding with the earthquake, the torrential rainfall significantly reduced the accessibility to the valley for nearly two days. Lesser known by the public is that the evening before the quake the weathermen set the chance of rain at only about thirty percent and projected that some areas could receive a quarter inch of rain, while others throughout the valley wouldn't see a drop.

Instead, the front met unexpectedly warmer air than projected, and a heavy tropical system developed and persisted over the valley for nearly twenty hours. The rainfall measured nine-point-three inches at Shenandoah National Park ranger station at the Swift Run Gap entrance. Though not official, areas further northwest, at lower elevation more central in the valley, were estimated to have received upward of twelve inches. Creeks and rivers surged, and due to the damage from the earthquake, many waterways ran in new and unexpected directions. The flooding at certain low points in the valley quickly became life threatening.

This double-pronged set of unusual variables may explain the lack of communication that was possible with areas beyond the mountains, and certainly explained the delayed emergency response. Some townspeople in Pineville would suggest something else influenced their extended period of isolation, though none of those claims have ever been substantiated by any scientific evidence.

Had it been ten or fifteen degrees cooler that autumn day in the Shenandoah valley, the area might have set a new record for snowfall. But it was not, so it did not, and instead the rain continued to fall and the rivers and creeks continued to rise and the towns remained cut off from the rest of the state.

Above are the facts that we know to be true, that anyone can verify with a simple internet query. Below is the rest of the story.

I've changed some names, but not all. I've changed some places, but not by too much. Mostly just enough to protect the few fools who would try to seek out these places… to their own demise.

After countless hours of research, I almost threw it all away. But one factor stayed my hand. It is important that *HER* story is told to the public. It is one that deserves to be told, even if it is dangerous. Even if it makes some folks toss and turn at night. But what follows is what I've determined to be the truth. Or close enough to make no difference. Many may call this account a fairy tale. Pure speculative fantasy fiction. And that's fine. I would have too, if I hadn't done the interviews, hadn't visited the town, hadn't hiked the old Virginian trails, hadn't seen the hidden cabin. So I can't call it fiction, even though some nights, I really wish I could.

So, instead, I'll call it what it really is.

A tribute.

To Morgan.

Prologue

October Thirtieth, 12:08 a.m.

A silver-haired man in a loosened tie eased back into the depths of a well-worn leather chair, careful not to spill his steaming cup of tea. He set aside the hot mug and turned his attention to his novel, flipping page by page to find where he had left off. The soft swish of the shadow-thin pages ruffled through the air, faster and faster, as he proceeded along through the story in double time, seeing only a few short words, knowing he'd seen them before.

Swish, swish, swish.

He stopped, flipped backward a single page. The backward turn was softer, gentler, a curious half-ruffle, more attentive, not quite committed to a full turn back.

He found his spot.

He lifted the leather book to his nose, inhaling the forever-scent of the ancient thin paper, noting just a hint of vanilla and the salty, oily smell of the ink of a civilization over a thousand years hence extinguished. He smiled and lifted his mug. He wafted the tea under his nose, exchanging the smell of extinction with that of chai and cinnamon, feeling warm, wet air against his upper lip.

Tilting his head, he glanced at the dead body in the corner of the room. He stared, as if waiting to see movement, but nothing stirred across the cabin, especially not the corpse. He sighed, focused back onto his book, disregarding the dead body with the strange black stitching etched across the throat.

Rain began to fall outside, and the drops landed fast and heavy against the wooden deck and against the timber roof, on the tall juniper trees and even taller maple trees. The rain drenched the whole mountain meadow, falling so heavy and loud and thick that the drops themselves seemed to meld together into a single sheet of water as infinite as the moon, never ceasing or pausing, just drowning out the entire world.

Drowning out the world, save one noise.

A heavy thud.

It lifted the faintest smile to the man's lips. A singular knock, insistent and curious and reverberating, from beyond the thick hardwood door that led to the basement of the cabin. A solid beam of wood was levered across the door earlier in the day, and now it rattled with the strength of the knocking.

Thud.

The man swished over another page, and the knocking continued. The heavy wood rattled, and the man in the cozy leather chair sipped his chai, the faint echo of a smile still lingering on his face. The swishing of the pages continued, as did the torrential downpour of the rain, as did the regular thumping, rattling knocks against the basement door. The corpse in the corner continued to lay in the corner, unmoving, as corpses usually do.

Swish.
Thud.
Swish.

Thud.

CRACK.

The world shook.

The wooden beams groaned, straining under the stress of holding the walls together as the ground underneath rocked, threatening to topple the whole cabin.

Something loosened behind the basement door, deep in the ground, from within the bowels of the mountain. A great bulk of something shook free. What had once been just a small crevice became a gaping vacuum of empty space, a wide tunnel connecting to a great, dark cavern hidden deep in the earth's underbelly.

The shaking continued for nearly three minutes and all the while the man sat in the leather chair with his legs crossed, the book resting gently on his lap, a hint of a smile turning the corner of his lips, waiting.

Part One
Wolves

Chapter 1

October Third, 6:27 p.m.

Red maple and brown oak leaves chased each other through the air, crinkling and spinning in the musical rustle of the autumn wind. As they swirled, they whispered of an ancient magic in a language only Morgan could hear, if she listened exactly right.

Though she watched them, playing in the twilight breeze, delirious after being shorn free from the twigs and branches that had held them dear and nourished them all spring and summer long, she did not reach out and indulge in the mystical golden resonance of their aura. They floated for a moment, daring gravity to take them, or perhaps for the auburn-haired woman with the soft green eyes to reach out and embrace them, but the wind picked up and the leaves raced off toward the midnight purple mountains at the horizon.

Morgan shuddered at the sudden cold.

She shifted the bag of vegetables into her left arm and used her right to pull her sweater tighter around her neck.

"Thank you again, Mr. Crawford," she said to the flannel-wearing farmer with the balding head and thick gray mustache.

"Like I told you last week, and the week before that,

it's just Tom, dear."

"My grandmamma raised a polite young lady, Mr. Crawford."

"Polite young ladies are supposed to listen to their elders, not stubbornly insist on calling old men Mister." Tom raised his eyebrows. "That includes grumpy old farmers, I think."

She smiled, checked her watch, almost dumped her bag of produce. "I'm sorry I made you wait. I would have been here sooner…"

"But you were too busy watching the leaves blow off in the wind?"

She tried to keep her smile, but it cracked and faded. "No, I was too busy… just… too busy. Come on, Joey!"

A white and black dog trotted out from the apple trees. His tongue hung lopsided out of his mouth as he tromped closer, heading toward the small silver sedan parked next to the two humans. The mutt paused in the grass, just at the edge of the driveway, sniffed, and then whined.

"Tire yourself out yet?" Morgan asked.

The dog whined back, wagging his tail. Morgan opened her car door, but he darted off in the other direction, back out toward the trees.

"No! Joey, stop! Joey, get back here!"

Joey did not get back here, did not stop, did not even slow down.

She tossed her full bag of veggies into the front seat, slammed the door, and took off after him. Her unbuttoned sweater fluttered out behind her like a cloak as the October winds gusted through the orchard.

She should never have let Alex talk her into adopting the animal. And then he'd gone and left her with him, left her with all the cats and *his* dog and the bills, and the big house out in the forest with all the land that he promised he would clear and never did.

Morgan slipped and fell, and her hand sunk into a pile of manure.

"Oh," she murmured.

Quick as silver, the dog was back at her side and he licked her face and his head cocked, and it seemed he could tell something was wrong as he sat down next to her. He wagged his tail but did not run off.

Tom Crawford limped over, one painful step at a time. He reached down and helped her stand up. Offered her a rag from his overalls. "Just a little bit of compost, that's all."

She wiped her hand off and quickly handed his rag back to him. "Thank you. Now come, Joey." She grabbed the dog by the collar and hauled him back toward the car, saying, "You don't run off, not for a second! Do not leave me, Joey. You can't run off and leave me too."

"You know," Tom hollered, limping after her, unable to keep up, "my table is always open, dear. For dinner… or just to talk."

"Thanks, Mr. Crawford, but I've got to get back home." She did not look back.

Tom exhaled deeply, loud enough for Morgan to stop to listen to what he said next.

"This valley, it's not right. It's not easy on folks." Tom hesitated, as if he had another thing to add on the tip of his tongue.

Here we go.

"You don't have to go through this alone," he said in a clear, flat voice. Morgan had already stopped

6

walking. Now she looked back at him. He nodded his head, met her eyes. "You *aren't* going through this alone."

She wasn't sure if there were tears in his eyes because at that moment her own tears were welling up, and she wiped roughly at them. She snapped around, opened the car door, urged the dog in, and then turned back to the farmer.

Mr. Crawford tried one more time. "I've been marinating pork chops since dawn. Old family recipe. Plenty to go around…"

Deep breath.

"I really do appreciate it, Tom, but… I just, um… not tonight, alright? Sometime soon, I will take you up on that offer." She saw the disappointment grow on his face. Added, "I promise. Just not tonight, okay?"

"Sometime real soon, I hope."

She got in the car, dabbed at her eyes with the back of her wrists, and inhaled slowly.

In through the nose, out through the mouth.

She would not have a full on break down in front of Tom Crawford.

In through the nose, out through the mouth.

She backed out of the farmer's long driveway and drove toward home.

The wind blew leaves across her windshield. As they rushed past, they pulsed with the sweet memories of magic that she could almost reach out and touch, but she did not notice them.

She barely even noticed the winding curves of the road as she followed it hypnotically up and down and around the hilly fields. She did not notice the cows all huddled together, facing outward in a circle, as she came around a gentle bend that led toward the foot of the mountains. She did not spare a second glance at the moon, bright red and full, peeking over the mountains to the east, catching the last arcing slice of the sun as it set into the mountains at the opposite horizon. The fields and the last vestiges of daylight vanished in a flash as she whipped around another bend and dropped into a thick cluster of gloomy woods.

The last stretch to her home was nothing but trees and shadows. Her headlights flashed across dark green bushes and dark tree trunks around the next bend and illuminated a big deer.

In the middle of the road.

Morgan slammed on her brakes, Joey smashed into the front passenger seat, and the bag of veggies tipped over and spilled out onto the floormats. The deer just stared at them for a moment, blinking vacantly at the car idling just feet away. Joey shook off his stupor, saw the deer, and started barking.

The deer lunged back into the forest.

"Quiet, Joey. It's gone. Quiet. Joseph! Enough!"

The dog quit barking but whined, looking at her and then back out into the dark woods where the deer had disappeared.

Normally when this happened, with her heart beating in her chest, Morgan would call Alex so he could calm her down and talk to her while she finished driving home. But Alex didn't answer calls anymore, so she sighed, continued around the bend, and drove carefully and slowly the rest of the way home.

Before she pulled into her driveway, she paused at her mailbox and pulled out three envelopes.

Ambulance bill. Hospital bill. Debt consolidation

scam.

She only had a few more days before some of her bills would end up in collections. Part of her worried. Another part of her couldn't care at all. All the burdensome legal ramifications of bankruptcy might be a nice distraction from the darkness of her depression.

Joey whined, wondering why they were stopped when he could see their house from the road.

"He's not going to be there, Joey."

How could she make him understand?

"He's gone, Joey!"

The dog whimpered with excitement as she pulled up onto the gravel drive and thumped his tail faster as she came to a stop, and it broke her heart.

Joey couldn't understand.

Couldn't understand what a gun with eleven bullets in it instead of twelve meant. Didn't understand why they were sleeping in the guest bedroom and why she didn't use the big bathroom anymore. Didn't understand why it still smelt like Alex, but he was never home anymore, would never be home again, why she cried when she pulled out the winter jackets and buried her head in the big one that Alex used to wear when he would shovel snow off her car in the morning before work.

No, Joey couldn't understand that, so Joey leapt out of the car as soon as she let him out and darted up the deck stairs and sat at the front door, tail going back and forth, sweeping an innocent, hopeful triangle behind his butt, thinking 'Tonight is the night, tonight is the night, tonight is the night. Dad will be home tonight.'

She sighed and wiped her eyes and leaned in and reloaded the veggies one at a time back into the bag, her head pressed against the seat as she rooted around on the floor mats. Joey started barking.

"I said he's not there!"

She felt the final onion just on her fingertips, but she couldn't quite reach it. She adjusted and stretched out her hand... Joey's barking got louder, closer, and more frantic.

What the hell was the matter with the dog?

The car jolted sideways, slamming Morgan in the shins, knocking her legs out behind her, wrenching the breath out of her lungs. A massive vice-like hand gripped her ankle, yanked her upward and tossed her haphazardly into the air. She crashed down into the lawn some twenty yards away, her skull bouncing hard off the ground. She blinked, trying to clear her head. She was in the middle of the lawn.

How was she in the middle of the lawn?

Joey yelped. She looked over as a massive furry brown *thing* slapped Joey halfway across the yard. Bear, she thought, in a detached, concussed sort-of-way, but it was clearly not a bear.

It was taller and thinner than a bear and it looked more wolf than bear and it looked more demonic than either wolf or bear and it glared at her with ferocious golden eyes. It took a step toward her, and she could see it had a thick scar running up its ribs onto its neck, could see sinewy muscles under brown fur, could see absurdly large white teeth inside a snarling lupine mouth. Could see a torn piece of her mail haphazardly dangling from its sickeningly large, clawed hands.

A scream got stuck in her throat.

Fear flooded her mind, pushing out the fog of the concussion. She knew she needed to act, before the monster turned her and Joey into dinner. But she felt pressed frozen into the ground.

Joey found his courage before she did. The dog barked and lunged at the monster. The beast leapt toward Joey.

"No!"

She pushed out her hands, fingers dancing, wrists snapping with an instinctual twist. The wind gusted behind her, and she heard a musical sizzling *zap* and the demon-wolf-thing, mere moments from striking Joey, yelped and leapt back, fleeing for the woods. Joey barked at it and chased it to the edge of the property but did not follow it past the tree line. Morgan ran for the front door, pulling the keys from her sweater pocket.

"Joey, come!"

She fumbled at the deadbolt. She tried the wrong key at first in her panic, flipped and flipped the key chain around, almost dropped the key chain completely, found the right key, jammed it at the door and it bounced off the hole and then it bounced off the hole again and she knew the beast-monster must be emerging from the woods by now, surely it was coming for her, blood-red slobber dripping off its fangs, and she realized she still was using the wrong key and she groaned and then she found it, the correct key, finally—*thank god*—but her hands trembled and the key wouldn't slide in the hole, and then the keys slipped out from her sweaty fingers and they dropped onto the deck, and then, as if in slow motion, gravity pulled them through a crack between the wood planks and the blackness under the deck consumed them.

She wanted to scream and yell and pound on the door.

Focus.

She heard rustling in the woods.

Joey began barking again at her side.

It's coming.

In through the nose, out through the mouth.

She pressed two fingers against the keyhole, extended her other hand out into the air, flicked her fingers, and visualized the lock turning.

Remember.

Remember the old ways.

Remember what your father forbid.

The door unlocked.

She threw it open. Joey dashed inside. She dashed inside.

Slammed the door. Twisted the deadbolt, twisted the doorknob lock, stumbled back toward the center of the living room.

Nothing came bounding up and knocking against the walls. The house was silent. She could hear the fall winds rushing around her home, but no creature stirred outside. No beast-monster had rushed out of the woods to blow the house down, let alone come stomping and snarling up her stairs to tear through the front door or smash through the windows.

After a few minutes of staring numbly, she eased herself down onto the edge of the couch.

Maybe it was just a big, starving bear.

Maybe it had been rabid.

Maybe it had been Joey that scared it off.

But none of those things were true, and she knew it. It had *not* been a bear; bears don't have long fingers that grab ankles. It had *not* been rabid; rabid things are unwell, but not malevolent, not vile, not demonic. It had *not* been Joey who scared it off; it had been her, with a surge of something that she didn't even let herself think about anymore, let alone practice. The same *something* that she used to unlock her door without a key. Joey certainly didn't do that. Morgan had done that.

She reached for her phone, but it was not in her pocket. It was probably lying in the middle of the front yard. Her car door was still hanging open, and the little interior light was still shining.

She could get her keys from under the deck in the morning once the sun came up. But if she didn't go out and close her door, her car battery would be dead in the morning. And if she didn't get her phone, she couldn't call for help, or call the police to report a 'bear' attack.

If you had fought for a landline, you wouldn't need to go get your cell phone. You'd be able to call for help right now.

She needed to call, right?

Someone else could be attacked by that… thing. Someone needed to do something. But what would she say to the sheriff?

Hi, I'd like to report that a demon-wolf-monster attacked me.

What would the police do? Other than maybe throwing her in the mental hospital. 'Poor widow Morgan,' they'd say, 'she finally snapped.'

She saw the creature in her mind's eye, nearly eight feet of thick muscles coated in brown fur, dinner-plate-sized hands with whistle-sharp claws, treacherous gray scar slashed across its ribs.

One step at a time.

She needed to get the phone.

She stood up from the couch. Joey whined at her.

Shadow, the black cat with the crooked tail, meowed

and cut in front of her. She glanced out the front windows again. Nothing moved. She would go quickly. She would be right back. She would call the police. And then when the sun came up, everything would be okay again.

Well, not okay.

It would still be pitiful, depressing, and meaningless, but it would be ordinarily depressing again. She fought with enough monstrous thoughts in her own head, she was not cut out for dealing with any other monsters.

Once upon a time, maybe she was, but not now.

Deep breath, Morgan. You can do this.

Find the phone, shut the car door, run back upstairs, call the police. Then forget this ever happened.

She reached out, twisted the deadbolt, and threw open the door.

Chapter 2

October Third, 6:42 p.m.

Just over three hours into a six-hour road trip and Max already wanted a beer. He picked up his cell phone and glanced at the service bars. One lone bar popped up and then dropped away. Still nothing came through, and the last message he tried to send stuck out with a little red exclamation point next to it. He scowled and tossed the phone into the passenger seat. He'd adapted to the technology, but that didn't mean he liked it.

Thick clouds, rolling hills, and an incoming cold front had transformed what might have been a scenic sunset drive into a frustrating gray drive through a darkening veil of fog and shadow. The forest trees flickered past his windows like the flipping pages of a black sketchbook. Only there was no hidden image behind those trees. Just more trees and darkness and boredom.

Max had made multiple mistakes on this trip, which he usually didn't make, but he blamed the office secretary. Truth was, though, he *could* have waited to leave until the morning. He *could* have packed thoroughly and checked the weather, and pre-downloaded his podcasts in case of bad service, and he *could* have confirmed with Eric that no one else from the company had already reached out to these customers.

But that attitude wasn't what made him the top annuities man in the Capital region.

He didn't even bother to stop off at his newest apartment. Instead of planning and proactively checking the online sales database, he grabbed his spare suit and tie from the office, bought two neon-green energy drinks with enough caffeine to wake a dead elephant and escaped out of DC before almost everyone else did. Traffic still sucked, but it *could* have sucked tremendously worse, and therefore Max indulged in a little smirk as he crawled out on I-61 at forty miles an hour, thinking he'd be in Charleston, West Virginia before midnight. Quick shower and shave and an early morning meeting would put him on track to be back in DC in time for a couple Friday afternoon beers before dinner, and if he upsold the client just a hair above what they were asking for, he'd win tickets to the football game Sunday night.

Someone else may have already had dibs on the client, but, well, Max wasn't in sales to make friends, and forgiveness was always better than permission. He could care less if he pissed off anyone on the sales team. He'd felt that way from the beginning of the job.

They found his nickname inscribed on his old Army satchel during one of his first weeks.

'Maximum Grim.'

AKA the Grim Reaper. His soldier buddies called him Grim for short. The sales team would never know where the nickname really came from, nor what it had come to truly mean, but ever since they discovered the alias Max had heard them whispering it in the office.

'Max Grim,' as temperamental as a summer storm.

'Max Grim,' the asshole who didn't play nice with

guest speakers at team meetings.

'Max Grim,' who gave one syllable answers to complex, open-ended questions.

It was fitting, because he closed deals as consistently as the Grim Reaper harvested souls and because he was a grim son-of-a-bitch. And so, if that's what they thought, then that's how Max acted. Someone else hadn't been answering their calls on a late Thursday afternoon in the office, call transfers to Max, Max gets the deal.

Snooze, you lose. 'Maximum Grim' steals another one before the weekend.

But now Max wasn't feeling so great about the decision to leave town early and drive through the night. The fog was getting thicker and Max couldn't zone out on the drive like he usually did. The mountain roads were winding back and forth, tight corners with big blind spots and nothing on the radio except old country music that sounded suspiciously like gospel.

He snapped the music off. Tossed his sunglasses over into the passenger seat. Too dark for those now.

Three different mountain ranges, four different state parks to make it to Charleston. Who knew there was still this much untamed wilderness east of the Mississippi? Max hadn't seen a stop light in forty miles, let alone a gas station or a place to eat.

All trees and mountains and long, twisting roads.

If only he could get one of his serial killer podcasts going, that would really brighten up the evening. And if he saw a gas station with cold beer, he might just call his most recent ex-girlfriend and apologize.

Well, let's not get carried away.

He glanced at his phone again and surprisingly he had one little bar. No 5G, and no LTE, but the lone bar floated there, unwavering. Maybe enough to try to push through his message to Eric. That way at least someone knew he was out of town and wouldn't be logging in or checking emails first thing tomorrow. A pang of loneliness slipped through him. If he didn't say anything to his boss, nobody would notice him missing for ten days. He had vacation next week, so they'd all think he kicked off on a Thursday for a long weekend before a week off. Classic Grim, just disappear, not say goodbye to anyone.

"Better to have no one to worry, that way you have no one to hurt," he murmured out of habit, glancing at his own dark eyes in the rearview mirror.

—You are talking to yourself again, Maximillian.—

Max scowled as he curved down out of the mountain pass and into a foggy valley. He passed a reflective blue sign that read:

Historic Pineville, Virginia, 1.75 miles, *Come for the history, stay for the people.*

I'm not coming for history or staying for shit.

Ahead, a fluorescent neon sign flickered above a rural gas station.

He pulled into the small parking lot and drew up behind a red truck blocking the one and only gas pump. No one stood around outside. Max walked inside to piss and buy a six pack.

He did not actually contemplate calling his ex.

A greasy, acne-covered twenty-something-year-old behind the counter looked up when he walked in, nodded at him, and went back to reading a magazine. The owner of the red truck must have been the big ol' boy standing in the snack aisle, contemplating the nutritional value between the ho-hos and the twinkies. Max walked through the lobby, and the big man looked over, stared right at him. Max stared back until he walked around the corner and then into the restroom.

It was about as dirty as you'd expect. The last annual cleaning had clearly been skipped, and a lot of grimy messages had been smeared haphazard across the walls. Thankfully, Max could stand to do the business he needed to do. As he peed, he perused the words nearby.

The usual 'Mike sucks' and 'for a good time, I call your mom' messages were plentiful, spaced out neatly by some very artistic illustrations of male and female genitalia. One message in spray paint that crowded almost the whole sidewall said, 'don't fear the moon, fear the witches,' which Max found rather misplaced amongst all the other sexually explicit language.

'*Don't fear the moon, fear the witches.*'

Sounded like a heavy metal lyric.

Max finished, looked at the nasty sink, and decided to skip out on washing his hands. His junk was surely cleaner than *that* faucet handle.

He used his foot to pry open the door and shuffled out of the bathroom. The red truck owner was standing at the counter. He had decided to go with both the ho-ho and the twinkie and had gotten a bag of beef jerky to round out his meal.

Max meandered over to the beer cooler. Eighteen packs of Pal light and Grainer light took up the bulk of the cooler.

Christ. He really was in the middle of nowhere.

He scanned up higher and saw six packs of Pal heavy and Tierra Montana and something called Pineville Porter by a brewery called 'The Dugout.' It looked dark and crafty so he grabbed that and walked over to the counter.

"That it?" The cashier asked.

"Yup," Max replied.

"That dude out there." The cashier gulped and then gestured out toward the parking lot. The other customer was standing by Max's blue ford fusion, lumbering around, peeking in the windows. "Don't listen to him if he says anything, man. Just leave."

"What?"

"Uh, he's been acting strange lately," the cashier said, sliding the pack of beer back to Max. He rubbed his neck, nervous, then continued. "He loitered around in here, man, 'til you pulled in." The boy's voice cracked as he spoke the last words. "I would just get in your car and leave."

Small town weirdos.

Max nodded at the teenager with sarcastic gravitas then walked outside.

He pulled one of the glass bottles out, twisted the top off and sucked back three solid gulps standing on the curb, and then walked over to his car.

"See anything in there you like?" Max asked.

The man didn't move at first, just kept staring. Max was about to ask him again when he finally stood up to his full height and looked back over his shoulder.

"Ain't never seen one of these here hybrids before. What's that mean, you don't need no gas?" His voice was slow and halting. Like English was a second language. But he looked like a thoroughbred hillbilly that had never left the mountains of Virginia, so Max pegged him for grasping only one language, and barely just.

What really is the point of post-elementary education, anyway? Hit the basics, addition, subtraction, get that third-grade diploma, and then help sling moonshine and meth with your older cousin Daryll. A classic backwoods story.

"No, friend," Max said, slowly, making sure the man understood him. "I still need gas. That's why I parked behind you at the *gas pump* while you were looking for your dinner."

The big man scratched his belly, looking Max up and down. "You know," he said, "around here, we say it ain't nice to be a smartass to strangers."

Max snorted and met his eyes, "Yeah well, round where I'm from it *isn't* nice to stare in somebody else's car."

The big man smiled wide. Tobacco-stained teeth, crooked and flat, glistened under the halogen lights. His head was as square as a picture frame and his neck was as thick as an NFL offensive lineman. Max had to admit, if he did miraculously make it to high school, he definitely would have made varsity.

He reached out a fat hand. "Name's Victor. Folks round here call me Vic."

Max looked at the hand but didn't take it.

The redneck chuckled, put his hand back in his pocket. "Alright, then, be that way. Best to remember your manners out here in the country, though, I'll say that. Now you have a good night, stranger, hear?"

Max just stared back until Victor turned and walked away. He lumbered back to his truck, took his sweet time getting in and starting it up. The truck idled for a while, but it never pulled away from the pump. Max leaned on his hood and waited. Drank his beer, tried to remember *his manners*.

And his anger management.

After he had finished his beer, the truck was still wheezing in front of the pump. Max ran his tongue along his teeth, enjoying the feeling of sharpness when his tongue grazed his canines. Anger management had never been easy for Max. Even more so lately.

He strode up to the truck window. The big man was fiddling with his bag of beef jerky, trying to open it.

Max smacked his hand against the glass. "Move out of the fucking way!"

Vic didn't flinch. He turned and smiled at Max. He reached over and cranked down his window, one slow turn at a time.

Of course, he had a crank window.

"Excuse me? I couldn't hear you through the glass."

"Yes, you could hear me. Quit with the thick-skulled, tough guy, small-town bullshit. Get your truck out of the way of the pump."

The big man smiled even wider. "That ain't very polite. You're going to have to ask nice."

Max took a deep breath.

Goosfraba.

Victor probably had a revolver in his glove box and would love to point it at somebody.

"Please," Max said, grinding his teeth, feeling the rays of the full moon shining down on him, "move your fucking truck up, *sir*."

The big man looked at himself in the rearview mirror, his eyes glazed over, and he muttered, "I do oppose my patience to his fury, and am arm'd to suffer with a quietness of spirit, the very tyranny and rage of his." He itched his nose, took a substantial chunk of jerky, and stuffed it in his mouth. His eyes turned back to Max, no longer hazy, and said, "I'll move it in a little while. Just you sit back in your fancy hybrid and wait your turn."

Max furrowed his eyebrows together.

Victor just took another big chomp of jerky.

Calm. Be calm.

Goosfraba.

Goosfraba.

Use your words.

"Reading furnishes the mind only with materials of knowledge, it is thinking that makes what we read ours," Max said, drawing from his own unusual wealth of useless literary quotes. "I'd suggest you stop memorizing Shakespeare and start thinking about being less of an asshole to out-of-towners."

Max held the redneck's eyes for a lingering moment, waiting to see if the hillbilly had another smart comeback or another book to quote, which he seemingly did not, so Max walked back to his car. He sat the six pack down on the passenger seat. He pulled another beer from the case, hit the push-to-start, and reversed out of the gas station. Truth was, he had at least another sixty to seventy miles before empty. No reason to make a scene or to lose control at some backwoods gas station. Especially with alcohol in him.

—I really wanted you to lose control, Maximillian.—

But I didn't, Grim.

That was a win.

He took a long slug of beer number two and hit 'Continue' on his map display. He looked up in his rear-view mirror and saw the red ford truck pull out and follow him. Max shook his head in disbelief.

Grim smiled.

Chapter 3

October Third, 8:19 p.m.

Morgan didn't see the creature as she raced down her front deck steps, didn't see it when she made it to her car. She didn't see the creature when she slammed shut the car door, deciding her spilled veggies would not be bothered with until daylight. She didn't see the creature as she swept through her front yard, moving toward the crumpled grass where she had been tossed. She almost gave up searching but then remembered her bracelet that Alex had gotten her, the one that had a little charm and when you squeezed it… her phone buzzed and lit up in the grass a few paces away. She didn't see the creature when she bent down and scooped up her phone.

But the creature saw her.

And smelt her. And wanted her.

Its eyes, if they were caught in a flashlight or headlight beam, would shine golden amber, like most nocturnal carnivores, but no light illuminated them now.

It had circled her property, followed the tree line, and smelt the urine spots of the overweight domestic dog. The creature laid up in the bramble at the high side of her front yard. Watched her come around her house and descend to her car. It crept, one paw at a time, through the darkness toward her.

But it hesitated.

She'd sent invisible fire from her hands, somehow.

The invisible fire hurt. Cautioned from another direct attack.

The creature dropped down, waiting in the darkness. The woman took her little box of light and dashed back toward her home. The creature mused as it rose back up, turned, and trotted back into the underbrush.

Was the pain and fear of the invisible fire familiar?

Was there an ancient memory of that power buried somewhere in its mind?

The creature's primal brain turned, rusty and grinding, out of practice, dredging up the oldest of its memories.

The past.

There had been fear. Fear of the warrior shouts of the painted men. The painted men who had once hunted this valley. The painted men felt familiar.

The creature loped along on all fours, staying in the deepest shadows. As it moved, it thought of long-gone hunting grounds.

The painted men. So long since the creature's mind turned to memories of them. Images and sounds leapt through its consciousness. Nights of brightest star light, far gone from the hazy nights the creature stalked in now. Summer meadows illuminated by millions of fireflies, mesmerizing in their flickering dances. Then high-pitched screeches echoing across the valley. Melded silver on arrow tips and spear points.

Searing physical wounds that left permanent scars.

The creature felt the old familiar itch in the scar along its ribs.

But the painted men did not have the power to cast invisible fire.

The creature stopped to smell a scent trail. A rabbit. Still warm and close. Nearby. The creature pressed its snout down, centimeters from the ground. Inhaled. Fear and protein and wet fur. And dirt. An adult rabbit, smart enough to leave the trail when it heard the creature coming. The creature snorted and soil blasted out from the ground. Too confident to flee. Just hiding, waiting for the predator to pass it by. It could hear its heart beating nearby. Could almost taste the tawny softness of its fur upon its tongue. The creature took a step to the left and sniffed again. Then it spun, lunged into the wild thorn bushes, snapped its jaws down, hard. The rabbit had no time to squeal. Its flesh melted through sharp teeth, the bones crunched and the creature chewed only twice, and then swallowed.

It trotted on. The creature padded across a cold creek and up another hill. The memories unfolded just as images and echoes of pain, but they were there and the creature remembered.

No, it was not the painted men who cast the invisible fire.

It had been the snake-woman.

It had been during the early times, when the painted men first arrived in the valley. The snake-woman burnt its insides. The ageless one. With bones in her hair and around her neck. She had breathed smoke and drew shapes in the air. And smelt *different*, not just of warmth and sustenance, like other mammals. She was unique, and she had known the creature, somehow, had called it by its true name and cursed it to these hills. Cursed it to desire human flesh, more than any other, unendingly.

The creature had fled from her. For uncountable moons the creature fed on smaller prey, and tread lightly where humans walked.

But the snake-woman's smell eventually faded, and the creature found the taste of man flesh again and had no longer been afraid. The man flesh was fatter now and often foul, but their flesh still pleased more than any other.

The creature had almost forgotten fear. Forgotten the pain of the burning invisible fire.

But this new human.

Yes, at first, she smelt different than the ancient snake-woman. The creature had not thought to smell too closely. To smell for the past, hidden underneath the artificial odors, the pungent perfumes and soaps and falseness and her own fear. The woman exuded the special aroma, unique from all other humans.

Like all mammalian prey, she smelt of iron and panic, but her odor also contained the snake-woman smell that sparked the ancient fear in the creature. A four-layer fragrance that nothing should have all at once. Wormy, damp soil; frigid, alpine blizzards; charred volcanic lava; and oyster beds at lowest tide. The impossible odor of those who could breathe smoke, draw colorful shapes in the air, and cast fire with their minds.

Yes, the creature could recognize it now, under the camouflage of her new human smell she had the smell of the ageless one, the smell of the snake-woman who still lived, isolated in the deepest woods, and kept the creature under this curse. The creature and its kin.

The creature halted its loping at the top of a high, treeless mountain peak.

Its kin. The pack.

It had once had a pack. A family.

Now it just had the two old men. They were allies.

Not family.

The rest were gone, dust and bone, broken and scattered across the valley.

Now a new snake-woman had returned. A new snake-woman who smelt of pain and fear but who also smelt of earth, air, fire, and water, all at once.

It was too much for the predator's mind to comprehend. The visions and the memories and the pain and the fog of something… more… something before even the painted men, before even the snake-woman… swirled inside the creature's brain.

It sat on its brown-furred haunches, tilted its snout into the air, spotted the glowing white disc in the sky, and howled.

****

Morgan's blood froze in her veins. The howl cut across the night air, remorse and melody and malice all swirling inside the dreadful call reverberating through the valley. The pain that haunted the howl felt far too familiar for Morgan's liking.

The phone in her hand made a muffled noise and drew Morgan back to her call. She lifted it back to her ear.

"—ell the Sheriff, what you just told me."

"Sorry, Maud, I didn't catch all that. Something howling out here tonight on the mountain."

"Goodness, girl, you heard that cry all the way out in your hollow? Must be a whole pack of them talking to each other tonight across the valley."

"I didn't think there were any wolves east of the Mississippi."

"Well, darling, the politicians say they ain't because the farmers make a darn bunch o' racket if they admit wild wolves be back in the mountains. So, what they do is, they call them coywolves, half-coyote half-wolf, some black burnt bologna if you ask me. That's all wolf we're hearing now. Big wolf, by my guess."

Morgan heard the gruff voice of the sheriff in the background, talking over a continuous click-clack noise but couldn't make out what he said, nor the noise that muffled him.

"Shut your voodoo Cajun mouth, Sheriff, quit playing with that old thing and come take the darn phone. That poor girl Morgan had a fright up on her property—sounds like a bear done attacked her and her dog in the yard."

Morgan waited, phone held tightly to her ear.

Click. Clack. Click. Click. Clack.

"Sheriff, would you quit poking at that thing and get your lazy behind over here and talk to your constituent? She is going to vote your double-wide behind back to Louisiana."

The clicking sounds ceased. The groans of an overweight man standing up replaced them.

"Maud, that'll be the day, when someone else runs for Sheriff. Who'd you say this was, that newly widowed girl up yonder in Bacon Hollow?"

"Yes, now don't go being insensitive and mentioning hcr dcad husband and come take this gosh darn call."

Morgan frowned as the old woman handed over the phone.

"Sheriff Jeffery here. What's all this about, Mrs. Reaves? You got a bear up there giving you and the animals trouble?"

Chapter 4

Max made a couple of double backs and turned down multiple side roads, but the truck stayed on his tail the whole time. Didn't try to hide it at all. At first, Max thought he'd just give the truck a run all the way over to the far side of the next mountain, but eventually Max would have to stop to get gas, so he decided he might as well get to it. His drill sergeant, lifetimes ago, had told him, "Ain't nothing got easier by waiting around worrying about it."

He circled all the way back to the gas station where he'd first come across the red pickup truck. He pulled in, stopped at the one lonely pump, and got out. He was onto his fourth beer at this point, and he swirled it in his hand as he pumped gas and watched the old truck pull in behind him. Max felt closer to Grim and farther from Maximillian with four beers in him. He shouldn't be drinking this much, out here in the middle of nowhere, and he knew it. Especially this time of the month.

But knowing you got a problem is a hell of a lot different than managing that problem.

Right after he heard the pump handle click, the gas station lobby lights went dark, followed quickly by the neon 'Open' sign. It flickered, then went out.

The red truck inched uncomfortably close to Max's

bumper before the hillbilly brought it to a complete stop and shifted into park. The big man got out, still slow moving, and stared at Max.

Max stared right back.

The breeze had picked up, the wind gusting down off the mountain. The flagpole chain was dangling loose, and the metal clanged loudly against metal.

Clang. Clang. Clang.

"I was worried you might get lost out on the roads this time a night. Wondering if you needed directions?"

Max raised a single eyebrow. "You were following me around for thirty minutes to make sure I didn't need directions?"

Clang.

"We do that sort of thing out here: help take care of folks. Even city folks that don't shake hands and have a ten o'clock shadow, dark eyes, and a bad attitude."

In the distance, an eerie howl carried down the mountain with the wind. It was the same howl Max had heard lifetimes ago, on another continent.

Clang.

Clang.

The hairs on the back of Max's neck stood upright. His ears tingled. He couldn't help but cast a furtive glance toward the moon. He swallowed hard and clenched his fists.

Clang.

Clang.

He did not expect that trigger, not here, not now.

Keep it together, Grim.

—Let me out, Maximillian. It's been so long.—

Goosfraba.

Max looked at the beer in his hand and tipped out

31

the remaining third.

Lose it now, the career's gone. The bank accounts. This identity. Everything.

—Let me out, Maximillian. You know its time.—

He hadn't prepared. He was nowhere near any of his hideouts.

Clang. Clang.

Clang. Clang.

Vic chuckled. "Take 'er easy, I'm not the cops. Don't have to dump your beer."

Max wasn't listening; he was concentrating on his own mind.

The wind gusted. The pole chain clanged even louder.

Clang, clang, clang!

Clang, clang, clang!

What were the odds of running into another one, way out here?

Don't give in.

—Let me out!—

"You look sick, city boy. Want to hop in my truck? I can take you somewhere safe."

Goosfraba.

The wind whistled now, pushing trash and debris across the parking lot, sending the metal chain into a frenzy, knocking again and again against the pole.

Clang! Clang! Clang!

Clang! Clang! Clang!

Max could barely think straight.

"Goosfraba," he said out loud, holding his hands up and pressing them against his ears. He felt a magnetism from overhead, pulling on his eyes, begging for him to turn and look up.

Clang! Clang! Clang!

"Boy, you need a real man to protect you from the big bad wolves?"

—LET ME EAT HIM, MAXIMILLIAN!—

Fuck it.

Max craned his neck, stared at the moon, felt the cold primal iron rippling below the surface. This time of the month, it was always so easy. Just sitting there in the sky, beaming down an intoxicating, hypnotic ray of pure lunar ecstasy. Max could slip right into Grim, no effort at all. He didn't really even have to try to turn. He just had to stop resisting.

So, he stopped resisting.

It hurt whenever it happened, but despite the pain, shedding his human flesh felt sublime.

The bones snapped in his fingers, bigger bones splintered in his hands; his wrists dislocated as larger, thicker muscles exploded across his forearms. Jet black fur pushed out like barbwire across his skin. His mouth tore open, stretching wide, the skin at his lips splitting, a bloody gash slicing along his cheek lines to allow his mouth to continue to gape larger and larger.

From the tips of his fingers steel-sharp claws emerged, pushing off his human nails like old, dried skin. His eyes stung and his face felt pinched and a spasm shot down his spine. His calves trembled and his legs gave out and he crumpled toward the ground, head banging off the car door on the way down.

For a moment he lay on the asphalt, writhing, screaming, snarling. But a moment later he stood back up, over nine-feet-tall, pain forgotten.

In fact, he had forgotten almost all of his human thoughts and feelings.

He saw nothing but a fat, ugly prey item standing nearby.

But this prey item smiled at him, and the prey item's eyes were suddenly sharp with intelligence that had been hidden there just moments before.

"The only defense against the world is a thorough knowledge of it. And I know just what you are, beast."

The prey pulled out a small silver tube and raised it to his lips.

Grim lunged, snarling, six-inch incisors flashing in the midnight air.

His senses were cranked up to eleven, and he instinctually swatted the bee-sized dart as it flew toward him. The needle punctured the leathery pad that had grown over his fleshy palm. Grim scratched it out with his other paw, still focused on the man nearby, gluttonous to rend apart his fatty flesh.

He paused.

He blinked, slowly.

He felt groggy.

Where was his prey?

The moon above him rippled like a reflection in a black pond, wavering in the air. The ground below him wobbled, asphalt suddenly transformed to lumpy mud. The clanging metal chain seemed dampened, almost muted. He couldn't feel the wind across his fur.

Grim sniffed and snorted and sneezed, and dropped to all four paws, trying to focus.

The big man whipped back around from behind the truck, raised the pipe to his lips.

Grim's black fur stood up on end, spiking in ridges between his massive shoulders. His jowls pulled back and he growled. The second dart flashed toward him.

He ducked.

The dart whistled by, nearly grazing one of his ears. Grim lurched toward the truck, his pulse throbbing in his head, thumping louder with each strong heartbeat. His vision was fading fast. Everything nearby was either gray or black lumps, and the lumps were blending together quickly.

Grim's nose, however, was less affected by whatever drug was coursing through his body. Maximillian might know. Grim only knew that he still smelt the cocky redneck, hiding behind his tailgate. Grim didn't have the confidence in his usual dexterity to leap over the vehicle and dodge more darts, considering he was all but blind.

He was still a big beast though, so he smashed right into the truck, throwing his shoulder hard into the bed, snarling in anger.

The pickup spun sideways, a weak human leg bone snapped, Victor squealed in pain. Grim heard the silver pipe clatter and roll out into the middle of the parking lot.

Grim stalked around the truck, staggering slightly, smelling piss, shit, and blood.

"A hex upon you, beast! The witch-sisters of Angavor will—"

Grim didn't know the witch-sisters, and he didn't stop to think if he should. He could taste the big man's fear, as palpable to him as the fog in the valley.

He fell upon his prey, his fangs piercing Vic's doughy neck, and in one strong bite he ripped his throat out. Wet blood gushed onto Grim's snout and fur as he swallowed. He leaned in and with another snap of his jaws he severed the spinal cord at the stem of the man's brain. Grim shook viciously, then tossed the decapitated head into the air.

It flew across the road, flipping over and over, blood spraying out the gory bottom like a deflating water balloon. It landed in the meadow thirty yards away.

The gray eyes, still wide and wild with fear, blinked twice before the life faded out of them.

Grim swallowed two mouthfuls of warm flesh from the bloody stump of the man's neck, but the enjoyment was gone. He was too drugged and too exposed, and the man-flesh tasted sour. Tasted like it had been dead for years already. He looked around inside his own thoughts, fighting to find the portal back to the human mind, back to Maximillian, just to find a path away from the drugs, but he was too far gone, too deep in the primal carnivore brain, and all Grim could think to do was trot into the ancient Appalachian woods and disappear into the deepest, darkest shadows and hope the drug wore off soon.

Chapter 5

Morgan drove to work in a daze the next morning.

Joey panted next to her, his nose aimed out the window, early morning sunlight bouncing golden rays across his spotted snout. The tree branches were barren, a smattering few leaves remained, bright yellow and deep rust and pumpkin orange in color, happily wagging in the morning breeze. Surely thinking, if leaves could think, that this would be the perfect day to set sail into the skies.

Morgan felt their warmth as she drove through the forest, a wave of positivity and golden power exuding from the deep woods.

She pushed the warmth away.

She hung onto a shield of darkness that would not let the light in. It was a cloak of defense, and it protected her from being hurt, in the way a lead bunker protects someone from sunburn, and it was a cloak that did not let go. It hung on her shoulders, thick, wet, leathery, like oversized bat wings. Each day she felt them tightening around her. Soon the wings would fuse together and seal her in a cocoon.

No, not a cocoon.

A coffin.

A blue sedan and then a red truck whipped around

the corner ahead of her. A massive dent decorated the rear of the pickup truck. Almost no one drove this far out on this road, back toward her isolated home in Bacon Hollow.

If the warmth of the forest was a gentle wave pulsating around her, the two cars brought with them a tsunami wave of dark energy and danger. She had to grip the steering wheel with two hands and tug hard to correct away from being pulled into it.

Joey yelped as two tires went off the asphalt and dipped into the steep ditch that ran alongside the road. Morgan fought the sudden yank in the opposite direction, pulled hard back to the left, and her two front tires grabbed hold of the road and whipped her front end into the middle of the street.

Back tires skidded. Smoked. Screeched. Backward. Sideways. Forward.

Sideways.

She came to a halt and held her head.

It hurt. She didn't remember hitting her head.

That potentially made *two* concussions in under twelve hours.

Not great.

Joey wasn't in the front seat.

Oh god.

Joey wasn't in the front seat.

No.

Joey whined and Morgan saw the dog in the back, four paws splayed out wide, head coming up and turning to her. He stood up, a little wobblily, stretched out his snout and licked her on the face. He stepped forward and she rubbed his ears and skull, feeling for any injuries. He just whined again and licked her.

He hopped forward into the front seat and gave a snort and a shake. She could almost hear his thoughts:

That was scary. Let's not do that again, Mom.

He plopped down and looked out the window. His mouth dropped open and he began panting happily.

If only Morgan could forget things so quickly and easily.

She turned and gazed back down the road where the two vehicles had disappeared. They had not stopped to check if she was alright. They had just raced on into the deeper parts of the forest. She hadn't picked up such a strong manifestation of evil aura since… well… since her father had arrived to take her away from her grandmother's house in St Louis.

Why was she sensing things again?

She had given all of that up. She had almost convinced herself there had never been anything to give up in the first place.

And now. The attack of the wolf-bear-demon-thing. The vehicles' evil auras bouncing her off the road. Sixteen-year-old Morgan stirred inside her.

We should follow it. What if someone needs our help?

Thirty-three-year-old Morgan responded. *We can't help anyone. Not even those closest to us. Not even ourselves. Remember?*

She gently pressed on the gas and turned away from the direction the car and truck had gone.

She straightened out and drove toward town, dropping Joey off at 'Dogs' Delight Daycare' on the way in.

All the while she fumed with her guilty conscious, the conscious that manifested itself as her younger self, the one that kept pestering her thoughts, insisting that she should always be doing something brave and stupid. That conscious sat like a little virgin angel on her shoulder and had no knowledge of the current reality, yet still whispered dumb, virtuous ideas into her head.

She parked in the employee garage of Pineville's only doctor's office, which doubled as an urgent care, and tripled as a hospital when needed. Her fingernails had dug so fiercely into the steering wheel as she drove that when she finally parked she had to pluck each finger one at a time out of the little gouges she had left in the leather.

The steering wheel looked like a prop from a horror movie. Something the young heroine hangs onto for dear life but ultimately is wrenched out by the monster after the car careens off into the woods. The detectives find it the next day, smashed in half, wrapped around a tree, but by then it's too late for unnamed, pretty female victim.

End Scene One.

Morgan shuddered at coming so close to being the Unnamed Female Victim twice in the past twelve hours. She wouldn't stand for that.

She couldn't even stand the finger-gouge evidence she had left behind on the leather steering wheel.

She reached out her left hand, feeling warmth from the woods, the warmth that she denied earlier. She beckoned with her fingers, triggering each fingertip at just the right moment, feeling the air for that warm, golden tension that reacted to her touch, found it, and grasped a strand of it. It surged inside her, sparkling with electrifying energy. She twirled the golden threads, pulling together a thick cord of power that she fed directly into the veins in her palm. In her mind, she threaded it down, straight into her own heart, as she had been taught, and then wound it back out to her other hand. She flicked that sizzling golden energy in her hand toward the steering wheel.

The leather gouges laced themselves together, one quick stitch at a time, until the steering wheel looked wholly new. Morgan pushed the extra golden energy back out of her body, into the town and the woods beyond, not wanting to hold onto it any longer than she needed to. That power could maybe stitch her broken heart back together too, if she focused.

But she would not give in to the call.

The dark wings settled back over her instead, the painful shield of sorrow that felt like justice, and she turned and trudged toward the parking garage elevator.

She didn't deserve the spark of joy that her grandmother's magic brought.

And she didn't want to relive the memories it invoked.

He left you.

Left her and everyone else who still had a heartbeat.

The elevator dinged, the doors opened, and Morgan stepped inside.

He left her, she didn't know why; it felt like a punch in the stomach every time her thoughts turned to him. She blamed herself, she hadn't seen his pain; she had muted herself to her grandmother's magic—earth's ancient magic—and by doing so she had muted herself to everyone else's feelings too. Including her husband's.

And now he was gone.

The bell dinged, the elevator doors opened, and her shift in the small-town medical facility yanked her out of her thoughts and threw her violently into reality.

"Help me!" someone yelled. "My wife's been attacked!"

Morgan burst into the lobby and saw the blank, gravestone gray face of a woman destined for death.

Dr. Williams was already there. She shouted something that Morgan didn't comprehend while taking the injured woman from the husband and laying her atop a gurney, a handful of gauze being pressed into a large slash across the thigh.

Morgan rushed to them. She couldn't find a pulse. Morgan began compressions there in the lobby. A unit of blood was rushed in by an intern and Dr. Williams hung it while she called for staff to clear a room for them.

They never made it.

The nasal passageway and mouth were gashed open and the clotting blood, loose teeth, and bone shards compromised the victim's airway. Suction didn't help. CPR was impossible. Due to the severity of the slash, traditional intubation was impossible and a tracheotomy had to be performed in the middle of the hallway. The patient was swaddled in blankets when she arrived, as she must have been shaking uncontrollably on the drive into town, but her body was limp and still as Dr. Williams took a fifteen blade and mosquito scissors and gently sliced open a window of skin and tissue at the second tracheal ring. With fast precision the doctor inserted a tracheal tube through the hole in the flesh.

"I still can't get a heartbeat," Morgan groaned between gritted teeth.

"I need a crash cart!" Dr. Williams shouted to no one in particular. She took over compressions, but while she and Morgan switched, the delicately placed tracheal tube became dislodged. Morgan released pressure on an exposed artery in the thigh to try to reinsert the trach tube. Another bandage of gauze sloughed off, more blood oozing from a separate gash at the victim's wrist. Morgan couldn't reinsert the trach tube as the passageway flooded with blood. The other nurse couldn't suction the blood out faster than it refilled. There was no clean pathway. They turned and looked up at the doctor, both nurses feeling beyond helpless.

The doctor's face mirrored theirs.

Dr. Williams ceased compressions, stepped back, and scanned the victim's body. Heartbeat monitors squealed. The victim lay still. No effort for breath. Barely any blood left to circulate, even if the heart could beat to circulate it.

Dr. Williams checked her watch, declared, "Time of death, seven-twenty-six A.M."

The husband, who had collapsed to his knees in the corner, let out a guttural sob.

Morgan removed her gloves. She got a silent nod of instruction from Dr. Williams.

Morgan went to the grieving husband. She got down on her knees with him. He looked at her. Panicked. Afraid. She didn't have any words to say, but she didn't leave him. She sat there with him, in his pain. He wouldn't be alone while he dealt with losing his spouse.

She was there. She didn't say anything. But she knew just how important it was that she was there.

Dr. Williams left the deceased body and bee-lined for the young sheriff deputy, Bunkum, who had bullied his way into the hallway while they were still trying to save the victim's life.

Animal mauling's severe enough to kill don't happen often, and Sheriff Jeffery apparently wanted to determine if this was an attempt to cover up a domestic violence incident. Morgan overheard Dr. Williams give Bunkum a piece of her mind.

"These wounds were inflicted by an *animal* with *claws*," the doctor stated, holding up her hands and pantomiming an aggressive claw swipe, rather near the deputy's face, "and unless the husband trained a pack of grizzly bears to murder his wife, he had nothing to do with this. Now, the husband is in shock, and overwhelmed with grief, and may have minor wounds himself, so please tell Sheriff Jeffery and Mayor Fraser I don't want you out here, haunting my office. I want you to wait outside in the parking lot and let me do my job. We may admit him overnight, so why don't you go investigate some double-parked cars by the coffee shop, like you do best, and come back tomorrow."

Dr. Vickie Williams turned on her heel and strode down the hallway. Bunkum itched his nose and then meandered off in the opposite direction.

Later, the autopsy would posit that a single massive canine, perhaps a bull mastiff or large rottweiler, not a pack of grizzly bears, had caused the wounds that led to the patient's death by exsanguination.

Morgan didn't need to wait for the autopsy results. She knew at the time it wasn't domestic violence or some rabid bear or dog. She knew it wasn't a coyote pack or a bobcat or a mountain lion. She knew in the deepest part of her soul that it was the same demon-wolf-creature that had attacked and almost killed her last night. And it made her feel even more guilty.

I could have stopped it.

Her sixteen-year-old self would certainly have thought so. Now, she wasn't so sure.

But she was sure she should have tried.

Morgan stayed with the husband and as he cried, Morgan whispered, "I'm sorry, I'm so sorry."

She knew his pain, and her own remorse churned inside of her, and she felt her jaw tightening, and suddenly she felt a strong new force of energy pulsing through the air. It danced around amongst the threads of golden energy that were always there. She felt this new energy calling to her, these ultra-thin red vibrating threads of high-strung power that lived in the very shadows of the golden threads. She'd never felt them before, but she felt them now, seeking out her fingertips, wanting to be used. The usual golden threads were just hovering there, like a constant backdrop in any setting. But these shadow threads, this new energy, wasn't just a backdrop. It was knocking against her body, running along her skin, whispering to her:

Use me, please, use me. If you use me you will be able to stop the beast in the woods. Just reach out your fingers and pluck me out of the air.

Morgan shook her head and brought her focus back to the grieving husband. She rubbed his shoulder, and said, "I'm sorry," one final time. The fine zig-zagging red threads snapped and disappeared and Morgan sensed nothing hiding in the backdrop any longer. She stood up and helped the husband stand. She walked him to the nearest chair, helped him sit down, and said, "Someone will be back to check on you soon, I promise. We aren't abandoning you. Someone will be right back to check you out."

The husband did not acknowledge that Morgan had said anything at all.

Morgan walked away, frowning. Was she relieved

the new red energy had disappeared as fast as it had arrived? Or was she disappointed? She wasn't sure she wanted to know the answer.

Chapter 6

September Fourteenth, 1944, 3:15 p.m.

In his memory, her hair glistened like fresh honey, golden and glossy, cascading down her shoulders in a slow tumble for eternity. It washed over him when he picked her up, the fragrance enveloping him. If he closed his eyes and breathed deeply, he could conjure her smell into his mind, even when she was far away. Sweet and floral, with just a touch of pumpkin, cinnamon, and apple. She smelt like sunshine and autumn harvest.

He closed his eyes and smelled her hair before he boarded the bus that took him to Fort Benning, closed his eyes and smelled her hair before he climbed aboard the USS Wasp, smelled her hair before he leapt from an airplane over France, smelled her hair before he signed a document agreeing to chase down Nazi intelligence officers across eastern Europe.

But when he found himself spending day after day in the rainy streets of Budapest, digging through newspapers looking for potential codes hidden within the articles, closing his eyes, desperately trying to recall the smell of his daughter Virginia's hair, he just couldn't find that aroma in his mind any longer. He could barely even conjure her image in his mind's eye. He had been gone too long. His daughter was as much a figment of his imagination now as was the very real, flesh and blood

German spy, Hans Claus Günter.

Max had been assigned to find Mr. Günter, but for many months he had found nothing but smoke and whispers.

Günter led Maximillian across Europe in a game of cat and cat, where each hunted the other, with Günter carrying a critical piece of information regarding the location of captured allied spies. Maximillian eventually became the last of the active American operatives with orders to find him.

If Günter killed Maximillian, he killed the last operative tracking him down. If Max caught him and *persuaded* intel from him, he could find the hidden prison that held his colleagues. American, British, and French spies were captured and held in this top-secret facility and Maximillian knew if he couldn't find Günter they would likely be tortured and killed, their bodies unceremoniously dumped in a mass grave somewhere.

The war against the Germans had turned, territories were being liberated, inch by inch, and Hitler was back-pedaling. But the captured special operatives would still be gaffed and gutted before the Nazis let them go free. If the Axis powers were going to lose the war, they would take their enemies' best men with them, if they could.

Max was their last hope of a possible escape.

The rain was unceasing the day he met Hans.

Max hustled down a cobblestone alley, his boots splashing through deep puddles, his bowler hat pulled low across his dark eyebrows, not looking around as he should have. He just wanted out of the damn rain.

A firm hand gripped Max by the shoulder, freezing him in place.

He turned and met the blue eyes of a Nazi officer.

The edge of a knife pressed firm up against his throat.

He had been made, somehow, despite nearly eighteen months of work and caution.

"Wenn du schreist, schlitze ich dir die Kehle auf." *If you scream, I will slit your throat.*

Max did not scream, but he did fight back.

Quick as silver, he swatted at the knife blade and drew his Luger with his other hand. He fired and the bullet screamed upward, missing his own face by inches, passing right through the face of the German. The man's scrambled brain matter ejected from the top of his head in a stringy mess, his body went limp and he collapsed onto the wet street.

As blood and brain flowed into the grooves between the cobblestones, Max pulled a watertight metal box from the man's interior jacket pocket. The box contained a small letter, folded over twice. Max bent over it, shielding it from the rain with his body. He gently unfolded it. A single sentence had been written on the parchment:

'Wir laden Sie zu einem besonderen Abend voller Folter, Rache und Hexerei ein.'*We invite you to a special evening of torture, revenge, and witchcraft.*

Below the message, a set of coordinates and a date.

Maximillian memorized it using a mnemonic trick he'd been taught in his crash course at spook school, then folded the note back into its little metal box, then tucked the box back inside the dead man's jacket. Max stood up and turned to flee the scene.

Three more Nazi men rushed at him from the nearest alleyway.

Max sprinted, hard, but one of the Nazis was faster. He crashed into Max and they tumbled into the street.

Max threw an elbow and a punch and the Nazi punched back and tried to grab him around the neck. Max scrambled out of his grip only to receive a haymaker to his chin as the next Nazi arrived at their scrum. Max maintained consciousness somehow, pushed himself back up off the cobblestones, nose broken, bottom lip bleeding profusely, and turned to face the three Nazis.

Two leveled their Lugers at him. The third, the one who had not fought Max at all, smiled.

"*Strong, American, but stupid. We don't want to kill you, we just want to take you for a ride in the country.*"

"I'm not going anywhere with you, so you'll have to kill me."

"Nein." The officer turned to the man at his left. "*Tie him up. Don't be gentle.*"

The two men holstered their weapons. One withdrew a set of handcuffs, the other slipped on a pair of brass knuckles.

Max spit blood at their boots, smiled, and charged.

Five minutes later his arms were contorted behind him, cuffs clanked around his wrists, and he was shoved into the back seat of a Type 82 Kübelwagen. His body felt broken in about twelve separate places. But the two Nazi soldiers were also bloodied and bruised and Max smirked through his swollen mouth. He wasn't the only one who felt broken, he was sure of that.

The German officer riding alongside him smirked back. In stilted English he said, "Where are my manners, Max? I forgot introduction. Ich bin Hans Claus Günter. I want you to know. I caught you. Not the other way around. Soon you will wish I had killed you, as well."

By Max's best guess, they were taking him toward Transylvania. The set of coordinates on the letter corresponded to a location outside Cluj, deep in the Carpathian Mountains. Max couldn't think of anything large and specific that matched that area, meaning perhaps they were taking him to the secret Axis prison he had been hunting for. If so, he would find the jail after all. Just as another prisoner, not as a liberator.

They drove mostly by night, and though they stopped and got out, occasionally changing drivers, Max stayed locked in the back of the car. They fed him occasionally, usually the cold, uneaten leftovers of their previous meal.

When the Kübelwagen began climbing in altitude, weaving in and out of dark forests, Max knew his guess was right.

Max had heard of the folklore myths in that part of the world. That chunk of territory seemed to change hands every hundred years or so for the last thousand years. A more notorious land of mysticism and legend Maximillian did not know. But at the time, he had no reason to believe in the whisperings of its dark lore. He worried more about his Nazi captors than the myths and legends of Transylvania.

Until he saw the castle.

Hans elbowed him, waking him up, and gestured out the window as they rounded a steep mountain road.

"There, Max. Das ist dein neuer Käfig. Käfig means home." The other German's laughed, but Max just stared.

Käfig translated to cage, not home.

Bedecked with burning torches in the windows, demonic stone gargoyles on the battlement towers, a cast iron gate and drawbridge over an honest-to-God moat, the castle at the top of the mountain raised goosebumps across Max's skin.

As they got closer Max heard music echoing across the stone walls. It did not sound like German propaganda songs; it sounded more like orchestral music from an Italian opera. When they pulled up to the gate, Max could see the silhouette of a massive bear, lean with starvation, a sparkling chain looped around its back leg, pacing across the lawn in the distance. Occasionally, it would stand on its two back legs and sniff at the air.

A man stepped out of the gatehouse. He saluted and uttered 'Heil Hitler,' but he was not dressed in Nazi attire. He wore a long, hooded cloak and long, black leather gloves and tall, black leather boots. As he approached the car he tossed back his hood, revealing a hawkish face graffitied in black and gray tattoos, geometrical and swirling across every inch of his exposed skin. He smiled at them as he leaned inside the vehicle.

Hans said in German to the bizarre guard, "*Another one for the ceremony.*"

The guard said to Max in crisp English, "We are pleased to have you join us, American."

The guard signaled to another man stationed inside the gatehouse, and Max heard mechanical grinding and watched the iron bars swing open. The car crossed the moat and continued up the drive toward the front entrance of the castle. The thick wooden front door was reinforced with iron bracing and looked as if it weighed a thousand pounds. Hans exited the vehicle, circled around, and opened the door for Max. He grabbed Max by the upper arm and hauled him out. The skinny bear growled at them from somewhere nearby. Hans quickened his pace and rushed them up to the door. He pounded hard, three times.

The door swung open. Another cloaked and hooded man, tattooed with the same black and gray swirls, stood at the door, holding a gas lamp in his hand. He stepped aside and beckoned them in.

The interior of the castle was remarkably dark. Max doubted it had electricity. Just torches in the windows and gas lamps in the hallways.

Hans did not step inside with Max. When Max looked back, Hans smiled and said, "*See you in a month, American. Then you will beg for me to shoot you. Right between your nasty American eyes.*"

****

October Fourth, 2:16 p.m.

Max woke up in a sunlit glade, in an American forest, a gurgling creek lapping against his fingertips, an angry little squirrel chattering at him from a nearby tree. He immediately recognized he was far from the torturous Transylvanian castle that had harbored him so many years ago.

He was nude, and muddy, and his head hurt. He remained motionless, going through a mental checklist as he assessed the rest of his body. He didn't feel bloated and gorged, so at least he knew he hadn't eaten something large in his other form last night. He thought hard and struggled to remember.

Grim rarely divulged his nocturnal meanderings.

It had been ten years. A record for Max. Nine years stable at his most recent job. For sure, another record. He'd gotten arrogant, lackadaisical. He'd made serious money; he had substantial funds in the Max Rosewood account. Of course, he still had his genuine Sanderson family trust, slowly building. But he had left so much on the table by changing the night before without properly preparing first.

Max groaned.

He remembered having multiple beers, and driving around aimlessly, trying to avoid something or someone.

So stupid.

So weak.

How had he let it happen?

He sat bolt upright out of the mud when he remembered the rest.

The other howl. There was another werewolf nearby. And the Shakespeare-quoting hillbilly. The hillbilly had known what Max was, somehow, had been trying to trigger him and elicit the change. Max had been poisoned, but Grim still managed to tear the man's head clean off. Max remembered that. And then he went and ran into the woods, leaving behind his car and the victim's truck at the kill site.

Christ, Grim, you've really outdone yourself this time.

Half the FBI and every state trooper in Virginia would probably have an APB out on him by now. They'd be looking for him everywhere.

Well, they'd be looking for Max Rosewood.

Ten years. It'd been a good run.

Goodbye, Max Rosewood. Hello… somebody.

He needed another identity. Another life.

Max was too hungover from his recent change to concoct a name for his next alias.

Abandoning an identity by necessity, as opposed to 'retiring' an identity by choosing a time and place, added an extra level of difficulty and lots of layers of frustration. Especially if that identity has been pegged as a psychopathic killer and that identity's face—which happened to be Max's real face—was being splashed all over the five o'clock news. Not exactly ideal for the *real* Max Sanderson. His next alias would need to be very discreet. And he probably would need to grow out his beard and wear thick rimmed glasses for a while.

At least the beard part would be easy. The hair grew on the bottom half of his face as if he were *always* in his other form.

Max groaned again and rubbed his eyes. He spent two years in Europe, under the best training that the US military offered, learning how to live a life as someone he really wasn't. After that, he had built up almost sixty years of experience pretending to be different men in their mid-thirties. He could do it again.

Hell, he would *always* have to do it again. Nine years was probably close to the high end of how long he could stay in any job before folks got to be suspicious anyway. Max just wished he'd planned the ending better. If he were smarter, earlier, he'd be a multi-millionaire already. But instead, he was naked, muddy, and on the run.

Something else bothered him. Giving up the Max Rosewood identity was inevitable, a part of the cursed cycle Max was stuck in. But there was another werewolf and a dead redneck werewolf hunter, all right in these woods, in the middle of Virginia. Smack dab in a seriously isolated valley between some thick mountain ranges. In the short fifteen minutes he'd spent at the gas station while he was passing through Pineville he had met a werewolf-hunter and had been tricked into transforming.

Hell of a coincidence.

Spook school lessons drifted back to him. 'When coincidences start stacking, someone or *something* is stacking them on purpose.'

Why had Max felt compelled to rush all the way across Virginia in the middle of the night close to a full moon, anyway? Why had he chosen last night of all nights to push the limit with his beers?

Questions for him to figure out once he had figured out the simple stuff. Like clothes and a hideout and a way to make it back to one of his stash points. Shelter and food and clean water.

He ached all over, as was usual, but he still stood up. He looked down at the creek and saw his shimmering reflection in the running water. He had scratches and leaf matter scattered across his taut skin, and his whole body was smeared in mud.

He high stepped through the weeds and splashed into the middle of the water. Only three feet deep, it was freezing cold and it shocked Max as he crouched down, stealing his breath away. He scrubbed at his body, breathing deeply, focused on enjoying his discomfort. He scrubbed and scrubbed and washed his body clean. His sins wouldn't wash off, but he still scrubbed, thinking of them, wishing he might one day scrub them clean, too.

He stood up, sopping and shivering, but mud-free. He trudged out of the gurgling creek and paused at the bank. He sniffed at the air, then scowled. Eyebrows furrowed and eyes dark, he decided to follow the creek upstream. He dripped dry as he walked, and his nudeness didn't bother him. It was a crisp, autumn day and the sunshine that made it through the tree branches warmed his skin without overheating him. Aside from being naked, homeless, and completely lost, it was a rather pleasant little walk along a babbling brook.

He'd had worse walks after much worse nights.

Chapter 7

October Fourth, 2:19 p.m.

Morgan sat in the corner of the break room. She forced down lukewarm black tea in large gulps.

She usually never drank black tea, preferring the less jitter-inducing green variety, but she had a long night ahead of her and needed to build up her energy reserves. She held the cup close to her face, smelling the stale fragrances as the steam wafted across her nose and cheeks. The tea was nothing like the fresh herbal tea her grandmother would make from her own garden, but it was caffeinated, and it still held a little warmth, and that would have to be enough for now.

"Hey, girl," Dr. Vickie Williams said, sweeping into the room, heading straight for the fridge. "How are you doing?"

She poked around in the fridge and eventually found something edible amongst all the expired and long-forgotten food. She turned back around, yogurt cup in hand, and looked at Morgan. "I said, hey, girl, how are you doing? Now you say, hey, girl, I'm living the dream, then I say, if this is a dream, wake me the hell up. You can't just sit there. You gotta talk to me, so I can pretend I'm listening, and then vice versa. Your silent, moody Morgan card expired at the end of last month, remember?"

Morgan cracked a smile. "Hi Dr. Williams, I'm fine, how about you?"

Dr. Williams frowned, "Uh huh, fine, she says. Sure. That woman we lost this morning still sitting with you?"

"No, I think it's—" *the victim's husband, my husband, the monster, the dented truck, the emergence of new, mysterious threads of magical power* "—just one of those days, Dr. Williams."

"I feel that." Vickie stabbed a spoon into her yogurt and took a big bite. She spoke through mouthfuls, "I definitely feel that. My babies were going crazy last night. We heard a wolf howl, and they were up all night, pacing around the house, little fur standing on end, yapping out the windows. Which kept *me* up all night. They never behave like that. Then this morning, that lady shows up, mauled to death by… something. I've never heard of a bear doing anything like that out here. Not the way she looked. I know it's not our job to speculate… but damn."

"Yeah," Morgan said quietly, "Yeah. Damn about sums it up. I didn't even think we had wolves out here, let alone—uh, big, man-eating ones."

"What do you think that was howling last night? A cow? A chicken? Your dog ever meow at you? Your cats ever moo? Wolves howl. I heard a howl. We got wolves. Mayor Fraser and his cronies like Sheriff Jeffrey just don't want to admit it till after the next election cycle."

"You know, I've heard that twice now in as many days."

"Just lying to the good people of this community, that's what they do, so they don't have to get off their asses and do something about it."

Morgan raised her eyebrows. "Maybe you should

run for mayor."

"Black woman doctor running for mayor in the mountains of rural Virginia? Damn, you might be onto something, Morgan. If only I was gay, I could hit a trifecta for racism, sexism, and homophobia. Set a record of lowest votes ever received in Pineville. You want to be my campaign manager?"

"I wouldn't be so quick to doubt this town,"

Vickie Williams snorted. "You really see Victor Frank scratching a checkmark next to my name?"

Morgan smiled. "We just need to convince his… *demographic*. I'll start lining up some town halls."

"We've only got the one town hall, and it's probably already booked for bingo."

"Tough luck."

"I came in here for a little small talk. You know, weather, dinner plans. But I'm going to leave with a schedule for kissing babies. You suck at small talk."

Morgan covered her heart with her hand in mock gravitas. "Me? No good at small talk? I'm… speechless."

Vickie mimed playing the drums with her yogurt cup and spoon. "Ba-Dum-Tish. You're just yanking my chain. I'm not going to stand here and be yanked around by one of my favorite nurses when I have dumbass patients that are going to yank me around the rest of the day. Thought we were on the same team, but nuh-uh, not Morgan, no, she out here doing her own thing, acting mopey, making puns, scheming up political agendas."

Vickie finished her yogurt, two-stepped sideways, pretended to dribble the empty plastic yogurt cup off the floor and then tossed it across the room.

"Kobe!" she shouted, hands held frozen in midair.

The yogurt cup swooshed perfectly through the small trash can lid and Vickie said, "Looks like it's going to be a good afternoon, at least. Chin up, huh?"

Morgan responded, "The basketball thing may be a little on the nose, don't you think? Voters are going to see right through it."

Dr. Williams smiled. "I am who I am, Morgan. I won't start my campaign lying to the good people of this town." She then disappeared out the break room door.

Morgan finished her tea in silence, feeling strangely melancholy, thoughts running in all different directions, torn between the normalcy of joking around with Dr. Williams and the new manifestations of evil waiting for her once she clocked out and left the office. She thought about wolves and monsters and old dented trucks. Eventually, inevitably, her thoughts turned to Alex, and then they came to a crashing halt. Today, thinking of Alex made her more angry than sad.

He had been so selfish.

When he checked himself out—for good—he had left her behind, left her to clean up their life. And in a way, it was all his fault she was now having to deal with all of this on her own. When they were together she could almost pretend she was a normal wife, with a normal, happy life. Someone who didn't have secret powers and a dark past and a broken womb.

"Oh," Dr. Williams added, sticking her head back in the doorway, jarring Morgan back to the present. "Jenny told me we have a same-day new patient, needs to be brought back to room three. Said they asked for you, says they are your neighbor or something. Do you mind snagging them early and figuring out what their deal is?"

****

Morgan walked behind the receptionist desk, peering out into the lobby. She saw two old men and a middle-aged woman. None of them looked familiar, and she definitely didn't have any nearby neighbors who would know her. She had close to ten acres and her land was surrounded by hundreds of acres of private hunting property in every direction. Safe to say no one was walking over to borrow a cup of sugar anytime soon.

She scooped up her tablet, typed in her code and pulled up the appointment window. She clicked on the time slot and the new patient's name popped up.

She smiled, glad for some reason to see which patient she would be taking back. She crossed around the desk and opened the door to the waiting room.

"Vera Saez?"

The only woman in the room popped up, smiled at Morgan, and strode over to her. "Hi," she said, sticking out her hand, smiling.

"Hi," Morgan said, juggling her tablet into her other hand, taken aback at just how cheery and forward her patient was acting. Morgan reached out with her free hand and shook Vera's, reminding herself to immediately wash it before she touched anything else.

"I'm Morgan. Now, uh, we're going to go down to the end of the hallway, go left and into the very first room on your right."

Vera strode briskly forward, tall boot heels clicking against the vinyl flooring. She had long, highlighted blonde hair, and her tan skin was practically glowing. She looked in perfect health, closer to an Olympic volleyball player than a sick patient worthy of a same-day appointment. But Morgan just shrugged and followed her back to the room.

Once they were in the room and Morgan shut the door, she said, "So I hear that I'm your neighbor?" Morgan walked to the sink, sat down the tablet, and washed her hands.

Vera smiled. "Well, no, not really. I'm not technically your neighbor and honestly…" Vera raised her voice half an octave and said, apologetically, "I'm not sick either. *Estoy completamente sana.* Very healthy. I just wanted to chat with you."

Morgan cocked her head and paused for a moment before she continued to dry her hands. "Well, okay. I didn't think you looked sick. So, how do you know me, and what's so important you lied to get a doctor's appointment and took a slot from someone who may actually need our help?"

Vera smiled softly. She sat down on the examination table in the center of the room, adjusted her skirt, and crossed her legs. "I do need help, Morgan, just not from a doctor. *De ti.* From you."

Morgan picked up her tablet. She turned to face the woman straight on. She tapped her fingers along the back of the tablet, irritation rising. "Look, I'm a nurse. My job is to help sick people. You just told me you are not sick." Morgan took a long, slow breath, and then spoke, trying to keep the edge out of her voice. "What do you need from me? And why should I help a stranger who tricked her way in here?"

Vera's feet dangled about a foot up off the floor, and she swung them back and forth, smiling at Morgan all the while. The picture of happy innocence. "I like you," she said, meeting Morgan's eyes. "Straight to the point."

Morgan stared back. Her finger tapping along the back of the tablet increased in speed.

"Look Morgan, I've done this before, and it can be overwhelming. Can you sit down in that chair there?"

"No," Morgan said. "I'm going to stay standing and if things don't start making sense, I'm going to be walking out of here. Tell me what this is about."

Vera nodded solemnly. "If you insist. *Te lo adverti*."

Morgan's pointer finger practically raced against the back of the tablet now. She tightened her lips together and pushed the tip of her tongue against the back of her teeth.

"I know you were attacked last night. And I know what attacked you," Vera said. "And, most important of all, I know you performed magic to defend yourself."

Morgan's stomach did a summersault. Nausea struck her at once, and goosebumps rocketed up her back. Her fingers flinched and she dropped the tablet.

It tumbled toward the ground.

It stopped in mid-air.

It hovered there for a moment, just floating.

Then it rose all the way back up to Morgan's frozen hand. She squeezed her fingers around it instinctually as it bumped into her palm. Morgan's eyes flicked over to the cheery Latin woman, smiling, on her examination table. She was holding a smooth wooden stick in her right hand. With an eyebrow raised playfully, she jerked her stick up with a quick snap motion.

The tablet lurched up; Morgan barely hung on.

Morgan stared and Vera just smiled back, cocking her head ever so slightly to the side. Morgan realized her mouth was hanging open and she snapped it shut.

Vera said, "You are a witch, Morgan. And you are not the only one."

Morgan didn't say anything. She took a deep breath,

turned quietly toward the door, and walked out.

She strode down the hallway, pace picking up. If she walked fast enough, her thoughts couldn't catch up to her.

She was almost to the elevator when she heard Dr. Williams's voice cut across the hallway, "Morgan, where are you going?"

Morgan pretended not to hear her. She couldn't process this. She halted at the elevator doors, reached out and pressed the down button.

No one could force her to slip back into her old past, into a world of evil and magic and—

No.

She had left all of that behind a lifetime ago. It cost her grandmother her life. She may have lost Alex by closing and locking that pandora's box. Now that he was gone, there was no reason to ever open it again. And yet, some cheery woman was sitting in her examination room, holding a wand, confiding to her that she was a witch, and revealing that she knew Morgan was one too.

"Morgan, are you alright? Is there a patient in that room?"

A bell chimed, the doors slid open, Morgan stepped inside. She turned and pressed 'Parking,' then looked up at her boss. Dr. Williams raised her hands in the air, still at the far end of the hallway, palms up. "Is there some emergency? Will you be back? What's going on?"

The elevator chimed again. The doors began to slide shut.

They almost closed, then they shuttered and bounced open. As if an invisible hand had stopped them from closing.

"Morgan!" Dr. Williams strode down the hallway

toward her, concern etched across her brow.

Morgan reached out and poked 'Close Door'. It began to shut again but bounced open as it had before.

"Morgan!" Dr Williams was almost to the elevator, her voice was more irritated now than concerned.

Morgan pressed and pressed and pressed the button, and this time the doors slid all the way shut. Morgan leaned back against the wall, covering her face with her hands.

The bell chimed, the doors opened, Morgan rushed into the basement parking garage, heading toward her car in the far corner.

This all had to be a dream.

"Didn't you get the letters?" Vera's voice echoed off the concrete walls.

Morgan spun in a circle, seeing no one. She picked up the pace, almost sprinting. She rounded the garage corner, saw Vera leaning casually against Morgan's own car, and froze.

How did she get down here?

"I asked," Vera said, looking at Morgan, "Didn't you get the letters?"

Morgan muttered, "Letters?"

Vera looked confused, almost as confused as Morgan. "Yes, you know, from the owls. From the castle? You know the one. We thought you just didn't want to come."

Morgan slowly shook her head. She did know the one. She loved reading the books as a kid. "I... I never got any letters."

Vera's solemn face cracked into a smile and then she burst out laughing, holding her hands over her stomach. "*Lo siento, lo siento.* I'm sorry, I'm sorry, I couldn't resist. The way you ran off, I wanted to lighten the mood." Vera giggled some more and tried to cover her mouth with her hands to calm herself down. "Oh my—your face! *Casi me orino*!"

Morgan just blinked, standing in the middle of the parking garage. She felt faint.

"It's just so similar," Vera continued. "I mean, it's hard to come across any other way!" Vera took a deep breath and shook her head. "*Lo siento,* that was cruel! We didn't send any letters. There's no American University of Witchcraft or Virginia Community College of Magic or nothing like that. Nobody knows *anything* about you. We just found out about you and your spell craft yesterday."

Morgan stammered, "Find out about me?"

"We have a little cabin in the woods, near Bacon Hollow, and our coven meets there every couple of weeks, you know, just for some R and R and sisterhood, channeling good energy, urging positive forces into the world. We brew herbal teas, do yoga, concoct love potions, brew up the occasional hex for cheating boyfriends or nosy foxes that want to steal our chickens. Fun little trivial things. And when you tapped into the Source; we could feel it! *Tomaste mucho poder,* Morgan, *todo por ti mismo*. So much power."

Coven?

Morgan still didn't know what to say. She met Vera's eyes, hazelnut brown, big and doe-like; She felt a warm innocence exuding from them. Her whole disposition, casually leaning back against Morgan's car with her hands resting halfway in her jacket pockets, radiated authenticity. Oozed tranquility.

Morgan reached out and sensed the hidden golden

vibrations in the air, felt them shimmering around Vera's body. There were no zig-zagging red threads accumulating around her. No repellent forces.

Vera's tone shifted and she said, more solemnly, "You don't have to probe my aura, Morgan. It's not polite to do that to other witches. *Pero, puedo simpatizar*. I understand. I know this is a lot. I thought I was the only woman in the entire world who had my powers. Then Hailey found me, and introduced me to Ulta, the high priestess of the coven."

High Priestess?

Vera continued, "*Escúchame*. Come over here. Sit down on your hood here and listen to me."

Morgan took a few careful strides forward, coming within a few feet of Vera, but she did not lean against her car.

Vera said, "Morgan. We don't really have time to do the whole ignore me and try to pretend I never was here routine. I know how scary this is, because I was scared too, when I first found out. But we don't have the time for you to go home, to drink a bottle of tequila, to wake up tomorrow morning and think I had just been some crazy loon, to think maybe you imagined my magic that I showed you. Because I'd be there tomorrow, waiting for you again, and we'd go through all of this again, and I'd finally convince you *que yo no soy loca*. I say all of this, because that's what I did, Morgan, when Hailey found me. So let's fast forward through all that. We just don't have that kind of time, and it's a little played out, really, if we are being honest. You are a witch. I'm a witch. We aren't the only ones. *Eso sí que e*s."

"Uh?"

"*Eso sí que es*. It is what it is."

Morgan shook her head side to side, every inch of her body trying very much to say no. To doubt. To go back in time ten minutes. But instead, she whispered, "Okay."

"Okay. Yes, Morgan, okay. It is okay. Believe me when I tell you, it's okay. Finding out about the other witches… it's been absolutely wonderful for me. Having this coven, it's like a light in the darkness. I think you would find tremendous support there, like I did. It's basically just one big support group for women like us. Actually, it's become more of a sisterhood than anything else. And to think, you've been living here in the woods, just a few miles away from our retreat, and no one ever crossed paths with you! You must very rarely use your gifts, huh?"

Morgan nodded, just barely, and murmured, "No, I… really don't. I… I don't want to use them. I don't like to use them."

"But they saved your life last night!"

Morgan barely nodded again, reliving the attack in her mind. "I suppose they did."

"*Escúchame,* Morgan. You can't run away from this, or from us. Not that you should want to! But whether you want to or not, I'm afraid you are going to *have* to use your gifts. I wasn't joking when I said I needed your help. *We* need your help. There are monsters in Pineville, which you learned the hard way last night."

Morgan swallowed. "What am I supposed to do about it? Why can't the sheriff or your… uh, coven stop that… that… that thing?"

"That *thing* is a werewolf, Morgan. *Nahual.* And there are more than one of them here. Maybe many of them. And we *are* going to stop them."

Morgan glanced around the dim parking garage. She didn't see anyone eavesdropping. Still, she felt compelled to whisper her response to Vera. "Werewolves?"

"Yes. Sheriff Jeffrey and his useless Deputy Bunkum can't stop them, but we *can*. We just need you, because right now, we only have four members."

"Four members?"

"Yes, Morgan. Four members."

"What difference does that make?"

"Morgan, haven't you read any books or watched any movies or anything? We can't complete a pentagram with four witches. We need a fifth."

"Pentagram?"

"*Si, Cotorra*. You are starting to sound more like a parrot than a person. Pentagram. *Pentagrama. Estrella satánica*. You know, upside down devil star that riles up the Catholics. Five-pointed star needs five witches. Five times five, our power increases. Five women, coven binds and never ceases. This will be the first time we gather as five and we can use our craft against evil. Actual evil. Werewolves, Morgan. *Se necesita magia para romper la maldición*. To break the curse. No more casting spells just to conjure *tierra fértil* or rain clouds or to wipe the short-term memory of creepy old men. Pineville needs us to come together and defend our town."

Werewolves. Pentagrams. High Priestesses.
Sisters.

Morgan reached out her hand toward her car, tried to steady herself, tried to lean against the hood. Her head was swimming.

Vera leapt over to her, seeing too late what was

about to happen.

Morgan's hand slipped right down the hood, her body missed the car and she tumbled onto the cold pavement. She lay there for a moment, then gathered herself and leaned back against the front tire of her car.

In through the nose, out through the mouth.

In through the nose, out through the mouth.

I'm not alone anymore, Grandmama. There are more like us.

More like me.

Her mouth cracked into a grin, and she laughed. She honest-to-goodness, full-on belly laughed.

Vera's concern vanished; a beaming smile emerged again. Morgan laughed even harder, and Vera started giggling at Morgan, laying on the ground like that, laughing like a maniac.

"I missed the car," Morgan wheezed between gasps of air, trying and failing to stop laughing. "I missed the whole car! You warned me!"

"Yes," Vera said, laughing heartily herself, reaching out her hand. "Everyone always misses the chair. You missed a whole car." She helped Morgan up to her feet. "Now let's go back inside, tell that confused doctor lady some white lie, and make a plan for you to meet the rest of your sisters."

Chapter 8

September Thirtieth, 1944, 9:15 p.m.

Max remained still, calming his breathing, as he heard the guards beating their way toward him.

He estimated it had been twenty some days since he'd been imprisoned in the occult Nazi castle, but he had no way of truly telling. There were no windows near Max's cell, and they fed him at odd hours and with strange plates of food. He'd feel like he'd been starving, unfed, for hours unending, and then a maggoty loaf of bread would arrive through the iron bars. Then, after he had made himself sick trying to choke down the vile rotten bread, a bowl of piping hot beef and onion soup would appear.

He knew these tactics were used to break men. Twist up someone's sense of time and place and identity and they'll break far quicker than if you just slapped them around a little. Pain galvanized the strongest men, men like Max, showed them they were valuable and worth the effort. Physical pain helped strong men keep their secrets. Pain made men angry. Anger made firm men firmer in their beliefs. Made them prideful. Max could build brick houses in his mind to distract himself from beatings but sitting alone in the dark with his own thoughts, for what might be an eternity, that was the true torture.

They did more, though, than just abandon him in the infinite darkness.

Twice he had been blindfolded, yanked outside, and shuffled into a line with the other prisoners. If anyone spoke, they said, then one of them would be chosen at random and shot in the back of the head.

No one spoke.

They would remove all their blindfolds—always revealing it to be the middle of the night—and pick a strong, defiant man. Someone who acted tough, who perhaps had stuck his chin out a little too far. Then they dragged that man into the castle lawn, lit up by torches and gas lanterns, while the others watched from the battlements above.

They forced the man to fight against the giant beast chained in the lawn.

This had happened twice, and Max had watched both men be easily struck down and then eaten alive by the creature.

When Max first arrived, his brain had written the creature off as a starving brown bear, acting as a sort of castle guard. Defense against escape attempts.

But bears don't howl at the moon in the middle of the night.

Whatever it was, it was more wolf than bear, and though it loped around on four legs, it fought the men on two legs most of the time, and it sliced flesh from bone with lightning speed and snarling aggression. It wasn't lean from starvation. It was lean with lupine muscle and whip-fast paws that could dismember a man before he could scream.

Bats and ghouls flooded Max's nightmares when the wolf-monster did not. The few times he managed to get any sleep he would be haunted by what his mind conjured. Giant, leathery-winged monsters transforming into Nazi officers. Prisoners abandoned in their cells, bones exposed across their arms and legs, strips of flesh dangling off like rotten cloth, calling out in raspy shrieks, desperate for food. Or perhaps just desperate to be allowed to die.

They slammed their exposed skulls against the iron bars, the shockingly white bone spiderwebbing with crisscrossing cracks, pinkish gray brain matter oozing out, and still they would shriek into the darkness.

Clang, clang, clang.

Shriek as their brains tumbled out of their broken heads, shriek as their eyeballs bulged out of their sockets, dangling by a bouncing worm of veins and nerves, shriek as they chewed their own tongues to a stump and swallowed the bloody paste for sustenance. Then they went back to smashing their skulls against the bars.

Clang, clang, clang.

The robed guards with the swirling tattoos showed up in his dreams as well, almost as often as they did during his waking hours. Max stopped being able to notice any tangible difference between dreaming and waking. At one point, one of the guards walked right through the iron bars of Max's own cell, as if the bars weren't there at all. His pale skin sparkled as he passed through the iron. The guard knelt over him, and his two front incisors seemed much too large and too sharp and then someone shouted from down the hall and the guard swept away, vanishing through the bars again like a poltergeist.

Max assumed he must be dreaming, seeing such an illusion, so he pinched himself, and it hurt and he felt like he was already awake. He stood up and walked to the bars and they were frozen solid, coated in ice where the man had passed through them.

Max did not sleep again for many hours.

This night the guards marched all the men out in unison, abandoning the charade of the blindfolds and subtlety. It was a night of surprises.

Surprise punches to the face. Surprise kicks to the knees. Max was drug past a new man wearing a Nazi officer uniform, and Max recognized Hans, smiling merrily as he drank from a glittering goblet. Hans asked if Max wanted to be shot between his *'nasty, American eyes,'* and Max bleakly replied, "Yes." Hans acted as if he hadn't heard him and Max was forced further along through the castle.

Very few prisoners were still alive. It was always so ghastly quiet, but Max never guessed there would only be seven others left. No prisoners stayed behind to watch whatever was about to happen from the battlement towers, as was usual. The bound men trudged forward, toward the lawn.

Toward their death.

Hans Claus Günter and his friends were the audience tonight. The final eight prisoners left alive were the entertainment.

As they exited onto the lawn Max saw torches spaced out to illuminate the entirety of the castle yard for whatever special festivities were about to occur. Max looked up and could see the Nazi audience looking down at them. The flickering shadows and glistening medals of the German officers shined down from the many windows and battlement towers. There must have been close to fifty men in attendance to watch the slaughter that was about to occur.

The ceremony that he had read about in the secret letter:

'We invite you to a special evening of torture, revenge, and witchcraft.'

Max ground his molars together to keep his jaw from chattering. Torture, revenge, and witchcraft. That did not bode well for them. And with his hands tied as they were, Max could do nothing but wait.

A tinny noise crackled from around the castle. Someone had hung metal speakers, big thick cords running between them, across the castle walls.

The speakers squealed and then a bounding voice echoed out. Max felt as though he knew the German language remarkably well, but the powerful, rapid speech of the speechmaker, combined with the tinny echo of the speaker-boxes rendered the whole thing untranslatable.

Or maybe it was fear that paralyzed Max's mind.

Either way, the German speech proceeded, pausing now and then to allow for a 'heil Hitler' or for general laughter and applause.

Max found his eyes racing across the yard, just beyond the shadows of the torches. He knew the monster was out there. Pacing in the darkness, waiting for its chain to be loosened, so it could devour the feast of men laid out for it.

"American." A sharp whisper from his left, a slight French accent. "When the creature arrives. Turn your back to *moi*. I will cut your binds."

Max whispered back, "Yes."

"If we live," the French man said, "you owe me a cigarette."

"Yes," Max whispered again.

The speakers squealed abruptly, the speech cut off, and Max glanced up.

Something silver glittered in the dark hallways above, shining out in flashes at the open windows. Someone screamed. Then, further down the hallway, another scream. And a deep, bestial growl.

A Romanian voice, speaking German, came across the speakers. And this time, Max could understand clearly.

"Danke fürs Kommen, Nazioffiziere. Dachtest du, Mutter Rumänien würde dir ihre dunkelsten Geheimnisse verraten ohne Folgen?" *Nazi Officers, thank you for coming. Did you really think Mother Romania would give up her darkest secrets without consequences?*

The mysterious man who had overtaken the microphone spoke without hurry, pausing to relish in each scream, waiting for the panicked gunfire to cease, before continuing.

Max whispered to the French man, "Now's as good a time as any, wouldn't you say?"

"*Oui*, American."

Max turned his back to the stranger and felt the binds around his wrists grow taut. Then he heard a scraping sound. The kind of sound a dull kitchen knife might make as it is drug across thick nylon rope.

The speaker continued, his voice echoing out all around them, booming from every speaker. "Es wird immer Konsequenzen geben, wenn Sie sich in die alten Flüche einmischen." *There will always be consequences when you meddle in the ancient curses.*

A carnivorous snarl erupted from the ground floor

window, very close to the lawn doorway. A German officer shouted, sprayed gunfire across the stone ceiling in a popping, arcing flash, and then fell silent.

"Tonight, we are the consequences. We set loose the beast that you stole from our deepest forest. We are the guardians against evil. For too long Transylvania has tolerated your dark experiments and occult research. That ends tonight."

There was no more shooting. No more screaming. Max tried to calm his breathing, to hear… something… moving in the dark. But the night had crashed into a deep silence. As if every man left standing was holding their breath.

Max felt his binds snap. He turned around and looked at the Frenchman who had helped him. His hands were still bound, and he held a glittering cross just with his two fingertips. Max plucked the silver cross from his fingers and began sawing hard at the ropes around the man's wrist.

The thick oak door that led to the bowels of the castle creaked. Then it thumped, hard, rattling on its stone hinges.

"Prisoners. Remember our name if you survive this night. Remember the Guild of the Silver Dawn. And know, wherever ancient evil is conjured, we shall follow, to snuff it out."

The iron bracing cracked and the hinges flew off the wall; the entire oaken door collapsed outward into the castle lawn. From the darkness stepped the gray-furred, eight-foot-tall beast of Max's nightmares.

The creature loped out, more graceful than Max remembered. For a monster of such primal malevolence, it moved with delicate, deadly, precision.

Max continued to carve at the binds around his French friend's wrists. The other men were running, hands still bound, shrieking into the night. The monster took two strides, leapt through the air, swiped a thick paw at one of the retreating men. The paw collided with the back of the man's head; Max heard a solid snap, and the man tumbled onto the ground, limp as boiled pasta.

The creature snorted, huffed, turned back to Max and the Frenchman. The eyes were gold and empty. It looked at them the way a lion looks at a baby gazelle. The pointed ears twitched as it focused in on the two men.

The beast had slaughtered enough to eat for a month. But the monster was not killing for food. The monster was simply killing. And these two men had not ran.

They were prey.

Still frozen in fright, Max carved with the jagged silver cross at his new friend's bound hands.

"Those of you who still witness, watch now, as our youngest knight frees the cursed soul of the evil creature your occult officers imprisoned."

Max saw a torch flicker in the stairwell leading back into the castle. A thin man, with a thin little black goatee, holding a ridiculously thin rapier, emerged from the shadows. He brandished a torch at the monster, and the beast turned away from Max and looked toward the young man.

The ropes snapped. The Frenchman tumbled forward, and the monster snapped its vision back toward them. It lunged forward and its jaws clamped over the Frenchman's head, neck, and left shoulder. It shook its wolfen head and gnashed its jaws and with a sickening *crunch*, the Frenchman's lower half separated and collapsed to the ground. The beast spat the head and shoulder down next to it. It turned its eyes to Max.

Max lunged at the beast. Not because he thought he could kill it. But because Max was not the breed of man who simply let fate happen to him. It seemed his fate was to die in the fangs and claws of this demonic creature. He wouldn't go down frozen in fear.

If death was upon him, Max was going out fighting.

He stabbed the silver cross at the beast.

The beast slashed at Max's body.

Max caught the blow in the shoulder. The monster caught the cross in its snapping snout.

It yelped; Max grunted. He crashed to the ground. He felt as if he'd been runover by a Panzer. He couldn't get up out of the dirt. The monster snarled, turned toward him, eyes narrowing. The silver cross had pierced the beast's left nostril and the wound sizzled and steamed, smoke drifting into the cold night air.

It took one massive step toward Max, baring its fangs.

A thin rapier thrust out from the creature's chest. The beast fell to its furry knees, whimpered in the general direction of the moon, and collapsed into the dead grass.

The young man with the black goatee poked around the carcass of the monster, looking down at Max.

Max grunted, and his vision faded. The darkness swam around him, and then took him. He was glad, for in that complete blackness no more haunted nightmares could curse his sleep.

He embraced the eternal darkness, and it embraced him back, like a mother would her long-lost son, whispering, *'Welcome home, welcome home, welcome home.'*

But that blackness was not infinite, as it should have been for a normal man.

Max awoke by a campfire.

He was surrounded by six people, one of them the goateed knight that had slayed the beast. They were having a fierce argument in Romanian. Max tried to concentrate, tried to listen. His head pounded in his effort, felt as though it would split in two. Max gave up, chose not to listen, not to translate, but rather to flee the pain and escape to the warm, welcoming blackness again.

This time though, it wasn't blackness he escaped to, but a sticky gray realm of fog. Max felt himself wavering there, still half alive, bumping along, being lugged in a horse drawn carriage, emerging and reemerging from a sleep that should have been unending. There was something raging within him. Something primal that refused to succumb to the blackness of eternity. The gray zone was a transitory place. His soul wanted to leave, to head toward that warm utter darkness at the far horizon. But something else, some other soul, pumped with the hunger for life and all its pleasures, pulled in the other direction. Back toward the loud, cold light at the far other horizon.

When Max would wake, he was fed raw horseflesh. And he ate it greedily. More Romanian arguments broke out.

Max found himself dumped outside an Allied army camp near the precipice of the Hürtgen Forest. He crawled the final two miles through the wild woods to the camp on his own.

When the first soldier found him, he said, "Holy

fuck. Johnson, get over here! Take a look at this fucking sonofabitch."

Thank God.

Americans.

****

October Fourth, 5:56 p.m.

The setting sun cast a peachy-violet hue over the few lingering clouds in the sky. Max lumbered along, eyes downcast on the small dirt trail he'd stumbled across earlier. He hoped the trail would lead him to a small road where he might figure out exactly where he was. As long as it didn't lead him back to a busy area where someone may recognize him as the missing and presumed dangerous Max Rosewood.

He needed to either set up camp or find an abandoned shelter, and soon. The sun set quickly in the valley, and the temperature would fall fast.

Not that Max could die from exposure.

But still, cold was cold, and Max would prefer not to collapse naked and fall asleep shivering under the stars his first night back after a transformation.

His foot hit asphalt and he looked down.

A paved road!

He took one more step and then saw headlights erupt from the twilight darkness. A car screeched; Max leapt. His shoulder crunched onto the roof of the car and his head cracked against the tailgate. He crashed onto the road in a heap, groaned, and then began to growl in pain.

Chapter 9

October Fourth, 5:29 p.m.

Morgan picked Joey up from day care, feeling drained emotionally and physically, but mentally wired, knowing she was riding some special kind of energy that could evaporate at any instant.

She had told Vera she would meet her and the other women—*witches, the other witches*—the next evening at The Dugout, a local brewery on the outskirts of Pineville. It was somewhere public where she would feel safe, and somewhere big enough and loud enough to hold a private conversation where no one might overhear. It had been her and Alex's favorite place, so naturally she hadn't been back in close to three months, but there weren't a lot of other options in Pineville.

Until then, though, the memory of persistent sixteen-year-old Morgan pestered thirty-three-year-old Morgan to begin her investigation. Vera had not mentioned the two vehicles that had raced past Morgan earlier in the morning, but somehow Morgan knew the red truck and the blue sedan were connected to the werewolf problem and could help point her and her new witch-sisters in the right direction.

Morgan reached out and felt for the tug of those new, zig-zagging red threads but she found only the usual layer of static golden filaments: the ancient, ever-present magic of old earth her grandmother had revealed to her.

Part of Morgan still felt the weariness of her day. It would be so easy to ignore her curiosity and her motivation, to just go home and pour herself a giant glass of white wine and fall asleep before she even finished it. Sleep was her favorite drug these days.

Sleep kept her from thinking about Alex, or work, and now it could help her forget about the werewolf and the blue car and the red truck with the seriously bad vibes, and the witch in the office who had cracked open a whole new world to Morgan. A whole new world that both scared and excited her. She wasn't sure she was ready to meet a group of women with powers like hers. Women who would finally understand her.

Darkness still shrouded her. Still wrapped its skeletal fingers around her, still wanted her to cast away any thoughts of new friendship. Any thoughts of new siblings to fill the gap of her lost family. No one knew what she had been through, after all. No one could help her. She should manage this on her own, because that was the way Depression with a capital D wanted her to handle it.

What really scared her, day in and day out, were the days that depression seemed to shout at her, instead of whisper. When it loudly reminded her of the gun that had eleven bullets in it and still sat next to the king size bed in the master bedroom. They'd released it back to her, after the investigation.

Here's the gun that your husband shot himself with. Still works just fine, if you're wondering. And oh yes, it's loaded. Anyhow, have a good night, ma'am.

Like they were tempting her.

She left it by the bed for protection, she lied to herself.

She didn't throw it away, didn't sell it. Just left it there. Gleaming in its deadly black powdered coat. *I'm here if you need me,* it whispered to her, late at night, its call as soft and smooth and seductive as a love affair. *I'm here when you're ready.*

But maybe it wasn't the gun.

Maybe it was her own itchy finger she was scared of. Because some nights, the itch was damn strong. And she knew, even if they didn't give the gun back, she still had the bottles of Vicodin and Oxycodone in the bathroom closet. Still had the rope in the attic. Still had the warm bath and Alex's antique straight-blade shave kit. Still had the car and the bottles of bourbon, and plenty of big thick trees on thin, dangerous country roads.

Lots of fun choices.

But Morgan was not the type to embrace easy choices, especially when she knew they were the wrong ones. The dangerous ones. The monstrous ones.

The easy way out is almost never the right way out.

'Put all of those nasty thoughts in a box and leave them outside,' her grandmother would say, if she were still alive.

Morgan had tweaked the phrase a little, shortening it up some so that it rolled off the tongue better, but the meaning was the same.

Fuck that noise.

There were *real* monsters out there, the kind with fangs and claws, and she needed to help her new witch-sisters slay them.

She wasn't alone. Not anymore. She had a mission

to accomplish, plans to keep. And she had witnessed a whole new layer of power unveil itself. Active red threads, vibrating on a shadow frequency below the warm golden threads her grandmother had taught her to find. She would find them again. And then she would use them.

She pressed her foot down on the gas and smiled as she took the next turn in the road a little too fast.

Her grandmother explained their access to magic as being similar to magnetism. That their secret power was simply a second 'magnetic field' that encompassed the planet. It was always there, invisible to the naked eye, but just like magnetism, specially-tuned objects could detect it. Except, instead of compasses, it was specially-tuned people. And if you knew how to quiet your mind and focus your energy exactly right you could find that second magnetism, hanging just behind the veil of reality. You could learn how to pull on the threads, pull on the very filaments of earth's secret magic, and channel it for your own purposes.

And Morgan felt those threads with each of her fingers now, better than she had as a teenager, back when she actively practiced. She had left it alone for so long, yet it came back to her, stronger than ever, more intuitive than ever before. She laid her senses upon the golden threads the way a spider feels the ornate strings of its silk with its eight legs, detecting a fly twitching in its web with the slightest vibration.

Morgan felt the golden threads now, twitching to different auras that had traveled through it. Morgan felt for the disturbance in those threads, the disturbance that had rippled along the road fourteen hours ago, when the blue car and the red truck had driven past her.

She pushed her gray civic even faster.

Joey sat in the passenger seat, watching her. He whined, a little afraid, but Morgan ignored him.

She stared ahead, ideas racing through her mind.

The truck with the big dent had left a trail. As she came closer to her own driveway, she could still sense the remnants of the truck's aura that continued deeper into the hollow, deeper into the forest, past her own home. Joey wagged his tail, happy to recognize their yard and driveway and know the car ride was over.

But she didn't pull in.

Morgan continued down the road, eyes half-closed, golden threads of magic tingling in the twilight air, teasing her to continue past her house. Joey whined. But the red threads were hiding out there somewhere, waiting for Morgan to come and find them again and use them to stop the werewolves.

She pushed down the gas, feeling a darkness that clashed with the blanket of natural magic. If she focused, she could distinguish the two conflicting forces and follow the path of disrupted magic as it continued deeper into the mountain woods. It carved a choppy path of rapids and turbulence through the otherwise still aura of calm golden magic that sat heavy across the forest.

She didn't have to do anything, she told herself, if she found the two cars. Just note where they were parked and then she could report it back to the coven tomorrow.

She accelerated faster, taking the corners aggressively, driving by sensation as much as sight.

A naked man stumbled out of the woods into her headlights. She slammed on her brakes, but she wasn't fast enough. He leapt as she crashed into him, his ankles hit her hood, his shoulder smashed into the roof of her car. He tumbled over her tailgate and flopped onto the road behind her.

Morgan gasped, covering her mouth with her hand. Joey didn't bark, he just whined, pacing around in the back seat, looking out the rear window.

Morgan blinked a few times and started muttering, "Oh, Christ. Oh, Jesus Christ. Oh, Jesus Christ."

Then her mind began piecing things together.

Naked man, middle of the woods.

She wasn't completely ignorant. Despite what Vera had said, she *had* seen some movies and she'd read plenty of books.

Naked man, middle of the woods, *the day after a werewolf attack.*

She steadied herself and hopped out of the car.

Pretty female victim? Please.

Not her.

She came around to the back of her trunk, arms raised, already grabbing hold of power, if she needed it.

Crumpled on the ground, a tall, muscular man, naked as the day he was born, groaned slightly. He had dark stubble on his cheeks, with a crop of short, dark hair and he was holding his head in his hands, rubbing his temples. He was not growing any fangs or claws. His glute and thigh and calf muscles were spasming in pain, flexing taut, but they weren't sprouting any fur.

"Ouch," he said, when he saw her standing over him. "You hit me."

"You jumped in front of me," Morgan snapped, still feeling confident in her assessment of the situation. "And what are you doing stalking around in the woods? Without any clothes?"

The man did not have an immediate answer. He

rolled onto his belly, grunted in pain, and then pushed himself up. As he stood, he covered himself with his hands, which was not entirely effective. Morgan tried not to look, at least, not more than a quick glance, before she deliberately kept her eyeline firmly set above his rather starkly defined abdomen muscles.

"Lady, um, how much news do you watch?"

"What the hell kind of suspicious question is that? I know a woman was killed last night, clawed, chewed, ripped all to pieces. By what—or maybe, by whom, I wonder?"

Fear and confusion washed over the man's face. He rubbed his eyebrows with one hand, thinking, sure to keep the other hand plastered over his delicate parts, not quite managing to achieve even halfway decent coverage, not that Morgan accidentally glanced down again.

"I… I don't think that was me," he finally said.

"You don't think? How can you not know? Answer my question, what the hell are you doing out here?"

Joey hopped out of the open driver door and trotted up next to her.

Curiously, Joey did not bark or even growl at the man. The dog happily wagged his tail, sticking his nose out, trying to smell the man as much as he could, without walking any closer to him than Morgan had.

The man knelt down and reached over with one hand and let the dog smell him, and then, when Joey inched closer, the man rubbed the dog's ears and said, "You've got a good boy here, huh?"

Morgan usually trusted Joey's sense of people, but right now, she felt like he was being a gullible fool.

The man looked up at Morgan, a little abashed, his

eyes' dark and pained and mysterious, and said, "Look, my name is Max. I need help. Nothing much, just some clothes, maybe, and a lift. To the nearest bus station, or as close as you can get me. I don't want to hurt anyone and I don't want to cause trouble."

Morgan rolled her eyes. He was full of shit. She reached into that second magnetism, and felt for Max's aura, and he felt…

Clean.

Pure.

Slightly broken.

Not consistent at all with the aura of the werewolf she had been attacked by the previous night. That had been predatory, feral, primal. Instinctual. But Vera had said there was more than one werewolf on the loose…

Morgan thought for a moment and then said, "Get in the back with the dog. And don't make any sudden movements."

The man smiled, relief and gratitude washing over his face. "Yes, ma'am."

Then Morgan thought of the size of the beast she had encountered the previous night. Of its strength and speed and ferociousness as it had attacked her and Joey. She glanced to the west, where the sky was darkening quickly.

"Actually," she clicked the lowest button on her key fob. "Get in the trunk."

Chapter 10

October Fourth, 6:07 p.m.

Max thumped along, cramped inside the tiny trunk, grunting in pain whenever they hit a large bump and his head smacked against the metal just inches above him.

—Fool.—

The woman clearly suspected him of something nefarious, but, ironically enough, she seemed to have no knowledge of the actual nefarious thing he had done the night before.

Max connected the dots as he rode along, his back cramping from squeezing into such a tight ball to fit into the trunk. The other werewolf, whose howl he had heard, must have made a kill the night before. Apparently some woman. Hadn't stuck around to eat her, though. At least not long enough to completely consume her. The lady who had run into Max with her car had either seen or heard of the wounds left on the victim's body. Judging by the scrubs she was wearing, and her visceral reaction to seeing Max emerging from the woods, she probably had seen the wounds personally.

So now, this med tech or nurse or doctor, or whoever she was, driving home like a racecar driver, crashes into Max. Max remembered his reflection from the creek earlier in the day. He certainly looked like a wild person, capable of anything. Perhaps capable of attacking and murdering that woman. So this nurse, who knows nothing of werewolves, Max Rosewood, or the murder he would be assumed to have committed at the gas station outside of town, suspects him of another heinous attack that Max did not actually commit.

Now he gets into her trunk, thinking, blindingly optimistically, that she'll take him to a bus station.

—She's taking us to the police, Maximillian.—
We don't know that for sure, Grim.

Truth was, though, she probably *was* taking him to the police. Small town sheriff operation, but the police, nonetheless. And the feds would be there, working on the missing Max Rosewood case. They would put it together faster than he could say, "Full moon."

His only option would be to transform again. And Grim would do a lot of damage during their escape. He would become notorious, probably attract the attention of the few secret operations in America that could *actually* kill him. And just like that, Max Rosewood, AKA Max Sanderson, AKA Maximum Grim, would go from an anonymous werewolf who keeps to himself to the biggest monster bounty on the whole damn continent.

Max remembered the Romanians, The Guild of the Silver Dawn, and their rapier-wielding knight. He wondered if they had an American outpost.

Max would prefer not to find out.

He needed to get out of the trunk before this woman arrived at the sheriff's office.

Why had he allowed himself to get into this trunk in the first place?

She'd been so convincing. So in control. She had a magnetism about her that had entranced Max. Almost hypnotized him. Like she had reached out with her mind and touched his soul.

—Don't lie to yourself, Maximillian. You foolishly trusted her because of her large eyes and got in her car because of her particular female shape that you find pleasing. Your primal human desires always get us in trouble.—

My primal desires, Grim? My primal desires are the ones that get us *in trouble?*

Arguing with his alter-ego would get him nowhere.

Max reached out and grasped for a pull hook or a lever or something. He groped around in the dark, exploring the edges of the trunk, but he found nothing. Maybe he could pop a taillight out, reach around and grab the handle from the outside?

The car slowed down. Turned onto gravel. Stopped. Shifted into park.

They'd only been driving for five minutes. No way they had reached civilization that fast.

The trunk popped open and the auburn-haired woman with the green eyes stared down at him. Her dog popped into view, front two paws landing on the rear bumper, snout poking in to lick Max, tail wagging behind him.

"Joey, back off and give him some space. Come on," she said to Max. "Get out."

He fended off the overly-friendly pooch, scooted and climbed and half-tumbled out of the trunk. He stood up to his full height and stretched, his back popping. Thank goodness she hadn't driven much further. He would have become a permanent hunchback if he stayed in that trunk any longer. He realized he was exposing himself again, quickly covering himself. He stared down at the commanding little woman. Her eyes were still

93

fierce, jaw still set tight.

The dog had zero of the suspicions that the woman did. Max had always had a thing for animals, but it increased exponentially after his transformation. He'd thought his wolfish scent would bother dogs, but instead he'd always found a connection—a kinship—with the canines he encountered.

This woman's dog was no different.

The mutt she called Joey wiggled his whole body back and forth, still smelling Max all over, just barely able to resist the urge to jump up and lick his face. Max reached down and gave the dog another ear rub, but he kept his eyes trained toward the woman.

Behind her, now that he was out of the trunk, he could see she had parked in the gravel driveway of an old country house. The house sat behind a big open front lawn, a long narrow strip of grass running along both sides toward the back. Thick woods surrounded the whole property.

The house itself looked quaint and a little run down, even though it had a new coat of gray paint on it. The rooms behind the dormers in the second story were dark, but they each had a single fake candle, fake flickering, at each window. The front deck was new too, strung up with little Edison lightbulbs, twinkling in the fall breeze, swaying back and forth.

It was a scene right out of a cliché autumn romance movie. Just missing a couple of carved jack-o-lanterns on the deck steps.

"Cute place," he said.

"Are you hurt?" she asked.

"Are you worrying about me?" Max deflected back.

"No," she said, stomping her foot down. "I'm not

worried about you, trust me on that. I'm wondering how someone *doesn't* get hurt when they get run over by a car."

"A speeding racecar, no less," Max said, raising his eyebrows. "And it did—"

Max stopped speaking and sniffed the air. Something lingered, some aroma that tingled his memory. Joey had stopped wiggling, and was now sniffing at the air in the same direction.

The breeze shifted, and Max lost the scent. Joey growled into the evening air, turning his nose this way and that, trying to locate the smell. But it was gone.

"Maybe we should go up to the house," Max said, scanning the tree line. "And maybe get me a… towel or something?"

She cast a quick glance at the trees, then snapped her attention back to Max.

"Stop being evasive. You need to explain yourself, now, before I call the police. I'm sure they'd be very interested in your alibi for last night."

Max sighed. He was very tired, slightly concerned about that particular smell being nearby, and even more concerned about being dragged down to the police station. He didn't want to get into a long back and forth with this brave, angry, *cute* woman. At least not until he got some sustenance in him. So far she had done him no wrong. In fact, she'd done nothing but the huge favor of taking him out of the woods and back to her home. He doubted he would do as much for a stranger. He just wanted to get out of her driveway, get a pair of pants, and sit down somewhere.

"I'm Max, by the way," he said, trying to add a little familiarity to take the edge out of her voice.

"You said that already," she snapped. "Now explain yourself."

"How about this? You get me that towel, or maybe even some shorts, alright, so I don't have to stand in your driveway naked any longer, get me a glass of water and something to eat, and we'll sit up on your deck and I'll explain this whole situation. I won't even come inside. I feel a little… self-conscious standing here barely covering myself being interrogated by you, alright? You are by far the most intimidating woman who has ever run me over and then thrown me in her trunk. And you won't even tell me your name."

"It's Morgan." She raised her eyebrows, seeming very doubtful of every word he said. "And you aren't acting very vulnerable or self-conscious, but, fine. I'll get you some clothes. Because *I* don't want *you* standing in *my* driveway naked, understand? And I want answers. Real ones."

Max shrugged. "Fair enough." He could tell her the truth. She wouldn't believe it anyway. As long as it led to him getting the hell out of this honky-tonk town and safely back to one of his hideouts, he'd tell her whatever she needed to hear.

Max followed her and Joey up the deck stairs, but he stayed outside as she unlocked the door and went into the house. Joey disappeared inside behind her. A few moments later the door sprung open and Morgan held out a pair of men's running shorts and a gray T-shirt. In her other hand she held a tall glass of ice water.

Max gratefully took the glass of water, drank it down in two gulps, crushed ice and all, then reached over and took the clothes from her. Her small hands disappeared back inside the house and Max quickly dressed. They were tight for him, and the shorts rode up a little high, but at least they were men's clothes.

He fell back onto one of the two rocking chairs on the deck. He swayed a little, forward and back, and took a deep breath. It might be a short-lived break from his life on the run, but it was peaceful here. Calm and simple. He took another deep breath, partially searching for the smell of that creature in the air. But it had drifted off. The twinkling lights were a nice touch. Max let his eyes drift close. Another deep breath.

Then he smelt something else and his eyes popped open.

He smelt copper.

Like she was hiding pennies in all her walls. He smelled the chemicals she'd used to try to get rid of the copper smell, too. Someone had tried to disguise the evidence in the house, but it was still tainted by the heavy odor. Max scowled. There was something this lady was hiding from him. Maybe something she was hiding from everyone.

About five minutes later she emerged back from the house, turkey, tomato, and mayo sandwich in one hand, something else inside her other hand, out of view.

Max smelt that too.

His senses weren't nearly as fine-tuned as when he transformed into his Grim alter-ego, but they were still much more developed than the average human.

She knew a lot more than he originally gave her credit for, and he frowned, worried he may have to hurt this woman and her dog, if she tried anything stupid. He really didn't want to do that.

"Do you need to call anyone? Is there anyone who might be worrying about you? Who might want to help you?" Morgan asked.

Max snorted and ignored answering her question. "What do you intend to do with that?"

"Do with this sandwich?" She held it up. "I intend to give it to you so you can eat it. You asked for food, didn't you?"

"The sandwich is nice," Max said. "But what do you intend to do with the small bar of silver in your other hand?"

Morgan did not speak. She met Max's eyes and her eyes flashed with both surprise and conviction. She was caught off guard by him smelling the metal, but she was not going to back down.

"You could try to shove it down my mouth, I suppose," Max pondered, wondering out loud, turning to look back out into the darkening lawn. "If you could force it down my throat, which you can't, it would melt my insides probably, boil me from the inside out. But, well, you don't look strong enough to do that. Not even if I stay human, let alone if I…" He glanced back at her and trailed off.

Morgan glared at him. "So you admit it. You are one of them. I swear, if you try to do anything to me, I am capable of much more—"

Max cut her off. "Relax!" He shook his head and said, "Yes. I am one of them. One of them…" He reached out his hand. "…who like turkey sandwiches."

He snatched the sandwich out of her fingers. And took a giant bite. "I'm starving," he said, barely slowing to breathe as he ate.

She makes a mean sandwich, Grim, gotta give her that.

When Max finished, he wiped his mouth and looked

back at her. "You already knew what I was, clearly. You knew I was one of them. Or at least, you suspected it, considering the weapon you chose to carry out here onto the deck. So why act so shocked?"

"This isn't my only weapon," she said, eyes flashing dangerously, reflecting the twinkling lights of the dangling Edison bulbs.

Max believed her. There was something … unusual about her. Something special. But he wasn't her enemy.

He didn't even want to be here.

He just needed to convince this strange woman to give him some money, take him to a bus station, and get him the hell out of this creepy valley town. And Step One was to convince her that he was not out to eat her or her friends anytime soon.

"Look," Max said, "I'm not out to eat you or your friends. I'm not going to change, okay? Yes, I am one of them. I can smell the flat bar of silver in your clenched fist, but you don't need it. We don't just change when a full moon touches our skin. We can control—" Max stopped abruptly, then rephrased his sentence. "Well, *I* can control it. I choose when I change. And I don't like changing. I don't want to do it." He took a deep breath and said, "I don't want to hurt anyone, especially a nice stranger who can give me a ride to the bus station."

"So why were you naked in the woods? Why did you change last night?"

Max thought for a moment, then answered. "Someone forced me to change last night."

"So you really weren't the one who attacked me here yesterday, were you?"

Max blew out his breath in a huff. One thing after another with this woman. It was starting to seem like she had more secrets than he did.

"Attack *you? You* were attacked by a werewolf last night? Right here? I thought you said someone else had been attacked."

"I'm the one asking the questions."

"How are you alive?"

"I said, I'm the one asking the questions. I fed you a sandwich and covered your naked butt. So, thanks for the concern, but I still get to ask the questions."

"Okay, Sherlock, relax." Max said, "No, I didn't attack you. I was nowhere near here when I transformed last night. And when I attack, I…" Max paused for a second, looked out into the darkness and then continued. "Let's just say, I don't miss. I attacked someone else. Some backwoods hillbilly, I think. It's hard for me to remember it all perfectly, but like I said, he was *trying* to get me to change. He knew what I was, somehow, and shot me with a dart full of poison. Nightshade, maybe, mixed with something else, I'm not sure. Not that that's an excuse to kill someone, but, well, yeah that's why I changed in the first place. It had been almost a decade since the last time I turned. Something strange, something almost paranormal, seemed to pull me here, seemed to want me to turn."

Morgan leaned back, her chair rocking slightly, while she thought. Max could smell her hair, and it reminded him of autumn harvest and his eyes started to water and he shook his head, trying to shake out the old memory he didn't want to unearth.

Morgan chuckled.

"What?" Max asked.

"You look like a dog. Shaking your head like that. You seemed to have picked up some habits from your other half."

—Don't make a connection, Maximillian.—

Better to have no one to worry, so you *have no one to hurt, I know.*

He turned back to her, and said, because he couldn't help it, "You told me your name, but we haven't properly shook hands yet." Max reached out his hand. "Shake this with your non-silver-bearing hand, if you don't mind, please. Don't want to burn myself."

Morgan raised her eyebrows at him. He kept his face dead serious.

She obliged, switching the silver from her right hand to her left before extending her palm out to him. His hand wrapped around hers like a baseball glove, but he made sure not to squeeze too hard. "Thank you, Morgan, for feeding and clothing me. It's a kindness that most strangers wouldn't do."

"I'm not fragile, Max. I'm the one who ran over a werewolf and stuffed it in my trunk."

Max smirked. "Well yes, but the werewolf went pretty willingly, if I remember correctly."

They sat in a comfortable silence for a few moments, thoughts wandering, then Max asked, "Where did this other woman get attacked?"

Morgan tilted her head, eyes glancing left, indicating to Max that she probably didn't know the answer to that question. But instead, she dodged giving him an answer at all. "Before I start answering your questions, I still have a few left myself."

"Right, right," Max said, inclining his head. "Go ahead."

"You attacked someone last night, right? Here's what I don't understand. I worked all day at the only medical facility within almost fifty miles of here. We treated only one trauma victim, a fifty-five-year-old female that I told you about. How come I didn't treat the man you attacked? Or at least hear about another victim coming through the hospital?"

Max met her eyes and said darkly, "Is the only morgue within fifty miles also at your medical office?"

"Yes." A quick response.

Max nodded his head. "Then yes, that is strange." *Was someone covering something up?*

Two abandoned vehicles at a gas station, blood everywhere, headless hillbilly corpse left in the middle of the parking lot. That doesn't just disappear. Not without fast, deliberate effort. If a civilian had found that carnage, the whole town would know by now.

Morgan murmured, sounding like she was talking to herself as much as she was talking to Max. "You said someone wanted you to change… *provoked* you to change."

"Yes."

"And that someone was the one you killed?"

"I'm not sure if he was the one pulling the strings, or if he was just a puppet in a grander plan that I don't understand yet. But yes, I killed him. Undoubtedly, I killed him. And I left behind a lot of… evidence at the scene of the crime."

"You drove here, right?"

"Before I changed, you mean? Yes."

"Which means your car is wherever you left it when you changed?"

"It should be. Out in the open. Which is why I assumed that by now my face would be plastered all over the five o'clock—"

"Wait!" The woman's green eyes widened, she looked over at Max, excited. "Do you drive a red truck? Or a blue sedan?"

Max felt his stomach tightening. So someone *had* discovered the cars. "Yup," he said. "I drove the car, the… dead man… yes, I think he drove an old red truck."

"Well, hot damn," she said, standing up, rubbing her temples. She muttered to herself, pacing the deck, then remembered Max existed. "I saw those two cars drive past me early this morning and I sensed—uh, I mean, I got a weird vibe from them. The truck had a big dent in the back. They were driving into the woods, past my house, on this very road." She pointed out into the darkness, toward the small country road that intersected her gravel driveway. "I was looking for them when I found you tonight."

"Okay, slow down for a second. My turn now. Why were you looking for two random cars *before* you met me? And did you see who was driving those cars? And don't forget, I also want to know how the hell you survived being attacked by a werewolf, let alone came out completely unscathed."

"I…" She hesitated.

"Come on, I showed you mine. Fur and claws and all." Max spread his big hands out in front of him, palms up. "You can tell me."

"I just felt there may be a connection between the werewolf that attacked me and the woman who was killed, and those cars. No one ever drives out past my house. It's all dense mountain forest beyond here. The big dent, the speed they were driving. It seemed suspicious, that's all."

Max nodded, then said, "And yourself? How'd you

survive?"

"It rushed at me in my front yard. I had Joey with me, which might have distracted it, maybe. I don't really know. We made it into the house, locked the door, before it caught us. Simple as that. That poor woman wasn't as lucky as me, I guess."

Max sniffed the air. He closed his eyes and sniffed again, smelling for that dangerous odor he had detected in the air earlier.

"You outran a werewolf from down there," Max pointed into the yard, "up the stairs, across the deck, and into your house before it could even touch you?"

Morgan shook her head. "I don't know if it even chased me up the stairs. I wasn't measuring the distance; I was too busy trying to run away from it. Too busy trying not to hyperventilate. I unlocked the door and then barricaded myself inside. I didn't hear or see the monster after that."

"Monster is kind of a derogatory word in my culture. It's kind of as bad as using a racist word, actually. Use werewolf, or just call us wolf-person. You could get cancelled for saying monster, these days."

Morgan frowned. "What? Really? I didn't mean to offend—Wait, you're pulling my leg."

Max didn't laugh, but he smiled.

Morgan narrowed her eyes at him. "Max don't joke with me. A woman is dead. And more might be dead, soon, if we don't do something."

Max coughed in surprise. "We?"

She nodded.

Max said, "Well, before there is a 'we,' I have one more question."

"Only fair, I guess. Go ahead."

"I smell something inside your house. Is there anything you may have forgotten to tell me about yourself? Anything that might have happened in this house? Anything that might have lured the werewolf here?"

Morgan's eyes looked hurt, but she spoke defensively. "No, there is nothing else. What do you smell? It's unnerving by the way, that stupid party trick of yours."

"I smell blood, Morgan. A whole lot of old blood. And the smell of bleach and vinegar and baking soda, lots of it. The kind of smells that one might associate with a violent crime. The kind of smells that might attract one of my kind." Max leaned forward. "So tell me, what are you hiding in there? And why are you not afraid of me? You want to talk about unnerving? Small little hundred-pound, five-foot-nothing chick, green fire in her eyes, unblinking in the face of a *monster* of unstoppable violence. What do you know about the shadowy world that my kind inhabit? Why did a werewolf try to attack you, way out here, in the middle of nowhere? And how did you actually stop it? Who the hell are you, really? Whose blood are you trying to hide in this house?"

"Enough!" Morgan's eyes watered and she slapped her hands down on the deck railing. "My husband shot himself! Months ago. Is that what you needed to know? My big, dark secret? It's that I'm widowed at thirty-three! And I'm not afraid of you, Max, because half of me doesn't even want to be here anymore! If it weren't for those fucking animals in there, I'd have picked up the gun and put a bullet through my brain the very night I came home and found him. That blood you smell is Alex's blood. The blood he splattered all across our bathroom tile. I didn't know it could attract a fucking werewolf. And yes, sonofabitch, you are right. I used bleach. I used vinegar. I used baking soda. You can still smell it? I can still see it! Every time I close my eyes, I see my husband's brains on the walls!"

She stormed inside, the screen door clanking shut behind her.

—*Smooth, Maximillian.*—
Shut the fuck up, Grim.

Chapter 11

October Fourth, 7:29 p.m.

Lancelot and Galahad hissed and then scattered when the screen door opened. Darting under the bed or scurrying for some other hiding place, no doubt. Shadow remained in Morgan's lap, still purring, but on alert. She heard Joey greeting Max in the foyer with heavy tail wagging and soft licks.

He had given her half an hour by herself.

She sat on the vinyl floor in the middle of the dark kitchen. She hadn't turned any lights on, the sun had fully set, and the whole house was almost pitch black now.

Max emerged from the foyer, snagged a chair from the dining room table, lifted it like it was nothing. He plopped it down in front of her in the middle of the kitchen. He turned his back to her, looked around. She guessed he must have night vision or something, because she couldn't see anything at all. Another werewolf trick, she supposed. Max walked over to the bar cabinet set along the far wall. Examined her wine rack. Examined the half-empty bourbon bottles.

"These his?" Max asked, tapping a finger against a bottle.

Morgan didn't respond.

Max left the bourbon alone, assuming correctly that

they were Alex's. He pulled two wine glasses off the shelf. Found her fancy corkscrew in the dark cabinet. Opened a bottle of something. Poured two big glasses.

He brought them over, handed one to Morgan. She reached up and took it. She still said nothing.

Max sat down in the chair. He sighed, took a big swallow of his wine.

Morgan could almost make out his face in the dark. The way the stubble ran along his jaw line. The way when he clenched his teeth, a firm muscle flexed and tightened in his cheeks, making his face grow taut. His dark brown eyes glowed in the sunset on the deck but now they smoldered black and mysterious in the dark. He was strong. And hurt. And built like a warrior from ages past.

She looked away, back to the wine glass in her hand. Thinking these ridiculous thoughts about the werewolf who she'd run over did her no good. At the end of the day, she needed him gone from her town, and he needed her to help him leave. That was it. Anything else was just fantasy. And she wasn't ready for fantasy. She'd already had too much excitement meeting another witch at her office. Adding a lone, rugged werewolf into the mix… it seemed like some crazy, adolescent dream.

She lifted her wine glass to her nose and smelled it. It was one of the red blends from Barboursville, a nearby winery over the mountains. A little closer to true civilization. It was her favorite.

Max spoke. "When I got back from the war, I wasn't really sure how I even made it home. They flew me from Germany to London to New York, then on to Louisville. I wasn't all there. Not really. Kept having these dreams. Dreams of the moon. Dreams of blood and screams and ghosts.

"Back then, you didn't know how much they might have told your family. Didn't know if anyone even knew you were still alive or not. When I landed, nobody was waiting for me. Ma was gone a long time by then. Pa gone right after I left. It was just my wife and my little girl who might have been waiting on me, but they hadn't heard word from me in close to a year. So I got off the plane. Didn't know a single face. Took a taxi. Served for six years, deployed in Europe for more than three straight. Took a taxi back to the house, on my own dime.

"When I pulled up, I almost told the driver to take me somewhere else. Every day. Every day of my immortal life, I wish I had told that taxi driver to take me somewhere else. Any-goddamn-where else. But instead, I got out. Taxi driver said 'Thank you for your service, young man.' Wouldn't take my money. People were good to veterans like that back then. Made me feel like everything was going to be alright. But after he pulled off and I was alone, standing in my old driveway by myself, holding my big, green duffel bag, I knew it wouldn't be alright. I knew there was something wrong. I just didn't know what.

"I walked up to the door and walked right in and my little girl saw me and she shouted, 'Daddy! Daddy,' she kept saying, 'Daddy, Daddy, Daddy,' but I hardly recognized her. She could barely say Da-da when I left. Now she looked halfway to being a grown woman. I called her Ginny when she was a little baby, but she wasn't Ginny anymore. She was all Virginia now. Her hair still smelt the same, though. And when that smell hit me, I just started crying, and she started crying, and her mother came running out of the laundry room, and she was already starting to cry. 'Maximillian,' she asked, 'You're home?' Like she couldn't really believe it.

"She had these yellow sunflowers sitting on the coffee table. Christ. I don't even remember the color of the house, or the wallpaper. I barely remember her anymore. But those yellow sunflowers were sitting there, and the afternoon sunlight was coming in, the kind of sunlight that catches the dust and makes it look like it's alive, swirling in the air, nature's gentle little afternoon spotlight. Aimed right on those sunflowers. I stared at those flowers as I hugged my baby girl and her momma, and I cried. I could have held them for an eternity, just staring at those flowers in the fading sunlight. I was home. For the first time in almost four years, I was home.

"But it wasn't the same. Or I wasn't. Both, I guess. I kept having dreams. Every night, they'd hit me. I'd dread falling asleep, because I knew what was coming for me in the dark after midnight. I had been home maybe two weeks when I woke up and I was screaming and I had my hands on my wife's throat. Virginia was shouting and shouting and beating me on the back. Pounding and pounding and pounding, her little fists, with all her little strength, trying to save her momma, pounding and pounding and pounding. Christ, I didn't know what happened. 'I was dreaming,' I muttered. But I saw their fear. The fear in their eyes. The fear of a husband. Fear of a father. A man can't have that. Can't think his family fears him like that.

"I slept outside on the ground that night. Like a dog. Next day I went and got a hammock, tied it up between the oak tree and the swing set out back. Slept in it for two weeks straight.

"I could tell they were talking about me. I didn't

blame them. But I kept having those fucking dreams. Having those visons of the moon. The visions of my fingers in somebody's flesh. Tearing at something, something secret, something buried deep inside the blood and the muscle, inside the very bones."

Max swallowed back the rest of his glass of wine. He sat it on the floor between his legs, in the dark. He sat silent for a long while. Just breathing. Morgan reached for him in her mind, felt for his aura and it was nothing but blackness. Not dark energy, or bad energy or golden, neutral energy. Empty. Completely void of any magic or hope. A cursed vacuum of space that she'd never felt before. He poured himself another big glass from the bottle, but he didn't take another sip.

After a while longer, he continued. "Virginia was nine years old. She woke up when I came in her room. I'd been sleeping out in that fucking hammock. Didn't know what might happen. I'd been dreaming and then I woke up. Full moon shining down on me. And then I got angry. Angry at God, angry at the war, angry at being alive. And something snapped in me. Like I went to this place in my head where none of that anger mattered. But when I got there, I couldn't get out. I was trapped there. And I turned. I changed.

"And I remember that night, Morgan.

"Sometimes, I don't remember. But that first night, the first night of my change, I remember it all. I stalked into her room, had to duck under the doorframe. I smelled flesh and blood and I wanted it. My nose brought me right to her, like I wasn't even in control, and I came up to her, real close. Real close to her face. Breathing in the smell of her, my eyes peering down at her. She looked right back into my golden eyes. I was full monster at this point. Fur and fangs, right in her face. But… *Christ*… she still said 'Daddy.' Somehow, she still squeaked out, 'Daddy?' in pure terror just before… just before… And I hesitated. When she said Daddy, I had my claws on her chest and I could smell her fear, that smell of vinegar and adrenaline and iron and I hesitated just for a moment and stared into her eyes. She knew it was me. She knew I was the monster in her room. And in my head I thought, 'Run, Ginny, run.'

"But it was too late. Another part of me, the stronger part, the more primal part, the predator part, wouldn't let her run. I pressed my claws down through the blanket, right into her chest. I couldn't resist. The aroma was too intoxicating. I lifted her little body out of her bed with one paw, and she was squirming and screaming and crying for her momma and I… I… I lifted her face right up to my mouth and I…"

"Stop." Morgan reached out and put her hand on Max's knee. "Stop Max. You don't have to relive this again."

"I relive that moment every day." Max put his face in his hands and took a ragged breath. "I didn't just kill my little baby girl…" He stifled another sob and then spoke, his voice threatening to break. "I ate her. Ate my own daughter. And then I ate her mother, too."

Morgan held one hand over her mouth. She felt bile building up in her throat, swallowed, tried to hold back vomit.

Max took a deep breath, and he spoke, his voice still shaky. "You know the most fucked up part, Morgan?"

She shook her head. Somehow, he saw her in the pitch-black kitchen.

"I can still taste them," he said.

He finally picked up his second glass of wine. Swallowed it all back.

"Ever since that day I've been fighting with that monster inside me. The creature that killed my family. But the real truth is that it's not some other creature. It's me. Just a *different* me. A primal, insatiable, Jungian me. But still me. I am the one who slaughtered them. I am the one that killed my family.

"I tried to kill myself for a while, tried plenty of different ways, but the monster didn't let that happen. We finally came to a kind of understanding. We don't kill innocent people, not anymore. We don't change unless we have to. The monster doesn't try to get out all the time; I don't try to find new ways to kill us both. I eat more rare steak, the monster whispers less violent urges into my head … I think, in a way, the monster part of me feels guilty about my family too. Didn't know who they were, back then."

Morgan didn't know what to say. She shivered, rubbed at her arms for warmth. The fall air outside had plummeted in temperature and Max had only shut the screen door.

Max straightened up in his chair. He rubbed a big hand down his face, dragging his callused fingers across his stubbly cheeks. "I'm sorry. I'm sorry for saying all that, Morgan. And I'm real sorry about your husband. But I want you to know: *he* chose to do this. Not you. You didn't kill him. I can smell the guilt on you. You are holding onto that guilt, the same way I am. But you don't deserve it. Trust me when I tell you, you don't want to hold onto that forever. I'm cursed, Morgan. I still remember what it sounded like, cracking into the bones of my own daughter. It was like the snap of a branch across your knee, but wetter. Like snapping a branch across your knee and finding gooey caramel inside. I remember the salty taste of her marrow. I deserve that guilt because I *am* that monster. You need to get me out of your town and I promise I'll never come back. And then you need to forgive yourself. Because you, Morgan—*you*—you aren't cursed like me. You aren't a monster. You didn't kill your husband. He did that to himself."

Morgan stood up in the dark. She laid a hand on Max's shoulder.

"I'm not taking you anywhere." She continued, "Not until you help me stop this other werewolf. The one still killing innocent people in my town. Because if you can help me do that, maybe you can realize you aren't that monster anymore, either."

Max was silent for a moment. He inhaled slowly and spoke without looking up. "Fine," he said. "I can do that. I can find this other werewolf, and I'll kill it and then you'll help me leave."

She squeezed his shoulder and only then did he look up at her in the dark, and she saw the pain burning in his eyes, felt sorrow within the void of his aura, and she felt an urge to take her other hand and put it across his face. She reached out.

Her fingernails hovered in midair. She felt the warmth of his face inches away. Felt it slide ever so closer to her fingertips. Then her fingers touched his face, and she dragged them across the stubble on his cheek. He kept his eyes on her. He stood up, slowly, and she kept her hand on his face as he rose.

Max's breath deepened. He inched closer—

Then he turned away from her, pulling back, and

stepped away further into the kitchen. He said, "Want me to sleep outside on the deck? It would be safest, I think. I understand if you—"

"No," she said. "Max, you aren't an animal that needs to be kept outside."

"Are you sure?" Max asked quietly, still looking away. Morgan didn't respond. He wasn't asking her, anyway, she knew.

He was asking himself.

****

October Fifth, 5:49 a.m.

Max woke up the following morning and sensed two warm lumps resting against his body. He felt more peaceful than he had in a long while.

He cracked open his eyes and saw two cats, one curled up in his lap, the other curled up in the little crevice between his ankles, both as cozy as could be. The first gray rays of dawn crept into the house. In the kitchen he heard the sound of a kettle beginning to boil. Max sat up and the cats scattered.

"Good morning." Morgan chirped, "Do you want any tea?"

It wasn't even six in the morning and this woman was already up, brewing tea.

Groggily, Max said, "Urgh."

"What?"

Slightly less groggily, Max said, "Coffee?"

Morgan didn't respond, but he heard her digging around in a pantry somewhere behind him.

The previous night, Morgan refused to let Max sleep outside. She insisted that he deserved a shower and a safe, warm place to sleep. She laid out a set of gray sweatpants for him and offered Max the master bedroom. Max didn't have to sleep outside, if she insisted she was okay with it, but Max would not be talked into being the first person to sleep in the master bed since her husband died.

So she slept in the guest bedroom, as she had since Alex passed, and Max took the couch.

"How do you like it?"

Max shook himself out of his reverie, responded, "Black is fine."

He watched her as she turned back to the counter, watched her chestnut hair bounce as she measured out coffee beans, watched the muscles in her upper back and shoulders stretch underneath her tank top as she lifted down a large French press from a high shelf, followed the curve of her body down toward her hips—

He tore his eyes away from her, throwing the idea out almost before it could fully form.

Better to have no one to worry, so you have no one to hurt.

—She wanted you, Maximillian, last night.—

Max tossed a thin orange blanket off, ignoring Grim's thought. Morgan must have laid it across him once he fell asleep. He stood up and strode over to the window and stretched, looking out across the yard. Joey was already outside, sniffing around by the side of the house, looking for a good spot to relieve himself.

Beyond the dog, beyond the lawn, above the tops of the tall trees and a layer of thick fog, a rounded mountain peak poked into the softening gray sky. The whole world was still.

A tranquil mountain sunrise, as picturesque as if Thomas Kinkade painted it himself.

"Here you go," Morgan said, joining him at the window.

Max took the mug of black coffee offered to him.

"I'm not a big coffee person," Morgan said, "but Alex was. I never had the heart to throw his stuff out. His bourbon or his coffee beans…"

"Or his sweatpants, thankfully, because there's no chance I could have fit in those pink yoga pants you're wearing."

Morgan snorted. "First of all, these are salmon, not pink. Second, I wish I had forced you to wear them, just so I could have seen that. A werewolf in yoga pants. The girls at work would never believe it."

Max blew on his coffee, adding, "I wouldn't recommend telling the girls at work about keeping werewolves in yoga pants under your roof. They might have you committed."

"Hell, they might believe me, the way things have been going lately. Plus, who knows what happened last night, with at least one other werewolf on the loose."

"Probably nothing," Max said. "If there is just one other werewolf out there, I doubt they would change two nights in a row."

"What do you mean? Why wouldn't they? It was still a full moon, right?"

"It doesn't quite work like that. It's not like in the movies. The full moon definitely adds pressure. But transforming, it gives you this… ah… the best way to describe it is like a powerful release."

Morgan looked up at him.

Max nodded. "I know what that sounds like, but I don't know any other way to describe it. There's this tension within you, this desire that you know is wrong but you want so, so bad, and the longer you go without 'releasing' it, the more it builds and builds… The full moon ramps that tension up even more." Max couldn't help but flick his gaze again toward Morgan. She met his gaze, green eyes unblinking, simmering with an inner heat that Max hadn't noticed until just then. Max looked down to her lips, then pulled his eyes away and turned back to the window.

"Anyway, my point is, unless this other person is a sociopath, they probably aren't changing every night. Once you transform and get that release, the tension is broken, and it takes a while to build back up again. They probably just had a rough day, felt a stronger urge than usual due to the full moon, and snapped. They tried to attack you, then attacked and killed someone else, and woke up somewhere isolated, on their own. Odds are they are laying low somewhere, afraid of what they might have done. Perhaps they don't even remember."

Morgan thought for a moment, then she said, "Last night you told me something was pulling you here. Some unnatural force was acting on you to change. Don't you think that could be influencing this other werewolf? Forcing them to change more often too? Or bringing others?"

Max shrugged, not convinced. "Possibly. But I didn't feel any urges to change last night." He took a cautionary sip of his coffee. "Damn, this is really good. I'm not just saying that. It really is very good coffee."

Morgan smiled and sighed. "I practiced a lot, making it for Alex, just the way he liked. Grind fresh every morning, don't let the water come to a full boil. Sprinkle in a touch of nutmeg with the grounds."

Max looked at Morgan. "He had great taste." They

both were silent. Max eventually continued. "It sounds like he was a lucky man to have you, Morgan. I'm not sure what demons he had, but I doubt they had anything to do with you."

Morgan nodded, but Max could see in her eyes she didn't fully accept what he said. Guilt still haunted her for his suicide. Morgan changed the subject. "Max, if you think you were called to be out here, if you think something is trying to get you to change, something brought you all the way to Pineville, don't you think there could be more going on here? More than just one other werewolf being called to our town?"

"That is a good question, and it's certainly possible." Max took another sip of his coffee. "But I have no way to know the answer. You would know better than me. Is there anything else going on in Pineville? Anything you've noticed or heard about that might be drawing us here? Anything else… paranormal? Supernatural?"

"No," Morgan said quickly. She shook her head, adding, "Not that I know of, anyway."

They stared out the window, and eventually Joey came tromping back up the deck stairs. Morgan let him in and Joey bee-lined for Max, tail wagging, happy to see his new friend up and awake.

"Can I be honest with you, Max?" Morgan asked, while Max rubbed Joey's ears.

"I would hope so," Max said, dead serious. "Werewolves are notoriously trustworthy."

"I don't think it's the werewolf in you that I find trustworthy. I think it's the human. And I don't know why, I can't really explain it, but I *do* trust you. And I want to tell you something."

Max didn't respond. He watched her, waiting for her to continue.

"I'm meeting with someone today, well, some people today, about this… situation. And I'm not sure if I should tell them about you. You don't seem to be a danger to our town, you don't even want to be here. But I'm afraid if I don't tell them, well, they may find out about you. It would look awfully suspicious if I'm caught hiding a werewolf from what might turn into a werewolf hunting committee."

Max thought for a minute. Then he said, "Who are you talking to who might believe that Pineville has a werewolf problem? Normal people don't believe in these things… Human instinct is to explain away the supernatural. To discredit the monsters in the shadows."

"I… I'm not sure I still can believe it, and I saw it with my own eyes."

Max waited for her to continue.

"But maybe these folks have seen things too… They came to me… they invited me."

"Well, don't tell them about me. You don't have to lie. Just don't even mention it. You haven't seen me change, for all you know, I'm just a homeless lunatic with a strange obsession with the moon."

"And a great sense of smell. And very resilient to being struck by moving cars."

"Coincidence," Max said. "Just don't bring me up. Go find out what they know tonight, and we can take it from there."

Morgan frowned. "That is one option."

"Do you have another?"

"Look, I think having a werewolf there could be very helpful. Don't roll your eyes. Last night you acted like you could take care of this on your own. So why not help us, if you're so confident? I know that it's not my place to tell your secret—"

"No," Max said firmly, "It's not."

Morgan pushed forward, "Look, I have to work today, and then tonight we are meeting at the local brewery to discuss what's been going on. If you want, you can stay here for the day. No one will look for you all the way out here. I normally take Joey to daycare, but you'll save me fifty bucks if you can stay home with him and watch him. I can come back here after work, pick you and Joey up, and you can come with me to the brewery for the meeting. If it seems dangerous, or if they aren't receptive toward you, I'll take you right out of there and straight to the bus station and buy you a ticket to wherever you want to go."

Max didn't hesitate to shut her down. "No."

"Damn it, Max, why not?"

"Morgan, the things I told you, I've never told anyone else. I keep my head down, I don't change, I try to live a simple, *human* life. I don't want to hunt another werewolf, but I would much rather do that than go to some community town hall and divulge all my secrets to a bunch of nosy country people with nothing better to do than gossip and complain. They won't believe me, but they still might throw me in jail. Or worse, Grim will feel trapped and I'll change again, and I'll kill innocent people. I'm not nice. I'm not a good person. I'm not some good Samaritan out here trying to rid the world—"

Morgan stepped backward, away from him. Her fingers on each hand were contorted in a strange shape at her sides.

Max noticed his chest heaving. He had turned toward her, had raised his voice, had lifted his fist into the air as he spoke, without even realizing his anger was building.

"I'm sorry." He took a deep breath and then another and then continued, his voice softer, "I don't want to hurt people, Morgan. I don't want to risk it. I *can't* risk it. If it is just you and me, working together to stop some other werewolf that can't control their instincts, fine, you lost your husband, I lost… everyone… We can track down this monster together and get it over with, no other innocent people involved or at risk. I'll help you out because you helped me out. That's the full breadth of my morality system. Favor for a favor. But no, I won't be joining up with the nosy neighborhood watch."

Morgan regained her confidence, kept pushing. "What if it's not a neighborhood watch? What if it is a group that can maybe help you? Not just to catch the monster, but help you deal with yours as well?"

Max titled his head. "What are you talking about, Morgan? What are you saying?"

Something red flickered in her green eyes.

Then it vanished.

"I'm not saying anything, Max. I'm just trying to be optimistic. Isn't that worth a try, for once?"

"No," Max said, firmly, "It's not. I'm not going."

Morgan huffed, turned on her heels, strode out of the room without a word.

Max sipped his coffee.

—And I'm the antisocial one, Maximillian?—

"Really is good coffee," Max muttered to himself, ignoring Grim's quip.

Five minutes later, Morgan stepped around the

corner, dressed in fresh scrubs, car keys jingling in her hand. She didn't look at Max as she walked past him into the foyer toward the front door.

"Come on, Joey. Want to go on a ride?"

"I can watch him," Max said quickly. "I really—"

"No, I don't want to inconvenience you, Max." She stepped out the front door, Joey ran out after her, and she finally looked up at him. "Feel free to stay or go, I don't give a shit. Just lock the door behind you when you leave." She slammed shut the door before Max could respond.

Chapter 12

October Fifth, 5:25 p.m.

Morgan shivered. The wind blowing off the mountain shook the treetops on her drive to the edge of town, and she knew chilly air waited for her outside the car. But still, she'd made a promise.

She left work a little early and made it to The Dugout before their arranged meeting time. Joey wagged his tail and whined from his spot in the passenger seat. He could see the dog park, just outside the brewery. Two other dogs were already bounding around beyond the gate. String lights ran along the fence, and the sun sat heavy on the horizon, glowing across the waving cornstalks, turning the farmland and the dog park and the remnants of the old baseball field into shades of soft golden yellow.

When The Dugout purchased the property, they replaced the home-side dugout with a massive pavilion. Though it looked open to the elements, the breezeways and door frames had been covered over with large glass windows and automatic sliding glass doors. Morgan could see inside, where the fireplace glowed orange, where the bartender laughed with two regulars, where the owner and the brewer sat at the far end of the bar, sipping two dark beers. No one else sat inside, unless she also counted Big Moose.

Just next to the baseball field once sat the old Moose Lodge. It had fallen into decay and sat empty for years, but at one point someone had gone in and stripped everything out of the building. The only thing they left behind was a giant boulder, rumored to be formed from ancient rock hauled out from the mountain forest. When The Dugout owners bought the property, they decided they liked the look of it. They hauled the old moose boulder inside their pavilion bar and then built up around it. Now Big Moose stood like a massive guardian mascot at the center of the bar's back wall, looking over all the patrons.

Morgan did not see Vera inside or at any of the outside picnic tables. Apparently no one else from her group had arrived early. In an hour the brewery would be busy: jam-packed, the dance floor full, and Morgan could hold her secret conversations with the rest of the women from the coven.

Until then she would tire Joey out at the dog park and brace herself for the conversation with a little liquid courage.

She ground her teeth, zipped up her jacket, and threw open the car door. She clipped Joey onto his leash and made room for him to hop down into the gravel. She walked him over toward the dog park, him whimpering and hopping the whole way. He wanted to see his old friends worse than she needed a drink.

It was close, though.

An all-white husky and two-tone brown boxer, both of whom Joey had made friends with before, paced inside the fence, wagging their tails, watching Joey trot closer. Morgan smiled at the short, friendly owner of the two dogs.

What was her name?

She remembered having long conversations about each other's dogs with her, but she hadn't seen her since Alex passed away. The woman waved at her as she walked into the first of the two gates.

"Hi, Morgan!" she said. "I'm so glad to see you out here!"

She still couldn't dredge up the woman's name, but she remembered the dogs.

"Looks like Balto and Tyson are happy to see us, too!"

Both dogs stood right up at the edge of the second gate, panting, tails wagging.

She unclipped Joey from his harness, threw open the second gate and the dog bolted into the park, racing immediately around the perimeter, looking over his shoulder to ensure both of his four-legged friends were hot on his tail.

Morgan stepped inside the gate. The woman smiled kindly at her, asking her, "So, how are you doing?"

"I'm doing well," she replied.

"I'm glad to hear that." The woman stared at Morgan, waiting for her to say more. The silence stretched on.

"Uh, I'm going to go grab a beer, mind if you watch Joey for a quick sec?"

"Of course not!" the woman said, beaming. She held up her half-full pint. "I always load up before I bring the dogs over."

"Smart," Morgan said, already turning toward the brewery.

She would endure an awkward conversation with the woman, but not without a beer in her hand. She would have to face the owner and the brewer, too, which would potentially be another difficult conversation. The owner and brewer had both been friends of theirs, had both shown up at Alex's funeral, and she hadn't said a word to either of them since.

She didn't mean to turn herself into a hermit over the last three months, but it seemed to be the case. Still, she couldn't hide forever, especially in this town, and she would have to get comfortable socializing again outside of work. Yes, she was a widow. Yes, no one knew how the hell to talk to her without being awkward. Yes, she appreciated their thoughts and prayers, as little good as they did.

The doors slid open and she strode in. The temperature was twenty degrees higher inside than outside; the warmth immediately cheered her spirits. The brewery smelt pungent, full of a rich, earthy smell. Philip and Craig must have been working on a new beer earlier in the day.

"Morgan!" Craig shouted. He walked over quickly, opened his arms, embraced her before she could even figure out something to say. He smelt like he may have been tasting a lot of beer before she arrived. "I'm glad to see you out and about," he said once he finally released her and stepped back, revealing Philip the brewer standing a couple of feet behind him.

Philip smiled and inclined his head, a little nervous at her presence, far less forward and far more sober than Craig, and said, "It's good to see you."

"It's good to see you both, too."

"Want a beer?"

"Hell yeah," she said.

The bartender filled a glass of Pineville Porter for

each of them. Craig waved away the money she tried to hand to the bartender, saying tonight he would hear nothing about her paying. They took their beers and walked outside.

After their gracious welcome there had been a moment of silence. No one said anything as they made their way toward the dog park. But as they crossed the gravel patio area and arrived at the fence Craig blurted out, "The last three months must have really sucked, Morgan, and I'm damned glad to see you." He pointed into the dog park, where Joey was hunched over, dropping a pile of poop in the tall grass in the corner, "But you still have to pick up Joey's turds. Dead husband doesn't mean we allow breaking the rules around here."

Philip's eyes shot open, but Morgan laughed, then Craig and Philip laughed and they felt like friends again. The awkwardness was broken; Morgan asked them questions about the brewery, and they responded cordially. Now that it had been mentioned, everyone was quite happy *not* to mention Alex again.

After one poop scoop, two more beers, and plenty of running around and butt sniffing, Morgan and a slightly-tired Joey reentered the brewery with Craig. Philip left for the parking lot, saying if he walked back in, he'd be stuck there all night.

Sure enough, the place was starting to swarm inside.

Two new bartenders were hustling at the bar, and the original bartender came bounding up to Craig as they walked in. "Hey, Craig, um, the water heater is doing that thing again."

"What thing?"

"Like, uh, not heating the water."

Craig gave Morgan a look and said, "Good luck with

your girls' night or whatever it is. Duty calls. Come find me if you need a break." As he walked off with the bartender, she heard him saying, "Did you flip the circuit like I told you last time?"

The bartender shook his head. "I forgot which one was which."

"They're labeled!" Craig filled up his pint glass again on his way toward the staff-only door.

Morgan skirted the edge of the crowd, looking for Vera, Joey tagging along behind, tail placidly wagging back and forth.

Morgan spotted Vera and another woman sitting at a small table in the back corner of the bar. Tucked into the corner as they were, they still struggled to keep a low profile.

The other woman with Vera seemed to be in her early twenties and she practically glowed in a bar full of mostly dark flannel and jeans. Her hair was bright pink, spiked on top, buzzed along the sides, and had two hard edges traced along the ridge of her skull. She shaved two dashes across one of her eyebrows to match the hard edges buzzed into her hair. She had high cheekbones and pale skin and an ink-black squid tentacle tattoo that rose up out of her sweater, curled around her long neck, and stopped just under her jawline. Upside down crosses dangled in her ears and a small silver nose ring curved around one nostril. Under the table, Morgan could see she even had bright pink sneakers that matched her hair.

Her eyes sat in heavy eyeshadow and eyeliner, looking very much like a stereotypical modern-day witch, and very much like she wasn't hiding herself from anyone.

"Morgan! *Bueno*! Good to see you," Vera said.

"Grab a seat! And who is this?" Joey sniffed at Vera and wagged his tail lazily as she rubbed his ears.

"This is Joey, he's super friendly."

The pink-haired lady squatted down near the dog, but Joey growled and stepped back.

"Joey, cut it out!" Morgan said. To the new woman, she said, "I'm so sorry, he's never like this." Morgan tugged on Joey's leash, but he continued growling.

The pink-haired woman said, "It's okay, sis. I rock a different style than this pup is used to, that's all. I'm not as scary as I look. Say, what is this?" She reached into her pocket and Joey's ears perked forward. He cocked his head sideways. She pulled out a milk bone. Joey's growl transformed to drool, and after taking the treat gently from her fingers, he was putty in her hands.

Joey laid down under the table; the three women sat around it.

"So," Morgan said, "I'm Morgan." She reached out her hand.

"I'm Ash. Well, I'm Ashley Rose Summers, but look at me, I only really vibe with the first three letters."

"Oh, well, fair enough. I guess I can… vibe with it." Morgan smiled, not quite sure she was using that word correctly. She felt kind of like a dork. Alex used to call her a dork all the time.

"Thank you, sweetie," Ash said and lifted her wine glass and took a small sip of the white wine she was drinking. "Vera tells me you have a certain connection to us."

Diving right into it, I guess.

"No one else meeting us? I thought there were two others coming?"

"Ulta, um, can't make it tonight. *Lo siento. Pero,*

Hailey will be here, I guess she's just running late."

Ash added, "Hailey is always running late, but usually for a good reason."

The house music cut off and a mic reverb screeched across the bar.

Ash and Vera both flinched, reached up, covered their ears. Morgan grimaced.

"Sorry!" Someone shouted. Then the reverb was balanced out, and a few hesitant strums of guitar chords thumped from the stage area at the front of the brewery. "Check, check."

The live music started and Morgan had to lean forward to try to hear the two girls. Joey whined under the table.

"Let's go outside!" Vera shouted.

Morgan glanced back as they walked outside; the dance floor was crowding already. She remembered nights with her and Alex, a few beers deep, him pulling her onto the dance floor, grinding like horny teenagers at prom during the fast songs, twirling to the steps they had rehearsed for their wedding during the slow songs, Alex holding her close, kissing her neck, his breath hot against her cheeks, whispering things he wanted to do to her in the car on the way home…

The cold air buffeted them as they crossed outside. One of the firepits sat unoccupied, and Morgan, Vera, and Ash beelined right to it.

Vera sat down on a wooden bench and Morgan sat down in the Adirondack seat across from her. Ash walked over to a wheelbarrow full of pre-cut logs, grabbed up two big pieces of cedar, lugged them back and set them into the firepit. It was already burning along nicely and would only grow bigger now.

Ash sat next to Vera and said to Morgan, "I kind of have a thing for fires."

"Sure, who doesn't?" Morgan said, looking around, seeing no one else anywhere nearby. The picnic tables were abandoned, far too cold to be outside without being right up next to a fire or a heater. The nearest firepit was thirty yards away. "Should be plenty private for us to talk."

Ash said, "Don't worry about private, Morgan. Trust me, people don't want to know us, don't want to listen, don't want to even consider there could be people like us. Most people in Pineville don't even look me in the eyes. They are afraid of different, but even worse than that, they are apathetic to everything that doesn't immediately involve them."

Morgan nodded. Pineville was old-fashioned like that. Like a trip back in time, Alex used to say.

Ash continued, "These people are so ignorant, so cut off from mother nature, so damn self-absorbed and self-obsessed, sucking the dick of capitalism at every turn, screwing Earth over in favor of microwavable meals full of slaughtered, caged, diseased animals, animals who barely make it to their teenage years, by the way, tortured into fattening up by force feeding—"

"*Mi amor!* We just met this woman, *por favor*, do not bombard her with every toxic problem you have in *tu cabeza a esta momento. Es importante* for me and Hailey *que ella se une a nuestro aquelarre*."

"Vera, sweetie, you are speaking Spanglish again."

"*Ah, lo siento, pero suenas loca!*"

Morgan interjected, "Actually, Vera, I understand what Ash is getting at. Maybe not as vehemently as her, but I get it. I'm not a full-blown vegetarian, but I don't eat that much meat, and it is kind of frustrating the way these big corporations treat the animals, like they are just products, not living creatures. Plus all the wild animals going extinct, the Arctic melting, corporate profits higher than ever." Morgan took a big gulp of her beer. She was almost done with her second. "How did you put it? Sucking the dick of capitalism? I've never heard it put that way before, but I'm definitely stealing that line."

Ash's grin grew wide, and Vera huffed and sat back. "You are lucky," Vera murmured. "*Que ella es loca como tu.*"

"Sweetie," Ash said to Vera, "I knew she would be like us. We are connected. We all have the same power. Our power emanates directly from the soul of our natural world. We know it is not coming from the damn oil companies or nuclear reactors or any of the other blood-sucking monopolies plaguing this planet. Our power comes from Mama Earth herself."

Morgan smiled. Ash was a little over the top. Well, not just a little over the top. Alex would probably say she had gone full 'crunchy-granola conspiracy hippy,' but Morgan dug it.

"Actually," Morgan said, "I've read nuclear is maybe the safest, best way to power the country right now."

Ash chuckled. "Well, I see you still have some way to go, sweetie. Nuclear reactors are unnatural, and if something happens, they could kill millions. They are not the solution."

"Better than burning fossil fuels."

Ash nodded. "But simply being better, that is not enough."

"My husband used to say, 'Don't let perfect stand in

the way of better.' I always liked that."

"Used to?" Vera interjected, "Divorced? *Pero…* What happened?"

"No, not divorced. Uh… he's dead, actually."

"Oh, *mi amor*. We didn't know."

Ash stared into the fire. "I knew." She looked up at Morgan. "I helped that idiot Sheriff and his dusty old secretary out with some IT stuff a while back. What, must be over three months now? I was there that afternoon. Converting the phones to digital when they got the call."

"Oh." Morgan didn't like someone else knowing her business, but at least Ash wasn't trying to hide the knowledge and pretend she knew nothing about it. It didn't seem to be in Ash's nature to be anything other than blunt.

Vera reached her hand out tentatively and then set it gently on Morgan's knee. "May I ask, what happened?"

"Suicide," Ash said, before Morgan could speak, still staring into the fire. Morgan's eyes instantly teared up.

She had said it so matter of fact.

Then, Ash added, "Fuck him for doing that to you."

"Ash!" Vera looked shocked. She covered her mouth. "*Por qué eres tan* cruel? That is her husband you are talking about!"

"Yeah, so? He left her." Ash looked up at Morgan. "My mother, she was like your husband. Couldn't handle the world. Didn't think life was worth the suffering it brought. So… she, uh, set Stevie, my little brother, 'free.' While I was at school. She was sitting in the living room when I got home. A big, bloody chef's knife sat across her lap. She had used it to slice her own throat.

134

The detectives said I was lucky. Said if I hadn't stayed late at school, she would have killed me too. They wrote in their report that her blood was much fresher than my brother's blood in the other room. She sat on the couch for at least a couple hours, waiting for me to walk through the door, so she could set me free too before she did it to herself. Eventually she must have said fuck it and killed herself, instead of waiting an extra hour for her only daughter."

"My god," Morgan said. "I'm sorry."

"Yeah, that bitch didn't have the patience to wait for me to come home." Ash's eyes smoldered, reflecting the raging fire in front of her. "I'm just pissed she wasn't alive when I got home. Because if I saw what she did to my little brother, I would have killed her. Killed her with my bare hands. Her cowardice took that away from me. Took away my vengeance."

Ash's eyes stayed locked on the glowing firepit. She hadn't moved them once.

Morgan remembered Farmer Tom Crawford's words, back at his produce stand the other evening. *'Something's not right with this valley.'*

Tragedy haunted Pineville.

Morgan and Alex had heard stories almost as soon as they moved to the small town. Now that she thought about it, she remembered that ten years ago, Mayor Fraser's young teenage daughter killed herself. She jumped off the bridge into the Shenandoah River. Alex had told her the story in hushed whispers the first time they attended a town hall meeting when they moved to Pineville.

They renamed the bridge after her, as a kind of memorial.

Morgan could see the bronze decal in her mind's eye. She drove past it whenever they left town to head south, back when they would go visit Alex's parents in Florida:

Cynthia's Bridge of Hope.
June 21st, 2009.
Stop. Think. Ask for help.
Someone WILL *miss you.*

How far back the tragedies went, Morgan couldn't say.

But maybe whatever was drawing the werewolves here, maybe it was drawing evil in general. Maybe Alex hadn't killed himself all on his own. Maybe something *pushed* him to do it.

Maybe it wasn't Morgan's fault she didn't notice him growing isolated. Didn't notice his struggle.

Morgan took a deep breath. "I can't bring back my husband. You can't bring back your brother. But according to what Vera said the other day, if we work together, maybe we can save some other folks in this town from losing *their* loved ones. Tell me how we can stop these monsters."

She thought of Max. Even though she told him she didn't care if he left, she hoped he stayed. She didn't know what she would do if the coven found out she was sheltering a werewolf, but she would cross that bridge when they came to it. Perhaps he was already on his way out, hitchhiking across the mountains.

Ash and Vera recognized someone behind Morgan.

Vera stood up and gestured. "Morgan, this is Hailey."

Morgan turned and saw the most stunning woman she'd ever seen in person.

Nearly six feet tall, with fire-red curly hair that tumbled down over her shoulders, she wore a deep cut beige V-neck that showed a lot of cleavage (especially for Pineville), skintight khakis, and a brown leather bomber jacket. Wound tightly at one side of her waist hung a brown whip. On her other side, a flat gray revolver in a small leather holster.

Morgan's first thought was she looked like an Irish super model, dressed up as a tomb raider for Halloween. But Halloween was still almost a month away.

"Hi, Morgan," Hailey said, stretching her manicured hand out to Morgan. She wore fingerless horseback riding gloves, and her nails were the same sparkling fiery orange as her hair. Not a single nail was scratched or scuffed.

"I hear you are going to be our fifth," she said, just a hint of an Irish accent sneaking out, "I can't wait to see what we're capable of, now that the coven is complete."

****

October Fifth, 11:44 p.m.

Morgan helped Craig and the last on-the-clock bartender clear the tables. Hailey, Ash, and Vera left together at closing time, exchanging numbers with Morgan, promising to meet up again later that week. Now that Morgan had met them, she agreed to join them for a séance in the woods where they could safely practice their powers and discuss what it would take to stop the werewolves entering the valley.

Morgan hated driving under the influence, so she stuck around after they left to sober up a little, and to get Craig's opinion on the girls. Being the brewery owner, he always had a good grasp on everyone that came through his doors.

"I can't get a good grasp on them, honestly," Craig said.

Morgan frowned.

Craig continued, "Some folks around here don't trust them. Mostly the ol' timers. But I think that's just based on how they dress, which isn't really a fair way to judge somebody. Vera has lived in the valley a long while, and Ash grew up here. How'd you meet them?"

"Oh, uh, it's like a grief group thing."

"Ah… well, they say it's good to talk about… um, stuff, I guess."

"Why do you sound less than convinced?"

"Oh, I don't know." Craig admitted, "I'm not good at that shit. I subscribe more to the Irish-style mental health philosophy."

"What's the Irish-style mental health philosophy?"

"I'm not an expert, yet, but it's mostly whiskey and beer based, as I understand it."

Morgan rolled her eyes. "Well, to each their own." She dropped off the last tub of empty pint glasses onto the bar and looked around. The tables were all clear. "That's about all I can do to help, unless you want to finally teach me how to close down the kegs in the back. I know you showed Alex once, but he never…" Morgan's voice faltered.

Craig opened his mouth to talk but couldn't find the words.

Morgan whispered, "Sorry, I didn't mean to, uh—his name just slipped out."

After a moment's hesitation Craig said, "Don't *ever* apologize, Morgan, for saying his name."

Morgan nodded. "Well, anyway, teach me next

time, maybe?"

"Alright, next time."

"Goodnight, Craig. Thanks for letting me stick around."

"Thanks for cleaning. Anyone who cleans can stay past closing, that's in the official Dugout handbook."

Morgan unlocked a weak smile from somewhere, and said, "Alex told me that lie, too, but I know he was just staying late to drink beers with you boys. Lord knows he wasn't doing any extra cleaning."

"Goodnight, Morgan. Drive safe, and honestly…" Craig scratched his chin, then said, "maybe, I think that grief group is a good idea. I think it's smart that you are spending time with those women. Just don't tell any of my regulars I told you that, ya' hear? I will firmly deny it if you do."

Morgan nodded. "Fair enough. I'll see you soon."

"I hope so. No more three-month absences."

"Deal."

She turned and left the brewery. She walked to her car through the gravel parking lot, a sleepy Joey trotting along at her side.

"You've had a big day, huh, boy?"

Joey twitched his ears and whined a little.

"Yeah, I'm tired too. Don't worry, we're going straight home and going straight to bed."

Joey wagged his tail, whined a little more in response to Morgan.

"I don't know if he'll still be there. Don't tell him this, but I hope he's there too."

Joey snorted, shook his ears.

"He doesn't have a phone, so if he's gone, he's gone. Don't get your hopes up, okay?"

Morgan opened the passenger seat and let Joey hop inside the car. She walked around to the driver's side door, swung it open, and collapsed into the front seat. She let out a big sigh and then leaned forward to start the car.

"Don't scream," said a deep voice from the back seat.

Morgan screamed anyway, and her scream was cut off by a callused hand around her mouth. "It's me, I'm not here to hurt you."

Max removed his hand. Only then did Morgan notice Joey had already clambered into the backseat, tail wagging happily, big block head laying on Max's lap. Her heart raced; she could feel her pulse thrumming like a percussion drum in her temples.

"Jesus, Max. That is not right. You can't do that to people! I feel like I'm going to have a heart attack." She glanced in the mirror, meeting his eyes. He didn't exactly look apologetic. "How did you even get all the way out here? It's like twenty miles back to my house."

"I found something today. Something you need to see."

"You really need to work on normal human interactions, Max." Morgan leaned forward, turned the keys. "This better be important."

Chapter 13

October Sixth, 12:30 a.m.

"Pull off here," Max said, gesturing toward an unlit side road. "Turn off your lights."

Only the dim running lights lit the gravel road. Small houses, rundown, old. Stacked up next to each other, most without much of a yard, and no streetlights anywhere in sight. Crumbling roofs, uneven foundations, collapsing sidewalls. Most of the houses would be condemned if they were inspected today. An old neighborhood in an abandoned stretch of Pineville that time had forgotten.

Morgan routinely drove right past this side street on her way home. She kept on the main highway, never gave the road a second glance or thought. Hidden behind a thick barricade of overgrown pine trees, most of the valley residents probably didn't even know the neighborhood still existed.

Just as the Pineville chamber of commerce intended.

"Stop here."

They came to a halt in front of the most dilapidated house on the street yet. The front door was blocked by a bulky heap of wood and cement rubble. Once, the home must have had a covered entryway above the front sidewalk. No longer. It had crumbled into a heaping pile of debris. Graffitied plywood sheets blocked out the windows. Patches of dead weeds stuck up between the cracks in the sidewalk.

More worrisome than the decay, though, was the flickering blue light that glowed through the gaps between the plywood and the windows.

"Max," Morgan whispered, even though the windows were rolled up in the car, "Someone's in there. This looks dangerous."

"Maybe, but you need to see. Come on." He threw open the back door. Morgan cracked the windows for Joey, and then hopped out.

"Okay, follow me and stay quiet. No one was here earlier, but I don't know what the neighbors might think if they see us."

Morgan glanced at the other houses and whispered, "If there are any other neighbors." She doubted there were. "Max, why are we here?"

"Come on, I'll tell you once we're inside."

They crept around the side of the house. Max pushed through the thorny, overgrown hedge without as much as a grunt. Morgan followed after, arms up to protect her face, pricking herself again and again across her forearms.

Why are you doing this?

Because it's an adventure. Sixteen-year-old Morgan.

Because Max led you here. Thirty-three-year-old Morgan.

But neither of those answers were wholly true. Sure, the mysterious man who literally crash-landed in her life was a compelling force, but Morgan's curiosity drove her onward more than Max's insistence. Something was happening to Pineville. Werewolves arriving, maybe in many numbers. Perhaps more on the way. A witch coven emerging and inviting her to join. New threads of red energy materializing out of the ether…

Morgan felt compelled to put the pieces together.

She ground her jaw tight and pushed through the remainder of the brush and emerged into an overgrown backyard. Pool furniture had been knocked over and scattered about, partially hidden by clumps of thick weeds. Max walked straight to the back doorway. Without knocking he turned the knob and pushed. Flickering blue light fell across him, and he raised his finger to Morgan. He gestured for her to follow, then walked inside.

Morgan took two fast breaths then strode in right behind him.

The inside of the house was filthy. It reeked of sweet, rotten fruit and unwashed bodies. But it didn't look abandoned. Looked well lived in by both rodents and vagrants. Nothing moved inside, however. They both listened. Heard nothing.

They tiptoed further into the house, Max whispering as they went, "When you left this morning, I got onto your laptop. I looked through the local news websites, trying to find anything I could about my incident at the gas station. I found plenty about your female victim who was attacked, but nothing on the man attacked and killed by Grim—by me, that is." Max stopped in the living room. Sleeping bags were strewn across worn down furniture. An old TV was lit, blasting a blue channel that simply said, 'No input found.' It had been hooked up by an extension cord that ran out a small gap in one of the plywood covered windows. "I hopped on Facebook to check—"

"You have a Facebook?"

"No. I used yours. It was already logged in."

"Wait—how'd you even get into my laptop?"

"It was just a pin code. On the laptop of a woman with multiple cats. You said Joey was Alex's, so I figured the cats were yours. I looked through the calendar in your office, found all the cat's birthdays highlighted throughout the year. Shadow looked the oldest, so I tried his birthday first. Zero. Two. One. Seven."

Morgan scowled at him. "Max, you are being exceptionally creepy tonight."

"I was a spy, Morgan. I hate to burst your bubble, but you weren't that tough to crack. I didn't download any viruses or log onto Chase and move all your savings into an offshore Cayman account, if that's what you are worried about."

"How did you know I bank with Chase?"

"It was on your favorites list, don't be paranoid."

"What, did you check my web history also?"

"No, I wasn't snooping on *you*. I was trying to track down the loose werewolf that attacked you. First thing we can assume: if there is no coverage at all on the gas station attack, someone must be covering something up out there. So I started with who I knew was there that night. A greasy, twenty-something night-shift gas station attendant."

"Okay, so, what did Facebook tell you?"

"Well, I found the gas station page, they'd tagged their new hire just six weeks ago with a welcome to the team picture. Clicked on his profile. Full name, with picture and everything. Ronald Greenburg. I swear, it's like people want to throw away their privacy these days.

Turns out he lost his phone and had to get a new phone number about six months ago. Helpfully, for all his friends and for me, he posted the new number publicly. I cross referenced his name and number on a background search website. The background check provided a list of known aliases, known addresses and a Class 1 misdemeanor for possession of drug paraphernalia two years ago in Richmond. The address that intrigued me the most was the local one, of course, and I was only more intrigued when I cross-referenced the local real estate property listings with the county. This address is owned by a man with the kid's same last name. Ran that guy back through the background check and found him. A couple more searches and I found out he died, just before little Ronnie got popped with the possession charge."

Morgan sighed. "Okay, so the night-shift gas station attendant in a small town has lost some family and used drugs and…" Morgan scanned the room again, "seems to be down on his luck. How does that help us?"

"On its own, it doesn't. But when you dig, you dig. You don't just look for your own biases or hope for a smoking gun. Let the details come to you, gather all that you can, then put the mystery together with all the different parts you've gathered."

"Thanks for the free detective lesson," Morgan said dryly.

"When I came by here this afternoon, the place was abandoned, and the TV was turned off. But I saw the extension cord, tried the remote, and it worked. That dusty black box underneath it? That's a video game console. It works too. Ronnie's been here recently, hiding out maybe, and been jacking power from somewhere."

"Okay…"

"I flipped the input and left the TV on when I left, that way when we came back, if the blue was still lit up, I could be pretty confident no one had come back. Or if they had, they'd left again in a hurry. I also found this." Max stepped over a crumpled pile of dirty clothes and a pizza box and pointed down. "Like I said, you don't hope for a smoking gun, but that doesn't mean you might not stumble into one."

A piece of paper, yellowed and weathered and slightly frayed at the edges, rolled up halfway on itself sat on the coffee table. As if it had been rolled tightly at some point, it had tried to reroll back into its original shape. A segment of blood red twine lay underneath it.

"It's a note, and it sure as hell looks out of place in a room like this, wouldn't you say?"

"For sure."

"Come over here and read it, but don't move it from where it is."

Morgan stepped toward the coffee table, but her foot caught on something that threw her off balance. Max caught her as she stumbled into him, but not before her face smashed into his chest.

"Thanks," she said, looking up at him.

"Try to be careful," he said, his breath warm against her. "We don't want anyone to know we came back here." He steadied her, pushed her upright, away from him.

Morgan cleared her throat, murmured, "Says the guy who left the TV on the last time he left."

Max frowned. "That was because—"

"I know, relax, I'm messing with you." Morgan tried

to ignore the intoxicating whiff of his body aroma. It had been of sweat and pine and something… feral. Something wild. Like he'd been running through the deep woods all afternoon. And considering she hadn't left Max with a car, that must have been exactly how he'd gotten from her house to this house and then to the brewery across town. Morgan pulled a pen out from her scrub pocket, pressed down on the unrolled edge of the paper, and squinted to see the note. It had been written in heavy black ink:

Ronald,

Pass the attached letter to the man we discussed. He drives a blue Ford Fusion. DO NOT speak to him or anyone else who may enter the gas station late at night on the third of October. Once you deliver the note, close the gas station and leave town. Do not read HIS *note. Do not mention* THIS *note. Do not mention our previous meeting to anyone. Remember, you also need to paint a message on the bathroom wall. Burn* THIS NOTE *once you've memorized the graffiti for the bathroom.*

VC and BS

Spray paint the following:

DON'T FEAR THE MOON, FEAR THE WITCH.
SHE IS A CURSE UPON THIS LAND.
LEAVE NOW OR FALL UNDER HER SPELL.

Morgan's heart started to beat even faster. The mention of a witch made her stomach crawl, but seeing those initials flustered her even more. Surely it was just a coincidence that her father's initials were also BS. She held her emotions in check and turned to Max.

"They knew you were coming. Whoever VC and BS

are. They were planning for it."

"Yes." Max seemed calm, but Morgan felt anxiety creeping within his aura.

"This is not exactly a normal note to leave for a tweaker."

"No," Max said, eyes on her. "And opens up way more questions than answers. Who knows me? How did they expect me to come through Pineville that night? Who else are they drawing here? And why the dramatics about the witch?"

Morgan pressed her fingers against her forehead, thinking. And hiding the creeping dose of anxiety building within her.

Was she the witch? Did they know her, too? Or were one of the other women she'd met earlier that night the witch they were referencing?

If BS stands for Benjamin Shroud, he'd certainly know your powers…

She shook her head. Her father was nowhere near Pineville. He couldn't find her; she'd made sure of that.

Max continued, "The note also tells us that Ronald did not follow instructions very well."

Morgan took a deep breath, forced herself to stay in the present, to not let her thoughts run toward the dark past, where memories of her father haunted her.

She looked at Max. "I assume you didn't get handed a note at the gas station?"

"No. And he only left the first line of the message on the wall in the bathroom. My memories are still a little shaky from that night, since I transformed less than an hour later. But I remember seeing the graffiti. I remember the message. 'Don't fear the moon, fear the witches.' Plural. Nothing else about curses or spells or whatever else."

"Why would he write only half the message, and write it wrong?"

"I don't know. Seems like a hell of a mistake to make, even for a tweaker. But he talked to me, too. Warned me about the big hillbilly who ended up trying to capture me once I—er, once Grim took over. Ron tried to convince me to leave town, now that I think about it. But he didn't give me the note intended for me."

"Don't suppose that note is around here somewhere?"

"No, I looked everywhere for—" Max cut himself off and held up a finger. Morgan strained her ears but couldn't hear anything. Max whispered, "Joey is growling out there."

Then Joey wasn't growling but barking, ferociously, and the barks cut through the thin plywood covering the broken windows. Max didn't bother to run back through the house. He kicked a sheet of plywood right off the front window with inhuman strength and then leapt through the opening.

In the dim light Morgan saw two things in a single instant.

One, a young man that looked a lot like gas station attendant Ron Greenburg in a large hoody and backpack, sprinting away in terror down the street.

Two, Max, much faster than Ron, running him down like a predator. His strides were quick, his arms pumped powerfully, cords stood out taut on his rigid neck. Ronnie glanced back in pure fear. The kid was white as a ghost.

Joey continued to bark in alarm. If anyone had been sleeping in any of the neighboring houses, they weren't any longer. Morgan clambered out of the window and rushed over to her car. She calmed Joey down the best she could, though it took nearly a minute to get him to cease howling and yelping. With the racket Joey had made, Morgan wouldn't be surprised if one of the remaining residents had called the cops. She and Max needed to get out of the neighborhood, and fast.

She turned and saw that the kid hadn't made it very far. Max had him pinned in the middle of someone's front yard.

He was shrieking in mortal terror, "Don't eat me! Don't eat—" and then Max clamped a large hand over his mouth. Morgan ran to them.

"Max, we have to get out of here."

"Not yet." Max had contorted Ronnie's forearm around his back, and now twisted it agonizingly upward toward the rear of his head. "Don't scream, Ronnie. No one is going to eat you. I am going to let you go, but don't scream or run, or I *will* eat you."

Max released him. Ron flipped around, his panicky eyes darting back and forth between Morgan and the man who'd caught him. "You're… you're… you're like the wolf-dude, man."

"Not right now. Right now, I want to help you."

"Help me? Christ, I don't want help, man. I don't want to get involved with anymore shit, man. I want out, man, I told those old guys, I want out. Then I told the spooky woman I want out. I don't want to be involved in any of this, man."

"Involved in what, Ronnie? Weren't you supposed to leave town?"

"And go where? Be homeless somewhere else? Did they put you up to this? What are you, like their wolf-man enforcer?"

"I think I was supposed to be their victim, like you might be if you stay around here. Where is my note, Ronnie? Why didn't you give me my note? Who were these men? Who are VC and BS?"

"How the hell am I supposed to know, man? They had drugs, they wanted me to do shit. One of them had evil eyes. Like he could stare into my soul, man. They said what I had to do was really important. Like some trippy evil was coming to town. I don't know, man. But then some lady, she like called to me or something, man, like in my dreams. But it wasn't a dream. It was real. Like a real dream, you know, and she seemed a lot nicer than they were. She wasn't evil. She was like, on my side, man. She told me to burn your note. Told me to follow the rest of their instructions, but only kind of, pretend-like, like I fucked it up or something. And that she'd protect me. That was a fucking lie, clearly!" Ronnie looked around spasmodically, as if his protection might swoop out of the darkness and rescue him at any moment.

Nothing moved, save the branches in the trees, swaying in the wind.

Max and Morgan exchanged a look.

Max tightened his fists around the straps on Ronnie's backpack. He shook him, asked, "Think, kid, who were these men? What did they look like? Did they have names?"

Ronnie stammered, "I don't know, I don't know, man, I don't know."

Max continued, "And this woman from your dream? What did she say to you? Did she know these men? Did she have a name?"

Ronnie's stammering dissolved into hysterics and blathering.

Max growled, "I'm getting hungry, Ronnie…"

Ronnie's eyes rolled into the back of his head. "Ben…" he murmured, his voice barely a rasp louder than the wind. "She said not to trust the man named Benjamin…"

The kid's eyelids fluttered and he went limp.

"Fuck," Max murmured. He dropped the passed out tweaker onto the lawn. "Okay, let's get the hell out of here."

Morgan felt like she was going to puke. Her father's name. She hadn't imagined it. Her knees almost buckled out from underneath her.

Benjamin.

The kid's description sure sounded like her father.

"One of them had evil eyes, like he could stare into my soul…"

Still just a coincidence, Morgan?

"Morgan, come on!"

Focus.

In through the nose, out through the mouth.

"What about the kid?" Morgan managed. "You just going to leave him there?"

"He'll live. It won't be the first time he wakes up in a strange yard, I'd guess."

Max strode back toward the car. Morgan looked back at Ronnie. She felt for him in her mind, found an aura of confusion and paranoia under his unconsciousness. He was alive, for now, and she could see his chest rising and falling, rhythmic and deep, if a little fast.

Morgan left him in the dirt. She had her own

problems to deal with.

They got into Morgan's car and drove to the cul-de-sac at the end of the road. They spun around, raced back to the highway turnoff, then sped toward Morgan's place.

Max murmured, as much to himself as to Morgan, "How could they know I was coming before I even did?"

Morgan shook her head but didn't reply.

Her own thoughts raced too fast for her to think about anyone else's problems.

How did Father find me?

****

October Sixth, 5:34 a.m.

Max didn't sleep well.

When Morgan rose to let Joey out, Max was already up, filling a teapot with water for her. Morgan hadn't spoken much after they returned to the house the night before. And Max hadn't made much effort to start a dialogue.

While Morgan made coffee and tea, Max walked around outside in the pre-dawn twilight with Joey, thinking, smelling the mountain air.

—We could still leave, Maximillian.—

They know us, Grim. They know you. *Shouldn't that concern you?*

—Leave Morgan. Leave Pineville. Leave America. Find meat somewhere else. Forget them.—

That was certainly the easiest path forward. And for so long, Max had taken the easy path, and it had led him nowhere. He'd managed to keep Grim under control and to live a lonely, human life. To exist in the world without hurting others.

But that's all he did. Exist. Drift. Build up a little wealth and then float to a new town, start the good fight over again with a never-ending drinking problem in tow.

Morgan joined him outside, handing over a cup of coffee. She didn't say anything. She sipped her tea and they continued to stroll around the property. Joey tromped back and forth, sniffing and snorting, occasionally chasing a rabbit from one bush to another.

"You still want to leave?" Morgan asked, her voice soft. Max's hyper-tuned ears almost detected a faint tremble in her question that she tried to suppress.

"I don't know," Max said. "I don't really know what the hell I'm involved in. But I don't like the idea of strangers knowing my secret. Knowing my moves before I do. I feel like a pawn in someone else's chess match."

Morgan nodded. "I…" She scratched behind her neck, then cleared her throat. "For so long, Max, this town seemed like it was a refuge for me—for us. Alex and I. A place frozen in time, where nothing really ever happened, where we could hide out from the rest of the world. Alex found it for us. Had all these grand plans for starting a family and building a homestead in rural America. Getting away from the big city. And I just went with it, because I needed a new start. But now I'm here, without him, and all of a sudden Pineville isn't some quaint historic town in a quiet mountain valley. It's… I don't know, maybe it is cursed. But whatever it is, even if it's not a hideout for me any longer, I can't just leave. I feel connected somehow. Like it's my home, even if I don't recognize it."

"You put down roots, that makes sense."

"But I didn't. Not really. I don't have close friends here. I have a nice boss, friendly co-workers, and some acquaintances, but that's it. It's all surface level. I shouldn't feel connected to this place, not logically. I can't rationally explain why I want to be—No. Not want. Why I *need* to be here."

Max stopped walking and looked down at her.

"But I do need to be here. Maybe now more than ever. I feel it. Just thinking of leaving, I can't even process the idea." She turned and met Max's eyes. "If you want out, I'll take you out of here. I'm not holding you hostage. You want a bus ticket far, far away, I'll get you one. But tell me this, honestly, after last night, of seeing just how involved you may already be in this, do you still feel like you can leave? Could you really get on that bus?" She didn't finish the rest of that question, but Max saw it in her eyes.

Could you really get on that bus and leave me here to deal with this on my own?

Max drank his coffee. He thought about her question. He turned it over in his mind, but he didn't answer right away.

"I don't know," he said, at last. "Truth is, I feel like whatever decision I make, it'll end up getting someone killed. I'm worried if I stay here, that person might be you."

"I am not some damsel in distress, Max, and I sure as hell won't be used as a scapegoat for you to justify running away from your problems, again."

Max raised his eyebrows. "Tell me how you really feel, Morgan."

"I'm sorry. I know that's harsh. But this is my town. I saved you from jail. I saved myself from the other werewolf. I am going to solve this mystery and save this town, no matter what it costs, because that's who my grandmother raised me to be. It's who Alex would want me to be. So, I need you to think about who you want to be. Do you want to be the man that gets on that bus, looking for another place to hide, or do you want to be the man who helps me save Pineville?"

Max turned away, thinking.

He walked back toward the house, and Morgan walked alongside him. She didn't pressure him for an answer, just padded along beside him, occasionally tossing a ball for Joey.

The morning breeze was chilly, but the ground was even colder. The near frozen clay soil numbed Max's toes and heels as he strolled barefoot back toward the house. Morgan wore slippers, but Max didn't bother to find shoes for himself. Truth was, he enjoyed the sensation. The stinging pain made him feel human, despite the immortal lycanthropic blood that pumped through his veins.

As they walked up the deck stairs, Max said, "For what it's worth, there is a bit of good news I haven't mentioned yet."

"After our night last night, what possible good news could we have?"

"Yesterday was the last night of the full moon. We've got three weeks before the moon is bright enough to start amplifying the transformations again. Odds are, we've got a respite before another werewolf attack. Gives me some time to research VC and BS and this witch woman… if she even exists…" Max watched Morgan, seeing if she gave away any reaction.

"So you'll stay, then?"

"I'll stay," Max said. "I guess I'm done running, at least for a little while."

Morgan flashed a small smile and reached out her hand. "Partners, for at least one more lunar cycle?"

Max chuckled. He took her hand, squeezed it, firmer than he had the first time. "Partners," he said, eyes on her.

—She's still hiding something from you, Maximillian.—

I know it, Grim. She might be the key to all of this.

Chapter 14

October Thirtieth, 12:24 a.m.

Crack.

The world shook.

The wooden beams groaned, straining under the stress of holding the walls together as the ground underneath rocked, threatening to topple the whole cabin.

The shaking continued for nearly three minutes, and all the while, Benjamin Shroud sat in the leather chair, legs crossed, book resting gently on his lap, waiting.

When the ground ceased tearing itself apart, the faint smile dancing across Benjamin's face grew wide. He waited, his brow low and thick and dark, half-moon shadows under his eyes, and felt no aftershocks that might crumble the cabin. He stood. His eyes sizzled, electric green. He strode across the room, heels cracking against the wooden floor. His tie was loosened for the time that he waited. He pulled it taut now, up against his collar, enjoying the sensation of tightness that he applied to his own neck. He did not spare a glance for the corpse still lying dead in the corner.

The rain had not ceased during the quake. Now it seemed to fall as torrentially as the world had ever known, as thick and fast as even old Noah once saw.

Crack.

The wooden brace had splintered.

The tunnel had opened, as Benjamin knew it would after the ritual. His knight had had to be sacrificed, and his pawns scattered, but he'd pushed all the pieces to the center of the board, and they'd triggered the endgame.

Now his own endgame began.

It would soon join him, teeth all fangs, eyes all daggers, legs all scales and fur and whiskers.

He waited for it, as others had done. He knew what would come from behind that door, and what fear he should feel. But he smiled, nonetheless. For he'd lived so long, fear was a forgotten memory, a concept that intrigued, but did not truly illicit any real emotion. Fear was for the forgotten. For the time-bound. For the weak. The current world had forgotten the most primal of fears. The fears of ancient, unknown evils.

That fear would be left for his daughter.

Fear was what he inspired when his lips cracked open, when his white eyes flashed in the night, when the world turned in their beds, nightmares in their minds, shadows dancing across the walls of their imaginations.

One in ten-thousand, they didn't imagine. They awoke, and they shivered, and they told themselves the dancing shades and the glimmering eyes and the silhouette of ancient evil was naught but a hallucination. One in ten-thousand, they were wrong.

Benjamin still held the mug of tea in his hands. Cold now. But he finished the remnants, swirled the dregs, glanced at what remained at the bottom of the clay vessel.

Crack.

His attention was drawn away. The creature would join him very soon. It would have to answer Benjamin's questions, and then it would choose to spare him or consume his soul. The silver-haired man chuckled at the thought.

His soul. The creature would choke and die if it tried to swallow his soul, for that amount of evil blackness could not be swallowed, not even by it.

He turned his attention back to the dregs at the bottom of his mug. They revealed the blurry shape of a creature, perhaps, if one were to squint just right. The first Rorschach, long played with by mystics and prophets and seers, well before science endowed the concept with a name.

Benjamin smirked. At each side, he saw a wing, blossoming out. A thick vertical smear in the center defined a sort of torso, a sort of mammalian body. At the head of the Rorschach-creature two clumps of tealeaf particles formed a set of triangular ears. There was a conspicuous blankness where the mouth should set. Two upside down crescents, sharp as needles, hung into that blankness, as if ready to strike whatever may stray too close.

Crack.

Crack.

Benjamin smiled fuller, this time creasing open his lips, revealing his own set of fangs.

Crack.

The braced basement door crashed open.

The Fallen emerged, vile, cruel, and unworldly.

It hissed and spat; its many legs barraged across the cabin, smashing floor panels and walls, struggling for purchase.

It was unaccustomed to the surface world, but it hungered, nonetheless.

"My Lord," Benjamin said, bowing, dodging a blind sweeping strike of a front leg, remaining as calm as the mountains themselves, unflinching at the void of light and life that now karoomed through the cabin, seeking sustenance. "Your sister-daughter, Vexulta, has emerged once again. To feed, I presume."

The Fallen paused, hesitated, blinked its many eyes. In guttural English, along with a hundred other tongues, vibrating across many planes of existence, words erupted into the air.

"What of her?"

"She has added a new member to her coven. A unique human. A mortal, but born of immortal blood, and trained in the dark arts of your sister-daughters. Vexulta may kill this one, in her fury. That would displease me."

"Why should I care, blood-fiend, of your displeasure?"

"I send you many sacrifices, my Lord, before their time is due. I want to happily continue my servitude. Search your memory. I am one of the eldest of my kind."

"You are one of the eldest grains of sand in the desert of my prison, and you send me nothing but husks. The sister-daughters do as they wish and consume if they hunger. As do I."

The Fallen pressed its many mouths forward, sought with many tongues the taste of the nearby soul.

The silver-haired man vanished with a chuckle and a pinch and a few flaps of gentle air that beat against The Fallen's scaly skin. The Fallen no longer sensed prey, nor a worthy conversation. It shuddered, hissed, undulated its fangs, tasting the air.

The Fallen maneuvered back through the broken

door, down into the cave, down into the crack that ran to the core of the world, murmuring in ancient tongues, disgruntled at being awoken. The many legs scuttled it downward and downward, deeper into the earth, where the warmth of the molten core beckoned it closer to true comfort. Where skin and fur boiled, and souls shrieked, and the sound of pain drowned out all The Fallen's primordial thoughts and regrets.

Benjamin returned in a flash of leathery wings and dropped back onto the cabin floor. In one hand, he held a small vial, the black ooze within bubbling in discontent.

"The life-force of the fallen child of Gaia," the man whispered, eyeing the goo. "No cost is too great, I'm afraid, dear daughter. And you have misbehaved terribly of late…" He tittered to himself, then vanished, leaving the cabin empty once again, save the corpse in the corner.

Rain continued to fall, and the first growl of distant thunder rolled toward the cabin.

****

Part Two
Witches

Chapter 15

October Tenth, 7:34 p.m.

Morgan didn't know why she kept her secret from Max.

Not at first.

At first, it was just a feeling that she had, deeper and stronger than the guilty feeling she had for lying to him.

It wasn't really a lie. Thirty-three-year-old Morgan.

Lying by omission is still lying. Sixteen-year-old Morgan.

She certainly felt an instinctual urge to tell him. To confide in him the way he'd confided in her about his… wolf-condition, the very first night. She knew her entanglements with magic could be part of the solution to the riddles they were facing in Pineville. She knew her "grief group" could hold the answers that they both sought.

But she knew, deep down, she couldn't tell him.

Not yet.

She realized why one night, staring at him across the room while he rubbed his eyes in front of the computer. The way he absent-mindedly stroked Shadow's ears when he wasn't paying attention. The way he examined the dishes after he washed them, double-checking they were whistle-clean. She realized she couldn't tell him her secret, because if she told him, he'd leave.

And if he left, she'd be alone again in her home. Her own selfish reason, true, but not her only reason.

If he left, she couldn't cure him of his curse.

Max deserved to be human again. He deserved to find someone—not her, certainly not her, certainly not someone with as much tragedy and fatherly complications as her—to make happy. He deserved the chance to work through his guilt and his PTSD and have a chance at some sort of family again.

Because if Morgan couldn't get that for herself, she could get it for Max.

Since she had met Hailey, Vera, and Ash, she'd mulled the idea of breaking Max's curse over and over in her head. Maybe, if the coven worked together, they could find an answer to his lycanthropy. Find a way to separate the werewolf from the man, permanently.

Despite everything running through her mind since she had discovered her father may be hunting her down, she'd kept this optimism for Max. She was a healer at heart. It's why she'd chosen nursing all those years ago. She wanted to heal Pineville, and heal Max. Maybe, she admitted, that would be what it took for her to accept healing herself.

She hadn't journaled since middle school. Her whole adult life she kept an agenda book, tracked important dates on a calendar in her office, and wrote out grocery lists on a magnetic whiteboard on her fridge, but for nearly two decades she'd kept herself away from journaling her thoughts and emotions.

Maybe because she knew once she started, she wouldn't be able to quit.

Her mind tended to pragmatism. Logically followed

one thought to another. She was a pro/con list kind of girl. To see everything visually allowed her to grasp different chaotic variables and organize them into a semblance of a structure.

So, when it seemed like every different aspect of her personal and professional life, past and present, and even the near-future, was about to crash together at a violent intersection, Morgan bought a leatherbound journal, sat in her car after work, and started figuring out how to balance it all.

First, she listed out the main problem that she knew for sure she needed to solve:

Problem: Pineville has AT LEAST *one werewolf on the loose. More may be arriving or already have arrived. Someone or something may be bringing them here. The valley residents are in danger until these werewolves are stopped and whatever is bringing them here is found.*

Second, she wrote out the complex variables, or clues that were pressing up against each other, to try to get them segmented into their own clean boxes so that she could visualize them and then succinctly deal with them.

1. Max is a werewolf, but he (for now?) is not a threat. He claims to control his ability to transform. (I believe he can) He was somehow summoned to this valley. He was tricked into transforming, survived a poisoning attempt and killed someone at the Pineville Gas Station on Route 1. He escaped the trap set for him and luckily found me. He is safe at my home where he is hiding out.

2. A coven of witches (names: Vera, Ash, Hailey, Ulta) secretly meet in the forest outside of Pineville. They've been meeting for the last three years. They are also aware of the werewolves in Pineville. They can detect when I perform magic (all magic?) and want to work with me to stop the werewolves. (Should I join their coven?) They seem well-intentioned, but I am suspicious that one or more of them may be misleading me.

3. Two men with the initials VC and BS convinced/coerced gas-station employee Ron Greenburg to assist them in communicating and/or potentially trapping Max (and other werewolves?) for unknown purposes. Are these men responsible for summoning the werewolves to Pineville?

4. A woman (one of the witches?) convinced Ron Greenburg not to follow through with the plans forced upon him by VC and BS (Is this how Max escaped the gas station situation?) Is this the woman summoning werewolves? Or is this the woman trying to stop them from coming?

5. BS's first name may be Benjamin, per the interrogation of Ron Greenburg. ~~This matches my father's first name and last initial and could suggest his presence in Pineville. He was never supposed to be able to find me. If he stays here, he will do much worse evil than any werewolves ever~~

Morgan stared at the last line she'd written, where she'd scratched out the implications about her father being involved. She sat the pen down in the middle of the open journal. She rubbed at her temples. This last clue had been the variable she'd been struggling with the most.

If werewolves were being drawn to Pineville, and mysterious figures were using them as pawns for their own chess game, as Max had put it, Morgan could find a way to wrap her mind around all of that. If that was the case, then that meant Morgan could count herself as just another chess piece. A surprise queen on the board who could move on her own, with powers no other pieces on the board had access to.

She would be the outsider, the one who wasn't from this valley, the outlier who may be able intercede and turn the tide to help the town.

But if her father were here…

If her father were here, then Morgan became the reason for the problems Pineville faced. No doubt, if her father was here, it meant he was here to finish what he started when he ripped Morgan away from her grandmother. Benjamin Shroud's whole career—if you could call it that—was built around crushing out magic wherever it bubbled up. He could allow nothing to threaten his underground empire.

When he realized there were two witches in his own family, hiding right under his nose, he acted swiftly and viciously.

Morgan felt the only reason she'd been kept alive was because she was his daughter, and he believed he could stamp the magic out of her through sheer force of will.

And, she hated to admit it, he'd been right.

He'd crushed her desire to ever dabble in magic again. When Alex came along, a lifeline to escape Benjamin's domineering control, Morgan grabbed on. She took it, sought out a normal life with him.

Benjamin had allowed it since Alex was harmless. Innocent. The opposite of a threat. Alex could care for Morgan, and Benjamin Shroud could abandon whatever twisted sense of responsibility he had for his human daughter.

Morgan confided in Alex about her resentment to her father, but never to the reasoning behind it. Alex accepted it, unconditionally. He never pressed.

Together they built Morgan's new identity. Alex helped her become a citizen, with a new social security number, and a new last name. His last name. Together they worked to escape Benjamin Shroud, so if he ever changed his mind, if he ever came looking for his only daughter Morgan, he wouldn't be able to find her.

Alex worked nearly sixty hours a week while Morgan got her nursing degree.

They found Pineville. The perfect, idyllic place to build a new life. A new home. And for almost four years, Pineville hadn't disappointed them.

Then, three months ago, out of the blue, Alex put the barrel of a handgun in his mouth, pulled the trigger, and turned Morgan's world upside down again.

Morgan slammed shut the journal and threw it against the passenger door. It ricocheted hard and fell onto the floorboards.

In through the nose, out through the mouth.

Something rushed through the car, traced a tingling sensation across her skin.

Morgan sensed the red threads of power, suddenly revealing themselves to her again. Zig-zagging vibrations, appearing out of thin air, rippling with promises of power and mystery and desire.

Morgan reached out her left hand.

She twitched her fingers. She felt the static touch of the golden threads of power, the ones she could always sense. She ignored them. She pinched her fingers in a unique way, felt them seize hold around the red magic vibrating in the background. Felt heat. Felt strength. Felt confidence thrumming in the static air, waiting to be harnessed.

She was done avoiding magic. She'd avoided it for years, and her husband was dead, her new hometown was prowling with witches and werewolves, and her father had hunted her down, after all this time.

Magic—not journaling—was her way out.

She let the zigzagging red threads inside of her. Let the magic surge through her fingers, into her palm, race through her veins and flood her body with a wholly new sense of power.

Morgan didn't understand it, but she didn't need to.

It was there for her. To help her. To empower her to protect herself, and to protect Max, and to protect the rest of the women in the coven.

To fuel her.

If her father was in Pineville…

If it was him who was pulling the strings…

He'd have hell to pay.

Morgan cranked the keys in the ignition. The engine roared, she threw the car in drive, and she raced out of downtown Pineville.

She had witch-sisters to meet, magic to cast, and revenge on her mind.

****

October Tenth, 7:39 p.m.

Max left Joey inside, patting him on the head as he walked out the door.

"Sorry, boy," Max said, "But tonight, I'm flying solo."

Morgan and Max had established a semblance of a routine over the last week. Max watched Joey during the day, did research online and explored the nearby forest. Morgan went to work, sometimes for close to sixteen hours at a time, came home, and they discussed whatever theories Max had concocted during the day. So far, they'd discovered nothing new since the note at Ron Greenburg's, and Max felt stuck at a dead end.

Ronnie had disappeared. No more sightings, no more news. Max couldn't even smell a trail when he returned to the neighborhood. The kid had vanished without a trace. The police didn't give a shit, according to Morgan, because he was the type to take off and leave town. Good riddance, Sheriff Jeffrey had said, essentially. Max hoped Sheriff Jeffrey was right. He hoped the kid had high-tailed it to the big city, but Max felt a more sinister ending had come to the twenty-something gas station attendant.

Despite plenty of time spent in front of the computer, Max also couldn't pierce the veil on either of the initials they'd discovered at Ron Greenburg's hideout.

Neither VC nor BS were connected to anything relevant in the town or any of the valley's history as far as Max could determine. They were both as good as ghosts, haunting the town, invisible to detection.

The rumored witch-woman was just as hard to find, if not harder. Max had his own theories, involving Morgan, but they were nothing more than theories. He couldn't prove anything, and he spent most of his time with her. He hoped she would eventually relinquish her secrets of her own accord.

So far, she had not.

The longer time went on, the more evident it became Max would have to dig out her secrets himself.

He trotted off the deck, felt the hard clay soil hit his feet, and began to jog.

His endurance was unnatural, stoked by the untamed energy of his alter ego that lived within him. And that night, he did not have too far to go.

Chapter 16

October Tenth, 8:05 p.m.

"We've got a long hike ahead of us?" Morgan asked, staring at the dark trail that disappeared into the mountain forest.

Ash sighed, nodded. "Yeah."

They'd parked their cars at the trailhead. Apparently, Ulta, Hailey, and Vera had already gone ahead to set up the séance. They left Ash behind to wait for Morgan.

Ash added awkwardly, almost apologetically, "They weren't totally sure you'd make it."

"I wasn't either," Morgan admitted. "But we are all in this together, for Pineville, right? I'm glad you waited for me."

"Sis, I wouldn't walk out to this séance by myself in the middle of the day, and I've been there loads of times. I definitely wouldn't make you do it after nightfall on your own."

Morgan flicked on a dim flashlight. The light flickered twice then extinguished.

"Shit," Morgan said in the darkness.

She heard Ash rustling with something in her jacket. "This'll due better, I think." Ash suddenly stood in a reddish glow, the illumination growing outward from a small stick held in her hand. "Electronics seem to break out here when we gather. Looks like the effect might already be setting in."

Morgan smiled at her, her breath momentarily quickening at the sight of magic. It was simple, yes, but it was only the second person she'd ever seen perform magic other than her grandmother. Morgan's stomach bubbled with childlike wonder.

But when she looked where Ash aimed her wand, fear cut into wonderment, turned her elation into anxiety.

The glowing wand illuminated nothing more than twisting, leafless branches around a shrinking tunnel of darkness into the black woods.

Morgan swallowed, cleared her throat, and asked, "So, you both have wands? You and Vera?"

"Yes," Ash said. "What magical relic do you use to draw in your power?"

Morgan said, "Uh, I—"

"Vera and I carry petrified Elderwood wands. Ulta gave them to us when we first came to her cabin. Said they were carved by some ancient Mohican shaman, but I forget the name. Hailey claims to have a special wand of her own, but I haven't seen it. She mostly just uses that whip you saw her carrying. What about your artifact? A ring, maybe? Or a necklace?"

"I, uh—" *Be honest, for Christ sakes, for once, Morgan "*—I don't have any artifact."

Ash stared at Morgan. "You're telling me that you just harvest magic straight from the Source, right into your body?"

"Well, yeah. Since I was a teenager. My grandmother taught me how to feel for it, how to find it in the wind, find it in the stillness of the air, find it in the leaves and the trees... how to access it, how to... she would always say, 'Tame it inside yourself and aim it back out.' I've always done that. I didn't know there was any other way."

I didn't even know there was anyone else casting magic, let alone doing it differently than me, a week ago.

Ash shook her head. "Morgan, I think that's something special."

"Is that bad?"

"Bad? No! Strange, I think. Rare, maybe. I've never heard of anything like it. Ulta might be able to do it, I suppose, but she's… well, I'm not supposed to… uh, let's just say, she has a power source all of her own, straight from Gaia. But for you? For a normal, mortal human to just reach right into the Source and pluck the magic out yourself? That is something really remarkable. Course, I'm pretty fucking new to all of this, so I don't know too much either…" Her voice drifted off.

"Well," Morgan said. "Shall we go ahead?"

"Right," Ash said, and stepped onto the dirt trail. They walked forward in silence.

The trees seemed to reach in toward the trail, almost as if they wanted to snag anyone foolish enough to follow the path at night, to stop them from proceeding forward.

"So tell me: how did you meet these girls? When did you join the coven?"

"Oh, sis, it's a long story."

"It's a long hike, you told me. And the silence is creeping me out."

Ash smiled, and then she began to ramble. Once she started, she couldn't seem to stop. Morgan forgot, until just then, Ash was still a kid, really, compared to her. Twenty-four-years-old and thirty-three-years-old felt like eons apart.

"Growing up, I idolized the Salem witches, the first women of the new American frontier who pushed back against the patriarchy, hundreds of years ago. They knew to be caught even gossiping about witchcraft was heresy. To practice risked being condemned to a torturous death, but they still did it. They were my heroes. They knew what they did was forbidden back then, and they earned the title of witches just for their courage alone. But I never believed any of them performed any real, actual magic. I figured they were just murdering their abusive husbands with poisonous plants they found in the woods, fucking hot Native American warriors, teaching their daughters to read more than just the Bible... you know, classic '*evil*' witch behavior. Shit that I would do if I was born back then."

Ash flicked quotation marks in the air with her hands when she said evil. Morgan listened to her story closely. She never thought about ancient witches, never connected the dots between them and herself. But then again, Morgan had had her own grandmother as a witch mentor. Ash had no one. She had to find her mentors in history.

The forest was growing stranger as they hiked, the branches more gnarled and twisted, spiraling in unnatural curves, the wood blacker, the creeping vines more suffocatingly dense around the trees. The evergreen trees, the juniper and the pine slowly vanished. Only twisted walnut and oak and maple remained. Spanish moss, almost unheard of in Virginia, especially in the higher mountain elevations in November, tumbled out of the oak tree limbs in thick globs.

Ash continued, oblivious to the changes, or maybe

just familiar with them. "Anyway, after the incident with my mother, I started looking for more… uh, practicing knowledge and less history. First I read 'The Malleus Maleficarum,' then 'The Discoverie of Witchcraft,' which were supposed to be these powerful, historical texts. But really, they were just fifteenth century old dudes mansplaining things they didn't understand. But those books led me to the 'Key of Solomon,' which seemed to outline some real magic. I was hooked. I read about the 'Book of Soyga,' and the 'Voynich Manuscript,' which they say might have been edited and annotated by Merlin himself. That led me down a rabbit hole about sects of necromancers that robbed the graves of King Arthur and Merlin and his knights. They may have been the ones to unearth Merlin's very own grimoire. That ended up being confiscated—well, plundered, really, by Viking witch-hunters, who traded it to a Muslim diplomat in exchange for his service in some great quest or another, who then brought it back to Baghdad in the tenth century." Ash turned and looked at Morgan. "They saved their literature, and saved the literature of other cultures that came into their hands. That's how we know so much about the Vikings, even though they kept very little writing themselves."

Morgan noticed their path now led more downhill than uphill. The ground grew squishier, the hard packed clay replaced with earthy, churned black soil, almost marsh-like. A mist descended over them, thick and heavy, and warm. It had been such a cold night in town, Morgan had been worried about frost and maybe ice on the roads the next morning, but now, far after sundown, the air temperature seemed to be warming up as they walked deeper into the woods. Patches of green and purple fungus clung to the bases of trees. Mushrooms started to dot their path here and there, protruding up from black piles of mushy rotten leaves.

"Did you know that all the major ancient civilizations, from all across the globe, have evidence depicting the practice of occult magic by witches? Women from every region on Earth, united in their quest for secret power… and being slandered at every turn for it. But the reality is, a lot of them, those women, they found it. Found the source of magic that permeates our world. Ancient Mesopotamia, Ancient Egypt, the Mayans, the Aztecs, the Greeks, the Mongols, the Huns, I'm sure I'm forgetting a bunch. And they all have concurrent folktales. The archetypical *'evil'* women, shunned by society, casting black magic on those that deserve it. The stories are skewed to fit their unique culture's perspective and society, but it's the same premise, every time. All these cultures knew about the occult and feared these groups of witch-doctors, fae-spirits, shamans, sorceresses, medicine-women, whatever, they all were the same really, just semantics and time periods that distinguished them. Outcast members of a chauvinistic society that, in some form or another, either battled the supernatural or tried to control it, channel it for their own personal gain."

Ash sighed. "All those special women of history, and I could never cast an ounce of magic. I'd never wanted anything so bad in my life, but I couldn't levitate a blade of grass, couldn't light candles, couldn't read a single grasshopper's thoughts. No matter how many ancient texts I chanted from. No matter how many different spell books I found, when I practiced their dark arts, nothing happened. I was a magic historian, maybe, but I wasn't a witch. I wanted to be a witch, Morgan."

Ash scratched her free hand against the back of her head, hesitating in her storytelling. She stepped over a rotten, fallen log, then continued her narrative.

"Eventually I got so mad, I threw it all out, gave it all up. My family had been dead for a year. I'd been avoiding dealing with that trauma by burying myself in the hunt for some sort of key to a magical escape. But it never came. I never found it. I got low, depressed. Started smoking weed and drinking and then doing blow, then I started doing the really hard stuff. Smack was my substitute for magic, I guess. For a little while it *was* magic to me. I dropped out of school my senior year. I did some nasty things when I needed to score, Morgan."

She paused for a moment. She stopped walking, stopped talking. Stared into the dark. Morgan thought about Ronnie, the missing gas station clerk, who also found himself hooked on drugs and then tangled up in a magical, violent conspiracy. Another victim of Pineville's dark pressures.

Ash started walking again and returned to her tale. "When I thought about what my life was, before I got sober, I thought about ending it all. I even slit my wrists. A couple times, Morgan, I slit my wrists. But I never dug deep enough, I guess. Didn't have my heart committed to it. Just didn't have it in me. There was this… *fire*, inside of me, even though I thought it was all extinguished after I gave up chasing magic. But this fire, this anger, it refused to go out, even when the rest of me wanted to." Ash frowned, then covered her mouth. "Is this too much? I'm sorry, I'm just, like, basically trauma dumping my whole life onto you, no filter."

Morgan nodded. "It's okay. It's really okay. What

happened next?"

"Hailey found me. Saved me, I should say. Recruited me for an internship in Charlottesville at the University of Virginia. It was a fresh start, a way out. And it was in some really interesting academic occult research. I had practically homeschooled my way to a master's degree in that already. Somehow all my visits to the online databases at the school, in that field, had sent a flag up the department to someone. That someone happened to be Hailey. She helped me graduate Pineville High, without having to physically go back. Helped me apply to grants and scholarships, and I got them all. Turned my summer internship into a chance at a four-year degree. On campus, Hailey and I would meet up about once a month. She took me under her wing, academically, but I picked up something else about her. Something she was hiding. My Spidey-witch-senses went off, you could say, and my old ways came back to me. I snuck up to the top of her department building, intending just to snoop around a little, during a thunderstorm one night. I assumed everyone would be gone. Her office was on the highest floor, it looked out over the stadium and the campus, toward the Shenandoah mountains in the distance. Her office door was locked, but something flickered inside, behind the frosted glass window in the door. I picked the lock, second nature to me from my druggie days, and cracked the door.

"Hailey had scrawled a big red pentagram across the floor of her office. She had at least a hundred candles flickering across the ground. She was meditating in the center of the star. And she was floating. Upside down. Floating upside down, Morgan, legs crossed, Indian-style—I mean, Native American style—I mean, well you know, crisscross applesauce style. Very creepy. Her lips were moving, but she wasn't speaking out loud, as far as I could tell. She would listen to something I couldn't hear, then respond, then listen again. Her hair, still as thick and red as you saw it the other night, floated in thin air below her. I… couldn't believe it. All my life I'd been looking for witches and now, here's this gorgeous adult woman, far prettier than me, smarter than me, more cultured than me, a real nerdy-librarian type, full of pep and positivity, classic sorority president, comes from a lot of money, exercises at four-thirty in the morning, never drinks, straight edge, perfect daddy's little girl— you know the type. And she's a witch! She was performing real magic!"

Ash smiled, glanced back at Morgan.

"I couldn't help myself. I stepped right into the room. Whispered, 'Oh my god.' Hailey's eyes cracked open, but she didn't act surprised. Like at all. She kind of smirked this half-smile at me, still upside down, and said, 'I knew it'd be you who'd catch me.' I just stared at her, thinking about all the different academic lectures we'd listened to, the different artifacts we'd found. And all of it under the guise of research. But Hailey wasn't researching, she was practicing. Learning. Honing her craft. 'Can you teach me?' I asked her, finally. I expected her to say no, but she just smiled. She rotated her body over in mid-air, turning from upside down to right side up. 'Sure,' she said, 'but it won't be easy.'

"'I don't care,' I told her. And I didn't. I'd do anything for that knowledge."

Ash paused at a strange tree, traced her wand light around its swirling, leafless branches. She shook her head, continued forward, passing by the tree, but giving it a wide berth.

"From there we continued our research, but we also began my training. My practice. We were both so busy already, especially Hailey, but she didn't hesitate to find time for me and our witchcraft practice. Once I had my first wand, I finally started doing tiny amounts of magic. Real magic! It electrified me. I ended up spending six years at UVA. Four years to get my bachelor's in history, another two to get a real master's in museum studies with an emphasis on occult texts. The whole time, I honed my craft. Then we came back here, where it all started. Because Hailey and I discovered evidence of a place of power, right here in the Appalachian woods, in the valley of my very own hometown. At the time I thought it was the world's most, like, unlikeliest coincidence. But now I believe more that it was fate, that it was Gaia herself, guiding me through all these trials to bring me back home, this time to a magical family of sisters. A whole batch of siblings for the one I lost as a kid. And to a real mother figure. One who could accept me. To Ulta."

Ash stopped for a moment, pointing her wand off the trail. The beam moved slowly across the unnatural landscape, stopped when it hit a willow tree. The thin, leafless limbs and branches draped all the way to the ground in most spots, so thick Morgan couldn't see the trunk of the tree.

"Ah. Here we go," Ash stepped off the dirt trail, walked toward the willow tree. Morgan took a step to follow her, then stopped. From somewhere behind them, she heard the crack of a stick.

Her head snapped around. Saw nothing but blackness. "Did you hear that?" Morgan whispered.

Ash turned to answer, then they both heard a call from ahead of them.

"Girls! Over here, come on!"

Ash and Morgan hustled toward the sound of Vera's voice. They emerged from the dense forest into an open meadow.

Fireflies zapped in the sky, thousands of bugs flashing in the darkness, outshining the glow of the stars behind them. Something flickered in Morgan's mind, some scientific fact she'd known since she was little girl: Fireflies only emerge on warm summer nights, not in autumn, and definitely not with a chill in the air. Yet, Morgan realized, the chill in the air had vanished. And the insects twinkled all the same, ignorant of the calendar, dancing in the night air, flashing their song of love above the meadow.

The beauty of it all took Morgan's breath away. She'd never seen the sky so clear. Never seen so many fireflies at once.

Below the lightning bugs, Vera and Hailey waited. A smoldering campfire glowed in the middle of the meadow. As Morgan drew closer, she noticed a large black cauldron had been set atop the glowing red embers.

"Are we brewing potions tonight?" Morgan asked. Her words sounded hollow, more nervous than jovial.

Hailey smiled a gorgeous smile, and answered simply, "Oh, yes."

When Morgan arrived beside the fire, she saw that a pentagram had been dug into the soil, with the cauldron sitting at the heart of the five cornered star. At the tip of each corner, large burlap bags had been set. From the light of Ash's wand, and the glow of the embers, Morgan could just make out that some of the bags seemed damp and stained near their base. A shiver ran down her spine, despite the warmth of the night.

Morgan didn't want to know what lay within the bags.

Hailey added, "I've gathered all the ingredients we will need, save one. Ulta should be returning soon with the last ingredient."

Out of the dark forest, robed in a gown of silken green and a cape of velvet black, a kindly woman, early in her senior years, stepped into view. Her salt and pepper hair fell haphazardly down over her ears, curling out before reaching her shoulders. Her skin was fair, just slightly wrinkled, and her eyes were a twinkling purplish black. She leaned on a long walking stick, had a bit of a hunch and a belly, and her steps were short and precise, as if she needed to take caution not to fall on the uneven ground.

"Ah, finally, my dear Morgan, we meet," she said, her voice honey-sweet. No malice dripped between her words, but Morgan detected—*felt, really instinctually felt*—disingenuousness in her sugary demeanor. "It's so good to see your face here in my meadow."

As she drew closer, Morgan noticed she carried a small bag tied together at her waist with blood red twine and a large burlap bag that seemed to wiggle on its own.

Morgan extended her hand to her. "It's good to meet you properly, Ulta."

The woman stretched out her arms wide, leaving her walking stick standing straight up where she let it go, and embraced Morgan with a gentle hug.

"Sisters don't shake hands, my dear, and neither do I."

Morgan hesitantly hugged her back and felt an

instant warmth of nostalgia and comfort wash over her.

Her eyes begin to water with the joy of it. Embracing Ulta felt like embracing her grandmother in a peaceful reunion in the afterlife. Ulta was shorter than Morgan, felt delicate and fragile but so full of love and warmth that Morgan wondered how she'd never met this woman earlier in life. It felt as if Ulta had cared for her since she'd been born. She felt like she could close her eyes and pass away into death with complete serenity.

Morgan pulled away hard, blinking, trying to clear away any evidence that she'd come so close to crying.

She'd felt that peace only once before, and it scared her. That peace was not a good kind of peace. She'd felt that peace on one of her lowest nights after Alex passed away. Had been after many glasses of wine and had come from staring a little too longingly and too dreamily at the matte-black revolver sitting on the nightstand.

Morgan cleared her head.

Focus.

In through the nose, out through the mouth.

Don't let her enchant you.

Morgan was here for a reason.

To stop the werewolves. To cure Max. To find the reason Pineville was haunted by tragedy. She was investigating them, not the other way around. She would find out the extent of their powers. And if they were working with her father, or against him, she'd get to the bottom of it.

Morgan felt a chill run down her spine as she looked into Ulta's eyes.

She knows the curse.

Maybe she IS *the curse.*

Then maybe she has the answer to it, too.

Ulta tittered away, unassuming, small steps leading her toward the cauldron at the center of the pentagram. "Hailey, dearie, did you already fill the cauldron with the mist of the mountain? Concentrate it down to a boil?"

Hailey nodded, answering in the way one might their hard-of-hearing elderly relative. "Yes, Ulta, I did."

Ulta stood at one point of the star. "Then everyone, circle around, take your places."

"Wait a minute," Morgan said. "I'm not here to just stand on a corner and be your fifth puppet. I want to know what we are doing out here. What are we brewing? Vera told me you all needed *me*. If you need *me* in this coven, you need to answer some of *my* questions, first."

Her heart pounded with adrenaline, but she did not let it show in her eyes. Morgan felt the tingle of red threads of power rushing around her skin, felt the thrumming pulses of the golden filaments of her grandmother's magic alongside. She could call on them both in an instant if she needed to.

But she did not need to.

"Morgan, dearie, we cannot begin any discussions until the sacraments are complete. We aren't trying to fool you, or make you do anything you don't want to do. But we must first clear the meadow of any dark spirits, must cleanse our sacred cauldron of any impurities, and must thank Gaia for giving us her gifts to use tonight."

Vera added, "Do not worry, *mi amor*. We all want to stop the werewolves. We will say our incantation and then we will answer your questions."

Morgan nodded, lowering her defenses, but just slightly. "Alright then."

She stepped onto her point on the star.

The four women spread their palms wide in front of

185

them, tilted their heads toward the flickering fireflies above. Morgan copied their motion. Then they began to chant:

"From yonder woods and verdant glade,
under silver moon or darkest shade,
by brooks that babble or falls' cascade,
grant us Gaia, your celestial aid.
We seek thy wisdom and thy grace
and thy leave to retrace
thine steps upon this earthen space.
Elements four, fire, water, earth and air,
lend us your power, grant us our prayer.
By oak and ash and hawthorn's might,
cleanse the air for ancient rite,
and grant Mother Earth's favor
upon the witch-sisters of Angavor!"

Morgan felt a ripple of power run through the magic threads that hung dense but unseen in the air. She looked around and saw no visible change. Vera, Ash, Hailey, and Ulta stared serenely at the cauldron at the center of the pentagram. Hailey pulled a small bundle of herbs from within her brown leather jacket and tossed it to Morgan.

"Want to do the honors and sage the space for us?"

Vera asked, "Do you need a match?"

Is this a test?

Morgan performed the simple flick of her fingers, took in only the golden magic she needed, and cast a ray of sparks across one end of the sage.

"No," Morgan said, lips held neutral, trying hard to act neither confident nor nervous as the smoke billowed off the herb.

She'd never 'saged' anything before, but she'd seen

it done in movies and on television. She waved it around her at arm's length, then passed it to her right, to Ash. The younger woman took the bundle, wafted it about and then passed it on.

After they'd all passed the burning herb about, Vera extinguished it with a wave of her wand and set it gently into the dirt.

"Now," Morgan asked, "May I ask my questions?"

Ulta nodded. "Anything you'd like, dearie."

She bit her bottom lip, thinking. She and Max had spent so much time looking for clues and evidence, and all the answers to their mystery could potentially be right in front of her now, waiting for the right questions. She just didn't know where to start.

She decided to cut to the chase. "What in the hell is going on?"

Ulta asked back, sweetly, "Whatever do you mean?"

"What do I mean? What do I *mean*? I was attacked by a werewolf! Another woman wasn't so lucky, she was killed by one. Then I find out that you four have been practicing magic here, some of you for decades! This isn't some off-brand movie playing on the horror channel! This is our town! This is Pineville. Pineville, the town that has the lowest per capita crime rate in the state, but one of the highest homicide and suicide rates across the whole country. Tell me how that makes sense? Something has been going wrong here long before these monsters showed up! Tell me why I shouldn't think it's you all?"

Ulta smiled, looked at Morgan like she was a lost puppy. "My dear, I've been practicing magic in these woods for a long time. I don't want to scare you, but monsters, they come and go. This valley, this forest, this is my home, too, just as it is yours. Remind me again how long you've lived here?"

Morgan stammered "Uh, close to four years, but I don't—"

"Ah, well, I don't want to date myself, but I've been here for well over fifty years. And I don't want anything harming my people, any more than you do. Now, if you'll allow us to brew the wolfsbane and nightshade potion, we can show you just how adamantly we are opposed to those beasts invading my valley."

"Wait," Morgan said, holding up her hand. She took a deep breath. "Do you know Benjamin Shroud?"

She looked between the four women and they all looked truly bewildered. No one revealed any recognition.

"And what about Ron Greenburg?"

Ash's eyebrows lifted up in surprise before she forced them back down. Vera looked at Morgan with confusion. "Who are these people you are talking about Morgan?"

"Ron Greenburg is the night-shift gas station attendant. According to the police, he skipped town a week ago."

Hailey's question: "Do you think he's a werewolf, Morgan?" She watched Morgan's face, judging her the same way Morgan was judging the others.

She shook her head. "No, but I think he's involved, somehow."

"What makes you think the gas station clerk is involved?" Hailey again. Eyes narrowed.

Morgan had walked herself into a potential trap. If she revealed more, she might give herself away. How indeed, if no one knew about Max and his incident at the gas station other than Max and Ron.

She edged her way out. "Mysterious disappearances in small towns aren't normal. I'm just trying to put together the pieces."

"Morgan, dearie. I can assure you, the five of us together, we can brew a concoction that will cause such a repellent odor to the beasts, they won't be caught within five hundred miles of this valley. If another single attack happens, we will gather back at my cabin and dive deeper into whatever strange bait may be luring the werewolves here. But for now, let's try it my way."

Morgan ran her tongue along her teeth, thinking. She relented, nodded her head. "What do we need to do?"

Hailey unfurled the whip from her waist. She flicked it out to the side, uncoiling it to its full length, then cracked it behind her, then snapped it down against the red embers.

Flames erupted at the base of the black cauldron.

Ulta said, "Each of you, one at a time, will reach into the burlap sack at your feet. Morgan, you start." Morgan did as she was told, her hand moving slowly in anticipation of whatever gross, damp thing she might find at the bottom of the sack.

Morgan felt something rigid. She gripped it between two fingers and pulled it out. Sparkling in the reflection from the red embers, she held a fern sprig unlike anything she'd ever seen before. The center vein was firm, bark-like, covered in a silver powder that emitted a soft glow of its own. The leaves unfurled around it and glistened, as if covered in a metallic sheen.

"Morgan, dearie, I need you to read out the incantation that Ash is handing you, then strip the sprig of its leaves and add them to the cauldron."

Morgan took the proffered leather book from Ash. She read from the open page, "Silverdust Fern, powder burn, lupine dread, begin to spread." She ran her closed fist along the fern sprig, ripping off the leaves as she went. Her hand suddenly flashed with pain, but she gritted her teeth and dropped the leaves into the softly bubbling cauldron. The bubbles accelerated and the steam thickened.

Morgan looked at her palm. A thick stripe of a red welt was rising. She looked up and saw Hailey watching her. "Stings a little," she said, "but you'll be alright."

"Hush now!" Ulta said, urgently, "Now Morgan, pass Ash back the book."

Morgan did so, and watched as Ash pulled her own ingredient from the bag at her feet. Hers was far viler than Morgan's. It looked like red slime, with wriggling seaweed inside.

Ash held it out over the cauldron, spoke, "Foxblood moss, rare and sacred, drained by one consumed by hatred," She seemed surprised by the final line, but nonetheless she tightened her fist, her knuckles whitening, and the red ooze splattered into the cauldron. Red steam belched out, and Ash drew back, coughing.

"Do not leave your mark!" threatened Ulta, her voice snapping from kindly crone to fearsome hag and then snapping back with a gentle, "Please, Ashley Rose, do not leave your mark."

Vera went next, taking the leather book and squeamishly reaching into her bag. Her face flashed with relief as her hand reached the bottom. She pulled out a clump of herbs, looking similar to the sage they had passed earlier.

"Moonwort, wolfsbane root, nightshade fruit. Poisons all, but do not stall. Add them third, without a word." Vera's eyes widened when she finished speaking. "Oh, pero no, porque I spoke the spell, pero—"

"That's why we read first and then speak, dearie. Think through the line again, keep it in your head, and drop them in."

Vera dropped the clump of herbs and the red steam lessened, though the cauldron continued to bubble turbulently.

Ulta took the fourth and fifth ingredients, recanting her lines from memory, not needing to read from the ancient tome. "Rattlesnake venom, dripped off the tongue, apple seed smoke exhaled from living lung."

From her sack at her waist Ulta pulled out a corncob pipe, apparently already packed with ground apple seeds. She lit the pipe with her finger, the small flame flickered green, then she inhaled deeply. While holding her breath, she lunged her hand into the bag at her feet. She pulled out a writhing snake by the head, tail whipping frantically, the sound of its rattle echoing across the meadow.

"Holy fuck!" Ash said.

"Jesus Christ," Morgan whispered, her stomach threatening to unload her dinner.

Ulta did not blink an eye. She brought the snake's scaly face right up to her lips. She kissed the creature, then opened her mouth. She squeezed tightly against the rattlesnake's neck. The snake's jaws unhinged, massive hypodermic needle-looking fangs undulated out. The snake thrust its head forward, striking toward Ulta's face, coming just centimeters away from landing a deadly blow. The fangs dripped heavily with venom. Ulta stuck her tongue out and caught one… two… three drops before pulling the snake away. She stuffed the serpent back down into the burlap bag, flashed ravenous raven-colored eyes toward Morgan that looked infinitely younger than they had an instant before, then leaned over the cauldron.

Ulta stuck out her tongue again, let the rattlesnake venom drop. One… two… three… right into the mixture. The red steam turned mustard yellow, smelling awful. Only then did Ulta exhale, blowing a smoke ring and then a thick train of apple seed smoke down through the ring and into the cauldron.

The steam ceased to rise. The bubbling calmed to a slow, melodious churn.

"Show off," muttered Hailey, smiling in what seemed to be pure awe of the older witch. She reached into her burlap bag and pulled out an oversized but innocent looking wooden spoon.

She read off her part of the incantation. "Swirl three times, harmless as pea vines, swirl five, none gathered shall survive."

She stirred her spoon in the cauldron, circling the potion. Morgan watched with horror as she swirled the mixture once, then twice, then a third time, suddenly fearing the red-headed witch might miscount… might stir the potion five times. But she did not. Morgan thought she might not have even stirred four times. Hailey removed the spoon. The cauldron gurgled, the potion suddenly churned and splatted and clearly some significant chemical reaction was occurring. The steam began rising, thicker and more pungent than ever.

Morgan looked between the girls. "Um, now what?"

Ulta scratched her head, thinking, all while the

steam continued to flood out, heavier and heavier, threatening to overwhelm them all. Hailey lifted the leather book, flipped the open page to the next.

She spoke, her voice cracking. "Now, uh, it looks like we leave." She stuffed the book down into her satchel and tossed it over her shoulder. "We leave quickly!" She jumped back from her spot on the pentagram. Morgan leapt backward, narrowly avoiding a splatter of potion that had gurgled over the edge and then belched outward. She began to feel like she couldn't breathe. Ash grabbed her hand, tugged her away from the cauldron.

"Come on, Morgan, run!"

They ran, Ash and Vera pointing their wand light ahead of them, illuminating the darkness as they fled from the toxic fumes. Morgan almost tripped and fell, but the other two girls held onto her, pulled her through the shadowy forest.

"What about Hailey and Ulta?"

"Trust me," Ash said, between heavy breaths, "They can take care of themselves."

Morgan didn't question her. She rushed onward, scrambling through the woods, desperate to get back to her car, to rush back to her home.

To see if the fumes would bother Max.

She hoped beyond hope it wouldn't hurt him.

In her heart, she worried he'd be dead by the time she reached him.

****

He looked dead, when she arrived. But his eyes' creased open on the couch, he murmured, "Late night," and rolled over, sleepily dragging his small pillow from under his head to on top of it. One of his strange habits.

She'd often find him asleep on the couch, head buried underneath his pillow.

He smelt like the forest again, and like sweat, and she figured he must have been out exploring earlier in the day, tuckering himself out with his almost daily marathons.

She almost woke him. Almost told him everything. Almost rushed him out of the valley, just to ensure the distant fumes did not bother him in the night. But he seemed peaceful, and he seemed like he desperately needed a full night of sleep. And the potion was supposed to deter werewolves from entering the valley. Not kill them.

She poured herself a glass of water, brushed her teeth and went to bed. She rubbed Joey's ears and thought about how she'd broach the subject of the witches, and her own powers, and the potential of her father's involvement to Max in the morning. Once he'd slept, she'd tell him everything she knew. No more lies.

Chapter 17

October Eleventh, 6:09 a.m.

Max couldn't wait any longer. He'd laid awake all night, seething. Now, he stared down at her, reached out his hand, nudged her chin, hard.

Her eyes snapped open.

Max growled, barely keeping his voice in check. "How did you know? Do you keep tabs on people like me? How long have I been tracked?" Max held up a single finger, jabbed it threateningly toward her face. "Don't fucking lie, Morgan. The lies are over."

"Max—I didn't know. I swear. Until you told me on the deck, I had no idea who you—"

"I said no more lies. I'm leaving. But I need to know. Who are VC and BS? Who else knows what I am?"

"Max, no one—"

"Those women, the witches you met with last night. Do they know about me?"

"Max, I was going to tell you, I just—"

Max grabbed her shoulders, squeezed them hard. Joey growled. Max had crossed a line.

"No more lies!" he whispered, the edge running through his voice so cold it sent chills down his own spine. Joey's ears flicked back and he whined submissively.

Morgan's eyes went from fear to anger in a flash.

She flicked her wrist, shoved out her flat palm and a tremendous force knocked him skidding out of the guest bedroom.

He stood up in the hallway, cocked his head. "What are you?" he whispered.

Morgan stood from the bed, the sheets falling down around her. Even in his anger, he noticed her. The way her hair tumbled messily over her ears, down her neck. The way her t-shirt hung against her breast. The way her legs climbed so high before they disappeared into the bottom of the shirt she slept in.

He felt a strange, pinching sensation on his hand and wrist.

The pinching became faster, more painful, like bee stings, over and over. Like someone was peppering him with thousands of microscopic needles. Morgan snapped her hand up into thin air. She twitched her fingers in an unnatural pattern.

Max's hands seized up; he stumbled backward. She walked out of the bedroom, somehow pushing him out in front of her, keeping him at a safe distance away.

His fingers cramped together, tightening into deformed fists.

His feet found purchase on the living room carpet, he leaned against the pressure, but he couldn't do anything. Some magnetic force seemed to repel him from her.

He looked down at his writhing hands, confused. And afraid, for he knew what would come next. With all his effort, he turned for the door.

The lock snapped shut on its own.

"I can't let you leave, Max. Not until I explain everything."

Don't panic, Grim.
—She's trapping us, Maximillian!—
Don't panic!
I should have left. Should've ran to the bus station and never looked back.

Fear ran through Max, and it made him sick. He could see the future, unraveling before him. Another dead woman at his hands. Another chance at family and hope and it would be slaughtered by his own claws and fangs.

Max looked at Morgan. She had both of her hands held out in front of her; her fingers traced unknown shapes in the air. They almost seemed to glow gold and red.

She said, "I don't want to hurt you. I really do believe you mean me no harm. But this town needs you…" She lifted slightly into the air, her heels losing contact with the ground. "I need you."

Run away from me, Morgan. Run.
—She's a witch, Maximillian!—

Max's arms yanked together, same as his legs, and he tumbled onto the ground.

"Morgan!" he snarled. His jaw had somehow been clamped shut, as if something forced an invisible muzzle over his mouth. He growled out his words from behind clenched teeth. "Run!"

"I just want to explain."

—Too late, she had her chance to explain, Maximillian.—

Max tried not to think about the moon, but he found it anyway, somewhere over eastern Asia, on the far side of the Earth.

—She's a witch!—

Grim. Please, God, no. Please, Grim.
—She's mine, Maximillian.—
****
October Eleventh, 6:14 a.m.

He shivered on her carpet, his arms raking across the ground, his legs twitching. He was having a seizure, induced no doubt by the surge of red magic she had shot into him.

She didn't feel the red zig-zag threads until they were suddenly buzzing all around her. They had leapt out of the background, from out of nowhere, the moment Max snarled at her and Joey. They pushed into her almost before she even reached out to them. They protected her, but she'd over-reacted.

Or *they'd* over-reacted.

They had swarmed her. Clouded her judgement. Why didn't she just tell him everything last night? Why did she feel the need to hide who she truly was?

And now the red threads of power were gone. Disappeared, just as fast as they arrived.

Max stopped shivering.

A second man, dead in her house, needing her to call emergency services.

What would she tell the sheriff this time?

Then Max's arms shot out, his flesh carving open, bones snapping and straightening, fur pushing out across the newly forming skin and muscle. She watched his skull shatter open, then watched it reform. Before she could wrap her mind around the carnage, the beast was standing up, finding its footing on its thick paws, growling, snapping, snarling. The head cracked against the ceiling as it stood upright.

Morgan only had time for one final spell before the transformation was complete.

She swooshed her hands toward Joey and the three cats. They yelped and hissed, but they also levitated. She slung them into the master bedroom, dropped them onto the big king bed, and then slammed shut the door.

She faced the massive werewolf.

Max had transformed into a bigger, darker-furred monster than the one she had met a week ago. That creature had been almost eight-feet, lean and quick and coated in brown fur. Max was now over nine-feet tall, forced to stand hunched over, shoulders brushing against the ceiling. His eyes were golden, but the rest of him was covered in jet black fur, save his sharp white teeth. His incisors jutted out over his snout, like a wild boar with an underbite. His back paws boasted one oversized claw each, arching out from his big toes, sharp enough and long enough to slice Morgan in half. No wonder he had been so confident that he could catch the other werewolf. He was a far more formidable predator than the other werewolf she had met.

And now she was trapped in her own house with him.

She reached out in her mind for Max's aura but found only anger and betrayal. And a hunger for vengeance.

Her next thought was of that bar of silver. She followed the golden threads, gathered them together. She needed more power for her next spell than she had ever used before. And, of course, the strumming red threads of power were gone again, vanished as quickly as they appeared, now that she really needed them.

But before she could even attempt to melt and

reshape the silver bar into a weapon, if that was even possible, Max jabbed a big paw at Morgan, far faster than she expected, knocking the wind out of her, sending her crashing back onto the couch. The couch tipped over and she tumbled with it. She squirmed backward on her elbows, desperate to get away from the monster. The werewolf stared at her, hunger and malice and violence burning through golden eyes.

She forgot the bar of silver, forgot any strategy at all. In pure panic she pushed out her hands and sent an instinctual blast of pure golden energy at the werewolf.

The same blast of direct magical energy had sent the smaller brown werewolf yelping and squealing, running into the woods.

Now, the black werewolf barely flinched.

The beast leapt, cleared the couch, and landed on top of her in a single pounce. His massive jaws snapped inches from her nose. He pinned her hands under his front claws. She couldn't move. Her wrists felt broken; she couldn't cast any more spells.

The werewolf snarled and growled and lifted his huge head. In another instant, the beast would strike down and spear those incisors into her face and neck. Morgan closed her eyes. There was nothing more she could do. She was dead. She hoped it would be quick. She had a fleeting thought of relief, thinking she would be joining Alex, she wouldn't have to worry about her father, would no longer be responsible for dealing with all the chaos and evil gathering in Pineville. Her last thought was guilt for never confiding in Alex for all those years, for lying to Max the past week, for forcing Max to change and kill her, which he would regret whenever he changed back from wolf to man.

The giant werewolf leaned down. Opened his jaws. Sniffed her face.

But he did not bite her.

He howled at the ceiling, frustration and confusion poured into his mournful howl. He leapt away from her, smashed through the front window, glass shattering out across the deck, and vaulted over the railing. Morgan popped up, dashed after him, saw his black furred haunches disappearing into the woods at the far side of the yard.

Morgan heard her father's voice in her head. A raspy, smarmy voice that she tried never to remember. But now his unwanted and unwarranted advice drifted back to her, as if he was speaking to her again, in the moment, the same as he had when he returned to St. Louis and took her away from her grandmother.

'Magic never helps, Morgan. Eventually, inevitably, magic only destroys. One day you'll understand that.'

It had certainly destroyed her chance of helping Maximillian. He'd never trust her now. And she didn't blame him.

Part Three
Knights and Monsters

Chapter 18

October Twenty-Ninth, 7:24 a.m.

Maximum Grim ran without purpose, without any direction. He ran just to run. The ground barely skimmed his paws. The piney air rushed past his snout, vibrating his whiskers. The foggy mountain woods felt like home.

Why Maximillian felt the need for civilization, Grim couldn't understand. Was there anything more refreshing than cold creek water, bubbling up from a deep mountain spring? Anything more comfortable than a three-month long nap in a warm cave, matted down with dead leaves, sealed off from the world by a thick wall of snow? Anything as joyous as running down a man—*or deer*—across an open meadow, anything as satisfying as feeding on warm flesh and marrow and knowing by the skill and strength of one's own body the hunt had been successful?

Grim had spent the last three weeks in complete control. Maximillian had given up, turned over the reins. They'd lived in the forest, feasted on boar and deer, slept in the shade during the day, stalked the forest at night.

And all three weeks, Grim behaved. He followed the rules that he and Max had agreed upon decades earlier.

Some days, Grim wondered if Max was still in there

at all. Some days, he wanted to break the rules, just to see if it got some sort of reaction out of his human alter-ego.

But Grim didn't want to push Maximillian to suicide again.

Grim had felt Maximillian screaming inside his own head when he pinned the witch woman to the floor. Her spells stung and made Grim's insides burn. Yet, his anger and ferocity were greater than her futile magic. Maximum Grim had wanted her head off her body, wanted to eat her brains right out of the top of her caved-in skull, but Maximillian just wanted to escape.

And Maximillian had caved. His weakness let them turn, and Grim had to save them both. But Grim knew if he killed the woman Maximillian would never forgive him, like those first two whom he'd consumed. Maximillian's human pack.

Grim hated to admit it, but the instinct to escape the witch's home had been just as strong as the instinct to kill her. Maybe even stronger. Fleeing into the woods felt good.

Sprinting fast on all fours through the ancient forest felt divine.

The last three weeks had been sublime.

Maximum Grim hadn't been set free in the daylight for nearly half a century. The sunshine, dissolved and softened by the mountain fog, reminded Grim of a past that he never truly had. Of an imagined time when he was pure wolf-beast. The foggy forest dredged up fictional memories of his ancient pack that worked together to bring down prey like wooly mammoths and giant ground sloths.

His kind once stood their own with sabretooth tigers.

Fought honorable battles with massive prehistoric cave bears, fifteen feet tall, stronger than a dozen of the half-domesticated black bears that now trundled across the American countryside.

Grim came to a halt in an open meadow and focused back on the present. A breeze brought an odor to his nostrils. That smell, the one Maximillian first smelt in Romania. It was nearby. Grim skulked low, hackles raised. But he wasn't afraid. He was cautious and wary, but perhaps more than both those, curious. He hadn't smelt anything like it since they first arrived in Pineville, nearly a month ago.

In fact, sniffing at the air again, Grim detected a new odor. The wind carried two scents, strong and pungent, but distinct. They smelt harmonious, like a chord being struck on a guitar. Two different scents, both the smell of werewolf fur and musk, but not quite alike. No, not two. More than two! Something had brought him to this meadow this day, something beyond his conscious mind. Maximum Grim wondered if coming to Pineville had all been a part of him coming to this very place…

Grim trotted along the tree line, circling the meadow, staying downwind of the odor, trying to get closer without giving away his own scent to the creatures. Their noses were as fine-tuned as his, no doubt.

Grim saw a big rock, jutting up out of the ground, with a fully nude woman sitting on top.

Thick and curly fire-red hair fell halfway down her back. She sat with her legs crisscrossed in front of her. Maximum Grim felt an ancestral, primal urge spark within him.

He started to creep forward.

Maximillian buzzed into Grim's head, finally showing up after all this time, suddenly whispering warnings, trying to get Grim's attention. But the werewolf's mind was focused only on the meadow and the woman sitting out before him. He smelt many wolfish smells in the air, and the red-headed naked woman on the rock was one of them. Maximillian's thoughts finally cut through to the werewolf mind.

Grim, remember the witch.

But Grim knew this nude woman wasn't some witch. She was another werewolf. Grim was about to walk out of the woods toward her, but Maximillian's words of caution echoed through the werewolf's mind. Grim hesitated for half an instant.

At that moment, three wild wolves trotted out of the far woods, bodies low, coming up toward the flat rock. They laid down at the foot of the rock, looking up at the woman. The young woman remained in her meditative position, did not even look down at the wolves.

Next, two gray werewolves, almost double the size of the wolves, emerged from a different section of the woods. They stood up on their back legs to inspect the woman, then dropped onto all fours and worked their way closer, joining the wolves at the edge of the rock. They sniffed at the wolves and the wolves sniffed back. The bigger of the two gray werewolves snapped at the wild wolves, stood up onto its back legs and snarled at them. It took a big step toward the wolves, and they flattened themselves onto the ground, whimpering, ears tucked back, tails curled underneath them.

Grim stared, transfixed. He felt a thrumming between his ears.

Five more werewolves emerged from all across the

tree line, all different shades and covered in different splotches of gray and white and brown, as well as a dozen or so more wolves. Soon the meadow was full of the lupine beasts, all encircled around the small woman sitting on the flat rock. The largest gray werewolf had snapped and snarled and growled at the bigger creatures and seemed to have placed himself at the closest space nearest the woman. Grim estimated the current alpha to be a little shorter than him, but more bulky, fuller across the chest and front paws. The rest were all smaller and would submit to him as easily as they did to this other werewolf. Grim wasn't sure if he could take the big gray alpha or not. But he wanted to try.

Then he heard the slightest vibration through the pads of his paws. It came from behind him.

He turned just a fraction and saw a small, dark brown werewolf lurking in the shadows behind him. It had a long scar running from its lower ribs up almost to its neck. It wasn't crouched to attack, but rather looked submissive, following along with the proceedings, the same as Maximum Grim. Grim's jowls pulled back, his instinct to snap and growl at the other beast was strong, but he didn't want to expose them both to the pack in the meadow. The brown werewolf slunk lower, submitting to him. Maximum Grim turned back to look at the woman on the rock, transfixed.

She stood up, her red curly hair shining in the fog-softened sunlight, as bright and thick as fox fur. She raised her hands over her head, stretched tall on the rock, lithe, exposing all of herself to the creatures surrounding her. She turned in a slow circle as she stretched, and when she turned toward Grim, her eyes flashed like brilliant emeralds. A deeper, starker green than

Morgan's eyes, the red-head's eyes twinkled with the primordial forest beauty of pine and juniper, seemed to beckon him nearer for a closer look. Freckles dotted her pale cheeks, softening the otherwise angular, stark face.

Maximum Grim took in all of her; sensed human Maximilian doing the same. He worked his vision up, starting with her bare feet that led to thin ankles to tight calf muscles, up muscled thighs that could probably run for miles, around curved, rounded hips, past a tuft of fire red curls at the base of an athletic, flat stomach, paused at her supple breasts, untouched by gravity, soft, pale as the moon, pink as a wild rose at their center, nipples tight and erect in the cool mountain air, then continued, across her thin collarbones hiding just under a millimeter of skin, to a strong neck that held a proud, almost fierce, face. Her eyes, when Grim reached them, seemed to bore into him, as if she'd watched him as he consumed her whole appearance.

Maximillian's warning thoughts of caution evaporated. Both man and beast wanted her, wanted to stride into the meadow and tear apart the big gray werewolf and then take her upon the rock. Take her as a woman and then force her to change, to take her again as the beautiful, predatory beast that she truly was.

The brown werewolf grabbed Grim's back ankle.

Maximum Grim had been about to take one small step closer. His paw froze in mid-air when he felt the other werewolf's touch.

But in that half-instant the allure was lost, the woman's eyes disconnected from his, she continued her turn. Grim settled back, still feeling the urges, but content to wait and see what happened next.

She changed.

Her flesh melted.

Not painfully and spasmodically, as it did when Maximillian shifted into Grim, but effortlessly, like it was nothing but a change of clothes, and orange fur erupted across her body, and her ears grew and her human shape shifted into that of a monstrous wolfwoman, over eight feet tall, as exquisite as anything Maximum Grim had ever laid his golden eyes upon.

She leapt, more graceful than any of the other werewolves there, over the pack, and ran out of the meadow, fast as a hare, more vulpine than canine, and the whole pack, over twenty strong, werewolves and wolves alike, chased at her heels, following her lead, wherever she intended to take them.

Maximum Grim again felt the thrumming in his head, again wanted to leap from the woods and chase the pack down, to run at her side and prove his dominance, but again the small brown werewolf reached out and swatted at his ankles.

The brown werewolf scampered off in the other direction, away from the pack. It stopped and looked back at Maximum Grim. The giant black werewolf whined, glancing at the rock in the meadow where the female werewolf had stood. But Maximillian's thoughts buzzed inside Grim's head, seeming to have slipped back to caution, offering the advice to follow the small, brown werewolf, who clearly had more caution and sense about him than Grim and the rest of the others.

Grim huffed, then turned and snorted at the brown werewolf. A growl lingered in his throat but the brown werewolf sneezed, dipped its head and Grim was content. They trotted along through the woods, heading higher up into the mountains, instead of down into the hollow, as the rest of the werewolves had done.

****

October Twenty-Ninth, 2:24 p.m.

Maximum Grim followed the brown werewolf for half a day, eventually coming to a high mountain lake.

Hawks circled the water, a few fluffy white clouds drifted by, but all else was still. The trees were bare, save the pines, and the lake was clear as crystal, the sky as blue as robins' eggs, and Grim felt overwhelmed with tranquility. He sniffed at the water's edge then took a few steps forward, paws tentatively dipping into the cold water, bringing him deeper one step at a time. A sparkling rainbow trout swam underneath him and Grim instinctually lunged for it. His jaws snapped closed, empty. He pulled his snout back out of the lake and shook himself off, spraying lake water out all around him.

He spied the brown werewolf at the edge of the bank. Hunched down on the sand, it peeled a filet off a fish that it had managed to catch. It swallowed back the meat, scales and all. Then it flipped the fish over, stripped the other filet off, ate it, then tossed aside the head and the bones.

It promptly stepped back out into the water, delicately setting each paw down, causing almost zero ripples as it waded out. Once the creature reached about a three-foot depth, it lowered the very tip of its snout to the water's surface, and then reached out its right front paw ever so slowly, hovering above the surface, razor tipped claws mere millimeters from breaking the water tension. The werewolf froze there, still as an ancient stone, until the claws flashed down into the water and then reemerged, flapping fish dangling from the tips of the paw. The werewolf brought the fish between its jaws and stashed it there gently. It repeated this hunting technique twice more, then with three juicy fish flopping in its mouth, it retreated out of the water, almost daintily, as if not to get any more wet than necessary. It squatted down on the sandy bank, spat out the fish, and looked toward Maximum Grim.

It looked at the fish and then it looked back at Grim.

—I hunt my own food.—

Grim turned away and circled the lake in the other direction. He saw a large turtle scrambling down off a log and lunged after it. The turtle shell didn't stand much chance against the werewolf's jaws, but the amphibious creature was covered in algae and it slipped right through Grim's paws and disappeared into the deeper waters of the lake.

Grim spent another twenty minutes fishing and poking around the edge of the lake. He eventually managed to snag a large catfish and he trotted proudly all the way back to the brown werewolf to show off his catch.

The brown werewolf watched as he approached, diverting his gaze from direct eye contact.

The wriggling catfish made for a delicious lunch. Maximum Grim ate it all, including the tiny, sharp fishbones. He then sniffed out and ate the trout heads off the bony fish skeletons that the brown werewolf had discarded. He approached the lakeside and lapped thirstily at the cool water.

He inhaled the clean mountain air. He felt the sun warming the black fur on his back, felt the lake water cooling his front two paws. His appetite was satiated and he wandered back onto the shore, intending to doze in the sand for the remainder of the afternoon, as his ancestors had once done. The high heat of the day was no time for an apex predator to hunt or travel.

—*You are still with me, Maximillian?*—

Yes, Grim, I'm here, for now.

—*I am not giving up control. Not yet, I won't.*—

I don't want you to give up control.

—*I don't believe you!*—

Grim, why would I want to take back over while another werewolf is just fifteen feet away, staring right at us?

—*I... don't know.*—

And should you nap while another werewolf is around?

—*I can do what I want. I'm bigger.*—

It could be dangerous.

—*The brown one is weak. And small.*—

It's crafty and smart.

—*Why did it bring us out here?*—

You have to figure that out. And then turn the keys back over to me only when you think it is safe. I'll stay with you as long as I can, but I might not last much longer.

—*Because you are weak and small, like the brown one.*—

Yes, maybe so. But you and me, we are still on the same team. Not the brown one. We don't know that yet.

Grim growled slightly, acquiescing in his own way. This startled the brown werewolf, who looked up frightened at the big black werewolf at its side.

Who was the human inside the brown werewolf,

Grim wondered? Was he weak and small, like Maximillian?

Grim snorted and pawed at the sandy ground, which felt cool on his paw pads. But he would not give in to the desire to snooze. He paced back and forth and growled again at the brown werewolf, this time in a fierce, questioning manner. The brown werewolf stood up, hackles raised and growled back.

Maximum Grim stood all the way up to his full height, also raising his hackles and snarling, revealing his full set of gleaming white teeth. He pushed out his massive chest, raised his hulking shoulders, kicked at the dirt with one back paw; his large, curved claw glinted in the sunlight, sharp-tipped point flashing bright as it caught the reflection of the sun off the lake's calm water.

The brown werewolf fell back to four paws and loped away from the lake, whimpering, looking back at its spot in the cool sand, mournful to skip its usual afternoon nap.

Maximum Grim pounced after it and growled and nipped at its haunches but did not bite hard enough to draw blood. The brown werewolf sped up, sniffing at the air. Catching a scent, it turned more northerly, heading even higher up the mountain, leading Grim… somewhere.

****

Three hours later, with the sun's bottom edge dissolving into the horizon, the scarred, brown werewolf scrambled up over a boulder and crested the top of the large mountain ridge. The last few miles, as they worked their way higher and further north had been rocky and slippery, treacherous for a werewolf to climb, impossible for any human without equipment and years of rock-climbing experience. Before crossing the final ten yards to the top Grim took a moment to look back across the valley.

From this height on the western ridge, he could see the whole valley laid out below him, including the few winding roads that connected Pineville and the farmlands in the valley to the outside world beyond the mountains. Only one road led through the eastern mountains. This same road carved through the town and led back up and out through the western stretch of mountains.

Grim realized that the whole valley was almost entirely encircled by tall mountains. The eastern and western ridges came together north of the town, wrapping three sides of Pineville in thick, mountainous terrain. The largest road leading in and out of Pineville, a four-lane highway that blazed due south, crossed over the powerful, deep Shenandoah River on an old steel bridge that flashed rusty orange in the setting sunlight.

Maximum Grim huffed. An urge to howl rose up deep inside his chest, but he pushed it down, and turned away.

He climbed the final boulder, following the claw marks left by the other werewolf. He leapt the final five yards and landed at the top of the mountain summit. He smelt silver nearby.

An old stone cabin stood resolute upon the peak.

The Blue Ridge Mountain range stretched out into the west, a jagged line across the horizon. The nearer mountains were sharp edged against the sky, further mountains just blueish lumps, cresting like pods of giant whales as far into the hazy distance as Grim could gaze.

He turned his attention to closer things.

The brown werewolf stood hunched over on all fours near the wooden door of the stone-walled cabin. The shack looked as ancient as the Blue Ridge mountains themselves. It could not be more than 400 square feet inside, if that, though it was certainly sturdy, to hold up for so long at the top of a ragged, wind-blown peak.

Inside. The silver must be inside the shack.

Who would build such an outpost here, in such an impossible place?

The door creaked open and an old, thin man with a gray goatee emerged, wobbly, bracing himself upon a gnarled walking staff. On his hip hung a thin silver rapier, sparkling, shining in the setting sun.

Maximum Grim snarled, but the old man smiled back.

With a cracking voice, and a strong Romanian accent, he spoke. "Maximillian, how pleased I am to see you here, now, at the crux of things, when I need more help than ever before."

Maximum Grim's fur stood on end, but somehow this old man knew Maximillian, knew him even through this shaggy, black-furred form.

Still, he wore a silver sword.

—He could hunt werewolves! Maximillian? Are you hearing this?—

Grim looked for Maximillian inside his own head, but his human alter-ego had fallen silent again. Grim turned and listened as the old man spoke.

"I'm hunting far worse than Nazis and werewolves, this time, I'm afraid," the thin old man said, as if hearing Grim's thoughts. "A far more ancient and far more primal evil has infected this place. I've had to ally myself with an old enemy to try to stop her. This whole valley is haunted by an evil older than mankind itself."

I'm here, Grim, I'm listening.

The man waved his staff vaguely down toward Pineville, and then continued. "There is an evil here that bubbles up from the very depths of the underworld, spawn of the malevolent demon, The Fallen, who came and fell before the rest and made his place in the bowels of our world."

Grim could sense Maximillian now, and they both focused, taking in the information each in their own way. Grim sniffed at the air, watched the man's crinkled gray eyes. Max listened. As the man spoke Grim watched for signs of deceit or trickery. He saw only wisdom and fear and truth in the old man's eyes.

"Vexulta, the ancient one, the snake-demon of the old mountains and hills, sister-daughter of The Fallen, the first of his dark sibling-spawn, has claimed this place. Vexulta, high priestess of the Angavor witch-sisters, she burrows here. Feasts upon the life force of the valley. She must be stopped. Before she drains this town of all that is good and pure."

—Do you understand any of this, Maximillian?—

Not a fucking word, Grim.

Maximum Grim huffed, confused. He looked around, thinking again of how impossible it would be for any normal human to climb down off this rocky peak. His head hurt from all the words he couldn't understand, and his instinct to kill the old man with the silver sword just to shut him up was very strong. He had no desire to focus and try to decipher the meaning of what the Romanian knight was saying, so he made a snap decision.

—If I can't kill him, then I can't deal with him. Good

luck, Maximillian.—

Grim released control of his own consciousness like a toddler dropping a toy on a whim; the beast's body shuddered and collapsed.

Two minutes later, the brown werewolf had Max's delicate human ankle in its massive jaws. He dragged the unconscious body inside the stone shack as gently as a werewolf could, which it turns out, was not very gentle at all. Max's head thumped along the ground all the way inside.

The old man hobbled about in the shack, lashing together dried herbs hanging from the rafters, whispering incantations and recipes under his breath, lighting the herbs on fire, wafting the smoldering collection under Max's nose. When Max did not awake, the old man bonked his wooden staff against the knees and elbows of Max's body, tittering and mumbling as he did so.

After fifteen to twenty minutes of bodily abuse, the old man returned to his wooden table. He began smashing a pestle into a stone mortar, adding a pinch of unknown spices and a handful of unknown leaves and a sprinkling of some sort of dried berry that had been scattered across the table. He eventually succeeded in liquefying all of it into a pungent mush of purple-brown goo. He proceeded to pry open Max's lower jaw and dump the thick paste directly into the human's mouth. Max began to choke and cough and violently hack and this near-death experience seemed to rouse him from his slumber. He spat the muck from his mouth and wiped at his tongue.

"Urgh," Max said, spitting more remnants of the foul gunk onto the dirt floor.

"Ah," the man said. "My potion has awoken you."

The brown werewolf in the corner growled, staring at Max with flashing eyes that seemed to twinkle, reflecting the flickering orange candlelight. The beast remained seated, however, content just to watch and growl.

Maximillian had no clue where he was, nor why Grim had chosen this moment to change and slink away into his subconscious. The last few minutes with Grim were just a blur. Sometimes it could be whole hours that disappeared from his memory, so it could be worse. That said, Max had never woken up in such a strange place before.

"Where am I?" Max murmured, rubbing at his knees. They felt bruised and swollen, along with his elbows, for some unknown reason.

"In a stone shack at the top of a mountain with a very old acquaintance. A knight named Vlad Cosmin." The words trickled out in a familiar Romanian accent. "You've aged much better than I, Maximillian. I wish we could catch up, but we have a lot to cover, and very little time."

Chapter 19

October Twenty-Ninth, 8:24 p.m.

Morgan and Joey returned to the brewery, to celebrate.

She bumped into Farmer Tom Crawford. Had a beer with him. Bumped into Phillip, had a beer with him before he left.

Then she met the girls. It'd been three weeks. Max may have fled, but the witches hadn't. Their potion had worked. No one had been attacked. The full moon had risen into the sky two nights ago, and no one had seen or heard any sign of the werewolves returning.

And, even better news, Benjamin Shroud hadn't shown himself. Whoever this BS was, he must not be her father, as he'd disappeared along with the werewolves, all without ever confronting her.

Morgan drank her fourth beer on the dance floor with Vera. When Hailey arrived, they all were dancing. Once the music got too loud for Joey they went outside. Had more beer.

It was a cold night.

No one was outside. The only firepit lit was the one Ash had lit earlier. Vera, Hailey, and Morgan joined her, stood around the flames, hands out, trying to stay warm. Morgan worried about Joey, until she saw him flopped over under a bench, panting in the heat of the fire, happy as he'd been in a long while.

When Farmer Tom left, he waved goodbye to Morgan. She didn't see him wave. Too distracted by the conversation with her new sisters.

She heard him scream, though.

His shouts pierced the night air.

No.

She bolted into the parking lot. Adrenaline and fear sobered her up, fast.

The parking lot was bathed in an eerie blue-white glow from the overhead light poles. Morgan looked around the first row of cars. Saw nothing. She could hear the buzz of live music still, pulsing out from the brewery. The drums thumped. The guitar squealed.

She ran to the next row, skidded to a halt.

Twenty yards away, two gray werewolves were fighting with each other, tugging at something they both gripped in their mouths.

No, they shouldn't be here. We banished them.
We tried to banish them. We failed.

One of the monsters twisted its head, Morgan heard a wet ripping noise, and the beasts tumbled away from each other. The nearer werewolf turned toward her, the lower half of a gnawed human arm held in its jaws.

A shock of white bone jutted out from red oozing flesh. At the other side of the forearm, like the head of a dead bird after colliding with a window, hung a limp, lifeless hand. Blood seeped out of the wounds, soaking the werewolf's gray fur red before splattering onto the asphalt, a small puddle already forming between its massive paws.

The creature grunted at her.

She noticed the sharpness of its six-inch incisors,

clasped over top of the piece of meat. She noticed the fierce predator's eyes, locked onto hers. Eyes of pure gold, entranced by her beating heart, no longer even aware of the forearm clamped in its mouth.

She noticed frosty fear racing down her spine.

She noticed primal panic sinking into her stomach.

So much for the witch's potion.

Then she heard the crack of a whip, and turned to see Hailey, Vera, Ash, and Joey joining her, flanking her. Her dog and her sisters. They hadn't abandoned her.

Joey's snout bumped against her jeans, a reminder he was with her, that they were together against these monsters, then he aimed his snarling growl toward the two werewolves.

Hailey stepped forward, out in front of Morgan and Joey. She snapped the whip and it cracked loudly, the tip sizzling with sparks of red energy. The bigger werewolf also took a stride forward, dropping to all fours, the dismembered forearm falling with a thud onto the ground. The gray werewolf snarled, a heavy bass resonance vibrating deep in the creature's chest, almost making a harmony with the thumping drums still pounding out from the brewery taproom. Joey barked. Vera and Ash extended their wands.

The guitar squealed, a solo riff, screeching into the night.

Ash and Vera snapped their wrists and Morgan sensed—*no, felt*—zaps of magic rocket out toward the werewolves.

The monsters flinched and raised their arms, as if protecting themselves from being pelted by invisible rocks.

Hailey pressed the attack, lunging forward and

twisting her body, bringing the long whip around in a graceful arc. She cracked it forward right at the bigger werewolf. Fire-red energy shot visibly through the air, vibrating erratically as it raced across the lot, then slammed into the big werewolf's stomach. The beast yowled as it was knocked backward, tumbling onto the ground, nearly pummeling into its packmate.

The smaller werewolf sidestepped the bigger one and leapt toward Hailey, quick as a shadow. She drew back her whip, but not fast enough. The beast was swifter than seemed physically possible.

Morgan pushed out both her hands and twisted her wrists, grabbed all the golden energy and zigzagging red energy available—*it was back!*—within her aura and slashed it toward the monster.

The werewolf's jaws were inches from Hailey's face when Morgan's blast smashed into her, knocking her out of the way, sending her down into the gravel. Morgan grimaced. She'd meant to hit the beast, not the woman.

Hailey shrieked as she fell.

Vera was frozen in fear.

Ash acted.

The young witch sprang forward, wand swishing through the static air, pink shoes sidestepping just quick enough, eyes burning with focus and rage. The werewolf landed where she had just stood, turned toward her, got pummeled by wads of unfocused, angry magic right in the face. It staggered backward, paws in front of its snout, whining. It ducked down, enduring the blows across its thick neck and shoulders, then sprang forward again.

Vera snapped into action, bolstered Ash's attack, wand spryly jabbing forward. Spanish curses flew from her lips as fast as the spells she cast. The werewolf stumbled in its attack.

Morgan grabbed more red and golden magic from the air, this time channeled all that she had into a ball of energy, then pitched it straight at the werewolf as it lunged forward again.

The monster took the blow straight to the chest, flew backward, smashed into someone's car.

The bigger werewolf finally regained its footing twenty-five yards away. It glanced at the damaged car and at its beaten packmate, a whimpering crumple of fur. Then scanned the three women standing in its way.

It stepped forward, sniffed the air. Considered attacking them.

Hailey pushed herself up from the ground with a groan, dusted off her shoulders. She lifted the handle of her whip, and with a flick of her wrist, snapped it with a sound-barrier-breaking *crack*.

The four witches stood in front of the big werewolf, blocking it from approaching the brewery.

The drums joined back in with the guitar, the male singer wailed. The song pounded into its crescendo.

Hailey and the big werewolf stared at each other. Morgan could feel the searing heat from the tip of the whip where it lay coiled next to her, waiting to lash out again.

The werewolf snarled.

Hailey lifted the whip's handle at her side just an inch.

The big gray beast turned and raced off into the woods.

The smaller werewolf whined from its crumpled position on the ground. It staggered up, took two limping strides after its bigger packmate, then tripped, snout smacking down against the gravel.

Hailey's whip lifted up into the air and slashed down, ripping fur and thick callused skin from the werewolf's muscular back.

Hailey passed her whip into her left hand, then deftly snapped it out, wrapping the tip around the werewolf's nose. She tugged on the whip, turning the creature's head to face her. With her right hand she drew her gray revolver from its leather holster. The werewolf snarled and scrabbled in the gravel as it fought against the magical restraint wrapped around its snout. But it was beaten, and Hailey held its struggling throes easily. She did not strain, despite the giant beast pulling with all its evil strength against the whip, trying to escape.

The red-headed witch in the leather bomber jacket took two confident strides toward the werewolf, stomped the heel of her brown boot into its massive calf muscle, cranked back the hammer on her revolver, and aimed the thin barrel between the beast's pointed furry ears.

The creature stopped struggling. Stared right at Hailey. The predatory eyes flashed from angry to afraid.

Morgan could swear she saw betrayal in its eyes.

Hailey pulled the trigger, the muzzle flashed, once, then again.

In through the nose, out through the mouth.

In just seconds the monstrous beast, all fur and muscles and fangs and claws, melted away. A pale, flabby human remained behind in the gravel. Above the neck, there was only a lower jaw, along with a bit of scrambled flesh where once had been a face and a brain.

Morgan thought of a November jack-o-lantern, long past its prime, some teenager having put a boot through it, knocking the rotten flesh apart. Instead of pumpkin pulp, red blood and fatty flesh spilled out around the shattered skull, and instead of pumpkin seeds, pink brain matter and white bits of bone floated in the blood, bobbing in the bright crimson tide, remnants of a wolf monster turned back to man now turned to a pulpy, scarlet soup.

Morgan turned, almost puked. She'd seen a lot in her time as a nurse. Seen a lot more in the few years between leaving her grandmother's and then fleeing from her father. She'd seen almost this exact carnage three months earlier, in her own master bathroom, where her husband ended his own life.

But the gore still got to her. She'd thought she was numb to it since Alex. But this was too familiar, too brutal, too… cold.

The werewolf was human. Like Max. Cursed, out of control perhaps, but not evil. The beast inside him may have been malicious, but the man was just that. A man. This one was a wrinkly, lumpy man caught with a supernatural disease he couldn't control, abandoned by his packmate, shot down in the parking lot by a whip-wielding Irish bombshell and her coven of witches.

"Silver bullets," Hailey muttered, picking something shiny up out of the bloody gravel. "Usually does the trick, as long as you get the heart or the brain." She held the squished bullet in the air, where it sizzled and smoked in her fingers. She flicked it to the ground and blew on her pointer and her thumb. She holstered her pistol and then began to wind up her whip. "We need to get the hell out of here."

"Christ, Hailey," Ash said. "That was fucking gruesome." She stared down at the corpse, almost in disbelief at the scene in front of her. Ash reached down and felt for the upside-down cross hanging on her chest and instinctively rubbed at it with her thumb, murmuring something to herself no one could hear.

Vera, on the other hand, was already casting spells, turning her wand in little flicking dances, drawing in magic, aiming it at the dented car. The dent made a crinkly, screeching noise and the metal popped back out.

Joey whimpered from the next row of cars over, further from the brewery taproom.

Morgan rushed over, Ash right on her heels.

Tom Crawford lay in a bloody lump, shivering. Joey licked at his face, and the man groaned. Morgan pulled the dog away and turned the poor man's face toward hers.

His body was shredded and gashed, very few parts of him were still recognizable. His arm was completely torn off at the bicep. He had wrapped his flannel shirt around the wound, but it had bled through the thick cotton. He had taken his belt off but was not able to tighten the makeshift tourniquet around his upper arm with just one hand.

Morgan snatched the belt and looped it around the remainder of his arm. She pulled it painfully taut, prodded the metal tip at the buckle through the leather.

"Tom, are you with me?"

"Mr. Crawford, I believe," he coughed, "is more appropriate, my dear."

Morgan half-sobbed and half-laughed. "Tom, you are going to be okay. I'm here."

"I'm going to see Linda, Morgan. It's okay."

Ash floated behind Morgan and whispered to her, "You want me to… um, should I do anything?"

Morgan didn't respond. She locked her eyes with the old farmer. "I'm here with you, Tom. I'm here."

"I'm scared, Morgan."

"I know."

"I'm scared."

"I know, Tom."

"Linda went first. She was braver than me. She's waiting for me."

"Yes."

"I wanted to tell you about her."

"I know, I'm sorry."

"I'm scared."

"Yes. It's scary."

"Linda would have liked you, Morgan."

"I'm sure."

"She…" Tom coughed, and blood spewed from his lungs, but he continued speaking, "like you, I think," he finished.

"I'm sure she would have."

"I'm scared… for you, Morgan."

"It's okay, Tom. The town will be okay."

"No, it's never…" More bloody coughing, weaker now. "It's… doomed…"

"No. We are going to get rid of them. Somehow."

Tom tried to cough but his body just spasmed under Morgan's hands, his mouth opening and closing uselessly. She knew he had no chance of surviving. More than half his blood was on the cold gravel underneath him, no longer flowing through his veins.

"Don't join…" Tom gasped, choking on the blood filling his throat, "Don't fear… moon… fear…" He coughed again, one last burst of energy, blood flying from his lips. He reached out and pressed his bloody palm against Morgan's neck, grabbing her, pulling her close. "Fear!"

He coughed and his hand slackened and his eyes lolled, all focus lost. His head dropped hard onto the ground.

"Oh," Ash murmured from behind Morgan. "Oh, fuck."

Morgan held Thomas Crawford's body in her arms. She thought of his apple orchard and his grumpy patience with Joey, and the way he waited for her on market nights long past closing time.

In through the nose and out through the mouth.

She'd have time to grieve later.

She needed to contact Sheriff Jeffrey. This had gone too far. This was beyond them all. They needed… help. Something. The national guard, maybe. The FBI. Hell, she'd take Van Helsing or Sherlock Holmes at this point.

Anyone, as long as it wasn't just her and her new sisters.

Could Father stop the werewolves?

Maybe, but he's just as likely the reason they are here.

She stood up, pushed past Ash, and walked back toward Hailey and Vera. Hailey stood still as a statue, staring off into the woods where the other werewolf disappeared, deep in thought. Vera paced back and forth, murmuring to herself in Spanish.

Morgan rubbed her eyes. She was suddenly so tired. The buzz of the beers that had disappeared in the battle boiled back up with a vengeance.

The music inside The Dugout started again, a piano instead of a guitar this time in the background. A man wailed something about London, about eating Chinese takeout, about assaulting little old ladies late at night.

"We have to get out of here, now," Hailey said, as much to herself as anyone else. "Before someone finds us standing around two dead bodies. Let's get back to Ulta's cabin. She said to meet there if they returned. This is just the beginning."

Morgan asked, "What do you mean, just the beginning? This is way too far out of control already, Hailey."

"Fucking hell," Ash added.

"I'll explain it to you when we get back to the cabin and meet with Ulta. There must be something here, like we discussed at the last meeting. A relic, maybe. A source of power. Ash and I have been tracking it for years. Maybe it is in Pineville, after all, somewhere nearby, and it is drawing these creatures here. Maybe worse will come. Ulta will know what to do. She can stop them. But she needs our help to do it." Hailey straightened her jacket and adjusted her riding gloves, tugging them tighter onto her wrists.

Morgan whispered, "No, no, no. No! I've heard all this before, and it didn't work." With each no, her voice grew stronger. "We need to call the police. The dead werewolf is still a human, too. And this human might have had a family, might have had children. And that—" Morgan pointed to the forearm that was just gray flesh and bone lying in the gravel. "That belonged to Tom Crawford. The rest of him just died over there. We need to make sure his body is buried next to his wife Linda's, out—"

"Morgan, *mi amor, no hay tiempo para eso*. We have to stop these things, *nosotras no podemos cavar tumbas*."

"No time to dig graves," Hailey translated. "She's right."

"Sheriff Jeffrey knows me. We can call him, and Dr. Williams and—and… we can figure this out. Together. Hell, we should call a town hall, make sure everyone knows about these dangers, force the mayor and the town council to do something. We should have done this a month ago. More people might die tonight, Hailey!"

"And what, Morgan? I just shot this 'man.' Who would believe he was a werewolf? Should we confess we are witches, too, while we are at? They'll think we're crazy, Morgan! And even if they do believe we're witches, they'll burn us at the stake, like they've always done! Except this time, it'll be poison in our veins, instead of flames at our feet."

"What? Who cares about what happens to us, potentially years from now? People are dying!" Morgan pressed her fingers against her eyes, feeling the whole weight of the world crashing down onto her shoulders. She'd thought they were in the clear. And now…

Something wasn't adding up, but the buzz of red power and beer and golden magic and the rush of adrenaline was still scrambling up her thoughts.

Ash nodded. "I think she's right, Hailey. This isn't just about us."

Vera glanced between nurse Morgan, blood smeared across her scrubs and her skin, and the tall redhead in leather with a whip and a revolver strapped at her belt, twitching her fingers with impatience.

"All of you, look." Hailey prodded the dead body at the shoulder with her boot, turning the limp man over onto his back.

The body had an italicized tattooed inscription

across his chest, above his heart:

'Cynthia, the darkness may have taken you,
But I'll bring your light back into the world.'

Ash whispered, "No fucking way."

"Recognize that tattoo?" Hailey asked Morgan.

Morgan didn't say anything.

Ten years ago, Mayor Fraser's daughter killed herself, jumping off the bridge into the Shenandoah River. They'd renamed the bridge after her. Morgan had thought about him weeks ago, when they'd first discussed all the tragic things that had happened in Pineville's past.

"Christ." Morgan said.

Now the mayor lay dead in the middle of the parking lot, recently transformed back from his werewolf form.

"This goes deeper than any of you know. We can't risk calling the police."

Vera added, "*Te necesitamos.* You can help us. You can help Ulta. But we can't trust anyone else. No police. No town hall."

Ash stared at the body. "Un-fucking-believable." She ran her hands through her short pink hair, then covered her mouth. "No fucking way."

Hailey said, softer now, "You are right, Morgan. The town is in danger, and we can't wait. I'm sorry. I really thought we'd kept them away for good."

Morgan shook her head, still unsure. She had so many questions. How had no one else heard anything from the brewery? The music was loud, but could it be that loud? Someone would discover these bodies, and what would they think? Craig and Phillip knew Morgan had been at the brewery, they would assume she might have seen something. If she went missing into the woods, would she become a suspect?

Then again, more people could be attacked by more werewolves if she didn't act. If she just called the police like last time, another innocent person may die, just as had happened before… The investigation into the mauling death weeks ago had gone nowhere.

Morgan stammered out one last excuse. "What about… uh, Joey? What am I going to do with my dog?"

Hailey said, "Every witch needs a familiar."

Sixteen-year-old Morgan bubbled up inside her. The teenage girl who survived her evil father. And now she reminded Morgan of who she truly was. Of the strength she had inside her, all this time.

You've known from the beginning. You are the one to fix this. This is why Grandmama showed us these things. So we could stop this. Alex helped you hide. Alex showed you normal. Alex showed you what love could be. But Alex brought you here, and then Alex left you. Max forced you to confront your powers. To be the strongest version of yourself. Then Max left too. But he left you alive when he could have killed you.

You are still here for a reason.

Morgan nodded, more to herself than to her witch-sisters, and pulled the keys out of her pocket.

"Take me to Ulta's cabin," Morgan said. "No one else dies on our watch."

Chapter 20

October Twenty-Ninth, 8:57 p.m.

Max listened to the knight of the Silver Dawn, still rubbing at his knees, still unsure of just how much he should believe. Even if he did believe it, he was pretty sure he shouldn't care about it. This valley had chewed him up and spat him out. Grim had ran the show for close to three weeks. Max just needed to climb down the mountain on the other side, and he was gone. No more witches. No more mysterious werewolves, no more guilds recruiting him to fight their holy battles.

Grim had abandoned him for now, which meant Max was stuck on the top of the mountain, inside this dilapidated shack with the other brown werewolf and the old man, but Max had a pretty good idea of how to get Grim back.

"This valley rests just above one of the ancient hellfire cracks that stretch all the way to earth's underworld," the man said, waving his staff at a map of the world that had been stuck up on one of the walls. Certain locations across the globe were circled in red marker. Max saw two spots in Europe, three more in the Americas, another in central Asia, one at the heart of Antarctica. A question mark had been drawn there, the abbreviation EGAP scrawled in black pen nearby.

The knight droned on, rambling about ancient

creatures and mankind's place in the battle of good and evil, and some other occult bullshit.

Max tuned him out. His thoughts raced. He needed to get the hell out of this valley and the first step was getting down off the mountain. Morgan had lied to him. He wanted no part in saving her town.

He *definitely* wanted no part in saving humanity from some ambiguous world-consuming evil.

"Are you listening, Max?"

Max blinked. He was staring right at the old man and hadn't heard a word he'd said. "Oh, yes."

"Good, this is important." He continued on, pontificating about the 'real' dark ages, about the origins of werewolves and trolls and other wild shit, and how they all were spawn of some sort of eternal devil-monster, which Max figured was the real big bad in this whole situation, and something he had no desire to encounter.

Good luck to whoever ended up dealing with it. Certainly wouldn't be Max. He was planning his escape.

The heat from the wood stove was sweltering.

He felt like a child, strapped to a school desk, listening to one of his old history professor's monotone voice whining about ancient Greece or Rome or something. The knight certainly found the history of the dark arts subject interesting, but Max had more pressing problems. A part of him worried that if he did pay attention, he might start to feel sympathetic about Pineville, and then he might actually feel inclined to help. He wouldn't allow that. He was supposed to keep to himself, to stay low, to avoid shit like this. He wanted about two dozen beer right now, not to go save the world.

He knew logically that these prehistoric evils must

still exist, considering he'd been cursed to be one of them, and Max dealt with his personal curse every damn day. But he preferred to live his life as if he was the only werewolf in the whole world, and that if he managed it properly, it was almost like he didn't have a problem at all. Just a carnivorous spilt personality that lived in his head and complained about salads and insinuated rude bosses should be stalked into dark alleyways and eaten alive.

Yes, he'd done evil, vile, monstrous things, and he'd tried to be better. He'd tried to face who he was, and help Morgan protect Pineville.

But he saw how that had worked out.

Now, he would revert back to what he knew how to do. He would focus on being a normal man, keeping his nose out of trouble, and eventually retiring to Cape Cod and watching the sunrise and sunset for eternity in gentle peace. Maybe get a pet dog of his own.

A pet dog like Joey.

Joey.

Morgan.

If he left, they'd be the ones to suffer the consequences.

So be it, she lied.

All that evil, all that darkness that boiled up within him, he wanted to keep all of that in his past. He'd mistakenly revisited it once with Morgan already. That had been one too many times. He should never have let himself make a connection with her.

"Look," Max said, cutting the knight off. "I get it. This valley has some ancient demon witch thing with command of an army of werewolves, or some such, and me and flea-bag over there need to help you defeat it. But there's one problem. I don't want to. This whole ancient evil versus the last remnants of mankind's canine protectors or whatever, in the middle of a forgotten Appalachian valley, it's not happening. It's not my story. I'm leaving. I don't do ancient holy wars. It's just one of my non-negotiables. Sorry."

Max stood up, and the brown werewolf growled in the corner.

"It's humanity's story, Max. And humanity needs you. We *saved* you, Max."

Max looked at the old man and saw just how exhausted he truly looked. The knight looked near breaking. Max was his last hope.

"Max, *I* saved you," the knight pleaded, "Nearly eighty years ago. We let you move on with your life. Kept tabs on you from a distance. I know you remember, the night I saved you from the castle!"

"Saved me!" Max erupted. "You dropped me in the mud in a German forest to fend for myself! You allowed me to take this fucking curse back to America. Back to my family. If you'd let me die, my wife and child would have had long, fulfilling lives. Ginny would be a grandmother, somewhere, or a realtor, or a NASA astronaut for all I know. Instead, I… instead, she's dead because you *saved* me. Excuse me if I don't show enough gratitude."

The knight turned away and stared at the wall. Stared at the map with the red circles. He said softly, "There is another… creature here. He and I share a goal for this place. We have a common enemy. But he is not good, Max. His brand of evil is less chaotic, less far-reaching, but do not mistake. He is evil. I've been forced to work with him, to achieve our goal. I don't want to do this, but I swore an oath to root out black magic across the world. And so I do what I must, against all odds. Because my oath is sacred."

The knight turned and looked at Max. "Once upon a time, you swore an oath too, and accepted a duty to help the innocent. You were a soldier. I need that soldier, again, Max. This is a new war for you. A more important war than ever, and the most ancient of them all, but it's the same oath. Will you help us?"

"I was a soldier," Max said, and he stepped right up toward the old knight. The goateed man turned, faced him. Max saw his chance, and he felt like a prick, but he knew he had to take it. "Now, I'm just a cursed man with a drinking problem and anger issues."

He slammed his palm into the old man's chin. With his other hand he grabbed the pommel of the silver rapier, pulled it from the scabbard at the knight's waist. He dashed to the door, kicked it open and chucked the sword out into the night, off the mountain, down toward the valley below. The brown werewolf's low growl transformed into a menacing snarl as it lunged out of the shack.

Max turned around just as the brown werewolf reached him. The creature swiped out a big paw, raked it across his chest. Sent him crashing toward the cliff ledge. Max barely clung onto the ground, his feet tumbled out over the edge, dangling in mid-air.

Max grimaced in pain, but he also felt the full moon's rays radiating down across his body, hitting him, illuminating the whole mountain range in the intoxicating glow of reflected starlight. Max felt the familiar stir of anger and release building inside him. He pushed and pulled and clawed his way up the cliff's edge, spat out blood onto the ground. His body convulsed.

Maximum Grim stood up from the ground, snarling, ready to slaughter.

Grim landed two smashing strikes onto the brown werewolf before it cowered and yelped and ran in fear to the far side of the stone cabin. The knight watched from the shack, seemingly indifferent to the outcome of the scrap between the two werewolves.

"Are you going to leave us then, Max? Abandon this whole town? Abandon your werewolf packmate that saved you from enslavement? Abandon Morgan?"

Maximum Grim stopped, focused on the knight.

—*So they do know Morgan.*—

"She had nothing to do with you coming here, you know. She's just as oblivious as you. Another puppet in Benjamin Shroud's schemes."

Benjamin Shroud. BS.

Vlad Cosmin. VC.

They were the ones who used Ronnie. Who tried to leave a message for Max, no doubt to recruit him to this crusade.

They wanted to get to him before he ever turned, before he ran into the witches and their hillbilly werewolf-hunter.

Before he would ever meet Morgan.

"He'll use her for his own gain, then take her back. The cost of doing business with a creature of the night, like him. If you stay, if you help, maybe we can find a way to save her, too."

—*Maximillian?*—

We are leaving, Grim. We can get out of here, right now. We saw Morgan with the witches. This knight wants werewolves to fight them. We aren't being used for another war.

"Max, please," the knight begged.

Climb down the other side of this mountain, get us somewhere safe, and we'll have steak for a month. I swear. Fuck this whole valley.

—What about your witch friend?—

She lied to us, Grim. This knight is probably lying to us now.

—You didn't want me to kill her, even after she lied and attacked us. You stopped me.—

The knight said, "I've never seen a werewolf like you, Max, not in any of your species. You could lead the whole pack. You could lead them all."

Better to have no one to worry, that way you have no one to hurt.

Maximum Grim didn't fear anything. No werewolf pack, no witches, no ancient evils from the underworld, nothing.

Grim, Morgan doesn't want our help. She wouldn't have lied to us if she wanted our help.

—She lied to us because she's afraid. She begged for our help. The most honest she smelt was when she wanted you to stay and to help her.—

That's not an excuse.

—When you get scared, we just leave. Because you are weak. She took us in.—

Grim, we do not have to be responsible for Pineville. Nor the widowed witch. The town can sort it out on their own. She doesn't need us. We will just make things worse. The next time you see her, you may kill her as likely as help her.

—You are afraid.—

238

I'm looking out for us.
—We should stay and fight.—
We should escape while we can.
The knight asked, "What's it going to be, Max?"

Chapter 21

October Twenty-Ninth, 9:41 p.m.

Ulta's cabin in the woods was much further past Morgan's house than she expected. The paved road went on for at least three more miles, winding north, weaving over and around dark creeks, climbing up steep hills, then dropping back down into deeper, woodsy hollows. Eventually the road shrunk in on itself and grew very narrow, and then the asphalt ended completely and the road continued, nothing but dirt and gravel and small eyes flashing in the dark, skirting across the road. In the brief gleam of the headlights the tree trunks flashed like iron bars, pressing close on either side of the car, trapping Morgan, Ash, and Joey on their one-way path forward toward the coven's retreat… and Morgan's destiny.

Ash stared straight ahead, eyes dark, thoughts unreadable, her aura unprobeable.

Joey had whined when they drove past their home but now he had settled into a wary silence in the back seat. He sensed the anxious anticipation of the two women in the car with him.

Morgan had been half-tempted to pull in and change out of her bloody scrubs and drop the dog off, but for one, she wasn't ready for Ash to know where she lived, and for two, pulling into her own driveway after fleeing a murder scene seemed pretty reckless.

Almost as reckless as fleeing a murder scene and racing off into the dark forest with a witch, looking for a witch-priestess.

Morgan was anxious, but she was no longer afraid. And she certainly was not doubting herself. She'd done that for far too long, and she was past all that. In fact, her head still buzzing with the influx of the zigzagging red energy, Morgan realized that she was more confident than ever. In her powers. In her decision making. In her commitment to save the town.

And for the first time in months, she hadn't stopped for a minute to think about her depression, or her grief, or her guilt. She felt an electric sizzle of adrenaline and exhilaration and pure power.

She knew she hadn't killed Alex from the day she found his headless corpse in the master bath. But she hadn't truly *felt* innocent until this very moment. Alex died, and he chose that for himself. Some darkness may have pushed him over the edge.

So be it.

Morgan wouldn't let it continue.

She hadn't attacked Max; she protected herself from him. He grabbed her, after all, and he was so strong, even in his human form. His dark eyes were full of pain. And maybe something more. But he was gone now, disappeared back into anonymity.

And Lord knows, she certainly hadn't killed poor old Farmer Tom. She'd tried to save him.

Yes, together with her new *friends*, they'd killed the werewolf, who turned out to be Mayor Fraser. But they'd been forced to do that, to stop him from killing anyone else.

And to make sure no one else died, the werewolves all needed to be stopped. With Morgan joining the coven, it could be done. What was it that Hailey said? A place of power that might be luring the werewolves closer. Ulta could find it, and shut it off, with the coven's help.

As Morgan drove closer she sensed a stronger and stronger sense of growing power. Though her thoughts ran in her head, she still remained focused on the road, bumping along through gravel and potholes, ensuring not to drift an inch off either side.

"There," Ash said. "Turn there."

Morgan pressed on the brakes and stopped. She saw nothing but the single dirt road they were on, winding further into the mountain forest, nowhere to make a turn, left or right.

"See that red slash on the tree up ahead?"

Morgan squinted. Sure enough, scratched into the bark, a red gash. Little drizzles of scarlet sap dripped from the wound in the trunk. If Morgan didn't know better, she'd say the tree was bleeding.

"Just past that tree, on the right, there is a narrow little road. Turn there."

"Narrow?" Morgan asked. "Narrower than this?"

Ash nodded. "You'll see. It'll take us up to a mountain lake, and we can walk from there."

Morgan eased the car forward, flicked her blinker on.

Ash stifled a laugh, snorted instead, which only made her laugh louder. In between her cackling she stammered out, "You put on your blinker!"

"Shut up!" Morgan started giggling. "Shut up! It's a good habit!"

Ash put her hands up over her mouth. "I'm sorry.

But come on, sis! We are out in the middle of nowhere, I don't have to sense your aura to tell your tension is ratcheted up through the roof, you haven't said a word to me this whole drive, we are looking for a witch's cabin in the middle of the woods, potentially being hunted down by both cops and werewolves… and you flick on your blinker? Thank God you did, really, that way the fucking racoons know which direction you're turning."

Morgan bit on her tongue, frowned, and made a serious attempt to quit giggling. All attempts failed.

Ash said, "Oh, and the possum family, twenty yards back, they thank you for giving them plenty of time to hit their brakes." Ash continued to laugh, barely able to breathe, let alone speak.

Eventually their howls of laughter turned to giggles then to the sounds of them trying to catch their breath, trying not to burst into laughter once again.

It was nice to have someone to laugh with, someone along for this crazy adventure with Morgan. She thought, three weeks ago, that person would be Max. But that hadn't happened. Morgan needed sisterhood right now, not some passionate fling with a tall, dark-eyed, mysterious *werewolf.*

"Don't you dare tell Vera or Hailey about this," Morgan warned, still trying to catch her breath.

Ash said, "Oh, I'm telling them immediately!" They erupted into laughter again.

The windshield shattered.

Muscular furry arms reached in through the open front windshield and grabbed Ash by the neck. The young witch shrieked as a brown werewolf ripped her from the passenger seat, pulled her into the night.

Morgan heard a bone snap.

"No!"

The werewolf leapt out of the beam of the headlights, hauling Ash's limp body away with one clawed hand. Morgan felt hot tears in her eyes, but she recognized the creature's fur. It's size. The scar that ran along its ribs. It was the first werewolf that had attacked her and Joey. The werewolf that started all of this, a month ago.

Morgan furiously launched all the energy within her at the werewolf. She didn't pause to think about control or precision, she let the magic explode out of her, red and gold energy together, strong as a cannonball blast.

The brown werewolf deftly leapt out of the way, bouncing off a tree trunk, still latched onto Ash, refusing to let her go. The blast of golden red energy shattered the oak's mighty trunk, the tree wobbled, then tipped.

Falling right toward Morgan's car.

She thought of Joey in the backseat. Began pulling in energy.

The tree smashed down onto the car.

The front engine block and hood were decimated. The heavy trunk split the front half of the car in two.

The back half of the car remained untouched. A bubble of red and gold magic shimmered around Morgan. She wasn't sure how she even managed to pull off that spell.

The magical shield flickered; the tree crushed further onto the car. The roof groaned; the Civic door popped open under the tremendous pressure.

Morgan gritted her teeth, focused on keeping the shield intact for another few moments.

Joey whined. Morgan grabbed him by the collar; the protective bubble burst and they tumbled out of the car as the tree crumpled the remainder of her Civic into two very broken, very distinct, halves.

'Magic never helps, Morgan. Eventually, inevitably, magic only destroys. One day you'll understand that.'

Morgan saw the brown werewolf, still holding Ash's body, watching her and her dog from the shadows of the nearest trees.

Morgan shook her head, cleared her mind of intrusive thoughts. She pushed Joey behind her.

She needed more power, not less, and more focus, not more distractions. Her fingers twitched as she reached out and found the latent gold energy, found the zigzagging red threads of power dashing through the night air that seemed to be looking for her as much as she was looking for them.

Her blood boiled with how much red magic she drew into herself. If she didn't use it, she might erupt into flames. It raced through her veins, found little escape ports to seep out.

Her eyes bled glowing neon red, the fleshy tips of her fingers looked like gleaming crimson claws. Joey huddled behind her, whining at her feet.

"Put her down, you sonofabitch, or you'll get ten times the shock I gave you the last time we met."

The brown werewolf stared at the glowing red witch, then glanced at the smoldering stump where the giant oak tree had just stood, then looked back at Morgan. The creature dropped the body.

It fell and hit the dirt and collapsed into a heap. Morgan thought for sure Ash was already dead, but she wouldn't abandon her body.

Ash bounced up after just a half-second, wand in her hand, and scrambled to Morgan.

Morgan blinked. She stuttered out, "Are you okay?"

Ash groaned, whispered, "It broke my collar bone, but I'll live, I think." Ash added, "You know this one?"

"The one that attacked me a few weeks back," Morgan whispered. Then she asked, not taking her eyes off the brown werewolf, "Can we walk the rest of the way from here?"

"Well, we certainly aren't driving the rest of the way." Ash's eyes flicked toward the wreckage of Morgan's car. She took a deep breath, lifted her wand, aimed it at the werewolf. From the corner of her mouth, she said, "Your eyes are like, uh, glowing red, by the way. It's a serious vibe."

Morgan smirked, despite her body feeling close to bursting. She still hadn't released the energy she'd drawn into herself. But she had fully conjured her next spell in her mind, tweaking the magic inside her, visualizing precisely what she intended to do. She'd never done it before, but she was confident that she could do it, all the same. The golden energy might just be latent power, but the zigzagging red energy wanted to be shaped, yearned to be used in creative spells. It was unlike anything Morgan had ever experienced.

'Magic is as natural as the wind, Morgan. If you can control it, and you can focus, you can use it to do anything you can imagine. But you have to imagine it perfectly. You have to imagine it just exactly as you want it.'

Now, with this new energy, she could do more than her grandmother had ever conceived.

She thrust out her arms and links of red and gold chains exploded into the air, a pair of glittering handcuffs at the end of the chains snapping around the werewolf's wrists.

The magical chains clinked over the fur covered forearms and wound across the beast's chest, across its shoulders and wrists and ankles, and tugged.

The brown werewolf crashed to the ground. Despite its thrashing, it couldn't break loose.

Morgan declared, her voice calm and strong, "I am bringing you to someone who might be able to lift your curse. If you resist me, I'll sear off your fur and fix you like I did my dog. Are you going to resist?"

The werewolf whined in submission.

She lifted a finger, removed the chains from its ankles, but kept the rest secured.

"Lead the way," Morgan said to Ash.

"You are a fucking badass, you know that, right?"

Morgan smirked again, flicked her fingers, and the werewolf was tugged into line behind them, red glowing chains laced around its whole body.

Ash waved her wand with her right hand, whispered something, and her left arm lifted across her chest. She groaned a little, but the arm held firm against her body. She'd cast some sort of invisible sling for her broken clavicle.

Joey edged toward the werewolf cautiously and sniffed at the chained creature. The beast growled; Joey leapt back. The mutt looked up at Morgan in curiosity and confusion and whined.

"It's alright, Joey. You're safe." Morgan tightened the chains across the werewolf's chest. She turned to Ash, whispering, "The poor dog's going to need therapy worse than I do, after all this."

Ash chuckled, and together the four of them proceeded into the dark forest. Joey trotted along up front by Ash, tail somehow still wagging, Morgan followed right behind, the brown werewolf shuffled at the back of the pack, only able to take small steps, the magical restraints tight around its hips.

The chains around the werewolf gave off a limited reddish glow, but not enough to truly see by. The deeper they hiked into the forest, the closer the darkness seemed to gather. Ash used her wand as a torch again, and they continued deeper.

Just as before, the landscape began to shift. The temperate forest trees faded and warm, swamp-like conditions took over.

"I don't understand this forest. It's not like anything I've ever seen."

"I think," Ash said. "It has to do with the place of power nearby. But I'll ask Ulta when—"

A snap and the sound of leaves shuffling from behind them. Morgan whipped around. Someone had followed them, all this way from the road.

"Release the beast," an eastern-European voice exclaimed. The voice sounded old and tired but was nonetheless firm. The man continued, "I won't hurt you, and neither will the beast, if you listen to what I have to say. The werewolves are not your enemy."

A cloud of green vapor blossomed above them all.

The cloud flickered and shifted, shimmering, brightening in strange arcing rays. Like a miniature aurora borealis, concentrated directly over their heads. The light penetrated the misty woods, and Morgan saw an old man, gray mustache and goatee styled nobly across his face, one hand wrapped around a scuffed silver rapier, the other hand resting on a gnarled walking stick. His face gazed up at the glowing phenomenon, as surprised as the rest of them to be suddenly bathed in the ghostly green light.

"Is this you?" Morgan whispered.

"No fucking way," Ash whispered back.

"Is this him?" Morgan said, pointing to the skinny, old man, her lips curving down in doubt.

"No," Ash said, smiling now. "This is *her*."

The old man murmured to himself, his voice full of fear. "Vexulta. So be it." He looked toward the brown werewolf and said, regret in his eyes. "I am sorry, Abornazine."

A burst of emerald lightning slashed down out of the green vapor, striking the old man. Morgan turned away, blinded by the sudden flash of light. When she looked back, she was certain the man would be nothing but dust.

Instead, the old man still stood, wrapped in glowing green chains, similar to the chains Morgan had conjured and wrapped around the brown werewolf.

Out of the dark forest, robed in her traditional gown of silken green and a cape of black, Ulta emerged. She looked near the same as Morgan remembered from the séance, but she had grown lean. Her hunch was gone, and her belly was ghastly thin.

"It has been many years, Vlad Cosmin," Ulta said, nodding in welcome to the older man. "You are aging slower than most. Back again from the Scholomancc to try to kill me, I presume? One last great quest for the last knight of the Silver Dawn?"

The old man did not speak, but he nodded his head, slightly, in defiance, his wrinkled brows aimed down in anger.

Morgan's mind ran back to her night with Max, reading the note in the abandoned meth house.

Vlad Cosmin.

VC.

"Perhaps," she said, *hungrily*, "We can all sit down by my fireplace, eat some sweets, have a chat. We will keep no riddles from each other." She looked toward Morgan and her dark purple eyes seemed to linger on her, probing her aura, choking out her soul's darkest secrets, then she flashed her gaze across to the brown werewolf, who whimpered. She turned her unblinking stare back to the knight. "I'm impressed you managed to tame one of these feral beasts. But you must realize that to pit yourself against me here, in my very own enchanted forest, against my witch-sisters was foolish and futile."

The old man gurgled out a reply, "It's my duty to try."

The witch nodded, simply said, "And your fate to fail, it would seem."

She stepped into the center of the group, the green cloud still glowed and twinkled above their heads. As the rays of ethereal light washed over her, her face *transformed*, changed, flashed from countenance to countenance as the green shadows shifted over her. Ulta morphed, first to a stunning woman, then an ancient crone, then a regal elder, then an innocent face of a prepubescent girl. As her faces danced from one to another, she spoke, her voice changing as her faces did, each word a different octave, each syllable a different pitch.

"I'm quite certain that I am not at all what any of you believe me to be. I am more than that but I am less than that, and I shall not be defined by any simple definition. I'm neither as good as you hope, Vlad

Cosmin, nor as evil as you fear." She looked at Ash and her face solidified back to her first face, that of a mid-fifty-year-old woman, kindly, confident, *suddenly ravenous*, then calm again.

"Welcome back, Ashley Rose. Good to see you again, Morgan, dearie. Thank you for bringing these new friends with you. Now come along, we have much to do. I see our potion did not work as we had hoped." She was back to the sweet, elderly grandmother, tittering ahead, leading them all deeper into the heart of the dark forest.

Chapter 22

October Twenty-Ninth, 10:17 p.m.

Maximum Grim tried to follow them all, but the task became more difficult the closer Grim came to the cabin. The forest was changing somehow, altering into a different place entirely. More swamp than temperate forest. Grim noticed the smells first, the pungent stink of bacterial life growing in puddles and mud all around him, warmed by an unnatural heat. The sticky, sweet smell of rotten vegetables mingled with dead skunk, combined together with the stench of wet, vicious lupine creatures. He could detect each scent individually, but together, the air smelt like death, decay, and doom.

He pressed on.

Where before he tread on normal ground, loped past junipers and pine and maple trees, now he stalked past thick mossy oaks and had to traverse around foggy bogs. Strange, black-trunked trees, thick as redwoods, bedecked with massive human-sized spikes, grew up out of the bog water. The branches spiraled and twisted, curving in unnatural arcs, confusing the werewolf's sense of place.

Had he walked past these trees before?

The path he tried to follow wove him past carnivorous ferns that had traps large enough to catch rats, past bizarre, red-leafed bushes that held glowing pink fruit, past a hedge of cacti that shot little clumps of spikes from their trunks wherever their roots detected motion.

Grim traversed it all, a few quick-healing scrapes the only evidence of his struggle, then came to a halt. He stood at the foot of a black lake. A rotten wooden bridge, complete with a drooping rope for a handrail, stretched out over the lake, bobbing in the wind. His sharp werewolf eyesight allowed him to see through the mist across the lake to where the path continued back into the woods.

Maximum Grim reached out a hesitant paw, touched the water.

This was no crisp mountain lake. The water was warm, almost boiling. If bubbles started to drift to the surface, belching heat and gas, Grim wouldn't be surprised.

He backed up a few paces, looked around. Ignored his nose for a moment and took in the scenery with his eyes and his ears. This stretch of woods felt more ancient, untouched, and wilder than the rest of the forest he had explored over the last few hours.

He heard distant footsteps but couldn't be sure if they were beast or human. He saw big, black crows, hopping in the branches, uncomfortable, unable to rest with the werewolf so close by. He turned and looked out at the lake, saw something swimming in the black water. The muscular tail swished across the surface, back and forth, but the scaled head pushed straight forward, direct on its path, stopping for nothing.

An alligator. A big one.

In a mountain lake in Virginia.

Grim refocused on his nostrils, sniffed the air again,

trying to find the smell of Morgan, of her hair, to find that pleasant scent amongst the plethora of foul odors that hung in the air. For some reason, the smell of her hair held a valuable place in Maximilian's memories, deep in his heart, and therefore it was much easier to isolate and to follow. The stink of werewolves and dead prey lay across the land, growing more pungent now that he stood at the bank of the unnatural lake, but Grim could still isolate Morgan. She'd stepped onto this bridge, crossed toward the other side.

He worried he would get trapped if he exposed himself by crossing the bridge. If it could even hold his weight, which he doubted.

Still, it seemed an awful detour to go all the way around.

The black werewolf pondered his choices. Grim had chosen not to be a pawn for the Silver Dawn knight. If he had, he'd probably have been caught by the witch, same as Vlad Cosmin and the scarred, brown werewolf.

At the mountaintop, he'd listened to Maximilian's consciousness, despite his own instincts. He left the cabin, left the old knight and the scrappy brown werewolf, and climbed down the far side of the mountain, leaving the Pineville valley, intending never to return.

Grim sniffed out a herd of deer on his way down the other side, stalked them out into a mountain meadow. Spied a big stag standing amongst the does and the fawns.

Grim could have struck out, surprised one of the younger, less experienced prey items. But Grim didn't hunt that way. He emerged from the tree line, tall, monstrous, gleaming in the pale light of the moon, shiny black fur thick, claws sharp, roar guttural and frightful, eyes hungry.

The big buck flinched. Cast a glance at the herd around it. They panicked, fled, ran to the far side of the meadow. But they were slow. Many does waited for their fawns. Fawns tripped over their young, wobbly legs in pure terror.

In a few quick strides Grim could be upon any of them, fangs in their flesh, their neck clamped between his jaws, heartbeat dying upon his tongue.

The buck snorted, stepped forward, brandished its large rack of horns. It would stay and fight, huffing and stomping, protecting its family as they made their poor escape.

Grim respected it. He smelt its fear, the same terror-odor as all the rest. He could almost taste the desire the stag had to flee, panic bubbling up in its throat. But it had something else. An animalistic sense of honor, and confidence. Testosterone, maybe, but it wasn't just a chemical, hormonal choice the buck made. Other bucks with the same thick dose of testosterone in their veins may have fled. Not this one. This one had pride.

The buck had never seen a predator this big and fast, never heard a growl this ferocious, never smelt a more ancient, hungry carnivore.

It shook its antlers at the werewolf. It bellowed, it stomped, it pranced around, looking for an angle to charge the black-furred monster. All the while the buck made its show, the rest of the deer fled.

As these thoughts ran through Grim's primal mind, he felt Maximilian's consciousness squirming.

Grim wanted Maximilian to notice. Wanted Max to be there, conscious alongside him.

—The buck is brave, Maximillian, unlike you. It is afraid, but it still does its duty. Because it is the strongest. The strongest should never run. The strongest should fight. They should protect.—

Maximillian didn't respond. Instead, he relented, acquiesced, gave in. He slipped into Grim's subconscious, leaving the werewolf in complete control.

After Grim rushed the male deer, after he dodged the antlers with ease, after he tore the prey down to the ground and chewed out its windpipe, after he devoured the buck's heart and feasted on the warm flesh around the thighs and the neck, he howled at the moon, blood dripping down his chin.

Dominant, confident.

Looking for a real challenge.

No echoing howls returned. On this side of the mountain, Grim was the sole apex predator. Grim sniffed the air, smelt the rest of the deer herd in the distance, but they'd run far to the west, and it would require a long, fast trot to overtake them. The buck had done its job. Ensured with its sacrifice that its progeny would live on.

Grim would not allow this buck to be more honorable than he.

He knew where his challenge could be found. He knew where he belonged. Where he needed to make his stand.

He returned to the ancient shack. The knight and the brown werewolf were gone.

Grim descended into the valley, snout pressed close to the ground, his night vision and his fine-tuned olfactory glands guiding him back. Back toward the meadow where the vulpine female werewolf had been. From there he traced his own scent trail back to

Morgan's home. He sat under her deck, a giant black werewolf, curled up in the shadows against the front of her old house, staring out at the driveway, waiting for a small gray car to pull in.

He'd protect her. As he should have done from the beginning. Witch or not, she'd helped Maximilian, and therefore, Grim owed her the same. She may have lied, but she'd never wanted to trap Max. She'd known nothing of his problems until she slammed her car into him.

If she and her witch friends needed Grim to hunt down and kill other werewolves, he would do it. He would be the alpha of the pack and lead them away from the humans' small little town, if that's what Morgan desired. And if that plan ended up on the wrong side of the Silver Dawn knight and the old, brown werewolf, so be it. Maximum Grim would slaughter them. And if the ancient evil demon-witch-monster showed up as the knight had predicted, Grim would slaughter her too. He breathed easy. Unafraid. Patient.

He saw the headlights, saw her gray car. His night vision even allowed for him to see another woman in the passenger seat, black makeup smeared across her face, glittering jewelry pierced across her skin, her eyes dark with pain and anger, like his. The car did not slow, it went right on by, deeper into the northern woods.

Perhaps Maximillian would suggest they just wait for her to come back. But Grim did not. Grim always chose action over inaction. He did not like the look of the other woman, nor the thought of Morgan driving further into the forest. When the pack of werewolves left the meadow with the orange-furred female, they'd descended in that same direction.

Maximum Grim set off again, muscles strong and enduring, pushing the pace, chasing after the vehicle. He couldn't catch it unless they slowed down, but he could persist. He'd covered nearly fifty miles in just this day alone and could cover another fifty with ease if he needed.

He would follow their scent, and they'd eventually stop, and he'd catch up.

The next step, he'd figure out from there.

Eventually, Grim did catch up. He found her car smashed in half, a felled oak tree splitting the vehicle in two. The two witches were nowhere to be found, but Grim picked up the scent of Morgan's hair, and he followed the trail into the dark woods. He detected the scent of the brown werewolf and the scent of the old knight. They were together now, hiking deeper into the wilderness, all of them together with the old crone who'd cast green magic into the air.

Now, at the lakeside, Grim still mulled which direction would be quickest to circle the black body of water in his way and reach the trail at the far side. If he could circle quickly enough, he wouldn't lose her scent. And wherever she was headed, it couldn't be much further.

He chose north, rounded the lake, keeping the bank to his right side. The vegetation was dense, but his paws were callused, his fur thick enough to slough off thorns and prickers, his mind determined.

As he rounded the far point of the lake, he smelt something altogether out of place. It confused him.

He smelt his old blue car.

It had been a full month since he'd smelt his old blue car.

Maximilian had hung air fresheners from the rearview mirror, stashed them in the trunk and the back seat pockets, jammed them into the glove box and under the front mats. He'd been trying to disguise his own wolfy smell.

Grim knew that smell anywhere.

—What the hell is our car doing all the way out here, Maximilian?—

His alter ego did not respond. Did not even stir in the beast's mind.

Grim locked onto the aroma of the air fresheners, left the lake behind, tromped deeper into the woods. He'd catch up to Morgan soon enough. First, he needed to find out why his car had been moved to the middle of the woods.

As he left the lake, the forest faded back to normal.

The junipers and the pines returned, the soil shifted back to hard packed clay. The leafless tree branches were just leafless tree branches, the piles of dead leaves just natural piles of dead leaves, nothing vile and pungent buried underneath.

Grim reached a service road of some type. Maybe a fire access road. Across the thin strip of gravel and dirt, Grim saw two vehicles parked in the driveway of a small little wooden cabin on a steep hill. It looked spacious compared to the shack at the top of the mountain, but it was far from luxurious.

His blue Ford Fusion was in the driveway. So was the old red truck.

—They hid the cars all the way out here, Maximilian. Why'd they do that?—

No response.

Then the door to the cabin cracked open, a motion

sensor light triggered, flooded the front pathway with light.

The redneck who had poisoned Maximum Grim, the one who had had his head ripped off and tossed across the road, stepped out onto the front walkway, holding a bag of trash. Grim saw two thick bolts of black metal in his neck, and ugly, black stitching sewn across his throat.

—*Impossible.*—

He heard something crack behind him, loud, like a gun shot.

He turned around.

The naked red-head from the meadow, this time wearing leather clothes, stood behind him. She held a whip at the ready in her right hand.

"You weren't supposed to see that," she said.

Grim leapt at her, canines flashing.

The red-head snapped her whip and it sizzled, red and hot, and the tip struck him on the nose like snake fangs. A blast of weak magic pulsed from his nose down through his body.

He tumbled as he crashed into the ground but quickly rose, turned, snarled, lunged again, the whip struck him again in the nose, this time coiling around his whole snout, sealing his jaws shut.

Grim scratched and growled and shook viciously, but he couldn't throw off the whip. The red-head reeled him in, wrapping the whip around her arm, elbow to shoulder, like a Navy sailor. She took the whip handle into her left hand.

"So you are the giant, black-furred one," she said, eyeing Grim cautiously. "The one that Morgan met and didn't tell us about."

The red-head slowly reached for something with her

right hand, saying, "She shouldn't keep secrets from her sisters…" Grim pulled with all his might, straining his muscles, but the whip somehow held him in place. Magically held his head still.

From the inside pocket of her leather jacket, the red-head removed a slightly curved piece of smooth wood. It shone in the faint mist light, swirls of mahogany and cherry and a glimmer of some sort of big red jewel at its base.

She pointed the wand at Grim's face, he growled, unable to do anything else, and a beam of red light struck him in the forehead. His head snapped backward. His brain pounded inside his skull, like he'd just been hit by a locomotive.

He snarled, forced open his eyes despite the pain, and glared at her.

She smiled back. "Tough one, huh? Come now, don't be stubborn, this will only get more painful." She winked one emerald eye at him, a promiscuous smirk danced on her freckled face, and he remembered the way she looked, naked, stretching her supple body on the boulder in the meadow. "Do you like pain, beast?"

She barraged him again with a pulse of red light and Grim's head snapped back a second time. His vision faded and he collapsed into the dirt. His claws retreated to fingernails, black fur receded to dark stubble, golden predator eyes dimmed to human shades of brown.

Chapter 23

October Twenty-Ninth, 10:47 p.m.

Morgan stepped off the end of the rickety bridge, Joey right behind her. They followed Ash who followed behind Ulta, who walked behind the goateed old man and the brown werewolf. Ulta had wrapped her glowing green chains around the beast, allowing Morgan to release her own spell, to gather her strength back.

Morgan reached her hand down and Joey poked his cold nose against her palm. '*Still here,*' he seemed to say, '*Still with you, Mom, despite the scary monsters.*'

Ash asked, a little timid, "Ulta, why, um, why are the woods changing like this?"

The priestess did not turn back, but she answered, words as sweet as ever. "They are reverting back to an earlier version of themselves, Ashley Rose. From eons ago. The Source magic that flows from this place has… unnatural effects on the habitat."

Ulta led the way forward without any hesitation. She strayed close to dangerous creeping vines and thorny bushes, close to shadows that shifted and hissed, but they fell away as she drew near. Morgan followed the group around a dark corner and gulped.

The yard leading to the cabin was blanketed in pumpkins and gourds. Thousands of the fall harvest vegetables were sprawled out in front of the cabin. Here and there golden stalks of corn grew up between the squash. The night was still but the stalks of corn seemed to wiggle and flutter in a night breeze that hadn't blown.

The front path led through the garden, past the massive pumpkins, up to a spiraling set of wooden stairs.

At first, Morgan thought the cabin itself was hovering, levitating in mid-air, but then she saw a wide tree trunk extending down underneath the house into the ground.

The cabin was really just a big tree house.

A massive tree house with rooms jutting out here and there like an abstract Picasso painting. Each room seemed built with a different type of wood, each window carved in a different shape, no windows were equal sided squares. The whole house itself spiraled up and around the gargantuan tree trunk, giving the illusion that it had no top roof at all, just unending floors growing up and up into the tree branches above. More than one brick chimney curved out of the cabin, each one belching hot gray smoke. Many fires burned inside the home, but the windows glowed with a green light from inside, not the warm, soft orange of a welcoming fireplace. Moss and vines hung from the walls of the home, and they too fluttered in a nonexistent wind.

A black raven drifted down from high up in the tree house, croaked a greeting to them as it descended, landing on Ulta's outstretched arm.

"Welcome back," it croaked in a strained, throaty bird rasp. "Welcome back, welcome back, welcome back."

Ulta whispered something to it, stroked its smooth feathers. "It begins, it begins, it begins," it croaked, then stretched its wings out wide and soared off into the night air, cawing loudly, "It begins, it begins, it begins, it begins."

Morgan leaned over and whispered to Ash, "Relaxing retreat, huh? Where have you really brought me?"

Ash looked at her, then turned down her eyes. She said, "I'm sorry, Morgan. But we need you. You'd never come if we told you everything at the beginning, back at the brewery a month ago. Ulta will explain everything."

Morgan exhaled a ragged breath through her nose. She noticed the chained, goateed knight was staring at her, eyes wide, pleading. For what, Morgan hadn't a clue.

VC.

BS.

Morgan said to the knight, "Do you know my father? Is he your ally?"

The knight looked at Morgan, nodded his head a fraction, but spoke out loud so everyone could hear, "I don't know you, child. I don't know your father, either."

Ulta turned back to Morgan and spoke, "Don't fret about him, dearie. Your father can't step foot onto my property without my invitation. You are safe here. You are welcome to my home, dearie. You and Joey are invited to stay as long as you need. We will gather soon to begin the ritual that will banish the werewolves, permanently. First, though, perhaps we need to remove the masks of our two uninvited guests, to see who we are truly dealing with."

Ulta waved her wand and the brown werewolf began convulsing. The creature collapsed to the ground, its form shrinking, changing. A moment later a Native American man lay naked and unconscious in the mud.

The hair on his head was long and fell across his thin frame. Though he seemed muscular and fit, he looked very thin. There wasn't an ounce of body fat anywhere to be found.

The goateed knight trembled, but aside from his green chains vanishing from around him, nothing else about him changed.

He said, his old voice still firm, "You see, crone. I am no imposter, nor am I deceitful in my quest, as your spell has laid clear. It is no jest when I say I came here to strike you down and vanquish the evil that nests eternal upon this land."

Ulta scoffed, glanced at Morgan and Ash, rolling her eyes. She then turned and faced the old knight, looking at him the way a mother does a young toddler who misunderstood something.

"Vlad Cosmin, your conviction is authentic, of that I am sure." Aside, to Morgan and Ash, she said sweetly, "Perhaps we should have an early history lesson, before we go inside."

Kindly and patiently she said to the knight, "For thousands of years, old, 'brave,' men, full of conviction and certainty in their god and their moral superiority have circled the earth and brutalized others in the name of 'vanquishing evil.' These men wrote in their journals' similar thoughts, with the same lofty conviction, as you've just expressed to us. For instance, when European men invaded this poor boy's land four hundred years ago," Ulta gestured to the unconscious Native American man at Cosmin's feet, her voice shifting again, multiple voices flowing out of her, "and deliberately gifted them with blankets contaminated by small-pox patients."

Ulta's shadow seemed to grow larger as she

continued.

"When they massacred children on the banks of the Euphrates, they were convinced they were vanquishing evil. When they marched thousands into gas chambers, they were convinced they were vanquishing evil. When they thanked their god for sending a hurricane-sized swarm of locusts to consume all of a country's grain, condemning millions to starvation, they were convinced. When they proudly blame disastrous typhoons for a type of love they don't understand, they are convinced that evil is being vanquished. When they haul Grandmother Gaia's oldest oceanic protectors up by their tails across every harbor in the world, chop off their fins, boil their teeth, they are convinced. When they stack buffalo skulls so high the noontime sun can barely scrape by overhead, they are convinced. When they fly planes into buildings, when they blow themselves up, when they decimate children's hospitals, they are convinced that they are vanquishing evil. When they burn women for letting their hair be seen in public, or when they burn women for not letting their hair be seen in public, they believe they are vanquishing some sort of evil. But no…"

Now Ulta herself grew, green energy swirling around her like a cyclone, her body lifting into the air, her silky green and black robes billowing out, her face changing, each new face contorted into pure, tight-lipped rage.

"No, they are not. These men in power all sleep soundly at night, thinking to themselves, they are 'vanquishing evil.' Since Homo sapiens cracked open the last Neanderthal woman's skull, men who have sought to vanquish evil have accomplished nothing except to have been the most destructive, disgusting, monstrous force on this planet. Worse than any demon or ghoul that may lurk in the deepest shadows of this world, worse than any practitioner of the black arts. Worse even than the first malevolent creature of them all, my traitorous father, The Fallen, who at least consumes his souls without prejudice or partiality. Worse even than I, Ulta, truly named, Vexulta, the first-born sister-daughter of The Fallen, the protector of the ancient Appalachian Mountains, the witch-queen of the Blue Ridge, the Pineville Valley Hag-Viper, the Bell Witch, the Priestess Crone, leader of the Angavor witch-sisters, dispenser of depression, darkness, and doom!"

Vexulta's arms raised in front of her body, her hands twitched, green fire ignited above each of her fingers.

"Yes, Vlad Cosmin, you and men like you are quantifiably the worst force of destruction upon Gaia's green world. And when men like you are fool-hardy enough to wander into *my* lair and accuse *me* of evil when you should shatter every mirror you've ever crossed from the shame of who you are, you shall suffer the consequences. Your blind, white-knight convictions of superiority and righteousness are nothing but the hot stink of moral corruption, your sword nothing but a distraction from your small prick, your walking staff a symbol of mankind's inability to walk a righteous path on your own two feet. This is not some far-fetched story of fiction where good goes to battle versus evil, and an old white man with a gray beard dispenses the moral values from his place of superiority, oh no, Gaia's world is much more complex than that, and Pineville will not be any better off with you poking blindly after evil you don't understand. I only need one thing from you."

Vexulta's faces stopped shifting. Returned to her

first. Her rage still burned hot, but now she smiled.

"I need you to suffer for the foul deeds of men like you."

She pointed a finger at Vlad Cosmin and a stream of green flame doused the goateed knight. Cosmin screamed and shrieked as the flames burned across his body.

"Suffer for your conviction!"

Vexulta pointed four more fingers at him, they all gushed rivers of green fire down upon the body.

"Suffer for all the innocent women killed while men 'vanquished evil!'"

She pointed her other hand, dumping more green fire across his body.

"Suffer for Gaia's pain!"

His body spasmed, but Vexulta didn't let him fall. He stayed frozen upright, was forced to remain conscious, suffered the ferocity of the flames as his skin melted and his flesh bubbled and hissed. The smell of burning flesh turned Morgan's stomach, but she couldn't pull her eyes away.

"Suffer!"

Soon fleshy tendons popped, melted off the bone, great gobs of muscle and fat dripped onto the ground. More skeleton than human stood before them, internal organs sizzled out between exposed ribs, and the half-flesh, half-skull jaw spasmed, tried to continue to scream in pain.

"Suffer!" she bellowed. "Suffer for all of mankind!"

The fleshless legs eventually gave way, the corpse collapsed on itself, but the green flames continued to burn over the pile of bones. The knight's rapier melted in the heat, molten silver dripped across the smoldering heap. The wooden walking staff remained upright in the ground, unburnt. Untouched completely.

Vexulta turned, her size snapping back to normal as if it had never changed, the green cyclone mist vanished, the rage in her face lifted like a cloud passing over the sun. The flames vanished. Ulta again, no longer Vexulta.

"Alright, girls," Ulta smiled, words honey lavender sweet, "Did we learn our history lesson?"

Morgan looked at Ash, and the admiration in Ash's eyes scared her. But when Ulta turned her purple eyes toward Morgan, she just nodded along, withering in the elderly witch's stare.

"Good. Now, how about we continue inside?"

Ash wouldn't meet Morgan's eyes. She stepped forward, headed to the stairs. Joey whimpered. Morgan reached down and rubbed the dog's ears. Joey poked his nose against her hand.

She still felt strong, still felt the rush of red energy available all about her, and the strength of that magic thrummed beside her, softening the horrific scene she'd just witnessed. But even the new zigzagging layer of red magic couldn't convince her she would be entirely safe. The night had unraveled quickly into fantasy and terror.

Her car was destroyed, her farmer friend Tom was dead, the mayor was dead—who was also a werewolf— and more werewolves threatened everyone in Pineville. An ancient witch, far more powerful than Morgan, and seemingly far more homicidal, held the very fate of the valley in her hands.

And Morgan had to work tomorrow morning.

It felt unnatural to even think about going into work, but if she didn't make it, her absence would heighten the suspicions folks may have about her having something to do with the death of Tom Crawford and Mayor Fraser.

Morgan had no idea how to even get home, let alone to work the next morning, but she'd figure that out later. She needed to see the night through to the end. She followed after Ash, intent to make something positive out of the horror of the evening. If together the witches could save Pineville, perhaps it was worth teaming up with this ancient priestess and her ambiguous set of moral principles.

Morgan climbed the stairs, walked up to the circular, wooden door. Her world had changed beyond imagination since Alex died. And it was about to change even more. She'd trained for half a decade with her grandmother. She hoped those skills would be enough to stop the werewolves, save Pineville, and most important of all, get her and her poor dog home safe.

She entered the ancient witch's cabin.

She hoped Max was far, far away from Pineville by now.

****

October Twenty-Ninth, 11:17 p.m.

Max woke up with a pounding headache. He was lying in a soft bed, though he had no idea how he got there. He didn't remember anything from Grim's latest turn at the wheel. The last thing he remembered was standing at the top of the mountain with the old knight and the brown werewolf.

The room was pitch black, and Max couldn't hear anything.

He tried to lean up, but he hit his head on a little jingling bell, then realized he was strapped to the bed at his arms and legs. He could only wiggle around. He panicked, suddenly feeling trapped, but Grim was nowhere to be found. He couldn't communicate with the werewolf inside of him, and the path to unleashing him seemed locked away inside Max's own mind.

The door creaked open. A familiar voice said, "Awake already, huh?"

The redneck, Victor, somehow still alive. Maximum Grim had torn the man's head right off his shoulders.

Max was too stunned to speak.

"Hailey said you weren't to be allowed to wake up until morning. She said, 'Mr. Frank, he's a tough one. You might need to give him an extra dose in the middle of the night.' So I made up a big dose, just in case." His voice sounded slower than before, sounded almost slurred.

Max stammered, "How—how are you alive?"

Instead of answering, the redneck shuffled around to the far side of the bed. Max heard him pick something up, smelt a strange chemical in the air. He heard a plunging, suction noise.

A needle.

Max writhed but couldn't make any progress escaping out of his bonds.

"There, there," Victor said, grabbing Max by the back of his neck with a big hand, jabbing the needle into the side of Max's shoulder. He depressed the chemicals into the muscle, whispering, "Back to sleep. Not to wake until Hailey is back in the morning."

Max strained even more. He only had seconds to break free before the drugs might start to hit him. He had no idea who Hailey was, didn't intend on sticking around to find out.

Could really use some help here, Grim, if you can

271

hear me.

The redneck's grip tightened around Max's neck, twisted his head back toward him. "Hailey said, 'Mr. Frank, don't take no revenge out while I'm gone.' I promised I wouldn't."

Max heard knuckles crack. "This ain't revenge." A heavy fist crunched into his face, smashing his nose. It stung like hell.

Victor punched him again, this time in the stomach, knocking the air out of Max's lungs. "This ain't revenge, neither."

The next punch caught Max in the ear, but it didn't really hurt. In fact, Max smiled.

"This ain't nothing like the revenge you're going to get."

Max actually felt pretty good, despite being pummeled by the big redneck. A little loopy maybe. The bed was so damn comfortable. He would close his eyes for a minute, just to rest for a little, then he would escape.

The redneck let go of Max, stopped punching him. He shuffled back away from the bed, leaving Max snoring in the sheets. "Stupid wolf-man," Victor Frank said, rubbing at the base of his neck, feeling the stitching and the bolts that held his head onto his shoulders. "I'll tear your head off, soon, once the witch is done with you. Then we'll see how you like it."

Chapter 24

October Twenty-Ninth, 11:21 p.m.

The inside of Vexulta's cabin was as cozy and luxurious as the outside was creepy and unnatural.

The walls were covered in an eclectic fashion, barely a blank space available. Most of the area was taken up by homemade wooden shelves, stuffed with leatherbound books, intermixed with an occasional burning candle, a bottle of an unknown liquid, or a pile of quartz crystals. Dainty tables and chairs were scattered across the room. Sets of tea kettles and cups adorned most of the tables, along with snippets of some thorny flowers, cheese plates covered in lumps of things that weren't cheese, rolled up parchments and scrolls, and a map held down at all four corners by glittering geodes.

Small knots of twine floated through the air, flapping their oval loops like wings, sticking together like a flock. They drifted across the room, disappeared through a door at the far side.

A woodstove burned in the corner, and though it gave off a green hue, it also gave off warmth and *cheer*. Morgan's apprehension immediately lightened when she looked at it. The logs crackled and popped as if under any other normal flame, and the smell of burning cedar filled the air. From the ceiling, every herb imaginable hung in clumps, both dried and fresh, along with hundreds of other leafy twigs and flowers that Morgan couldn't identify.

Along the back wall a large table stretched, bending under the weight of all the assorted ingredients collected on top of it. Most of everything was sealed in glass jars, every manner of bug and reptile seemed collected there. When Morgan looked closer, she could see them moving, climbing around in their tiny terrariums, blinking their eyes, swishing their tails, stretching their insectoid wings. The focal piece of the room, hanging above the wall on the table, an old broom, hand woven, not a single twig out of place.

Vexulta entered; she'd aged fifteen years in her walk up the stairs. The face she wore now was wrinkled and her hair was far more gray than black. Her silky green robes were faded, more sage now than emerald, more drab than chic. She'd also regained her prodigious hunch, and teetered around the cabin, muttering to herself, picking small things up off one table and moving them to another, without any apparent method to her actions.

"Ashley Rose, my sweet sister, can you show Morgan to one of the guest rooms? And be careful walking through the greenhouse, something sinister seems to have slithered in there whilst I was away. Sphinx hasn't caught it yet."

Ash nodded, though Morgan saw a flash of frustration in her eyes. She hated that name, no matter who called her by it. Morgan heard a slobbery, chomping noise, and whipped her head behind her.

Joey had his paws up on one of the side tables, eating God-knows-what off a plate.

Morgan shouted, "No!"

Ulta murmured, "Oh, dear."

Morgan leapt over, grabbed Joey's collar, yanked him down off the table. Joey happily wagged his tail, licking his jowls. Morgan looked at the plate. Nothing was left but a smear of something vibrant green.

"I am so sorry!" Morgan said. The damn dog had been witness to all of the horrifying and terrifying experiences that Morgan had, yet of course, he was a dog, so he still had an appetite. Morgan shook her head in frustration. Joey trundled into a magical tree house, no fear, no hesitation, and ate the first big pile of goop that came to his mouth. "Was that, uh, poisonous?" she asked, heart beating hard in her chest.

Vexulta shrugged, murmuring, "I don't have any idea. Not to the alligators out at the lake. It's a solution of enchanted dragonfly wings. I burnt that batch, though."

"What was it supposed to do?"

Joey yelped; Morgan looked down.

Two sets of dragonfly wings bloomed out behind Joey's shoulders. Joey turned his head and sniffed them. They buzzed and vibrated through the air. Joey's tail began to wag. The wings accelerated their motion, Joey lifted up into the air, tail still wagging. He pawed his paws up and down, like he was swimming in water.

Morgan's mouth dropped open.

His wings tilted and he moved forward across the room. He clearly had no idea how to stop or change direction. He slowly buzzed forward until his head clunked into a shelf full of books on the far wall.

"That's what it's supposed to do." Ulta frowned, tottering after the flying dog. Morgan put her hands over her mouth, still speechless at the whole scene.

Joey twisted one set of wings, figured out that was how he could turn right, promptly smashed into another stack of books, this time knocking them all off onto the ground. Joey barked in excitement, his dragonfly wings snapped closed, folding parallel to his thick, furry torso. He smacked down to the ground, barely landing on his paws. His tail thumped happily against the wooden leg of a table, shaking a teacup near the edge right off onto the ground.

Morgan shot out her hand, caught the cup with a cushioned ball of golden magic, lifted it back up onto the table.

"Joey, come!"

The dog hopped into the air, the dragonfly wings snapped back out, he buzzed right at her. She snagged him out of mid-air, pushed him down onto the ground. Kept a hand on his collar.

"I'm so sorry," Morgan said. "I am so, so sorry, Ulta."

Joey's wings buzzed under her hand. He lifted up off the ground and Morgan shoved him back down to the floor. "Stay, Joey! Is this… uh, are these wings going to be permanent?"

She really hoped not.

And she hoped Ulta didn't hate dogs the same way she hated old white men.

The elderly witch just flapped her hands at Morgan. "Bah, how should I know? Lasts for the alligators about a month." She turned back to cleaning up the knocked-over books.

Morgan, Ash, and Joey climbed up and around the house, little sets of stairs leading up to each new room, slowly spiraling upward. Morgan hung onto Joey the whole way, despite his insistence to leap into the air and try to teach himself a crash course in insectoid flight.

They crossed through many rooms, each one more mysterious than the next. A lounge with bicycles hanging from the walls, a library complete with a sluggishly spinning globe that did not depict anything close to the current continents on earth, a greenhouse where they heard a rattle going off somewhere—they didn't stay to investigate—an all-white room with no furniture, no decorations, no windows at all, except a small black hole on the side wall. When Morgan glanced back she swore she saw a green finger with a nasty dirty claw sticking out of the hole, but it quickly pulled back inside.

The following room was just a long, cozy, hallway with two closed doors on either side and another far door at the end of the hall. Ash knocked on one of the doors.

"Who else could be here?" Morgan asked warily.

"Trust me," Ash said, "Always knock. Better safe than sorry."

Nobody responded, Ash twisted the knob and opened the door. They stepped into what could have been an Aspen ski-lodge loft. The walls were thick-cut timber, a white brick fireplace burned green flames in the corner, and a four-post bed with clean, white sheets beckoned Morgan to climb in and shut her eyes for a spell.

Morgan let go of Joey; the dog leapt from the doorway, buzzed his dragonfly wings, flew all the way to the bed, dropped on all fours onto the mattress. He sniffed the sheets, padded about in a circle three or four times, then curled into a ball and closed his eyes. He grumbled a little, then promptly began snoring.

Oh, to be as easy going as that dog.

She felt just about as tired as Joey, but she needed to keep her wits about her. And she needed to speak to Ash while they had a moment of privacy.

Ash said, "I'm going to go find Vera and Hailey. We'll be gathering in the room just past this one to perform the ritual. I'm sure we'll figure something out about what's drawing in the werewolves."

"Ash." Morgan thought for a moment, then whispered, "Don't you think it's pretty obvious that Vexulta could be behind the curse in Pineville?" Morgan was exhausted, exasperated, and couldn't believe Ash was acting like everything she'd seen and heard from the priestess was normal behavior. "Do you really think she wants to stop the werewolves?" Morgan asked. "I mean, she all but admitted she's been in this valley for centuries. You and Hailey found her when you went looking for your primordial source of power, right? I think she has some bigger scheme that the rest of you are blind to because she gave you these wands—gave you access to this extra power. I don't want to take that away from you, but stop and think, it's pretty obvious who is behind all of this... She may not be summoning the werewolves here, but she's for sure played a part in Pineville's tragic history."

"Pretty interesting theory, Morgan," Vexulta said, from just outside the doorway.

Morgan jumped, Ash whipped around; they both stared at the old witch.

Old was no longer accurate.

Her hunch was gone and her eyes glistened radiant royal purple. Her gown had brightened back to silken green and shimmering black. Her wrinkled face was now as smooth and fair as a cup of heavy cream, her mouth immaculately done in glittering shades of juicy purple and when she parted her moist lips her smile seemed to open a vacuum in space where her teeth glittered like white starlight.

Her gown was cut much shorter than before, an inverted *V* riding very high up her pale, flawless thigh. Morgan caught herself staring, despite her fear. She turned away, her face flushing cherry red. She'd never felt that way about a woman before, but she sure felt something for a brief moment.

"Your theory is not completely wrong," Ulta continued, "but it is missing some rather important context. Come now, Ashley Rose and Morgan. Vera is already waiting for us. I'm sure Hailey will be here soon. I can tell you a little more about myself, if you want to hear it."

She walked past them, continuing up the hallway. Ash snapped her eyes wide at Morgan, murmuring, "She can always hear you, here."

"Now you tell me," Morgan mouthed back.

They followed after her. From further up the hallway, Vexulta extended out her hand, snapping her fingers.

Ash's loose-fitting clothes disappeared into thin air. Morgan glanced down at herself, noticed her scrubs and underwear had vanished also. They were both stark naked.

Before she could move her arms to try to cover herself, a black robe slipped over her body. The length ended perfectly at her ankles. Ash received a similar robe, and a pointed black hat. Morgan reached up and, sure enough, felt a brimmed hat sitting on her head.

"Come along, girls," Vexulta said, her voice flowing down to them from the next room. "Some traditions are too important to abandon."

Ash and Morgan hustled the rest of the way down the hall, rustling in their new silky black robes.

The room of rituals had hundreds of candles burning. Some floated in midair, some were stacked along shelves along the wall, most were spread out across the floor. Vera sat, legs crossed, black robe donned, at a corner of a five-point star that had been scrawled onto the floor. She smiled at Morgan as she entered, gave her a little finger wave.

Vexulta gestured for Morgan and Ash to sit at adjacent points. Vexulta took her spot at the 'bottom' point of the star at the far side of the room.

Aside from the sputtering sound of candles burning, the room was deafeningly silent.

****

October Thirtieth, 12:00 a.m.

Max turned in his sleep, dreaming of a young girl whose hair smelt like the autumn harvest and whose eyes shone like wild sunflowers. He did not wake, nor toss fitfully, nor hear the intrusion coming from the main room of the cabin. He slept soundly as Victor Frank's recently reattached neck was punctured wide open, as the hillbilly's body was drug into the corner and tossed haphazardly there. He did not hear the teapot fill with water, did not wake as it was set upon the rusty stove. His eyes did not crease as the door to his room was slightly opened, as a silver-haired, middle-aged man with sparkling, electric eyes looked in upon him. His ears did not twitch, his nostrils did not flair, his lips did not quiver as the door was firmly shut again, and then locked.

He slept and rain began to fall.

****

October Thirtieth, 12:00 a.m.

The hour hand rolled past midnight downstairs, and the grandfather clock rang out twelve times, then twelve times again.

Morgan's hands rested on her knees, her palms turned upward.

Her eyes were closed. Her thoughts were focused. She barely heard the clock tolling. The three witches and the *priestess* each sat at their respective corner of the pentagram, waiting for the final member of the coven to arrive. Floating at the center of the hand-scrawled star were four small wands. They orbited each other, each wand infused with a different colored crystal shard. Red, green, blue, and gold.

Vexulta had affirmed to Morgan that Vexulta was not of mortal descent, not born as 'humans were.' That she was indeed the first daughter of a fallen demi-god, but that she'd repented against her own dark nature. Morgan struggled to wrap her mind around such a concept, but what other explanation did she have? What else could explain the place where they were now, the things she'd seen the last few nights?

"What is more admirable?" Ulta had asked Morgan, slyly, radiant violet eyes boring into her, "To be born pure of heart or to be born malevolent and malicious and yet still overcome the call to do evil through pure strength of will?"

Morgan hadn't known what to say. Those purple

eyes stayed locked on her, unblinking. After a moment of contemplation, Morgan answered. "The latter, I suppose."

Vexulta nodded, looked away, toward the other two witches. "I am not, by deliberate design, drawing these werewolves upon our valley. I suppose, though, they could be naturally drawn to this place of power, like moths to the flame. It's not happened before, but cursed beasts being drawn to a place of primordial magic makes sense. The flow of Gaia's energy bubbles up from a subterranean crack here in the valley, and we'd be fools to think no others have noticed. The holier-than-thou knight Vlad Cosmin would have succumbed to the temptation of this power. Perhaps, in his passion to exact blind justice, he would have become a greater danger to mankind than even myself. Surely, your father has been drawn here for the same reason, Morgan. But truly, I tell you, I am more human in mind now than I am in ancient spirit, and never have I been a mindless monster. I am simply something altogether *different*. I am a traitor only to my father, The Fallen, who betrayed Gaia at the dawn of Earth. I am cursed to consume the life force of this world for sustenance, as are all of my kind. But I've chosen to limit myself to the realm of this small valley, to starve myself, and consume only from the dark, tortured spirits who's lit wick is already flickering, about to go out. I do not want to vanquish the entirety of mortal spirit, as The Fallen does. I want to uplift the oppressed, the downtrodden, the weak. I am an agent of both Gaia and The Fallen. A grandchild of life and love, but sister-daughter to doom and despair. I do not suffer lightly the sins of the guilty, but I do not judge too harshly the flaws of the common folk. By my own self-imposed sacraments, I shall not directly enter the town, nor shall I directly kill nor rescue the innocent."

Vexulta gazed at the candles as she spoke.

"But since Gaia has sent me a new batch of magically-attuned sisters, I find it within the limits of my sacraments to imbue those of you who need to channel magic with the tools to channel magic. I can help you find and destroy the werewolves that descend upon my land. They are preying upon the innocent within my realm of enchantment, effectively eating of my own flock. Upon Hailey's arrival, we shall perform our ancient ritual, one that I perform once a millennia or so, and cast an enchantment across the valley, to protect Pineville once again. From all manners of creatures and ghouls, save me. Including your father, Morgan."

Morgan felt overwhelmed, light-headed.

"Including Benjamin Shroud, for as long as I am here to watch over the Blue-Ridge, I will not let him return here."

Morgan swallowed, nodding.

Hailey burst through the door, halfway covered by a black robe that she was still squirming into. She pulled it down past her bare hips and the robe fell to her ankles. Hailey rushed to her spot, still struggling to get her hand fully through one of the arm holes.

"Sorry! Sorry, everyone!"

Vexulta waited for Hailey to assume her meditative position, then spoke. "Gaia, Holy Mother of Earth, laid upon her land four different strains of magic, each imbued with powers and attributes unique from each other. These distinctive strains gave birth to atmosphere and to warmth, to sustenance and to hydration. Magic was the first true building block of life."

Vexulta looked at each of them in turn, first to Vera. "The enduring, patient power of water." The wand with the small blue shard drifted to Vera.

To Ash, "The raging destruction of fire."

To Hailey, "Wild nature, born of fertile earth,"

To Morgan, "Storm bringer and storm breaker, the capricious breath of air."

Each of the witches grasped their respective wands as they floated to them.

As soon as Morgan's fingertips grazed the wand she detected a minimal drop of golden magic within, already siphoned from the Source, ready to be used. It certainly wasn't a lot of power. But it was accessible. Anyone with a pulse and a cursory idea that the wand contained magic could just visualize, point, and cast.

It was a crude, weak tool.

"Each of you, sisters of Angavor, come to this sacred pentagram with access to one of these four powers. We shall now unite these powers and cast an enchantment upon the land that will persist for many centuries. To cleanse the darkness from Pineville Valley and give willpower to those tempted to ring the bells of their mortality. We will call home the lost, the weary, the troubled. And take their pains upon our own shoulders."

Vexulta looked around, met Morgan's open eyes. She gave her a small, sad smile, then continued her speech. Morgan squinted, thinking.

'We will call home the lost, the weary, the troubled.'

"Five witches, at five points, Gaia be our guide. Let no falsehoods or deception try to hide or divide the five who join together, now allied. Five by five, our power increases. No power of land nor sea shall attempt to cease us. So says the coven priestess, we begin, as Water releases."

Vera extended her wand toward the center of the pentagram, a pulse of gentle blue energy washed into the center of the star.

'Give willpower to those tempted to ring the bells of their mortality.'

"Let the burning rage of Fire ignite our request."

Ash extended her wand and exuded a weak beam of zigzagging red energy into the center of the pentagram.

Morgan's thoughts raced. This *non-mortal*, this witch-priestess-crone-ghoul, was sucking the life-force from the troubled inhabitants of Pineville, pushing those standing near a dark cliff right over the edge. And she was acting like she was doing this town some act of mercy. Some great sacrifice upon herself.

Alex.

She may as well have pulled the trigger herself.

"Add Gaia's untainted Air to help these powers coalesce."

Morgan, as previously instructed, raised her small wand, but she hesitated.

What could she do against this supernatural being? Daughter of a demi-god. It was like trying to stop a thunderstorm or a hurricane. Vexulta was a force of nature, haunting Pineville, feeding on the dark, troubled souls that lived there. Those left behind, like Ash and Morgan, would no doubt eventually suffer the same fate. It was a cycle of despair and depression, feeding an immortal monster that considered herself a protector.

Morgan had to end it. But she couldn't do it alone.

The other's had been gifted their magic from Vexulta, or had it dramatically enhanced, been given wands to siphon from the Source.

Well, Vera and Ash had.

She wasn't sure about Hailey.

Morgan opened her eyes. Vexulta's were closed shut. Morgan looked to Hailey, who was looking right back at her. Their green eyes locked together. Dark emerald with soft jade. Juniper and pine with sagebrush and spring lemongrass. Hailey raised her pointer finger to her lips, then nodded.

"Shhh," she seemed to say. *"I know. Go on."*

Morgan tightened her lips, added only the golden energy within the wand to the center of the pentagram. She did not send any magic from within herself. But she began gathering it, careful not to absorb any from the visible pool of magic gathering at the center of the pentagram, lest give herself away. Here, near the heart of the source of power in the valley, Morgan could draw in both the golden threads of Air, and the zigzagging red threads of Fire. She even detected the green magic of Earth, but it moved like molasses, required great strength to manipulate, let alone channel. Morgan didn't try to add that to her own stockade of magic.

The wand in her hand replenished its own magical reserves without command. It sucked up a small zap of Air magic from the room, filling up the shard with as much golden energy as it could hold. It was barely a fraction of the power Morgan pulled into herself.

Vexulta said, "Finish with the power of wild Earth added to the rest."

Hailey gestured softly with her small wand and sticky green energy crawled outward from the wand tip, slithered like heavy snakes and vines into the center.

The shifting blob of magic glimmered, now all four colors wriggled together, just inches off the ground, each unique in their texture and power. Erratic Fire energy, pulsing Water energy, deliberate, questing, sloughing Earth energy, and the latent, arcing rays of twinkling Air energy.

Morgan marveled at its beauty.

She glanced aside to see Vera and Ash also enraptured by the multicolored, ever-changing orb. Vexulta still had her eyes closed, her head lifted to the heavens, her hands held out to her side.

Morgan turned again, met Hailey's eyes a second time.

She mouthed, *"Trust me,"* and winked.

Vexulta snapped her head downward, shot her arms out, channeled glistening *violet* magic into a ball in front of her, bubbling and spitting like ooze from another planet.

Or from the underworld.

Morgan could sense the unnatural magic, felt revolted by it. This was not Gaia's magic. This was from… something else.

The Fallen.

Vexulta muttered, "And a touch of the infinite beyond, to *infest*."

Hailey slipped a second wand from her black sleeve. Morgan realized now why she'd struggled getting her arm into the robe earlier.

It had been a ploy.

A fist-sized ruby sat at the base of the wand. The wooden stick that grew out from there was smoothed and oiled, a twirl of different timber grains. Hailey pointed both her ruby wand and her smaller Earth-shard wand at the ball of purple ooze.

"Ar chaill tú mé, a dheirfiúr níos sine?" Hailey,

asked, Irish accent thicker than usual. Morgan had no clue what she said, guessing it was her native Gaelic tongue.

Hailey flicked her wrists, a powerful jolt of red Fire energy and a punch of green Earthen energy erupted from the wands.

"No!" Vexulta screamed.

The two bolts of energy flew toward the primordial purple ooze.

Morgan conjured a shield of gold in front of herself, Vera, and Ash.

At first, nothing happened, the roiling purple just absorbed the two beams of magic.

Then the violet ooze exploded.

A massive shockwave shuddered across the room, bounced off Morgan's shield and refracted downward, obliterating a large swath of the wood flooring in front of Vexulta. Morgan felt the trunk of the massive tree tremble, then felt the whole earth shake underneath her.

Vexulta's face changed, morphed, stretched. It was no longer human at all. It was long and bony and patches of rough, gray scales showed where the false human flesh had melted away. She had taken the full extent of the blast, but she still stood, bony arms outstretched, locked in a magical duel with Hailey.

Vexulta snarled, "Cailleach!"

Hailey smirked through her grimace of concentration, adding, "*Slat ruby gheimhridh, deirfiúr, ar mo ordú.*"

Morgan had no clue what they were saying, but she could see what they were dueling over. She watched as the quadratic-colored orb of magic slowly drifted out of the center of the pentagram, away from Hailey, toward

Vexulta.

The whole earth began to rock, the cabin itself creaked and trembled, the floor groaned and dropped half-a-foot with a startling jolt.

Hailey remained standing, though her knees buckled as the cabin bounced and she wavered, holding her wands outright. She was losing the magical tug-of-war.

"Sisters," she cried. "Help me!"

Vera and Ash both scrambled to their feet, extended their arms, but their wands refused to perform any magic. Morgan noticed the tiny shards of gemstones had shattered; the wands were nothing but wooden sticks now.

Morgan drew in Fire and Air, straight from the Source. She sought out the magic in the shattered gemstones of Water and Earth. Found remnants of that magic in the dust of the broken crystals. She connected with them all. She felt more Earth deep beneath her, felt her way to access it.

All four strains of magic were in the charged atmosphere of the room. And they were hers to channel and use.

In through the nose, out though the mouth.

She twisted her hands. All four strains of magic surged inside her. Water, Earth, Fire, and Air. Pulsing, throbbing, raging under her skin. Her fingers and toes clenched. The amount of power was far and away more than she thought she could ever handle.

Her body shivered, she almost convulsed with the strength of it all.

She had all the power she could hold within her veins. And she would use it all for her vengeance.

The orb was two thirds of the way toward Vexulta,

still roiling amorphously, but now stretching from solid sphere to an ovoid, tugging closer, glimmering in shades of blue and red and green and gold, pulling toward Vexulta. Hailey had lassoed a burning rope of pure Fire around the orb and had added a thin vine of Earth with her smaller wand, pulling with all her might to keep it away from Vexulta.

And failing.

"We can't let her get this magic," Hailey pleaded through gritted teeth. "It will strengthen her beyond measure!"

Morgan focused.

In through the nose, out through the mouth.

She visualized the magic she wanted to perform.

She remembered the man who loved her, the man she had loved back, unconditionally. She felt the ghostly echo of his kiss pressed against her neck. She felt the warmth of his arms around her still. In this very moment, Alex was with her. Or his spirit. Or his memory. Whatever version of him that remained was with her now, and he gave her confidence to act.

For Alex.

In her hand erupted a shimmering golden lance, sizzling with Fire from the tip to the tail. A river of Water and a vine of Earth wrapped around the shaft of the Air magic that held it together. Morgan launched it with all her strength.

Past the magical orb.

Directly into Vexulta's chest.

A horrible bestial screech ejected from the creature. Her pull on the orb of quadratic magic vanished.

The thing that once called itself Vexulta staggered, barely still on its feet—*no*, they were talons of black iron, no longer feet at all.

Morgan collapsed to her knees, all the magic spent from her veins. She'd poured everything into her strike. There was nothing left to sustain her but her own human will.

And that was draining fast.

The blob of four strains of magic tumbled back toward Hailey. She snapped her ruby wand toward it in a panic, siphoned it into the wood, down into the ruby. The stone glimmered as it absorbed the massive amount of energy. Hailey dropped her superfluous second wand, gripped her ruby wand with both hands. Her arms vibrated as they tried to contain and absorb all four elements of magic. The orb sizzled and pulsed, waves of power crashed up onto her fingers and wrists. Hailey screamed as she absorbed so much magic, both into her wand and her own veins. Her eyes flashed from dark, piney emerald to neon red, then aquamarine blue, then bright, blinding gold.

Vexulta shrieked again.

Morgan turned her head, with great effort.

Vexulta's ravenous eyes locked onto Morgan.

They did not blink.

Morgan was exposed, defeated, magic-less. She couldn't even sense magic in the Source to pull it into her, let alone cast it back out to protect herself.

Hailey was too busy trying to survive the conglomeration of magic infusing her and her wand. She wouldn't be able to save her.

Vexulta reached up with a shuddering, orcish arm, all gray and sinew and scales. Purple ooze bubbled into the air in front of her hand.

"You've made a terrible mistake, mortal," the

creature rasped, voice croaking and high-pitched and not-at-all human. She pointed her finger at Morgan, aiming the small ball of churning purple magic right at her. "You chose the wrong witch."

Wait for me, Alex. I'm coming.

"I told you a hundred fucking times, my name is not Ashley Rose, you ugly fucking hag."

A singular blast of zigzagging Fire shot directly at Vexulta, launched from across the room.

The red bolt struck Vexulta in the shin, her scaly gray leg flung backward and the witch-ghoul tumbled forward.

"It's Ash!"

Vexulta fell through the smoldering hole in the floor, shrieking as she plummeted downward, falling hundreds of feet, toward the trembling ground below.

Morgan's eyelids fluttered. The whole cabin was shaking, teetering, threatening to collapse.

She heard Vera crying, far, far off in the distance, saying, "*Mi amor*, Hailey, *mi amor*, are you alright?"

She closed her eyes. A second passed, or maybe minutes.

She heard, struggling to reopen her eyes, Ash ask, "What about Morgan?"

Hailey responded, "Leave her. We have to go, now, or we will die with her."

Something heavy cracked, the witches screamed.

More time swept past, or maybe only an instant. Morgan felt ready to sleep for an eternity. The whole world suddenly turned on its side, Morgan slid across the crumbling floor.

Blackness took her as she crashed toward oblivion.

****

She fought it off.

She was a survivor. Her grandmother did not go down without a fight. Neither would Morgan. No pretty, unnamed female victims here, remember? No one was left to save her, so she had to save herself, or die trying.

Trying was the important part.

She grabbed something, just before she fell. Or something grabbed her? She felt the echo of an arm. A memory of the touch of his fingers on her hand. Whose fingers?

Alex?

Max?

Benjamin?

She inhaled.

Exhaled.

Opened her eyes. The floor was mostly gone, Morgan remained on a small chunk by the far wall, tilted absurdly sideways, which creaked ominously. Her hand held a wooden board, half jutting up from the rest of the remaining floorboards. The rest of the witches were gone.

She was alone.

The witches had fallen to their death, maybe.

Escaped, hopefully.

Morgan inhaled again, put one clenched fist down against the shaking wooden floor. Pushed herself up to one knee.

'Magic never helps, Morgan. Eventually, inevitably, magic only destroys. One day you'll understand that.'

"Fuck you, Dad."

Morgan exhaled, pushed herself all the way to her feet.

Inhaled, reached out, found only latent golden

threads of magic, but they would be enough.

Exhaled. She could barely draw them in, she was so drained, but she took in what she could.

Inhaled. She took two tumbling steps down the embankment and leapt across the cavernous opening between her and the doorway.

Crashed through the doorframe, rolled into the next hallway.

Exhaled.

She limped forward, slammed into the door where Joey had been sleeping. She turned the knob, but the door was locked.

Why was the door locked?

Morgan jammed her finger against the door. The whole cabin shook again. To her left, the doorframe collapsed, the rest of the room beyond crumbled toward the ground, huge beams of wood and tile and brick crashed downward.

She visualized the lock turning, and the lock turned. She opened the door. Joey was there, bounding at her face, and he still had his wings, so he floated in midair. He was licking her cheeks, but he was also trembling, shaking, tail tucked between his back legs, petrified by the earthquake tearing apart the cabin.

Morgan could only think of one way to rescue the poor dog. She ran to the far window and heaved it open.

"Joey!" He leapt, buzzing toward her. She caught him in her arms, and then flung him outside. "I'll meet you downstairs! On the ground." She pointed down and then shut the window before Joey could rush back in. She heard his panicked, muffled barking from outside.

Morgan spun back around. She needed to work her way back down the spiral stairs, through the many different rooms, back outside and down onto the ground.

She darted back into the hallway, turned left, raced downward. She hopped over a collapsed chandelier, darted past another antique broom hung on the wall, ducked under a massive piece of timber that had cracked and fallen from above, sidestepped a tipped-over armoire. She turned down another set of stairs and almost fell into thin air.

The lower sections of the spiraling cabin had completely collapsed, fallen off the massive tree trunk. Hundreds of feet down, Morgan could see a huge pile of rubble. There was no way to escape. She climbed back up the stairs, on all fours, unsure what she should do next. Both ways, up and down, were gone. She was stuck on the last remaining clump of cabin still clinging to the tree trunk.

She heard more creaking, from just above her. The rest of the roof was about to give way. The last bit of cabin was about to crash to earth.

She was a witch, damnit! How could she not figure a way out of this?

In through the nose, out through the mouth.

She smirked.

It was her only chance.

She ran. Back past the armoire, underneath the massive timber beam. Back to the broom on the wall. Grabbed it. Yanked. It didn't budge. It was stuck fast.

She heard more creaking, then snapping, then a crack.

The roof fell in; she heaved backward with all her strength, hands gripped firmly on the broom.

It popped off the wall, came with her.

Morgan turned and fled, felt the remnants of the

cabin tumbling away from the tree trunk. The room tipped sideways, she crashed against the wall, which now was the floor.

She gasped, pushed herself back up. She could see open air just yards in front of her, heard massive destruction inches behind. The room tipped over further.

Something splintered; Morgan leapt.

The whole room was falling to the earth. She tumbled out into the open air, inches away from the crashing debris. As she fell, she tossed her leg over the old broom.

Plummeted downward.

No.

Everything else plummeted downward, debris and rubble crashed alongside her, fell to the earth, but Morgan hovered in mid-air.

Astride an antique wooden broom.

She smiled, despite herself. Brushed her hand across the brim of her pointed black hat, knocking the dirt and dust off.

She titled forward slightly, felt the broom respond to her touch. She injected it with just a gentle pulse of magic, felt the golden energy flowing from her fingertips into the enchanted piece of wood. She guided it left and then right, up and then down. It responded in controlled turns, dips, and climbs.

Joey barked, from above her. His dragonfly wings buzzed in the air, his silhouette flew between the treetops. He zipped down to her, licked her face, almost knocked her off the broom.

Morgan steadied herself, then looked down again. She saw a body lying near the big pile of debris.

She dipped down, soared low to the ground. Just

outside of the pile of rubble, the Native American man, the human who had transformed from the brown werewolf, lay unconscious.

She hopped off the broom, and the moment she did, it plopped onto the ground, all magical properties of defying gravity gone. She felt the man's neck, and his pulse thumped strong under her fingers.

Joey whined just above her, his wings still buzzing loudly. The ground shook again, the earth still quaking mightily. The pile of rubble threatened to shake loose, to tumble over the knocked-out human.

You've really got a thing for strays, huh?

Morgan turned the man onto his belly, then took the broom handle and worked it underneath him. She straddled the back half of the broom, then pushed Air into the antique wood.

The broom lifted into the air, the Native American man drooping over it like a pile of dirty laundry. Morgan adjusted herself on the back half of the handle.

The earth shook again, the giant pile of wood and debris tumbled toward them.

Morgan tilted the nose of her broom up, raced away from the destruction, up into the air. She flew up and up and launched out of the canopy of the trees and the whole valley stretched before her.

Joey buzzed past her, flew forward and she raced after him.

She had to be more careful than before, balancing a limp body across the front of the broom handle.

Joey really flew quite fast for a chubby mutt that didn't even have wings two hours ago. The wind rushed through her hair as she chased him down. Felt cool. Smelt of rain and the last breath of fall.

All wasn't over yet, there may still be werewolves to defeat, but Morgan felt confident. Vexulta, the priestess witch, the ancient ghoul who had been haunting this valley for centuries, was gone, defeated, and destroyed. Smote unto the ruin of her ancestral home. Vera, Ash, and Hailey had hopefully escaped. They would meet up somewhere, once they realized Morgan had survived, and together they would fend off the remaining werewolves. With Vexulta gone, Pineville could start to thrive again. To begin to heal.

When she finally caught up next to Joey, his tail thumped against her, his paws still tread air, as if he still thought he was swimming. Morgan carefully reached out and rubbed his ears, keeping the man who the old knight had called Abornazine balanced precariously on the tip of her flying broom.

She looked down, then back from where they had come. She saw nothing but black forest canopy. She had no idea where the witch cabin had been. Even if she wanted to go back, just to be extra cautious, to search for Vera and Ash and Hailey, she wouldn't be able to find them. The cabin was lost to Morgan. And down amongst the rubble, Vexulta was buried. If Ash or Vera or Hailey had escaped and survived, they'd be on their own until they found Morgan. She had no way to meet back up with them.

When she got back to the house, she'd sleep hard and fast, then wake up early and figure out who to call to try to bring her out to work. She could blame her car being totaled on the earthquake, which would net her some insurance money for a new car.

Silver linings.

The earthquake would surely make her next shift an

interesting day in town. Her heart sank as her thoughts turned to Thomas Crawford. Hopefully the kind farmer would be the only werewolf victim to turn up in the morning.

She turned her broom, aimed herself back toward where the town should be. It was suspiciously dark. She wondered if the earthquake had knocked out the whole town's power. She flew forward, drifting slowly down in height as the mountain descended toward the valley.

Behind her, thunder rumbled. The first few drops of rain started to fall.

"Great," Morgan whispered. "Come on, Joey. Let's try to find our way home."

Joey's tail whipped back and forth at the mention of home. He sniffed the air and then buzzed forward, and Morgan had to rush to keep up.

Part Four
Humans

Chapter 25

October Twenty-Ninth, 10:42 p.m.

"Sheriff office, this you, Craig, honey?"

"Yes, Maud, it's me. I need Sheriff Jeffrey down here. Now."

"Y'all told us last time that you could handle a couple of drunks over there, if they got to fighting. The ABC man told me—"

"No Maud, this is different. Remember Scott's wife, Sabrina, or Sidney, or whatever her name was?"

"Sandy, poor thing got mauled by a rabid bear, I heard. Same thing almost got nurse Morgan. 'Bout a month ago now."

"It wasn't no frickin' bear, Maud. I got Tom Crawford's body out here in my parking lot, with half his arm ripped off, bled to death. And another dead body, don't recognize his face, because his face, I mean his whole head... oh god, I think... But the tattoo... Maud, I think it's the mayor. I think the mayor is dead."

****

Craig and Phillip sat at the bar, steaming foam cups of black coffee in their hands. Phillip drank his to stay awake. Craig drank his to help him sober up. Neither man spoke. They just waited.

While Craig had waited for the sheriff and Phillip to

arrive, he brought all the patrons inside the brewery and asked everyone to stay put. Once Sheriff Jeffrey got sheets over the bodies and interviewed a handful of people, he escorted everyone out to their cars, told them to go straight home. Sheriff Jeffrey took statements from Craig and his lead bartender. The young man offered to stay but Craig sent him home once Phillip showed up.

Only Thomas Crawford's truck, Sheriff Jeffrey's squad car, and Craig and Phillip's SUVs remained behind.

Dr. Williams was on call, and she crawled out of the back of the ambulance when it arrived to examine the bodies with the sheriff. They told Craig and Phillip to stay inside the taproom while they completed the initial examination.

Phillip sipped his coffee. Craig stared straight ahead.

"You ever think there's something about this town, man?"

Craig didn't answer. He just stared at his cup of coffee.

"I mean. I met my ex-wife here, she convinced me to stay. Now I got a couple acres of land. Chickens, ducks, goats. Starting the bee thing this summer, for the honey. Plus, I'm making delicious beer, like award winning beer, man. Every other competition you let me enter, I win." He added quietly, "And, well, you."

Craig nodded. Lifted his coffee to his lips. Sipped it.

"Dreams coming true, man. You and me, we are making it. So tell me, why do I feel… smothered… like smothered, man, in… a dark fog? Why do I feel like I've got to fight to smile?"

Craig nodded. Sipped his coffee again.

"Say something, Craig. Am I crazy? What is going

on in this town?"

Craig pushed himself back from the bar. He walked away from Phillip, walked around the bar, chucked his almost full cup of coffee in the trash. Disappeared into the staff only door behind the bar.

Phillip sighed. Stared at his cup of coffee.

A few minutes later Craig reemerged from the back. He carried two glasses and a bottle of bourbon in his hands. Walked all the way back over to Phillip, sat back down, set down the glasses. Poured a heavy dose of amber liquor into both their glasses. He lifted his into the air, swirled it in front of his face, smelt it. Held it back up and looked at the viscosity, the way the liquid rolled in the glass, lapping against the rounded sides, just ever so slightly thicker than water or beer.

"I've saved this bourbon since my dad passed." He took a small sip. Held it in his mouth for a few moments. Swallowed, savored the heat of it. Sighed.

He looked at Phillip. "We used to watch a lot of westerns. Like classic westerns, you know? John Wayne, Clint Eastwood, shit like Tombstone with Doc Holiday and Wyatt Earp. I was obsessed with the saloons. Every town has a saloon. Every last western outpost has at least one bar to make sure the alcohol flows. The bartender always knows the town's business, always buddies with the heroes, but also knows how to talk to the outlaws. Always know who the good guys are and who the bad guys are. They run the most profitable business in the old westerns. Everybody went to the saloons. My brother wanted to be an outlaw. Wanted to make his own path. My dad, I think he connected with the sheriff or the marshal, usually. Old man, trying to bring order to chaos. I get it. But me? I was an entrepreneur for as long as I can remember. I connected with the saloons. They just made sense to me… Serving drinks to everybody. Good guys, bad guys, side characters, extras. The saloon always did good business."

Craig took a large sip from his glass. He closed his eyes, held it in his mouth for a moment, then sucked it down.

He continued, "I used to tell my dad I'd run a place like that. That I'd be the man who owned the saloon. I'd be the man who'd make his place the place to be in town. And we are. We're the saloon of Pineville, thanks to me, and thanks to you and your beer." He took another sip, this time sucking it right back. "But fuck if I know what that's really got me. Dad's gone now. Mom's mind is gone. Lose the old man, chaos ensues. There's some irony or symbolism or some shit in there somewhere. Matt's off in Alaska, which is probably the last place outlaws are thriving these days. But I'm in the saloon still. That's something the westerns never show. Once all the heroics go down. Once the town moves on. Once the gang leaves to the next adventure. The saloon stays."

Craig turned to the big moose boulder in the middle of the concrete-poured bar. "They say this lump of stone is as old as the mountains, Phillip. Seems like this valley, this place, this rock, has been here forever. Is that going to be us, someday, if we stay here?"

Phillip grunted and cocked his head. Waited for Craig to continue.

"I've never told anyone this… but well, honestly, when I heard Alex shot himself, when we went to the funeral and saw Morgan sitting in the corner, crying, her in-laws trying to comfort her, all I could think was damn. I get it. I get it. I fucking get it. The only difference between me and Alex… he just had that extra ounce of courage I never had. He had one finger that twitched down on the trigger. Mine never could…" Craig smiled as he stared at the remaining bourbon in his glass. "Well, I should say, mine hasn't yet."

Phillip scowled. "I should tell you not to think like that. But that feeling—I get that. When I heard about Alex, I was jealous, man. Isn't that fucked up?"

Craig just nodded.

Phillip smelt his glass of bourbon. Lifted it, swirled it, tasted it. "That really is good bourbon, man. Should I be pissed you keep a secret bottle of bourbon to drink at the brewery?"

Craig said, "Sometimes beer doesn't cut it, buddy."

Phillip took another sip. Smirked. "I get that."

Craig turned to Phillip. "Mom and Dad grew up in the valley. They were born in barns out in the mountains, Phillip. Back before Pineville was even big enough to be called Pineville. They saw some shit, worse than us. But they were tough. My dad used to say, when he drank, which was really, really rare. He used to say, as a toast, 'Don't let the demons get to you.' What do you think he meant by that?"

Phillip and Craig both sat silently for a moment. Eventually, Phillip said, "You do know what he meant. We both do."

"Yeah. Maybe we do." He lifted his glass. Drank the rest of his bourbon. "But why does it seem like every single person in this town is struggling with demons, Phillip?"

The door sliced open. Frigid air gusted inside. Dr. Williams and Sheriff Jeffrey strode inside and walked over. The door swooshed shut.

Sheriff Jeffrey took one look at the two men and said in his Cajun twang, "Y'all don't listen well, huh? I told you to drink coffee and sober the hell up, you boys found two dead bodies in the parking lot, and you pull out the heavy brown stuff."

Phillip inclined his head apologetically, Craig sucked his teeth and just stared at the Sheriff.

Dr. Williams intervened. "Look, guys, we need to know, was there anyone else in the parking lot? Anyone who might have been leaving just before this happened? Who might have seen suspicious behavior? Or displayed suspicious behavior. Jeffrey tells me nobody saw anything. That seems hard to believe."

Craig snapped back, "I already told our courageous law enforcement officer there all that. Yes, Morgan and Ash and the Spanish chick and that Irish professor lady from the university were all here, but they left just before the bodies were found. Something stinks here, Doc. First the attack on Morgan, followed by Sandy, followed by Tom and Fraser. We've got two dead people in town, slashed and tore all to hell, plus a dead mayor who doesn't have any of the same wounds, but his god-damn head was blown off and left in my parking lot…"

Dr. Vickie Williams cocked her head. "Well, Craig, that's the thing. The tattoo matches Mayor Fraser's tattoo, but when I bent down to examine it, it actually wasn't a tattoo. It seemed like a brand. The flesh was sizzled and burnt. Like someone burnt the skin, in the design of the mayor's tattoo for his daughter."

Craig asked, "Why would the mayor get a fucking brand instead of a tattoo?"

Vickie shook her head. "Fraser did get a regular tattoo, Craig."

Phillip coughed, choking on his bourbon. He looked back and forth between the sheriff and the doctor, incredulous. "Wait, what are you saying?"

The door sliced open again. More cold wind gusted inside. A tall man with a bald head, a gray pullover jacket and ironed khakis strode through the door and turned to look at the group.

"Does anyone want to tell me what in the hell is going on in my town? And why that fucking body out there has my tattoo on its chest?"

"Mayor Fraser. We were—"

The world shook.

Craig and Phillip leapt off their bar stools. The bottle of bourbon trembled. Craig reached out and grabbed it. Doctor Williams and Sheriff Jeffrey and Mayor Fraser all ducked down, covering their heads.

"Under the table!" Phillip shouted.

They stumbled their way to the nearest table, all while the ground underneath them rocked and churned. The whole brewery shook on its foundations, as if the very earth might crack open below their feet. Craig felt someone grab the bourbon bottle in his hand. He instinctually tightened his grip. Vickie raised her eyebrows at him and he let her take it. She pulled a big swallow from the bottle, handed it to the mayor who followed suit. They held onto each other as the whole valley shook. The lights flickered then went out. They only had the glow of the full moon to see by.

The quake seemed to last an eternity, and with each second it seemed more and more likely that the entire building would come down. Craig thought of his mom as dust and debris began to tumble down from the ceiling.

An explosive crack came from the bar. The concrete

bar on one side of the moose boulder splintered, fell to the ground with a crash. The moose boulder bucked now that it had room to wobble. The strange jutting head splintered, then cracked, then fell from the boulder. The head crashed onto the ground, stone striking concrete, smashing into rubble and dust.

The earthquake roared on. Craig felt sick, but it didn't stop him from taking his turn at swigging from the bottle of bourbon. Dr. Williams squeezed tightly onto Phillip's shoulders. The dust now blocked their view of the whole room. The mayor coughed, the sheriff covered his eyes with one hand, his knuckles on his other hand whitening around a table leg.

The shaking slowed, then stopped.

The world stilled.

Sluggishly, they all climbed out from underneath the table. The dust floated, drifting down lazily. The moonlight did little to illuminate the taproom. But an odd, greenish glow emanated from the bar, bathing them all in eerie light.

"What is that?" The sheriff asked.

Craig left the group first, waving his hand in front of his face, clearing the remaining dust. The boulder that had once been Big Moose still stood, now headless. At its core glistened a glowing, shining emerald. Craig walked up to it and reached out his hand. The emerald, almost the size of his fist, felt warm. There was a swirling light within the gem, pushing the green glow out into the brewery.

"Now that's something you don't see every day," Dr. Williams murmured.

Sheriff Jeffrey whispered, "No, that's something extra, right there."

Mayor Fraser cleared his throat, then said, "We just had a major earthquake. Double homicide. The goddamn power is out, probably across the whole town. We can gaze at the gem later. We need to go assess the damage and get the town together. Someone or something is killing my voters. I won't stand by idly while that happens. Dr. Williams, get back to the hospital. Set up a triage station and prepare for quake victims. Jeffrey, you come with me. We need to assess the damage and then I want you to find Morgan and bring her to the station. She was almost killed by whatever it is that is killing the townsfolk. And now, she disappears right before another murder occurs. I'm not a detective, but that sounds like a clue to me. Either that, or another potential victim. Craig, we will meet back here at five tomorrow for a town meeting. Sober your ass up and set your taproom up for a big crowd. Phillip, I want you to go check on the farmers. We'll catch up with you soon. Start spreading the word. Town meeting at The Dugout at five to discuss the quake damage, and the murders. My constituents need a leader. If I handle this right, I'll be mayor for the next decade. Let's go people, we've got a town to run."

"Morgan was here? My Morgan? Nurse Morgan?" Dr. Williams sounded truly scared for the first time that night.

Craig nodded.

Vickie Williams looked at the sheriff. "Find her, please, Jeffrey. She's been pretty shook up at work. She never told me she was almost attacked by whatever got Sandy. I'm worried for her."

Sheriff Jeffrey said, "I'll find her, Vickie. I promise."

The mayor, the doctor, and the sheriff left. Phillip

said to Craig, "You've got to admit, might not be for the right reasons, but the mayor knows how to handle a crisis, man."

"He's an asshole," Craig said. Thunder rumbled in the distance, long and grumbling. "I didn't think it was supposed to storm tonight."

Chapter 26

October Thirtieth, 5:54 a.m.

A loud noise woke her up before her alarm.

Morgan heard clattering, then something tumbling out of the pantry, crashing to the ground, and spilling. She got out of bed. It was just before six a.m. She'd slept maybe four hours.

Maybe.

When she came around the corner, she flipped the light switch, but the lights didn't respond. The power was still down. She could hear hard rain pounding against the roof.

The dawn was just cracking gray at the eastern horizon, and with the heavy clouds blocking most of it, the house was still very dark. Morgan flicked her flashlight on her phone, aiming it into the kitchen.

The Native American man, Abornazine, stood only feet away, crouched defensively, holding a kitchen knife in his hand.

Morgan gasped in surprise, then raised her hands, hopefully signaling to him she didn't want to hurt him. He brandished the knife like a dagger, as if he'd wielded something similar of that shape and size before.

Morgan kept her arms up, palms out. No weapons. No danger.

A gesture of submission, she hoped. She didn't want

to hurt the poor fellow. She wasn't sure if she could cure his lycanthropy, but she wanted to at least try to give him a chance at returning to society. The last thing she wanted to do was blast him with more magic and earn his distrust.

The way she had with Max.

Abornazine looked stressed, afraid, and tired. Probably like she did.

How was she going to communicate with him?

She noticed he'd stripped off the shirt she'd given him, and his stark muscles rippled underneath the orange blanket he'd tossed around his shoulders. He was thinner than seemed healthy, but not an ounce of it was anything but rip cord muscle and hairpin taut tendons. He emanated an aura of wild survival, something entirely different than anything she'd felt from anyone else she'd ever met, including Max.

He hadn't taken the pants off, though, for which Morgan was grateful. She'd seen enough naked post-transformation male appendages in the last month to last her a while.

Abornazine also held the white shirt that she'd given Max weeks ago.

He must have dug that out of the laundry room.

Why would he do that?

She pointed at his hand. He lifted the shirt up.

She asked, pointing, trying his name out, "Abornazine… Why do you have that?"

He slapped his chest, hard, and repeated, "Abornazine." Then he continued, speaking in a language she couldn't even try to write out phonetically, let alone repeat out loud. But he also held the shirt in front of his nose, smelling it, then repeated a phrase from his previous sentence. "Max ee mum. Max ee mum."

Morgan smiled suddenly, "Yes. Max. Maximillian." She nodded, pointing back at the shirt, "Do you know Max? Is that his smell?" She cracked a hopeful smile. Abornazine knew Max. Or the brown werewolf knew the big black werewolf that Max had transformed into. Maybe he was still around. Maybe she could still make things right with him. She ran into the laundry room and dug around in the laundry basket. Pulled out the pair of sweats that she let Max borrow.

She heard another crash. Rushed back into her kitchen and aimed her flashlight back to where she'd left Abornazine.

There was an eight-foot brown werewolf standing in her kitchen.

Morgan slapped her hand over her face.

This werewolf shit is growing old.

The werewolf still held the shirt, except now he held it in a clawed paw, and growled slightly when she reentered the room. Morgan heard tail thumping and wing buzzing coming from the bedroom, and then a big, whiny, canine yawn. Joey buzzed out of the bedroom, dual set of dragonfly wings still intact. He flew directly at the werewolf.

Morgan drew in more magic, sure she would have to cast a set of chains over the werewolf again.

But weirdly, the werewolf didn't growl at Joey. And Joey wagged his tail faster as he got closer, pawing his way, still flying like he swam, happily soaring through thin air. He thumped into the werewolf's furry shoulder, and the big brown beast smelt the dog while the dog smelt the werewolf's ear. Joey licked the big brown creature's cheek, and the werewolf lifted up a clawed paw and playfully thwapped the dog to the ground.

Joey's tail thumping accelerated even more. He circled around the werewolf's legs, trying to smell the creature's butt. The werewolf dropped to all fours on the ground and circled around behind Joey, acting almost exactly the same way, trying to smell Joey's butt, save the werewolf was probably three hundred pounds heavier, and slightly more predatory in proportion. The brown werewolf growled a little, showing his teeth, but Joey just flopped over onto his side and wiggled happily, trying to lick the werewolf on its snarling mouth. The brown werewolf ceased growling and sneezed, then returned to sniffing the dog's butt.

Morgan blinked, rubbed her eyes. She always said Joey could make friends with anyone, but this was a bit much…

She needed a cup of tea, and then she'd deal with the cryptological zoo animals she was harboring under her roof. One of her cats meowed, concerned and upset, from the kitchen table.

Morgan turned and said, "Don't you start!"

She went through her normal morning routine, despite her whole world feeling completely abnormal. Luckily, she had lit the wood stove last night, so she could set her teapot on it this morning for hot water, despite not having any electricity.

As she poured herself a mug of matcha, someone knocked at the front door.

At six in the morning.

Joey started barking, which startled the brown werewolf who growled and snapped and chased after Joey to the front door. Morgan pushed them both back, still a little wary of the brown werewolf, even if he seemed happy to be in their pack. Hard to imagine that this same creature had almost torn her and Joey to pieces a month ago. She'd come a long way since then. And so had the werewolf, it seemed.

"Go!" She pointed to the bedroom door.

Joey listened, hopped into the air, and buzzed back to the guest bedroom, swimming right over the living room furniture.

The brown werewolf emitted a low growl, still wanting to get out the front door at whoever had knocked. Morgan looked up at the formidable creature in the gray darkness. She had to crane her neck to meet his golden eyes. She snapped her fingers. A red bolt of energy sparked at her fingertips. The werewolf yelped and cried and leapt away in fear, rushing toward the bedroom, knocking over a lounge chair on the way.

Morgan sighed, waved a little magic toward the bedroom door, pulling it shut.

She opened the front door.

Sheriff Jeffrey stood on her deck, bundled in a thick raincoat, wearing his wide brimmed state-trooper-style hat. It was dumping buckets outside.

"Hello, Morgan."

"Sheriff," she said, "Want to come in out of the rain?"

"Actually, Morgan, I need you to come with me."

Morgan's stomach sank. They suspected her from last night.

"What do you mean, come with you? I've got to go in to work in a couple hours."

"You don't need to worry about work. What happened here?" The sheriff pointed to the turned over chair, then to the window. "Something break your window?"

Morgan had hung a blue tarp where werewolf Max had leapt through the front window to escape. "Dog accident."

"Your fat mutt did that?" Sheriff Jeffrey shook his head, then turned and looked in her driveway, where his cop car sat on its own. "And where's your car at, anyway?"

Fat was a little harsh.

"Totaled, last night, in the quake, out, uh, further in the mountains. I haven't had service to call a tow."

"Service is down all over town. Nobody has been able to get it back up and running. Those women you were with at The Dugout, they take you home last night?"

"Can I ask what business that is of yours?"

"Unfortunately, Morgan, it became my business around nine o'clock last night. I know you were with them at The Dugout. And I know that Ash and Vera have been going out past your place with that Hailey woman from the university." The rainfall picked up, falling even harder than before, and Sheriff Jeffrey had to raise his voice for Morgan to hear him.

"Morgan, we are holding a town hall at five tonight at The Dugout. The south bridge is close to flooding over, and 675 is closed eastbound at the gap and westbound at the pass. The town's cut off for a while. Mayor Fraser wants me to bring you back to the station to talk about what has been going on."

"The mayor?"

The sheriff inclined his head, chewed on his tongue. "Why does that surprise you?"

Morgan stammered, seeking an answer that would

explain away her surprise, "I'm just… you caught me off guard here, Jeffrey. Standing in the rain at my doorstep at six in the morning. Taking me down to the station, meeting with the mayor. It's a little much, isn't it? Plus, what about the earthquake? Don't you think the hospital needs all hands-on deck?"

"I'm sure it does. It's just a talk, Morgan. Afterward, if things line up, we will drop you off at the hospital. Dr. William's specifically asked me to make sure you are… treated right and brought to her as soon as possible."

Morgan exhaled.

If things line up.

She didn't have many options. If she refused to cooperate with the sheriff, her whole life may get turned even more upside down in Pineville… if that was even possible at this point. She still had friends here, new and old, and Dr. Williams needed her help.

Even though she certainly *could* stop the sheriff from bringing her in by force, she'd become a fugitive, and worse, be forced to hurt Sheriff Jeffrey. He was an innocent man, just trying to do his job.

Plus, if the mayor was alive… What did that mean? That Hailey had created a decoy?

Why would she do that?

She had said something like, *'This goes deeper than you know.'* She'd wanted Morgan to visit Vexulta at the cabin. She'd wanted Morgan not to alert the authorities.

Then Hailey absorbed the powerful spell at the ritual, instead of Vexulta. What had Vexulta said? *'You chose the wrong witch'*? Morgan thought the old crone had just been spitting vile curses at her whilst trying to kill her for helping Hailey. But maybe she was right.

As the cabin came down, after they defeated the

ancient witch that had haunted the valley for eons, Hailey had said, *'Leave her, Ash. We have to go, now, or we will die with her.'*

Hailey wanted the power for herself, and wanted to bury Morgan in the rubble with Vexulta, to get her out of the way…

Morgan had stopped Vexulta. But at what cost?

What had she unleashed upon Pineville instead?

"Alright," Morgan nodded, "Let me put something more reasonable on, let the dog out, and I'll be right down."

The sheriff nodded. She could see him peering around her house, eyes scanning across the rooms that he could see, and she thought for a moment he might ask to search her place. But instead he said, "See you in a minute," and turned and hustled back through the rain to his car.

Morgan's thoughts raced. She remembered the look of betrayal in the werewolf's eyes right before Hailey shot it. And the silver bullets. She'd all but smirked as she said it. How did she know so much about the werewolves, and already have silver bullets in her gun? Not exactly something you can buy at the ammo depot outlet. She wore leather gloves, had a whip, a powerful wand with a ruby stone the size of Morgan's fist, and a six-shooter revolver loaded with silver bullets.

Was Hailey the one calling the werewolves here? Using them as cover for her overthrow of Vexulta?

Morgan ran her hands through her hair.

Think.

In through the nose, out through the mouth.

Tonight was a full moon.

Morgan needed to figure out what the hell Hailey

was after, now that Vexulta was out of the way. And she'd need help. She wasn't sure if she could trust Vera or Ash. For all she knew, Hailey may have disposed of them already, the same way she thought she disposed of Morgan. The old knight Vlad Cosmin was dead, but Abornazine was still safe, hiding in Morgan's house. And it seemed, Abornazine knew Max.

Morgan brought all the clothes Max had worn and laid them in a pile by the guest bedroom. She whispered softly, coaxing the scarred werewolf out of hiding. Abornazine slinked out, bent down and sniffed the clothes. He looked up at her. Was there recognition in those eyes? Did he remember her saving his human form the night before? Did he trust her?

She whispered, "Find Max, if you can. Meet me back here. Good luck." The brown werewolf grunted, pushed its snout against her upraised palm.

She left the werewolf in the living room, but stuffed Joey into the side room with the cats and closed the door.

When she walked out onto the front deck, she made a show of turning around and locking the door. But she didn't lock it. She left it barely cracked open. She hustled down to the cop car, opened the passenger door, climbed inside.

Sheriff Jeffrey flipped the wipers on to their highest setting, threw the car in reverse, and pulled out of the driveway. Morgan glanced back as they drove away. She glimpsed the front door swing open and a furry brown snout, holding a white shirt in its mouth, emerge into the rain.

Chapter 27

October Thirtieth, 7:47 a.m.

Max woke up to the sound of heavy rain. The sun had risen, but the clouds were dark and heavy, and only limited gray light shone in through the half open window.

Scratchy ropes twisted around his wrists and ankles, dragging his limbs away from his body, securing each arm and leg to the respective thick wooden posts at the corners of the bed. He could lift his head slightly, but he saw a set of bells dangling just above him, so he kept his head flat on the pillow.

With the gray daylight, he could see around the room. It was sparse but decorated comfortably, clean linens on the bed, smooth wood furniture, well kept.

Max heard voices coming from beyond the door. From what he could discern, three separate women were conversing in the next room. They were speaking quickly and urgently about something. It sounded like the beginning of an argument.

Then one of the voices cut above the rest, thick with an Irish accent, which raised goosebumps across Max's skin.

"I decide what magic is valid to cast. Not either of you."

Another, younger-sounding woman argued back,

voice cracking in anger, "Necromancy is black magic, Hailey. We did a whole semester on it, together, remember—"

"I said, I decide, Ash."

'You decided to leave Morgan, too, and I still don't think that was right."

"She's dead, and that's the way it is. We couldn't have saved her. You would have died too. Yes, it's sad, but she's dead, alongside Vexulta. Morgan helped us defeat one of Gaia's elder witches, and she made a great sacrifice, but now she's gone and I won't hear any further arguments about her or going back to that place or about necromancy. We need Victor Frank, even if he is a shell of himself at this point."

The other woman huffed but said nothing else.

"You two have more important things to do if you want to keep your powers. Now. Go find me the relic, and report back to me."

One of the other female voices murmured something, Max couldn't make it out. His head swam.

Morgan's dead.

"When I gave you both your first wands, taught you your first spells, that's when! Both of you were nothing before me, so watch how you speak to me before you become nothing again. I'll take your magic away in a heartbeat. Don't test me."

Silence for a moment, then two sets of footsteps.

An outside door opened, then closed, and the footsteps hurriedly crunched through the wet fall leaves outside. The steps stopped, a door creaked open, followed by another and then old shocks sighed as two bodies climbed inside. The vehicle engine turned over, sounding just like the old red truck Vic drove.

The truck reversed out of a gravel driveway, the transmission groaned, then it pulled off, the sound of the engine slowly fading away, disappearing underneath the eternal noise of the pounding rain.

After a while, Max couldn't hear it rumbling at all anymore. There was no other traffic. Just the endless rain.

From outside his room, he heard the shambling footsteps of Victor Frank. The Irish woman said, "Vic, I don't know how you've managed to get yourself killed twice in the matter of less than a month. But if it happens again, I'm leaving you dead, you understand?"

Vic groaned… "It—uh, I don't really remember, miss Hailey, but I don't think it was a werewolf that got me."

"It had to be, you decaying lump of useless flesh. Nothing is missing. No doors are unlocked. The cabin is trashed and your neck wound was reopened. You must have not closed the gate to the pen. One of the werewolves escaped, and fortunately for you, after it killed you, it returned to the pack down in the den."

"I suppose that could be what happened."

"It is what happened, you dolt. Now go do something productive and bring down the werewolves' their next meal. But only give them a half serving. I want them hungry for tonight. They will have a new alpha, and I want them all primed for slaughter when the full moon rises."

Max swallowed. He shifted his focus. He needed to remember.

He needed to remember it all.

He dredged up memories from Grim, from chasing after Morgan and her witch friend, to smelling his own

Zach Stivers

car. To being caught by the redheaded witch. The one who masqueraded as a werewolf. She'd spoken to Grim, in an Irish accent.

The woman still outside the door must be her.

She'd somehow reincarnated the hillbilly. She'd sewn and bolted the head back on the body of Victor Frank, then tasked him with watching Max last night while she attended some other business. Then Max had been drugged, kept asleep all night long.

And here he was, trapped in the bed, still.

Max reeled, thinking about Morgan.

She sacrificed herself to stop some evil witch. Vlad Cosmin would be proud of her. He should have recruited her, not Max.

Max felt wave after wave of guilt wash over him. The first woman he let himself connect with for more than a one-night stand in the last decade, and within a month she was dead, since he wasn't there to help her or protect her.

Better to have no one to worry, so you have no one to hurt.

It was too late for that philosophy now.

You fled, and it got her killed.

Max sighed, tried to rub his hand across his forehead. But the twine was too tight, he couldn't reach his face. He couldn't rub his eyes. He couldn't hide the tear leaking down his cheek into the dark stubble of his beard.

The sorrow boiled into rage. He wanted to slip into Grim, but the werewolf's mind was nowhere to be found. Max couldn't even locate the moon in his mind. It felt like someone had surgically cut the werewolf out of his brain. Last month, Max might have rejoiced at such a

322

situation.

Now, it only angered him even more. Grim was a predatory monster, but he was also the other half of Max. And the last thing Max had close to family.

He pulled and pulled and twisted and felt the rope fraying against the corners of the wooden posts. The twine on his left arm snagged against the wood grain. Max yanked, and the twine frayed more. Two more hard yanks and the twine snapped. His left arm ripped free. He quickly reached around and untied his right arm and then sat up. He unbound his ankles and rolled out of the bed, landing deftly onto the wooden floor. He wanted to dart out of the window, but he was lost, deep in the woods, and the red truck was gone. If he could find the key fob to his blue fusion, he could escape that way.

So, he needed to explore the cabin beyond this room, find his keys, and avoid Victor Frank and the Irish werewolf-witch.

He padded over to the door, quiet as could be, and twisted the knob to test if it was locked. It turned easily. He cracked it open half an inch.

A rotten deer skull, with burning, radiant red eyes stared back through the crack at him.

He leapt back and the door creaked open. It swung on rusty hinges, and only then did Max notice the door itself was made of rotten wood, the floorboards beneath him were rotten, the ceiling rotten, riddled with holes. He frantically looked behind him.

The bed wasn't cozy, it wasn't made with clean white linen, it was rotten too, moldy and wrapped in dank rags and blankets, gray and brown and mossy pea green.

The smell of rain and fall leaves vanished, replaced with a ghastly aroma of sewage and expired maggot-filled meat.

Max covered his nose and fell to one knee.

Christ, it was too much.

The door fell fully open.

The freckled, red-headed woman with a devious smile, stood before him. She gestured casually with her arm, waving an oiled wooden wand with a red gem at its base.

He blinked.

The room was back to normal. The bed looked silky soft and fresh from the laundromat. The floors were warm and whole and smooth as polished mahogany. Maybe they *were* polished mahogany. The aroma of brown autumn leaves and fresh rain returned from outside.

"You look frightened, Max. Don't be scared. Please, come, sit back on the bed."

Her eyes sparkled emerald as she spoke, no longer blazing red, and she tossed her hair, thick and vibrant as fox fur, out of her face to keep eye contact with him. She crinkled her nose.

Max remembered her. The way she had stretched in the nude on the boulder in the meadow. The way she had smirked and winked when she caught him last night, leather whip wrapped around his snout.

"Now, what should I do with you?"

As Max stepped back toward the bed, he realized that this time, *he* was the stark naked one. He reached for the blankets and yanked them over his nudeness.

"Don't worry, I didn't look."

"You can save the act," he said, forcing a deep confidence into his voice that he didn't feel. "I heard you out there. And I remember everything. I remember you in the meadow, and in the forest last night."

She smirked. "If you remember me from the meadow, then I suppose I can admit, I did peek. Same as you did, I'm sure." She cocked her head and raised her eyebrows. "Glad to see you think I'm pretty."

Max shook his head. It felt like something wild was buzzing inside his own brain.

In a commanding, hypnotizing voice, the red head spoke. "Look at me, Maximillian."

Max tried not to, but his head turned, his eyes flashed up, despite every neuron in his brain resisting.

"That's a good boy." Her gaze bored into him. She had him at her beck and call, for as long as she wanted. He'd never blink again if that's what she wanted. Her eyes glittered like gemstones in an evergreen forest.

"I'm Cailleach. The youngest sister-daughter of the Fallen. Cursed to the Ould Sod across the Atlantic for eternity." She did a little curtsy, and for half-a-second her form… *flickered.* Her skin flashed brown and scaly, her hair turned to fire, her teeth to fangs. But half-a-second later, she flickered back, as beautiful as ever. "But look at me, now, Max. I've set myself free. If it's easier, you can just call me Hailey, it's my mortal name these days. We have to talk, Max. About what you are, and how I can help you, if you help me."

"Okay," Max said, and he gulped.

"It's fair to be wary of someone as beautiful and dangerous as myself. But if you help me get what I want, I'll help you get what you want."

She smiled at him then, her nose crinkled, her freckles seemed to pop.

"What is it that you want, Max?"

She took one step toward him. She dropped her arms

down, let her leather jacket fall to the ground behind her. She slid her finger under the strap of the dress, pushed it down over her shoulder, onto her arm. The dress slipped a little.

"You can tell me." She whispered, "You can tell me what you really want. Morgan's gone, Max. She's dead. She won't know."

Max didn't speak. His mind wasn't entirely his. She was inside there with him, her other form, her demon-witch form, fighting to steal his mind away. He fought for control, but he was losing.

"You don't have to say anything, Max," she said, her voice breathy, reaching out and yanking the blankets out of his hands, her eyes flicking downward. "I can see clearly what you want."

She lifted her finger to the final, thin piece of cloth by her neck, teased the fabric, then tugged the strap of her dress over her shoulder. It fell, then caught. Her taut, erect nipples caused just enough friction to hold the dress over her breasts for a moment.

She took another step.

The dress fell to the floor.

She was the mysterious beauty from the meadow again. Nude, vulpine, lithe. She shook her thick red hair and it fell loose across her shoulders, curls bouncing. Her eyes met his. She was so close Max could feel her heat.

He did want her—Or he felt like at least some part of him did.

She pounced on him, shoving him backward into the soft bed.

Yes. Don't think. Let your flesh decide. You do want her.

Then she answered, without speaking, from within

326

his own thoughts. 'I want you too, Max. I need you. Inside me. Right. Now.'

—This isn't right.—

Grim's voice, surfaced from out of nowhere.

Something ravenous flashed in Hailey's eyes as she realized he knew she was in his head. Her form *flickered*, just for an instant, and Max squeezed his own eyes shut, focused on overcoming her mental intrusion.

Get out!

Max shoved her out of his head and shoved her body off of his. She tumbled backwards, off the bed and onto the ground. For a moment, it felt like Grim had resurfaced, but he was gone again, still locked away somewhere. But in that brief moment, Max had kicked the demon-witch out of his mind.

She rose from the floor and chuckled, smiling a predator smile, gazing down at him with a bemused look in her eye. "So… you broke free of my hypnotism. You are awfully strong-willed, aren't you?"

Max glared back at her, setting his jaw tight.

Go on. Try to wriggle into my head again, witch.

Her coy smile turned to a hungry snarl; her bright white teeth became black fangs. Her seductive stare transformed into cold, reptilian hunger. A carnivorous creature, not human at all, not really. A monster, old as time, from the darkest pit in hell.

She took an unnaturally quick step forward and slashed her clawed hand at him. Stinging pain seared across Max's torso. He looked down and saw razor-thin red stripes traced across his bare chest. The pain didn't dull after a few moments, but instead grew sharper. It seemed to sting worse and worse, tendrils of pain stretching deeper into his body, stabbing at his nervous system.

Max clenched his body tight, trying and failing to overpower the pain.

She whispered, "Stop me, Max. Go on, transform. Fight back."

Max looked for Grim. Felt for the grip of cold iron tangled around his spine, the pull of the moon in orbit.

He found nothing but his own human fear.

She swiped her hand down again, and Max thrust his arms out, but his reaction time was much too slow. She carved another four strips of thin flesh out of his chest.

He lunged upwards, trying to get out of the vulnerable position he was in, but she knocked him back onto the bed, and her smile grew wider.

She slashed him again, this time across his abdomen. The pain was unimaginable. His vision swirled. He slammed his teeth together, grinding his jaw tight, doing everything in his power to keep from screaming. The pain was unreal. Unnatural.

As a human and as a werewolf he'd experienced plenty of painful wounds. The pain in just transforming from man to beast was exquisite, white-hot and brilliant in its intensity.

But the scratches on his body now were somehow far, far worse. It was as if the witch's claws weren't just deadly sharp, but toxic-tipped to induce the worst pain imaginable.

"Beg me to stop, Max."

He didn't respond, but glared back, meeting her eye to eye. He wouldn't give in.

She jabbed a single clawed finger into his shoulder, and he let out a shocked gasp. The wound radiated outward in deep throbs of searing pain.

There was nothing he could do to stop her. He may have kicked her out of his mind, but Grim was still locked away. He was human. And his soft flesh was vulnerable. He struggled to push her off, but with a single finger she held him pinned, naked, to the bed. She smiled down at him, her eyes pure venom. She twisted her finger deeper into the wound.

"Stop!" Max blurted out, tears welling up in his eyes.

"Stop what?" Her finger continued to twist, and Max felt nausea rising in his stomach. The pain was unbearable. Blackness radiated around the edges of his vision and began to overtake him. The monster-witch snapped her fingers on her other hand and the blackness vanished. "I won't let you escape the pain, Max. In your mind or not, I can make this pain eternal." She jabbed a second finger into the wound in his chest, sending another tearing rip of pain jolting through his body.

He almost retched. He couldn't take anymore. Her fingers were only an inch deep in his shoulder, but thousands of microscopic barbs seemed to be digging even deeper, each one racing up his neck and into his head, where they twisted and gouged and grated across his brain. His head pulsed worse than any migraine, his body throbbed worse than any physical pummeling he'd ever endured. Each of his nerves seemed to be fraying into infinite coils of pain.

His body had tried to shut down, and she'd kept him awake. He wanted death.

"Please… End it." Max choked out the words.

"End what?"

Through gritted teeth, Max moaned, "Stop… hurting… me."

"Oh, sure." She removed her finger, and the pain ceased. Gone, in an instant like it had never existed.

Max looked up.

Her face had softened, her claws had become hands again. Her body glistened. She stood calmly next to him, red hair rumpled and dangling over her shoulders, radiant in her nudity, looking as stunning and as human as he'd seen her in the open meadow. Looking nothing like the monster that had just doled out more pain than Max could even fathom.

"I can end you whenever I want," she whispered. "You broke free of my hypnotism, but it didn't matter, because I'm stronger than you, Max. You've got impressive willpower, but it's nothing compared to my true power." Her eyes *flickered*, raging red embers again, for just an instant. She reached over and drug a single finger across Max's chest. Goosebumps spread across his already healed skin. "And remember, death would be a mercy, compared to what I can do to you. So when I allow it, and I give you access back to your furry other half, remember the feeling of my claws on your skin." She pricked him, just barely, with a single human nail, and he felt a jolt of pain flash again into his abdomen. A single prick, worse than any stab wound.

She stepped backwards, smiling at him, where her dress lay crumpled in a heap. She pulled it up around her and fixed the straps over her shoulders as she spoke. "So here's the deal, champ. I get what I want, or you will suffer again. You know just how terrible that can be now. Whether you resist me or not. So be a good boy and quit fighting me. Who knows, you might end up having some fun in the long run. Certainly more fun than me having to teach you another lesson in pain. You have the power to lead my werewolf pack directly into Pineville. There's something green and glowing that I need, and there is no one left who is going to get in my way and stop me. Vexulta killed your pal Vlad Cosmin, the old knight, for me. And then Morgan helped me defeat Vexulta. And then I took out Morgan. See how that works? The whole town is mine for the taking now, Max. And I'm going to take it."

She walked to the doorway, glanced back over her shoulder, tossing her thick red hair. "Don't mope too long, I need my general strong and ready for battle tonight." She winked, then walked out the door. Closed it behind her and clicked the lock.

Max lay in the bed and stared at the ceiling. He remembered the pain, like an echo, reverberating through his bones.

Hell.

He was in hell. Trapped, deep in the middle of a wild forest, guarded by a dragon of a woman, and he couldn't escape. And part of him knew, for all his sins, he deserved this punishment.

Chapter 28

October Thirtieth, 8:11 a.m.

Morgan sat in the "interrogation room," which was really just an office, for close to an hour before she heard the mayor and the sheriff speaking outside the door. The mayor may have thought she couldn't hear them, but the walls were paper thin, and he rarely ever lowered his voice. He spoke loud and smooth, like he was behind a podium, even when he was in a tiny hallway with only one other person.

"I tell you, it's a monsoon out there, Jeffrey. And somewhere on the mountain there must have been a mudslide, because there's a whole new tributary of water dumping into the Shenandoah, and its cutting right across main street. I ain't never seen anything like it. I shut the bridge down because it's going to flood over any minute. You've got Morgan sweating in there?"

"I wouldn't say she's sweating; she's kind of pissed off she can't help Dr. Williams and the other nurses at the hospital."

"Yes, I understand. They need her too, I was just over there. Did you know Dr. Reynolds and his wife are on vacation in the Bahamas? Great timing on their part. It's just Dr. Vickie Williams, the receptionist and the two new girls. Vickie recruited Farmer Bill, and Phillip, and that 'Nam vet Charlie who lives on his own up in the woods to come down and do basic first aid in the lobby while she deals with the more seriously wounded."

"That bad, huh? Shit, maybe we should get over there and deal with Morgan later? What do you think, she's going to run off? The valley is blocked off at every exit. She'd need to be able to fly to get out of Pineville."

Morgan's eyebrow raised. She lowered it manually with her hand.

"Jeffrey, we need to talk to her. I can just feel it. Something's going on with her. Now, obviously we don't have any real evidence of anything, but we need to act like we know more than we actually do. She has just barely missed being killed twice now. She ain't that lucky. We need to put the squeeze on her. Tell her that Craig installed security cameras out in the parking lot."

Sheriff Jeffrey sipped at something, then said, "You weren't a detective in a past life, were you?"

"Huh? You just show me where that two-way mirror set up is, and I'll let you talk to her first."

"This isn't *Law and Order*, Fraser. This is Pineville. She's just right here in Deputy Bunkum's office."

"Oh, hell, why didn't you say so, Jeffrey? She can probably hear us out here. Let's just go in, then."

The mayor stormed through the door, followed by Jeffrey at a more leisurely pace, carrying a steaming thermos.

"Could you hear us out there, Morgan?"

Morgan grimaced, admitting with a hint of a smile, "Even if I hadn't, I wouldn't have fallen for the ol' Craig has installed security cameras trick."

"Well, hell. Okay, just be honest with me, Morgan. What is going on? What am I missing?"

Morgan shook her head, raised her hands. "I really

don't know. I know the same thing I knew when I told Maud and Sheriff Jeffrey that something like a bear attacked me and Joey. Am I understanding correctly? Did someone else get attacked?"

The mayor collapsed in the chair. "Yeah, someone was attacked. And now the town is close to flooding over, we've got no one to come and help us anytime soon, and no way to communicate beyond the mountains that we even need help. It's the darndest thing, I understand the internet and the phonelines and the power being out. But how in the hell can we not even raise someone on the old CV radios? It's like we're trapped inside some sort of weird... bubble. Totally isolated, totally on our own. This is a chance for me to lead this town, but if I bumble it, my career is over." Fraser shook his head, rubbed at the spot above his chest where Morgan knew his tattoo rested. "Cynthia wouldn't like that. We've got more good to do yet."

Jeffrey rolled his eyes behind the mayor's back.

Morgan said, "You can still be the mayor that brings the nurse in from out in the mountains, where she was trapped without a car, to help the hospital."

Mayor Fraser's face brightened at this.

Morgan continued, "I'm sure we can put you to work there too, it's a good photo op. Roll up the sleeves, show the town you're willing to do what it takes to help?"

The mayor inclined his head, smiling. "Now that is a good idea. Morgan—you and I will go over there immediately. Jeffrey, you get in one of them four-wheel trucks we got and circle the town. Check with the timber guys, see if we need to cut down any more trees or put together a crew to lay sandbags or put fires out anywhere. I feel like it may be too late for all that, but we need to protect what we can."

Jeffrey lifted his hat off the table and pulled it over his head. "Copy that."

Fraser continued, "We need to get Deputy Bunkum out on that tiny dirt road that crawls north into the mountains. If you follow it long enough, it actually meets up with an old fire access road. Little antique cabin sits out there, Victor Frank's place. That road actually goes up and over the northern mountain believe it or not. Have Bunkum make sure that old hillbilly is okay, and then send him over the mountain for help. Once he's out of the valley, maybe he can get a signal and let the outside world know just how bad we got hit. I want the National Guard and the state militia. If this rain doesn't let up, we're going to be evacuating people out of their second-floor windows, if they're lucky enough to have them."

Morgan swallowed. It was worse out there than she thought. Dr. Williams would need her help. But there were other things, maybe even more pressing, that Morgan needed to do to. To stop Hailey. And if Bunkum went out that way, he'd find Morgan's car, smashed under the giant tree. Who knows what else he might find.

Thunder rumbled overhead, and the rain fell even harder.

"If that's not a sign, I don't know what is." The mayor pushed back his chair and stood up. "Jeffrey, uncuff this woman, and let's save some lives."

"She was never cuffed, sir."

Morgan shrugged again, holding her uncuffed wrists up in the air.

"Oh, well, uh, alright then, come on."

Morgan stood up, walked around the desk, and followed the two men out of the office.

****

October Thirtieth, 9:22 a.m.

Max smelt them before he saw them. Morgan's dog Joey, and the brown werewolf—the small, scarred one that had led him to Vlad Cosmin.

What the hell were they doing out here?

He heard a noise, too, a strange one, just barely audible over the pounding rain. A buzzing sound, like the sound of a fly, just next to your ear.

Max turned his head, looked out the small window with the iron bars. He blinked, not trusting his vision. Next to the slinking brown werewolf loping forward in the rain, floated Joey, in mid-air.

Floating—No, not floating…

Flying.

Flying with a dual-set of dragonfly wings sprouting out from each side of him. Max had to smile. It was the most ridiculous thing he'd ever seen. The dog moved forward, paws turning underneath him uselessly, wings buzzing fast enough to push him along at the same pace as the brown werewolf next to him.

The werewolf and Joey came right up to the window. Max gently left the bed and met them at the window. The werewolf grunted, stuck its snout through the bars and bumped Max in the face. Joey did the same, except he licked Max, whimpering quietly in excitement, tail whipping so fast his whole body wobbled back and forth.

"I don't understand," Max said, rubbing Joey's ears, "But I guess I don't need to."

The brown werewolf reached out and grabbed the iron bars. Max sniffed again.

Dead flesh. Smelt it in the air. Then he heard blundering footsteps.

Max whispered, "Go, get out of here!"

Joey listened, buzzed straight up into the air, disappeared into the tree canopy.

The brown werewolf grunted, growled a little in disapproval. Then it caught the scent and turned.

But by then it was too late.

The big, lurching form of Victor Frank emerged around the corner of the cabin. His flesh was far grayer than before. His neck was still stitched together, two big iron bolts jutting out each side. The whole front of his flannel gray shirt was soaked in brown, dried blood.

"Pesky werewolves," Vic gurgled. His mouth didn't move very well, the skin of his face was turning green with rot and decay.

He lifted a blow pipe to his mouth, shot a dart at the brown werewolf.

The creature growled, snapped. Took two strides toward Victor. Then the werewolf crumpled to his knees, howled into the rainy forest, and collapsed.

"No escapes, today," Vic said, tottering forward. By the time he made it to his prey, the werewolf had transformed back to a skinny, five foot nothing Native American man with long, straight brown hair. Vic groaned as he bent down, but he scooped the man up and tossed him over his shoulder, as if the body were no heavier than a small child.

"Another one for the pack," he slurred, stumbling off, heading around the back of the cabin.

If only he could transform, Grim would tear that

son-of-a-bitch's head off all over again. In fact, if he could get out of here, Max would do it with his human hands if he had to.

Morgan was dead. Joey and the brown werewolf were his last allies. And now the old, brown werewolf was gone too. Max ground his teeth, turned around and started looking for things to help him escape. He didn't fear Victor Frank, but he feared more pain being dealt out by Hailey. He had to escape, no matter the cost. He wouldn't wallow in fear. He wouldn't let the demon-witch get away with all she had done.

Max felt the anger bubbling up inside him. He felt the white-hot rage pulsing at his temples. He didn't whisper *Goosfraba*, he didn't try to calm himself down.

No more anger management philosophy.

He embraced his anger.

Pain had nothing on his anger. Even her pain.

Able to change into a werewolf or not, he would not give up.

Chapter 29

October Thirtieth, 10:45 a.m.

Pineville's small hospital had installed a large generator over the summer and was able to keep most of the necessary pieces of equipment running after the power went out. One of the only large buildings in Pineville that had auxiliary lights shining through the windows had made it become the unofficial beacon for any injured or stranded survivors who needed help.

Morgan ran through the doors, found Dr. Williams and threw her arms around her.

An expression of relief washed across Vickie's face. "Thank god you're back. I— We need your help, Morgan."

"I'm here. You've got me. Point me in the right direction."

"I need you to run triage. No one else here knows how to diagnose and prioritize the severity of these injuries. They keep telling me bloody hands and feet need immediate attention, not the guy with the thready pulse and the blue lips. I need you to be the leader and create some sort of flexible system for priority needs. Phillip and Charlie and Bill can handle the minor wounds and small first aid things and pour hot water and get snacks and blankets and do all the little stuff for patients who aren't in severe need. I need me and the nurses working the worst victims. You make it happen."

Morgan gritted her teeth, nodded, and was off.

She fell into the work, running on adrenaline, glad to be of use. Secretly, when she could, she would inject gentle golden energy into the victims, giving their spirit and their bodies a surge of strength and vitality.

She didn't really have the skill to heal wounds with magic, but she had the ability to help push hearts and souls to hope. To optimism. To believing they would be okay.

In medicine, Morgan knew, sometimes that attitude could be the difference between recovery and death. And in this town, an infusion of optimism and hope would go a long way.

Hours later, which felt like only minutes, she looked up, wiping her sleeve against her sweating brow.

Philip and Charlie were standing at her side. So was Mayor Fraser. She didn't even notice, but he'd been there the whole time, helping Dr. Williams get supplies and transport patients.

"Nice work, everyone, but don't stop now. Who's next?"

Philip shook his head, "I don't know. We're caught up, finally. The rain is still coming down, but all the injured have been seen. The quake victims are all accounted for."

The mayor spoke up, agreeing with the brewer. "Yes, now we've got to start thinking about next steps. Battening down the hatches and, uh, preparing for tonight." He turned to veteran Charlie, and said, under his breath, "Would you mind stepping aside for a couple minutes, Charlie, so I could talk with Phillip and Morgan, privately?"

"Hell nah, I know what you want to talk about. The whole town does. Want to talk about what I heard killed Tom and killed Sandy. Might've killed someone else too, 'cept I heard nobody's identified the body, yet. I ain't stepping nowhere. What you want me to do, go stand in the storm like a turkey? What are you going to do, mayor? Ask the nurse and the beer man to fight the monsters? We got to get the hell out of this town."

Fraser just stared at the war veteran. Eventually, he said, "Well, uh, the bridge is out and the gaps are closed. What do you think we should do?"

"We still going to the brewery at five, right? Town meeting? We need to keep everyone together. Nobody outside, safety in numbers. Bunker down, man, bunker down. Keep a look out. Then as soon as we can, we get the national guard out here. Damn, ain't you the mayor?"

Morgan excused herself. Whatever they were doing, she needed to go do something else. Charlie, Phillip, and the mayor could figure out the hideout plans on their own.

She needed to find Hailey. And stop her. The werewolves were a symptom of Pineville's illness. Not the cause.

But first, she needed to say goodbye to someone.

"Dr. Williams?"

Vickie turned around from a patient. "One sec, Morg—"

"I just came to say I have to go. I'm going to go check on… something. But I'll be back here to relieve you by five, that way you can go to the town hall meeting."

"I'm staying right here, Morgan. I can't go anywhere. You go do what you need to get done, girl, then you go to the meeting. Afterward, you tell me what all we decide to do, okay? Sound like a plan?"

Morgan gave her another hug. Vickie was surprised for a moment, then she hugged her back. Really squeezed her. Whispered in her ear, "When I saw you out there, busting your ass, helping those folks, I finally felt like I had my old Morgan back. All the way back."

"Thank you," Morgan whispered. "I think I'm almost there."

"No almost, girl, you *all* the way back." She pulled her head away from Morgan, backing halfway out of the embrace. She looked her in the eye. "Whatever you are going to go do... good luck."

Morgan swallowed. She couldn't say anything. She nodded, turned, and ran.

Something inside her twisted. She felt the magic vibrations in the air, twisting, writhing. Someone else was using them.

Using the vibrating red threads. Using Fire.

Something was wrong. Where before the zig-zagging threads of Fire had swarmed her, had crawled all over her, now they were gone. Morgan felt for the magic in the atmosphere, felt a stirring of Earth, the latent layer of Air, and wave after wave of Water. Fire was barely there, distant, and it wanted no part of Morgan.

There was a component of emotional connection to magic, her grandmother had said. As a teenager, Morgan had never felt it. Now, though...

'It is a relationship with an energy we don't understand, but we can feel with our hearts.'

Right now, Morgan felt betrayal from the Fire magic.

She ran to the janitor closet. She didn't have time to

waste.

She yanked out a big trash can on wheels, tossed aside a mop, tossed aside a couple of bottles of bleach and cleaning solution.

Then she saw the broom.

It wasn't exactly the wooden antique from Vexulta's cabin.

It was a big push broom, made of plastic and cotton and the handle was bright neon yellow. Morgan looked down at her purple scrubs. Hell of a color combo.

She smiled, despite herself, despite the feeling of trouble in her gut. The feeling of anxiety for what was to come.

She wasn't a black robe and pointy hat type of witch. Not an antique broom riding witch that casted spells from a wand and mumbled incantations under her breath.

She was the granddaughter of a singularly special woman of Mother Earth who taught her how to harness magic the old ways, naturally, feeling for it in the atmosphere of the world. The widow of a good man who taught her how to love and be loved unconditionally, and finally, after all this time, how to forgive someone for giving up.

She was the daughter of a monster, too, just like Vexulta. Her father might not be The Fallen, but he was an evil, immortal bastard in his own right. And he may still be prowling around nearby Pineville. But she wasn't going to let Benjamin Shroud shape her life. Let him, or anything for that matter, pull her down into the darkness. She would not be another drain on this valley. She wouldn't feed on the life force of her neighbors. She wasn't Unnamed Pretty Female Victim. And she sure as hell wasn't the person that let the darkness and the evil take her and twist her into something she wasn't.

Yes, she was a witch.

She was the witch that was going to save Pineville.

She grabbed the push broom and ran down the hallway, shot upstairs—in complete darkness—stumbled and floundered up three flights to the roof.

When she threw open the door, the rain was pounding down as hard as ever.

But that didn't deter her.

The better to NOT see me by.

She reached her hand out, felt the strength of the rain drops. Felt their energy. Felt their pulse. She pulled golden threads and blue threads and green threads of magic from the world. From Gaia. She felt it, then, the connection.

The relationship.

Magic was the link between her and Gaia. Her oldest ancestor.

She could almost hear Gaia whispering to her. Telling her to take all the magic she needed. *Take and heal your heart. Things can be replaced. Memories live forever. Now go and do my will unto my enemies.*

Morgan swung her leg over, kicked off into the thunderstorm and flew into the gray sky, heading toward her home.

Lightning cracked just behind her; thunder exploded all around her. The rain drenched her, but it didn't matter. She raced over the town, headed north. When she got back to her house, she didn't know what she'd find. She hoped at least Abornazine. Maybe Max.

****

What she found instead was smoke and ruin.

Her house had gone up in flames.

It was a raging blaze, steaming in the rain. No flooding downpour was strong enough to put out such intense flames.

Joey. Shadow. Lancelot. Galahad.

No.

She plummeted to the earth, pulling up at the last second, then tumbled off her broom.

Her dog and her cats. She'd stuffed them into the side room. They were trapped. They were locked in the house. Burned alive.

Hailey did this.

She knew it in her very bones.

She screamed into the universe.

Then she heard meowing.

She looked behind her. Shadow hopped out from the trees, where he'd been hiding from the rain. Lancelot and Galahad followed after him.

"Oh, kitties, come here!" Tears ran down her face, but it made no noticeable difference, what with the pounding rain. She scooped up the cats, pressed their wet fur up against her face. They meowed at her, complaining about the rain and the burning house and when they would get their dinner. She kissed them and thanked Gaia they were alive.

Morgan heard barking from above her. Joey buzzed down, tail wagging, barking and whining at Morgan. He looked at the house and then back to Morgan.

The werewolf Abornazine must have let Joey out. Must have known how to open a door. He wanted his new friend Joey to come with him.

By leaving the door open, the animals had escaped.

The rest of her life, her home, was gone.

But her family was safe.

For now.

Joey barked and barked, buzzing back into the air, then turning back. Acting for all the world like he wanted Morgan to follow him.

Morgan didn't like leaving the cats in the storm, but she didn't have any options. They were outside cats as much as they were inside cats.

"Stay dry," she said, rubbing Shadow's ears. He meowed. "Look out for your brothers. Don't go far. I'll be back."

Shadow meowed grumpily again, then darted back into the underbrush at the tree line. Less wet over there, Morgan assumed. She scratched Lancelot and Galahad and then bopped them on the rear. They hustled after Shadow into the woods.

Joey barked; Morgan leapt onto her broom. "Go on then, Joey, lead me."

Morgan felt power sizzling in the air. She drew in magic. Air, Water and Earth. Fire threads danced away from her, but she'd win them over. She felt like she knew who was manipulating them, who was trying to deny her access to the explosive, volatile strain of magic.

Let her try.

She was coming for her.

****

October Thirtieth, 3:36 p.m.

Max thought for a long time, while he waited. Thought really hard. Asked himself what he owed this town. Asked himself why he should fight against Hailey, when it would be so easy to just go along with her, then escape her once she had what she wanted. Why in the world he would ever want to suffer the pain that he knew she could deal unto him at any time.

He could leave her behind, leave Pineville behind. Leave his old identity behind and finally get what he wanted.

Anonymity. To fade back into life, to pretend to be normal.

But is that what Max really wanted?

Max sat on his bed. Hands clasped together, hiding a small shank he'd whittled. He waited.

He listened.

When the red truck pulled back in, Max stayed silent.

He heard one of the girls report to Hailey what they'd learned. Her tongue rolled her r's and softened her l's.

"We found it, Hailey. You won't believe it. Under our noses, the entire time. The quake seems to have revealed it to everyone. Big Moose they call it, at The Dugout. Where we were, just last night. The rock, they say, it cracked in half. The enchanted emerald is glowing with power as we speak."

"Very good. The storm will break soon. The full moon will rise as the sun sets. We will gather the pack, set them loose upon the town. In the confusion, we will steal the stone, and craft an emerald Arch wand. Then we will have an unending supply of Fire *and* Earth energy, and we won't be limited to staying near places of power."

"And then I'll inherit the Ruby Arch wand, right? The wand of Fire?" another woman asked, the younger sounding one from before, based on what Max could hear.

"Yes. And after all the magnificent, devastating

magic you cast with it, you'll give it your name, written into the history of the world. The Ruby Wand of Ash, they'll call it. We will seek out the enchanted sapphire next, carve another wand for Vera. After that, those secret societies who seek to stop spellcasters and the supernatural will crumble before us. Dark cults and covens of witches and other vile, unnatural things who envy our power will either bend their knee or die in flame and be buried underneath the earth. By the time we are through, everyone will bow to the new trio of Witch-sisters of Angavor and their three unstoppable Arch wands."

Max wanted to warn the other women, to shout out from his cell, to tell them Hailey would betray them, just as she had her true sister, the one she called Vexulta. But something held Max's tongue.

Maybe fear.

Maybe the beginnings of a plan.

"There are two small problems, Hailey," Ash said, her voice lower than before.

"And what are those?"

"Well, one, basically everyone who wasn't injured by the earthquake will be at The Dugout tonight. They are holding their town meeting there. The mayor has enacted a curfew after sunset. Everyone is being strongly encouraged to remain at The Dugout or with injured family members at the hospital. The flooding has peaked, but most of the town is devastated. There are few places left that are safe. Lots of people will be in our way."

"They will either get out of our way, or they will be a sacrifice for our greater goals."

"The second, Hailey, is that Morgan is still alive."

Max's heart leapt.

"Yes, I felt her. Drawing power from the Source. I sent her a message. Pineville's no longer her home."

"Hailey, she should be with us. There are four Arch jewels, enchanted by Gaia. One for each strand of magic. We should have four witches. That's how the ancient lore is written. Four Arch wands. Not three."

"Oh, grow up. Not everything is a fairytale. Morgan is far too attached to this place. She doesn't have the ambition. I'm starting to worry that you've lost your *fire*, Ash. Has coming home been too much for you? Starting to care for the people here? Did Morgan rub off on you?"

"I don't give a fuck about these capitalist jack-offs, you know that," Ash insisted. "But Morgan, she's one of us. If she's not on our side, she will try to stop us. And she's strong."

"She doesn't have an Arch wand, Ash. Nor does she have the combined might of all four strains of Magic surging through her veins. I've been touched by the ritual, if you don't remember."

"I just think we should give her a chance."

Hailey sighed. "If we should cross paths, you can offer her our… *allegiance*… and if she accepts, I'll welcome her with open arms." Hailey clapped her hands, then spoke in a louder, more commanding tone. "Victor, we're leaving. We'll be back before five to unleash the pack. Try not to get yourself killed again. It's getting harder and harder to piece you back together."

"Yes, Ms. Hailey," came the grumbling reply.

"Now sisters, let's get ready for our debut to Pineville. Our coming out party, if you will. We do want everyone *spellbound* by our appearance, after all. And I think I know just the thing to get everyone's attention."

Max listened to them leave. They walked out into

the storm, but he didn't hear any car doors open. He heard three soft *swooshes,* and by the time he made it to the window to look for them, they were gone.

Chapter 30

October Thirtieth, 4:08 p.m.

Morgan and Joey dove low when they saw flashing blue and red lights. The rain had slowed, but not stopped, and Morgan guessed they were easier to see than before. She knew who those flashing lights belonged to. They dipped into the forest and proceeded quietly on foot toward the road. Joey seemed to understand, copying Morgan's body language, staying quiet and keeping his wings tucked against his body.

Deputy Bunkum stood next to Morgan's smashed car, chainsaw resting on the remainder of the front seat. Bunkum had made his way through about a third of the massive tree, and until he made it the rest of the way through, he wouldn't be able to pass the car in the road and head further north.

From what the mayor said, making it out of the mountains on this old northern dirt road would be the only way anyone could be alerted that Pineville needed serious aid.

Morgan thought about all the people in town. They were depending on Bunkum to make it out, to get help for the rest of the town.

And the deputy was stuck because of the destruction Morgan had caused.

Three dark figures zoomed through the gray sky

above the road.

"Well, I'll be…" Bunkum said, scratching his head, watching the three blurry silhouettes zip through mid-air toward town. "Ain't never seen that before…"

From the shadow of the forest Morgan sent a combination of magical threads of power into the crack of the tree that the deputy had already carved. She dialed the magic in so tightly it eventually exploded outward, and the tree trunk cracked at the weak point, snapping in twain.

"Hot damn!" Deputy Bunkum hollered, hopping out of the way as the trunk slowly tipped and rolled out of the road.

Morgan brought her push broom back under her legs, lifted off the ground a few inches, and started flying north, staying low, under the canopy of the pine trees.

"Come on, Joey. Let's go," she whispered.

The dog buzzed ahead of her, whining with a sense of urgency she felt in her bones.

Morgan followed after her dragonfly dog, hoping against hope he was leading her to Abornazine and Max.

****

October Thirtieth, 4:08 p.m.

Victor Frank began his paces, lumbering around, securing the house by completing laps around the inside of the cabin. Then he moved outside, stumbling around the exterior of the property, securing the perimeter, ensuring no other intruders were nearby and would catch him off guard. The steep incline of the hill and the pounding rain seemed to give him plenty of problems, but the massive lug would persist, machine-like, clambering around in the underbrush and the bramble, climbing up one side of the cabin, tumbling back down the other. Sometimes, as he passed by Max's window, Max thought about reaching out and grabbing him. He could shove the shank into the mostly-dead man's neck, finish the job, once again, and then break down the door, find his car keys, and high tail it out of dodge.

But instead, Max waited. The rain slowly decreased. It turned from a monsoon to a drizzle in about an hour.

He heard Victor Frank throw open the front door, come stomping back into the cabin, sopping wet. He heard the man moan a little as he struggled out of a heavy dripping coat. The wet jacket smacked onto the floor. Max heard Vic step toward the middle of the cabin, then heard a recliner chair creak. A book opened.

Max heard a familiar buzzing outside his window.

He turned, looked, saw.

Morgan.

She landed softly outside his window, Joey just behind her. Max couldn't contain his smile, but he held up his finger over his grinning lips.

"Quiet," he mouthed.

"Okay," she whispered back.

The recliner outside the door didn't creak.

"I thought you were dead," Max whispered.

"I thought you were gone," she whispered back.

"I was. But I came back."

"I see."

"I'm glad I came back," Max said.

"Yes, things look like they've really improved for you," Morgan said, examining Max's current jail cell.

"The hillbilly I killed at the gas station, the werewolf hunter, he is guarding this cabin."

"Excuse me?" Morgan asked.

"She brought him back. Hailey. The Irish witch. Black magic. Necromancy. I think she knows you. By the way, heads up, she's not happy you are still alive."

"Yeah, I pieced that together. She burnt down my house."

"Oh god, Morgan, I'm sorry."

"It's okay. The animals all made it. I'll process losing my home later. We have to get you out of here."

"No," Max said.

"What do you mean, no? I need your help, Max. You're the last person who can help me."

"I know. And I want to help you. But listen." Max gestured for her to come closer to the iron bars. He whispered conspiratorially into her ear, "They are going after an enchanted emerald in town. They can use it to make some sort of powerful wand. Hailey already has one—they call it an Arch wand. They were talking about being able to cast powerful, destructive spells with these wands."

Morgan nodded, understanding. "Yes," she said, "I've seen the one Hailey has."

"There are more of these enchanted jewels across the world, but one is right here in Pineville. A glowing emerald, stuck in some moose boulder or something. Does that ring a bell?"

"Yes," Morgan said, though her face grew more confused than ever. "At the brewery."

"Yes, that's what they're after. Hailey's gathered werewolves and wild wolves, plus the two other witches, and they're all headed for that brewery holding the emerald once the full moon rises."

"Well, then, even more reason for us to get you out of here. We need to get there first, and ready our defenses. Most of the town will be there tonight."

Max looked Morgan in the eyes. He wanted nothing more than to escape with her, to let her save him. Their faces were inches away from each other, separated by only cold iron bars. He could feel the warmth of her breath, smell her hair and her sweat. Her face was the opposite of Hailey's; Concern and empathy etched onto it, her smile was not voracious but conciliatory. Her eyes were welcoming, not predatory.

"Morgan, if you get me out of here, it'll just be the two of us against all of them. The whole pack of werewolves, and the three witches. She can hypnotize them, Morgan." Max's voice stuttered, thinking about her. About what she did to him. "She… she's got this power, Morgan. She can force you to do things… She can… hurt… in ways I didn't even think possible."

"Max," Morgan whispered, concern etching across her brow, "what happened?"

"Don't worry about what happened." Max shook his head. Morgan said she'd process losing her house later. He couldn't think about what had been done to him, not yet. "I'll tell you later about what happened. Right now, you need to hear what's to come. She wants me to lead the werewolf pack. She thinks she has me under her thumb, same as the rest. If you break me out of here, they'll know we're trying to stop them. They'll come after us with everything they've got."

"So, what's the alternative?"

Max sighed. Nodded his head, as if he needed to convince himself that the plan he concocted would truly work.

"I'll stay here. Pretend we never talked. I'll play her game and lead the pack of werewolves. I'm sure that's what she has in mind. If I can beat the current werewolf alpha, I'll be the pack leader. And when the moment is right, I'll turn on the witches. Most of the pack should turn with me. They'll follow the new alpha… hopefully. At the very least, it'll cause disarray, maybe give you a chance to strike. To take out Hailey. Once she goes down, the rest will scatter."

Morgan shook her head. "It's a terrible risk, Max."

"I've been running from every risk since I first turned, Morgan. I've finally found a reason to take one. To stand up for something."

"For Pineville?"

Max looked at Morgan. Her soft green eyes were nothing like Hailey's. They were warm, and caring, and light. They were the mountain fog on a spring morning. Full of hope, and magic, and future. And as she looked back at him, her figure did not flicker, her eyes did not flash ravenous. She was concerned, and worried, but she looked at Max, and she smiled, trying to give him some optimism and confidence that he didn't feel.

"For you," Max whispered. "Not for Pineville, Morgan. For you."

Morgan reached through the bars, her hands clasping behind Max's head. She pulled his face to the bars, centimeters from her own. Max hesitated for but a moment, then reached his hands through, brushed her wet hair off her brow, felt the smooth curve of her cheek, traced her jaw with his thumb. She turned her face up at his touch. He melted to hers.

Their lips met.

He kissed her, and she kissed him back, and his tongue brushed her tongue, and for a moment he was free. Free from his jail cell, free from his curse, from his near century long imprisonment on this world. As they kissed, something snapped in his mind, some mental wall that had been installed by an intruder.

The moon, in his mind, had returned.

Grim was back.

Max let the kiss linger for a moment longer, tasting the sweetness of her lips, then pulled away from her.

Iron bars still stood between them. Resolute, unbending.

"Are you sure you want to do this?" Morgan asked. "To stay here? To trust yourself to them? To her? We could still break you out. Come up with another plan."

"No," Max said, "I'm not sure it's going to work, but I'm doing it anyway. It's the best chance we've got. They will be coming. And if I do this, I might be able to save that little brown werewolf with the scar. He's on our side, too."

"Abornazine, that's his name. I met him… kind of."

"The witches may try to cause a distraction at the hospital, but their main force will be coming to The Dugout. They want that emerald."

Morgan threw her leg over her push broom. She kicked into the air, hovered a few inches off the ground. "I'll be waiting. I expect to see you there, Max." She hesitated, then added, with a smile, "I'd never kissed a werewolf before."

Max asked, "What'd you think?"

"I'm not sure." Morgan met his eyes and then she smiled, and it felt like the sun emerging for the first time from a winter of darkness. "I'd like to do it some more, I think."

Max didn't say anything. Morgan soared off into the gray sky. Joey whined and Max reached out and ruffled the dog's ears. "Go with your momma," he said. "I'll see you soon, buddy."

The dog's wings buzzed, recalibrated his direction, then Joey zoomed off, chasing after Morgan into the fading afternoon clouds.

Max turned away from the window, the remnants of a melancholy smile fading from his countenance. He rubbed his hands through his growing stubble. Closer to a beard, honestly, than stubble.

He ground his teeth, cracked his knuckles.

Ready or not, Grim, I need a big night out of you.

—I'll tear all their throats out, Maximillian.—

Chapter 31

October Thirtieth, 4:27 p.m.

Morgan saw Deputy Bunkum's car at the intersection of the fire access road and the narrow dirt mountain road. If he crossed the fire access road and continued up the dirt road further into the mountain, he'd eventually make it over the mountain, and back to civilization. If he turned down the fire access road, he'd come to Victor Frank's cabin on the hill, where Max was imprisoned. If he went that way, he'd either fudge up Max and Morgan's plan, or get himself killed.

Probably both.

Morgan drew in Air and Earth, felt Fire in the atmosphere, closer than before, more accessible, but she didn't need it yet. She wanted to let it come crawling back, wanted those zig-zagging red threads to trace along her skin, to plead for her to use them again before she would draw them in. She'd need all four strains of magic to even stand a chance against Hailey.

Morgan channeled a golden scythe in her mind, reinforced with a shaft of green earthen magic, and swept it through the trunk of the largest pine tree she could find that bordered the fire access road.

It fell across the road, smashing to the ground just inches away from Bunkum's slow cruiser.

A little closer than she wanted. But it would do the

trick. Bunkum couldn't make it the four miles down to the cabin by foot. He'd need to go to the top of the mountain himself to call for help. She watched from the shadowy canopy as the cruiser reversed, did a three-point turn in the middle of the intersection, and drove on, up into the thicker mountain forest.

Morgan checked her watch. Almost five o'clock. She had just enough time to keep herself and Joey hidden in the trees on their way back to town. It would take longer than flying above them, but she didn't want Hailey, Vera, and Ash to catch her and her dog alone. She wasn't ready for that confrontation yet.

First, she stopped by her house—well, the smoldering ruins of her house.

Morgan closed her eyes and sensed for the threads of magic that strummed in the late afternoon air. Followed them in her mind into the burning wreckage of her home. Located the bar of metal with the high melting point. Found Alex's collection of old coins. Using a surge of Air magic, she lifted them out of the ruins of the fire. Drew them to her and plopped them into a pile next to her broom. She watched as the rain fell onto the metal. The pile sizzled and steamed, slowly cooling. Once it had cooled enough not to burn, Morgan scooped the silver bar and the coins into her pocket.

Joey cocked his head side to side, watching her.

Morgan said to him, "You never know, boy, we may need them."

They wove their way back to town. Stayed low and darted in between old brick buildings when they had the opportunity, and when they thought for sure no one was looking, they buzzed up to the hospital roof from a nearby alleyway.

From there, with the rain finally gone, Morgan could see the devastation of Pineville.

The river roared across the southern edge of town, far wider than usual, with no bridge in sight. It had been completely washed out. The older buildings at the lower side of town all looked structurally damaged, large cracks running from their bases up the brick walls. Many had lost all their glass windows, shattered in their frames from the strength of the earthquake. Main street had transformed into a shallow creek bed, water ebbing down, feeding into the river. More men and women than Morgan expected still moved around down there, wading boots up to their knees, some carrying sticks, poking, and prodding in the water. Morgan frowned.

The western mountains were no longer shrouded in rain and clouds. The few clouds remaining exploded in sunset shades of pink and orange and purple at the horizon. Morgan looked the other direction. Where the moon would rise. The storm clouds still lingered there, for now. But the wind blew strong and soon the skies would clear, the sun would set completely, and a glowing full moon would rise over the valley.

They were running out of time. Morgan and Joey left the roof.

She stashed Joey in one of the abandoned upper rooms of the hospital with a big bowl of clean water and some chicken breast she pilfered from the break room fridge. She didn't want to put him at any more risk, and even though she may need to reveal her powers to the town to stop Hailey, she wasn't ready to do that just yet. Stomping around with a dragonfly-winged dog would lead to way too many questions and far too many distractions. And with her house burnt down, a small room at the hospital was the safest place she could think to keep him.

She jogged downstairs, rubbing her fingers against her brow, pondering where to begin, and how best to prepare.

****

October Thirtieth, 4:54 p.m.

Max stole a glance at the black woman in the scrubs and the white coat that the witches had kidnapped. She wasn't paying attention to him. Her hands were tied and locked behind her, Victor firmly pushing her forward up the hill. She glared at the three women who led the way, her face etched in anger, but hiding fear. Max knew who she must be.

They'd kidnapped Morgan's friend and boss, Dr. Vickie Williams.

He strode just off to the side of the witches. He maintained an aloofness, an attitude that he hoped conveyed something of begrudging acceptance. He wanted Hailey to believe he would shoulder his responsibility to take over the mantle of alpha. But that he wasn't happy about it. He didn't want to oversell his allegiance. If he did, they might suspect the trap he planned to spring.

They hiked up the steep hill for close to twenty minutes. The sunset sky smoldered, slowly darkening, the shadows growing stronger as they walked. Soon, the sun would dip below the mountains and Max could already feel the tug of the moon rising. Could sense it arcing up near the horizon, soon to slice into the air, hazy orange and full, illuminating the whole valley.

Max had a firm grip on his transformations. He

doubted the rest of the werewolves had such control. Under the bloodlust of the lunar rays, they'd be hard to lead, even harder to break and turn them against the three witches. Grim would not be able to show them logic or sense. He would just have to direct their violence against the real enemies. Not against the innocent townsfolk.

They paused when they reached the top of the hill. The trees fell away. A wood-rotted barn, leaning waywardly with the decay of time, rose up in the middle of the clearing.

Max could smell the beasts within.

Grim stirred.

Not yet.

Hailey needed to think she would be the one to set him free.

They walked forward. The three witches, in their matching black robes and black hats, threw open the sliding barn doors.

A large pit had been dug inside the barn, close to thirty feet deep. Silver barbwire encircled the whole den, including at a gated entrance where a gash of dirt-hewn stairs led down to the floor of the pit.

Max stepped into the barn, right up to the silver wire. Looked down inside.

Humans and wolves. Naked, feral-looking humans, most of them. Unused to not being in their lycanthropic form. They screamed and yelled when they saw Max at the precipice of their den. The wolves growled. Max noticed the Native American man, Abornazine. He stood off to the side, arms crossed. Staring up at Max, his eyes narrowed in concentration. Judging Max.

Probably thinking Max had betrayed him.

The young witch, Ash, said, "Let's get this over

with," and pointed her wand at the eastern side of the barn. She murmured some incantation and the whole barn exploded outward.

Timbers from the roof fell downward but a staticky, glowing blue shield pulsed around Max and the others, catching the debris. A few of the larger beams sort of phased through, and the Latin witch, Vera, groaned in concentration, her wand shaking in her unsteady hand.

"Useless," Hailey murmured, her ruby wand flashing out, neon red streaks of flame incinerating the logs that had penetrated the shield before they fell onto any of the humans or wolves in the pit.

The prisoners, both man and beast, howled and snarled in fear and anger.

With the barn in rubble around them, the harvest moon could be seen, slicing into the sky above the tree line. Max felt the hairs on the back of his neck stand up.

"Look at them, Dr. Williams. Look at what comes for your town," Hailey said, bemused.

"Don't call her doctor," Ash sneered. "She's a shill for the blood sucking health insurance companies. Drug dealer Vickie, paid by the suppliers, to hook the populace on the newest prescriptions."

Vickie raised her eyebrows in surprise, "Wait, what? You imprisoned a bunch of men in a pit with wild wolves, you're casting magic spells to wake the dead, kidnapping doctors, and plan on burning down my town, and I'm the bad guy because I've been working with Big Pharma?"

Hailey shrugged her shoulders, said, "What can I say? This new generation, huh?" The Irish witch continued, her voice rising a little above the snarls from the den below. "Alright, Vickie, make sure you watch.

This is the best part." She waved her wand toward Max, and then down toward the creatures in the den. Max felt a wave of nausea wash over him and felt something physically click in his mind.

Still ready, Grim?

No response.

Grim?

Hailey had cast a spell, flipping the door in his mind, thinking she was releasing the beast within him. But she hadn't realized Max had already regained his connection with his alter-ego. Now the werewolf was locked away again.

Shit.

The first unnatural howl rose from down within the den. One man collapsed to his knees, clawing and scratching at the flesh on his chest. Another bent sideways, crashing ribs first to the ground, spasming. Soon all the men were convulsing on the ground, their transformations an orgy of massacre and torture, blood and bone and skin-flaying, all in a muddy pit, screams and howls of primordial monsters from mankind's ancient past.

Max closed his eyes. The scene didn't disturb him. He was immune to that type of violence by now.

He needed to concentrate on something else.

On Morgan.

On her smile.

On her touch.

What about her kiss had set the beast within him free? She hadn't performed magic. All she'd done is reached out and kissed him.

No, it was more than that. She'd reached out and kissed him, without fear. Without judgment. Without anything but kindness and desire and… what?

Love?

How cheesy was that?

It couldn't just be love, could it?

Did he love someone he barely knew?

The five-foot-nothing chick with the soccer player body and the soft green eyes. The warmth inside her that made his heart race. All that warmth and desire to do good, to help someone even like Max, despite all the darkness that seemed to swirl around him.

Something clicked inside his mind.

—Love is ancient and primal, Maximillian. Like me.—

Max opened his eyes. He saw more than a dozen werewolves in the pit, ferocious beasts, anywhere from six to nearly nine-feet tall, fur thick and muscles thicker, fangs gleaming in snarling jaws. The wild wolves snapped and circled around them, each trying to find their place in the pecking order of the pack. Max saw the small brown werewolf, with the scar along the ribs, darting inside the den, avoiding the larger and more aggressive werewolves.

Max turned and looked to his side. Victor Frank wobbled at the edge, scowling down into the pit. His exposed skin was now all moldy and green, pure rot. The bolts in his neck seemed rusty. Clearly, his long-term survival was not a concern of the three witches.

"Disgusting animals," Vic gargled through his rotten throat.

Vera and Ash and Hailey stood nearby, holding Vickie Williams up. Hailey's hand held her chin, forcing her to look down upon the pack of monsters gathered below them.

Hailey turned her gaze to Max. "Well?"

Max frowned. "I'll lead your pack, witch. I'll get you what you want. But I don't want *you* as my reward. I want to leave. I want you to let me go. Let me go back to the shadows, and never find me again. I want anonymity. All I ever wanted."

Vickie groaned, hearing the rugged stranger agree to help the witches. She must have thought Max was her last hope.

Hailey scoffed. "Let's see if you can take the mantle first. If you do, I'll accept your terms."

Max looked back down into the pit. He saw the pack had found some structure. The big gray werewolf, almost as tall as Grim, but thicker, more bulldog in shape than wolf, stood at the center of the pack. He stared right up at Max.

Max said, "Oh, one last thing." He reached out and shoved Victor Frank into the pit. The hillbilly groaned as he tipped over the gate. Despite his frantic arm flailing, he could find nothing to grab onto. He screamed as he tumbled down the steep dirt banks all the way into the den. When he hit the ground he let out a guttural scream before the wolves and werewolves pounced on him.

Max stopped resisting the pull of the moon.

His body trembled, his skin boiled. His bones broke on their own, causing him to fall to the ground, grimacing in unbearable pain. He felt his consciousness slipping away, felt Grim sliding into the driver's seat. Max's tremors rolled his spasming body toward the edge of the pit, then over the precipice. He transformed as he fell, hitting the ground of the den with a painful smack.

A few nearby wolves snarled and leapt at him, as they had the zombie hillbilly.

Maximum Grim's thick, black-furred forearm shot out, snatched one wolf by the throat. He stood up and stalked to the circle of the wolfpack, nine-feet of pure primordial carnivore, holding out the whimpering wild canine with one massive paw. Grim tossed it casually to the ground, scattering a handful of other wolves that leapt and hopped away in fear.

Grim lifted his snout to the moon and howled.

The big gray werewolf marched up to Grim, snarling. The rest of the pack retreated back to the edge of the pit, giving the two largest amongst them as wide of a berth as possible.

Grim met the gray's eyes. They stared at each other, feeling one another out. Trying to gauge which werewolf might come out victorious in a battle. Neither blinked. They began to circle each other, both growling, waiting to see if the other would back out. If the other was bluffing.

Neither was.

They fought, as the harvest moon climbed into the night sky.

Maximum Grim was faster. He retained better fighting knowledge from Maximillian, better instincts of the predator. He had larger claws. Sharper fangs. A fiercer bite.

But the big gray werewolf could take every attack that the black werewolf could produce. The creature bled, but not much, and not from any vital areas. It took claw slashes to the thick shoulders, bites to the paws and the arms, but never the neck. And with each strike that Maximum Grim launched, he grew more tired. A half second slower. A half ounce less powerful.

The big gray werewolf absorbed the attacks, never

slowing, never flinching. Slashing methodically. Jaws snapping out, consistent, inevitable, unflagging. Maximum Grim had to put more and more energy into evading the attacks. His own attacks were less lethal, less surprising. They became mere feints, most of them, counters to avoid the gray werewolf's strikes.

If things continued as they were going, the big gray would wear him down to a panting, wheezing lump of fur, then rip out his throat.

Grim snarled in anger at the thought of losing, but the big gray stuck to its strategy. No impulse attacks, no impatience. Methodical, deliberate, plodding strikes, subtle turns to absorb blows without danger, and never a moment's hesitation to allow for rest.

He was as much a grizzled veteran as Grim and he knew, with patience, he would kill the taller, black-furred werewolf.

Grim, he's all beast. I watched the man, before he transformed. The human was nothing but a lumbering, feral neanderthal. He knows how to take a beating. His strategy is endurance and persistence. That's it.

—What of it, Maximilian?—

You won't beat him by pummeling him. He'll outlast you. You have to trick him.

—Tricking is for cowards. —

Tricking is for survival.

Grim growled. Continued his attack. But Max felt him letting up. Felt his strikes growing even slower than before. The black werewolf dodged another strike from the big gray, but this time, Grim knelt down in the dirt.

Panting.

The wolves behind him crept forward, snapped at his heels, sensing weakness.

Grim leapt up, but the gray werewolf struck him a massive swipe across the face. Grim didn't dodge at all.

He absorbed the full blow, stumbled, head spinning, dizziness threatening to steal away his vision. Fell into the dirt. He panted, but he didn't try to get up.

The gray werewolf swaggered over. Slashed Grim across the back with a kick of the back paw.

Grim barely flinched. He just lay there in the dirt. Panting. Bleeding.

Defeated.

The gray werewolf pressed a heavy paw down in between Grim's shoulder blades, big claw slicing into fur and flesh. The gray turned his snout up to the moon and howled in victory.

Fast as silver, Grim spun out from underneath the leg. Launched himself with everything he had.

The big gray pulled back, but not fast enough.

Maximum Grim snapped his massive fangs into the gray werewolf's neck. He clamped down, crashing to the ground, not letting go.

The wolves and werewolves smelt blood and death in the air. They growled and snapped and yipped at the encroaching edges around the fighters. The two werewolves rolled and tumbled in the dirt, sharp claws flashing wet and red in the night air, gray and black fur flying in tufts. But Grim never loosened the vice grip he had on the gray werewolf's throat.

The lack of oxygen eventually forced the gray werewolf to lay on its back, completely submitting to Grim.

Now let him go, Grim. You'll need him on your side later.

—*NO.*—

Maximum Grim tore the gray werewolf's throat out of its neck. He stood up, leaving the big gray dying on its back in the dirt. Blood dripped down from Grim's fangs into his fur around his jaws.

Maximum Grim howled at the moon as the blood ran in rivulets down his black-furred neck. The wolfpack swarmed the dead werewolf. They ripped and tore at the body, consuming the flesh as it morphed from werewolf to human.

Raggedy human bones were all that remained within just a few minutes.

Hailey stared down at Maximum Grim. She grinned in pleasure.

Grim, you remember the plan, right?

No response.

Right?

Grim ignored the sound of the weak human conscious blathering in his head.

The witch-demon swished her wand through the air and two antique brooms arrived at the side of Vera and Ash.

Hailey waved her wand again, and her flesh and cloak melted from around her, replaced with red and orange fur. She grew in size, and she stood above them, silhouetted by the big full moon, the most exquisite werewolf Maximum Grim had ever seen. With a swift claw strike she broke down the silver gate that trapped the pack within the den.

Grim led them up and out of the pit, snarling and snapping at whatever werewolf got too close to his side.

Vera pushed Vickie over her broom, then she and Ash lifted into the darkening sky.

Hailey, in her monstrous werewolf form, raced

ahead and the pack followed her down, through the ancient woods, toward the town of Pineville. Toward the enchanted emerald at The Dugout.

Blood lust pounded in Maximum Grim's head. He wanted flesh, needed it in his jaws, and the orange-furred werewolf ahead of him was leading the whole pack—*his pack*—to a feast.

Chapter 32

October Thirtieth, 4:49 p.m.

When Morgan emerged from the hospital stairwell, she knew something was wrong. When she left, the building had been full of noise and commotion. Now, silence reigned.

Morgan turned a corner and found one of the new nurses leaning up against the wall. Her hands were covering her face.

"What's happened?"

"Oh, Morgan, thank God. Where have you been?"

"I've—"

"Never mind, have you found her yet?"

"Found who?"

"Doctor Williams, obviously!"

"Doctor Williams?"

"Morgan, I'm sorry, I assumed the whole town knew. I—I thought you were out there looking for her, with the rest of them."

"Looking for her?" Morgan covered her mouth with her hand when she realized what they'd done. They'd taken her. Or killed her. Morgan's mind felt hollow. Her stomach threatened to turn over. Another good person gone, thanks to Morgan. Everyone who called themselves Morgan's friend or family, dead or gone… or soon to be in life-threatening danger.

The new nurse took a deep breath and continued, "She just vanished. I. I—I was only gone for a minute. I ran to get more gauze from another room, when I got back, she was gone. Poof into thin air. Like magic. Nobody has seen her since."

Morgan tightened her jaw. Another thought hit her, and she glanced at her watch.

"You said the rest of them are out searching for her? Who's the rest of them?"

"Yes, Maria and I stayed here, of course. To watch over the injured patients. A lot of the younger folks and the older folks stayed with their injured family members. The mayor instructed Sheriff Jeffrey to lead the search. He's got half the abled-bodied men and women in waders, sloshing through ankle deep water, spread out all across town, poking at the edges of the woods. Mayor Fraser is up at the brewery on the hill. If they find her or not, he said, they are meeting at The Dugout at five for the meeting."

At least the mayor knew enough to gather them back in before darkness fell. According to Max, the witches planned to waltz right into The Dugout and steal the enchanted emerald. If they managed to get the stone they'd be one step closer to doing even more dark magic, with more damning consequences, to even more innocent people.

The young nurse paused, then continued, her voice lower, "But Morgan, have you heard the whispers? No one is going into the woods. No one wants to be alone. The search is half-hearted, at best. Everyone is too afraid. Afraid of… whatever those things are, those—those monsters, coming out of the forest once the sun goes down. Someone told me, they said that you saw one—

Do you think that's what got Doctor Williams? Right here in the hospital?"

Morgan took the nurse by the shoulders. She looked in her eyes. "Listen, I need you to pull it together, okay? Doctor Williams is gone. It doesn't matter why. She's gone. So, you and Maria are in charge of the hospital now. I need you to get Maria and the two of you are going to take all the patients, and their family members and bring them all into the basement. Once you have everyone down there and you see that full moon rising over the pines, you lock the door, and don't unlock it for anyone. Blockade yourselves in there. Do not come out until morning. You understand?"

The nurse nodded, murmuring, "So they are real? You have seen them?"

Morgan answered, "Yes, they are real." She stepped away from the nurse, then said, "I'm going to stop them, but I need you to protect everyone while I do, okay?"

"How can you stop them?"

Morgan let the question linger in the air, then answered, "Just do your job, and I'll find a way to do mine."

She didn't wait for any further push back. She turned and ran down the hallway, toward the main entrance.

As she ran, she thought. Morgan didn't want to use fear to get the remainder of the town to safety. But she didn't have time for any other tactic. She needed everyone to gather back at The Dugout immediately. She pushed through the front doors onto the hospital landing.

The sun had dropped behind the mountains. The shadows of the night were growing, the sky fading fast from twilight purple to inky black. Morgan still wore her navy-blue rain jacket over her purple scrubs. While she stood at the top of the landing, debating what to do next, the wind whipped at the jacket, blowing it behind her, slapping against itself. She glanced back at her reflection in the glass doors.

With the hood tossed back as it was, and the wind gusting as it was, the dark blue rain jacket looked for all the world like a high collared cloak.

Vampiric, almost.

She frowned. She couldn't think about her father now.

One fact she knew was true. If she didn't get all the rescuers back to the Dugout, they'd still be near the woods by the time the moon rose. Considering she saw dozens of folks at the far edges of town, she doubted they'd all make it back by five. If they didn't, some would undoubtedly go missing themselves.

Morgan decided she needed to send a message, to everyone still out searching, that it was time to retreat.

She stepped down off the landing, entering into the calf-high water that flooded the street. She waded down two blocks, slower than she liked, and then stepped up off the street, out of the water and onto a bench. Only yards away from the bell tower, at the old brick church, the bench was high enough to be out of the water and close enough to execute her plan.

Many years ago, since the church sat silent for so long, the inner shaft and solid iron sphere had been removed from within the crown of the bell, effectively muting it. Morgan concentrated and lifted a large chunk of asphalt with her mind, then sent it flying up at the bell. At the same time she cast a brilliant ball of green and gold light into the air. The bell rang out, loud, reverberating, drawing everyone's attention back toward the center of the town. A moment later her magical firework exploded, green and gold explosions of energy spiraling outward, looking more fiercely destructive than jubilantly festive.

She heard shouts, then saw two men come wading into the street nearby.

She yelled, "Tell the others, we need to get to The Dugout, now!"

One of the men shouted something down the road behind them. The other just pushed on, wading up the next street, heading for the hill road that would take him up to The Dugout.

A few minutes later, as Morgan waded in the same general direction, she heard a mechanical rumbling coming up behind her. Sheriff Jeffrey, driving someone's lifted four-wheel drive truck, honked his horn at her. Three other men, including brewer Phillip, sat in the bed of the truck already.

Jeffrey rolled down his window, said, "Coming up to the brewery for the town meeting, Morgan? Will the injured folks at the hospital be alright with both you and Dr. Williams gone?"

"They'll be better off than the rest of us…" Morgan murmured, wading toward the truck stopped in the middle of the street.

"Sorry, what's that?"

"The other nurses have it under control," Morgan said, louder now. "I need to be at The Dugout with everyone else."

Jeffrey shrugged. "Alright then, hop in." Morgan stepped onto the back tire, Philip grabbed her wrist and she climbed into the bed of the truck.

****

October Thirtieth, 5:09 p.m.

The Dugout parking lot was packed. Philip told her, earlier in the day, before the river breached, they had hatched the plan to move as many cars up to the Dugout lot as possible, since it was situated at a higher elevation than most of the town.

With the power still out, and the remaining sunlight fading fast, Morgan could only see the flicker of candles and the beams of flashlights inside the brewery.

Along with an eerie green glow.

A *familiar* eerie green glow, the same that Vexulta emanated when she caught Vlad Cosmin. Morgan shook off the shiver running down her back and hopped off the back of the truck into the gravel lot.

Jeffrey, Philip, Morgan, and two other men walked up to the sliding glass door. It did not open. No power.

Duh.

Philip gripped the edges, pulled, and slid open the door. Flashlight beams blinded them. Morgan lifted her hand to cover her eyes.

"Guys! We've talked about this! Put the flashlights down!" Craig's voice echoed over the dull sounds of many people having many conversations. "Over here!" Craig called.

Jeffrey, Morgan, and Philip pushed through the crowd toward the sound of Craig's voice. Morgan heard the slithering whispers of gossip and conspiracy spreading through the townspeople as she walked past them. Rumors about her had been spreading, apparently, all day long.

When they reached Craig, Morgan saw he was

standing with Mayor Fraser, both men in front of the shattered boulder. Craig had tossed a sheet over the boulder, but the green glow from within still leaked out through the cloth. Craig grabbed Morgan's shoulder, pulled her to him, hugged her. "I thought you were gone, too. I don't suppose you have any idea what happened to Dr. Williams?"

Craig, Jeffrey, Fraser, and Philip all looked at Morgan. Expectant.

"No," Morgan said, eyes turning down.

Still lying, Morgan?

Father's voice in her head.

Or still hiding?

She hated how her most vulnerable thoughts always came to her in his voice. Even her inner dialogue couldn't shake off the horrible influence of him. Escaping him and hiding in the small, sleepy town of Pineville… it didn't help her at all.

She couldn't escape him. The same way she couldn't outrun who she really was.

It turned out, wherever she went, she'd always be haunted by her father. The same way Pineville had always been haunted. Until the monster was vanquished, no matter how far you ran, the monster would always be out there, threatening to find you.

The further you run, the deeper in the shadows that you hide, the more you disguise your own self, the worse the anxiety, the greater the fear, the more drawn-out the pain when the truth eventually catches up.

"Actually, yes," Morgan said, looking back up, meeting Craig's eyes. The others stared at her. "Yes, I think I do know what happened to Dr. Williams. And I do know what has been attacking folks… what has been emerging from the woods. I saw what killed Tom Crawford."

Morgan paused.

She heard something.

No, she felt it.

In the distance, threads of magic were vibrating, recoiling from something as it crashed toward The Dugout.

They were coming.

She was out of time.

She climbed up onto the half of the bar that was still standing. She shouted over the noise in the taproom.

"Hey! I have something to say!"

Some flashlight beams aimed toward her, spotlighting her standing above everyone else on the bar, but many others continued to talk.

Mayor Fraser climbed onto the bar next to Morgan, stuck two fingers in his mouth, and whistled loudly.

"Everybody! Listen up! We've had a hell of a day, and you all need to pat yourselves on the back. You've done an awe-inspiring job. I couldn't be prouder to call you all my neighbors. In times of crisis, after natural disasters, I find that Americans, especially Virginians, of all sex and race, show their true colors. Today, each and every one of us all bled red, white, and blue. Give yourselves a hand."

Morgan frowned. There was no time for damn political speeches, especially vain ones angling for reelection. But the town members were clapping and shaking each other's hands, smiling, and clinking their drinks together. The mayor was covered in grime, his button-down shirt was rolled up to his elbows. He wasn't campaigning. He was leading them. Inspiring them.

Building up some hope and confidence. Somehow, he knew Morgan was about to drop the other shoe. He wanted the townsfolk to be able to handle the news.

"But I'd be lying if I said the worst was behind us. Amongst all the hard work done today, I also heard a lot of gossiping. A lot of whispering about some rather dark, fantastical, horrific things. It should come as no surprise to anyone in this building that we've had at least three homicides in the past month. At least two of which have been caused by violent animal attacks. Today, Dr. Vickie Williams went missing from the hospital. We haven't seen her since. She's not the type of woman to run away. I… I don't know what happened to her. We don't know what animals could be behind these attacks. The truth is, we don't really know anything at all that's been occurring in the valley these last few nights. But I know who does. I spoke with her this morning, and I think she has more to say to us tonight. I won't waste any more time. Morgan Reaves has something she wants to tell you all. I'll let her take it from here."

Murmurs and whispers buzzed through the crowd, but they were quickly silenced. All the flashlights were aimed at her. Morgan blinked in the bright light, squinting a little to see the people standing in front of her.

Morgan saw many familiar faces in the crowd. Maud, the sheriff's office receptionist. Christina, the woman who ran the doggy daycare. The kind older lady who owned Balto and Tyson, Morgan still couldn't recall her name. Charlie, the Vietnam veteran. And right in front of her, staring up at her, Craig, Philip, and Sheriff Jeffrey.

They all looked at her.

For answers.

She drew in golden threads of power, flicking her fingers at her side, feeling the strength of that magic building within her. Her nerves didn't disappear, but her confidence grew. She was Morgan, the protector of this town. She'd come here with a purpose, even if she didn't know that purpose way back then.

Gaia had guided her to this moment. Her grandmother spoke of Gaia like an ancestor spirit, someone who looked over the world, and blessed certain individuals with gifts. Morgan had never really believed her magical awareness and ability came from some spirit like that. But as she stood on the bar, looking out at the hopeful faces of the town, she knew Gaia had brought her here. For this very moment. To defend Gaia's enchanted emerald. And to defend the people of Pineville.

She felt another ripple in the threads around the brewery. The pack was getting closer.

"Werewolves," Morgan said, letting the word hang in the air. A couple of townspeople chuckled, but most remained deathly silent. The laughter choked itself out.

"Werewolves have been gathering, right here in the forests around Pineville. They attacked Joey and I, before attacking and killing Sandy. They killed my friend Tom Crawford last night. That other body you've heard people whispering about? The one that can't be identified, because the head is gone? That was a werewolf, killed by shooting silver bullets into its skull. After death, it transformed back to its human form. The werewolves are coming back, in force, tonight. They are being led by a coven of evil witches, and they are coming right here, to The Dugout. To steal an enchanted emerald."

"She's lost it!"

"Fraser, get her off the bar!"

A timid, raspy voice cut across the deeper shouts of the men, "She's not lying!"

Everyone turned their heads, looking for the speaker.

Ronnie Greenburg stood up in the very back of the crowd. He barely lifted his head, and his greasy black hair hung down over his face. He looked very rough, the way a man looks when they've been on the run. Morgan thought he had skipped town, and so did the police.

Sheriff Jeffrey said, the Cajun drawl in his voice as strong as ever, "Ronnie, son, you and I need to have a talk."

Ronnie said, "I know, sheriff. But I have to say something first. A month ago, I got involved in all of this craziness. I still don't know what's all real and what's just been put into my head. But I know one thing for sure. I've seen one of these werewolves. I watched this out-of-towner transform into one at the gas station. At first I thought he was having a seizure or something, then—then… his body starts to—just, like, rip apart. On its own. His skin splits and his bones jut out, and then fur starts shooting out—When he stood up, he was huge, more wolf-like than human. Werewolf is the only way to describe it."

Morgan said, "Thank you, Ronnie."

The boy added, "I thought I had gone fucking crazy. I thought I'd finally dropped one too many tabs—"

"Alright, that's enough," Mayor Fraser cut in. "Look, Morgan—"

"As hard as this all may be to believe, I'm afraid it

383

is true." Morgan reached down and yanked the sheet off the boulder. The soft green glow transformed into a bright green floodlight, shining across the entirety of the taproom.

A few in the crowd gasped, the rest broke into conversations.

Morgan tossed the sheet back over the gem, continued speaking, her voice strong, cutting off any other side conversations. "That is what they want. That is what they are coming after. That is why they brought the werewolves here. They caused the earthquake last night, and during the quake the boulder split, revealing that ancient jewel at its heart. It's imbibed with magic in a way I don't understand. But I do know it's dangerous, and if Hailey, the witches' leader, gets her hands on it, she'll be unstoppable. And she won't be a threat just to us and our small town here in the valley. She'll be a danger to everyone. If we don't stop them—"

"Stop them?"

"How the hell can we stop werewolves?"

The whole crowd began shouting, arguing breaking out amongst them. Morgan had lost them. If they wouldn't listen, they wouldn't believe and if they didn't believe, they wouldn't prepare. They had mere minutes left. If they weren't ready for what was coming, they were doomed. They all were.

Mayor Fraser began to speak, "Now listen, folks, she may—"

Morgan cut him off. She wouldn't give up on the town, even if they would want to burn her at the stake after this was all over. She didn't need the mayor, or any man for that matter, to manage the crowd for her.

If they wouldn't believe what she said until they saw

it for themselves, so be it.

Her house was burnt to the ground. Her husband was dead. Her boss and best friend kidnapped and probably killed. And still, Morgan tried to hide who she truly was from the world. She kept the truth even from Max, who told her everything about his own secret life.

If she had revealed herself to him, that first night they met, together they may have resolved this issue before it ever came to this point.

She wouldn't miss any more chances to make things right.

No more.

No more lying.

No more hiding.

In through the nose, out through the mouth.

Morgan finally accepted the zigzagging Fire threads inside her body again, felt them racing through her veins, swirling, intermixing with Air and Water and Earth magic.

Morgan added a touch of deep Earth magic to her lungs when she spoke, adding unnatural volume and bass to her voice, ensuring she would gain the town people's full attention.

"Listen to me! What I say is true. I know it because I was there. I was with them. I'm as much to blame as the other three witches. We fought the werewolves in the parking lot after they ambushed and killed Tom Crawford. We caused the earthquake last night, during a ritual of magic that had unintended consequences. I know their magic is real, and I know we can stop it."

Morgan felt the coursing Fire threads, bouncing excitedly through her veins, seeking an exit.

"How?"

"Why should we believe you?"

"How can we stop them?"

She looked up from her hands, her eyes burning into the crowd. She lifted her left hand out in front of her, twirled her fingers in an elaborate dance, then snapped.

"I'm a witch, like them."

In the palm of her hand she conjured a pulsing blue ball of Water magic, and she spun it, and as it rotated she traced golden swirls of Air around it, then added vines of green Earth magic and flaming red meteors of Fire magic.

She felt the pack, then. Racing up out of the flood waters. Climbing the hill to the brewery.

Morgan glanced out the window. Above the eastern mountains, rising above the pines, an orange full moon rose into the sky.

They were out of time.

Morgan shot the roiling, multi-colored sphere into the air where it grew into a four-colored dome that encapsulated the entire taproom.

"They are here. And that shield will not protect us for long."

The crowd was stone quiet. A pin drop would shatter the silence. Morgan wondered if they'd call for her to be burned at the stake.

Mayor Fraser had taken two steps away from her, his heels almost entirely off the edge of the bar.

He took a deep breath, and spoke, his voice wavering only slightly, "Okay, Morgan. What do you want us to do?"

Morgan pulled the bar and coins of silver from her pockets.

Chapter 33

October Thirtieth, 5:59 p.m.

Maximum Grim brought the pack to a halt at the top of the hill. Sniffing cautiously, he took a few strides forward into the gravel parking lot.

They might have set traps.

But he didn't smell any treachery. He didn't smell any defenses at all.

From within the brewery, Grim smelt barley and yeast and hops, and lots of sweat. And fear. And a dash of silver, but hardly enough to be worried about.

His pack was two dozen strong, almost half of the pack true werewolves, the other half wild timber wolves, slowly having made their way from Wyoming to Virginia. Not to mention, he had the witch-werewolf at his side and the two witches flying on brooms above the pack to count amongst his own.

During their run to The Dugout, Grim had tried to make connections with his packmates. He exchanged sniffs with werewolves and wolves alike. He snarled at the few presumptuous enough to question his leadership, and they quickly fell back in line. He felt a connection to many of them already. A responsibility to protect them.

A responsibility to feed them.

The orange-furred werewolf, his equal at the head of the pack, stepped next to him and growled questioningly.

Grim wasn't sure why she growled, he didn't smell anything unusual…

A ball of multi-colored light expanded suddenly around the taproom. Shades of blue, red, green, and gold glimmered in the night air. Grim stepped back, wary.

—*Magic*.—

Werewolves hated magic. The orange werewolf snapped her teeth, growling. She stepped forward, her fur melted, her shape shrank and twisted.

Hailey stood before Grim. She wore her leather bomber jacket, her whip and her pistol hung at her hip. In her hand she carried the ruby wand.

She chuckled, murmuring to herself, "She still thinks she stands a chance…" Turning above her left shoulder, she called up to Vera, "Bring down the doctor."

Vera soared down, dismounting off her broom, shoving Vickie Williams onto the ground.

"*Mi amor*—" Vera began, but Hailey cut her off.

"No *mi amor*'s tonight, Vera. We've come too far now for your *mi amor*s."

She pointed her wand at Vickie. "Get up. I want you to tell the town something."

****

October Thirtieth, 6:11 p.m.

Everyone in the brewery watched as Vickie stumbled toward them. With the full moon rising above the pines, the silhouette of the entire pack could be seen behind her.

It did not look promising.

The werewolves were spread out in a line along the ground, at least a dozen of them, interspersed by wild wolves. The wolves were massive in their own right, their shoulders surely measured up to Morgan's chest. But compared to the werewolves that stood at least eight feet in height, they seemed miniscule. Morgan saw pointed ears above hulking shoulders, lined against the orange backdrop of the moon. She picked out the smallest, leanest werewolf, and the tallest, most muscular werewolf, both standing near the center, near Hailey.

The two werewolves *could* be Abornazine and Grim.

Maybe it was just wishful thinking. From her distance, she couldn't be sure.

Dr. Williams made it within fifty yards of the brewery doors. She paused there. Morgan hoped she wasn't injured, or hypnotized, but she couldn't be sure. She doubted Hailey would let her off without inflicting some sort of sick pain upon her.

Vickie called toward the brewery.

"Whoever is in there. They say whoever leaves now, whoever goes back down to the town, they'll let you leave. They'll stop the werewolves from hunting you and—from eating you. They say… They say now is your last chance to go. If you stay, they'll let the beasts…" She looked behind her shoulder. Morgan saw Hailey nod her head, encouraging Vickie to continue. "If you stay, they'll let the werewolves eat you alive."

Morgan looked to her right. Mayor Fraser and Sheriff Jeffrey looked back at Morgan. They were scared. But they were committed. Mayor Fraser rubbed the tattoo spot on his chest. The sheriff swallowed but held his handgun ready at his side. The gun hung steady, still. Not trembling.

Morgan looked to her left. Craig and Philip stood

alongside her, looking out at Vickie.

Craig whispered to Morgan, "I'm sorry. I take it back."

"What do you mean? You can't trust them, Craig. If you leave, they'll kill you."

"No, no, I mean, I take it back, I don't recommend joining their grief group."

Morgan cracked a smile. "Good idea. I think I'll just drink with you two after all this is over."

Philip said, "If the brewery survives, you mean."

"The saloon always makes it," Craig said, grinding his molars together. "The saloon endures."

Morgan nodded. "Thanks, guys, for staying."

"We're with you, Morgan. Blaze of glory, if it has to be. Besides, that's *my* fucking emerald."

"Our emerald," Philip muttered.

Craig smiled.

Morgan looked behind her.

Ronnie gave her a shaky thumbs up. Charlie saluted. The woman who owned Balto and Tyson smiled at her. "We're not going anywhere. We've got your back, Morgan," she said. "We always have."

Mayor Fraser said, "Go save Doctor Williams, Morgan. And we'll make sure, no matter what happens—"

"We won't let them get the emerald," Craig muttered. "Not in our saloon, they won't."

Morgan pushed open the sliding glass door.

In through the nose, out through the mouth.

She felt a sudden retraction of magic from the air around her. Earth, Fire, Air, and Water threads all pulled away from her, sucked toward the other witches. The glistening shield stayed in place, but the rest of the magic, the untapped threads of power, vanished.

Morgan looked toward Hailey. Even from fifty yards away, Morgan could see what she was doing.

She held her Arch wand in the air, and in front of her a tornado of magical energy began to swirl. She was sucking it all up with her ruby wand and dumping it into the cyclone. Vera and Ash floated on their brooms above her, watching.

Hailey had created a magical sink. In essence, a swirling magnet that could draw in and burn off nearly unlimited amounts of power. Morgan reached out, tried to access the violently spinning threads of magic from inside the tornado, but they were too strong, too chaotic.

She couldn't sense them individually, couldn't identify them.

She stood at the edge of her shield. Unable to refill her magic within her. A pack of werewolves and wild wolves encircled her. The town watched from the windows.

Hailey grabbed the handle of her whip in her left hand and snapped it out in front of her, igniting it with a burning, molten-lava-dripping dose of Fire magic. She could still access the threads of magic thanks to the ruby Arch wand. Morgan remembered the way the Air wand had been able to refill itself without prompt. The ruby wand could do that too, with exponentially more magical storage.

Morgan inhaled sharply through her nose. Spat onto the ground. She knew it wouldn't be easy.

Stick to the plan.

She stepped through her own shimmering shield, exposing herself to them. She gave Vickie a hopeful smile, felt the cautious hope bubble into the doctor's aura.

Morgan closed her eyes for a moment, felt the magic within her, the magic she'd drawn in before the witches had sucked it all away.

Without realizing she was doing it, Morgan began to lift into the air.

She floated up, and as she did, she felt the aura of the townspeople behind her. Wonder and awe and optimism bubbled out from the brewery walls. Morgan sensed the hope and prayers being sent toward her. It wasn't a source of magic, per se, but it buffeted the magic she already had within her. Strengthened her abilities.

Morgan never really needed the broom to fly, she realized, the same way she didn't need the wand to cast spells. It was only a conduit, an inanimate object that could be imbued with magic.

It was Gaia's magic that actually lifted Morgan. And Morgan herself became the conduit. She could touch the Source, directly, the way her grandmother had taught her.

Suddenly, Morgan felt the golden threads of Air magic in the cyclone. Identified them and ripped them out.

Morgan hung in the moonlit sky, silvery lunar rays beaming down on her, her navy-blue raincoat billowing out behind her. She sensed the golden threads rushing toward her, then felt them race within her, felt them available for her to use however she wanted.

She pumped magic up toward her face, and into the tips of her fingers. Luminous, golden light, bright as sunshine, bled from her eyes. Her fingers glowed so bright that they seemed transformed into golden claws.

She floated forward, toward the pack of

werewolves. Toward Hailey, Vera, and Ash.

When she came almost even with Vickie on the ground below her, Hailey called out, Irish accent thick with malice and bravado, "Are you sure you want to do this, Morgan?"

Ash said, "There's room for one more in the coven. Four Enchanted jewels. Four Arch wands. Are these people really worth dying for? They stand for everything that has corrupted Gaia's perfect world. They are letting her rot! Why save them?"

Morgan dropped to the ground, descending suddenly between Vickie and the witches.

"Run," Morgan urged, jaw tight.

Vickie sprinted.

Hailey snarled, and in a flash she transformed back to the massive orange werewolf, launching herself headlong toward Morgan, still carrying a Fire enchanted whip in a massive paw. Vera and Ash both launched unfocused spells at Vickie, trying to stop her from escaping.

Morgan reached out her hand, pulled the girl's spells off target and into her. She twirled her fingers, drank in their foolish gift of power.

The orange werewolf snarled in anger, cracking out the fiery whip.

Morgan raised her hands just in time, dumped magic into a brilliant golden shield to block the whip strike.

Hailey, the witch-werewolf, drew up in front of Morgan, standing almost twice her size. She lifted her snout in the air and howled.

The rest of the werewolves charged.

Morgan only had so much magic in her veins, and she'd used almost all of it on her golden shield.

She felt weak at the knees.

She glanced behind her. Vickie crossed inside the safety of the magic dome. Craig was pulling her into the taproom doors.

Stick to the plan.

In through the nose, out through the mouth.

Morgan raised her hands, dumping the last of her magic into the shield. She braced the glimmering gold with rivets of Fire and Water magic, repurposing the girls' magic into her own defense.

The orange werewolf spoke, voice monstrous and evil, half Hailey's Irish accent, half some other monster entirely. "I'll smash your futile shield into splinters of magical shard so small you'll never find them again, and then I'll eat your heart out of your chest."

She lifted her fiery whip into the air, preparing to slash it down onto Morgan again.

Maximum Grim took the end of the whip into his massive jaws, yanked it, and pulled Hailey backward, wrenching the orange werewolf's arm almost out of her shoulder socket. She spun around, and the giant black werewolf was upon her, snarling, snapping white fangs, slashing her with massive claws. Fiery orange fur tumbled with midnight black.

The rest of the wolfpack turned on each other, encircling Cailleach, the monster's true name, and Grim, ripping and tearing and biting each other.

Chaos.

Ash and Vera paused above the scrum of blood and claws and fangs. They hesitated, unsure how to help.

Morgan did not hesitate. She transformed her shield into two cannon balls connected by a golden chain.

She blasted the spell at them, knocked both of them

off their brooms. They crashed hard onto the ground. Morgan raced over to them, dodging past two snapping werewolves.

"Still sure you're on the right side, ladies?" Morgan asked, kneeling down next to the two witches. "You can still help me stop this craziness."

Vera said, "She'll take our wands, Morgan. And kill us too. *No puedes detenerla*. You can't stop her. Even Vexulta couldn't stop her."

Morgan lifted their wands from the ground. She detected a moderate amount of magic within them.

Ash spat at Morgan, "Sometimes you have to do the bad things, Morgan, for good results. One day, I'll be more powerful than any witch, and I'll restore—"

She flicked the wand and plastered a green gag around Ash's mouth. "That's enough out of you." She looked at Vera. "You could have been my sister. Instead, you chose enslavement to a tyrant." Morgan cast a gag around her mouth.

She filled her veins with the remainder of the magic in the wands, then snapped them in two. "Just fancy broken sticks, now." She flicked the sticks onto the ground and turned back to the werewolf scrum.

Things seemed to be going… riotously. The bulk of the wolves and the werewolves still fought, circled around Cailleach. Two dead wolves lay at either side of her.

She transformed back to her human form, ruby wand in hand, and shouted, "Enough!"

A massive shock wave of energy blasted the werewolves away from her.

The creatures were all flung backward, half of them transforming in mid-air back to humans. The humans hit the ground and did not move. Morgan raced back toward the taproom.

"Come on, Max! Abornazine!"

Hailey slashed her wand toward different werewolves, each strike knocking the creature out and transforming them back to humans.

She struck at Max and Abornazine multiple times, but Morgan shielded the two from each blow, casting Air, Fire, and Water magic into little shields to protect the two werewolves she knew were on her side.

Hailey raged, sending strike after strike and Morgan depleted her magic faster than she could refill it into herself. Max and Abornazine raced unharmed through the shimmering shield, Morgan right behind them. When she made it through, she turned and watched the evil, red-headed witch approach them.

Hailey strode right up to the shield and sneered at Morgan and the two werewolves that had betrayed her.

"This will not keep you safe for long. You don't have the strength to maintain it. That emerald will be mine."

Morgan swallowed. Her eyes flashed toward the big black werewolf at her side. He growled defiantly at the witch outside the bubble.

Morgan turned and walked back toward the taproom. Max and Abornazine followed her.

Chapter 34

October Thirtieth, 6:43 p.m.

Craig stumbled back from the two werewolves when they entered. Maximum Grim snarled at Craig but did not strike out at him or any of the other humans inside.

Grim felt defeated. He'd failed most of his pack. He and Abornazine may have survived their betrayal of Hailey, may have saved the doctor and Morgan, but they'd lost the rest. Either killed or knocked out, transformed back to humans, laying scattered outside the taproom. The few wolves left alive had fled, retreating back into the forest.

"You're sure these… things are on our side?" Philip asked.

Morgan answered, "I'm sure."

Grim stalked to the far corner of the bar, humans leaping for cover as he strode past. He saw Ronnie, glared at him until the boy ducked his head in shame. Grim stomped around in a circle a few times, then laid down, curled into a ball, and watched the humans.

"Is it ready?" Morgan asked. "We rescued Vickie, took out the two lesser witches, but Hailey is still out there, and she won't be kept out for much longer. I think I've bought us about as much time as I can."

"It's ready," Philip said, pulling a glowing green gem from behind the bar. He'd crudely attached it to one of the wooden tap handles using a lot of duct tape and twine. The handle gleamed, the wood freshly oiled. In flowing brown cursive, it read 'Pineville Porter.'

"Sorry," Philip said, "it's a little ugly. I didn't have time—"

"It's perfect," Morgan said. She took it into her hands, and her whole body shivered. "Wow," she said, after composing herself. "I can see why she wants this so bad."

Mayor Fraser placed his hand on Morgan's shoulder. "We've also decided who will be the ones to help you. The ones to strike her down."

"Who?"

"Me." Jeffrey was loading bullets into his duty revolver. For an older, slightly overweight man, his fingers moved with practiced dexterity. In his Cajun drawl he added, "I swore an oath, no *sorcière* will enchant my town while I'm on duty."

"And me. It's our civic duty, after all, to protect the public." Fraser rubbed the tattoo spot on his chest. "It's why I'm still here, I think."

Maximum Grim felt Max's consciousness awakening inside him.

You did fantastic, Grim.

The werewolf grumbled in response.

—I failed my pack.—

These people are your pack, too. You didn't fail them.

The werewolf blinked slowly, looking at Abornazine, who panted and wheezed in the other corner, then scanned the humans in the taproom.

—They are your pack, Maximilian.—

OUR *pack.*

The werewolf stretched, front paws reaching out, razor sharp claws scratching the wooden floor. Grim wanted to return to the action. Waiting around for humans to talk was tedious.

Morgan glanced again at Grim.

Grim felt that she, at least, was in his pack.

"Morgan," Craig said, from his lookout spot, "Somethings moving out there."

Morgan nodded. Grim stood from his place in the corner. The time for his revenge upon the evil witch was at hand. The werewolf snarled at no one in particular and leapt toward the door.

Abornazine followed him.

Grim didn't fully understand the human's plan. But he understood his role. Morgan and the humans would out-magic Hailey if they could. Grim and Abornazine would keep Cailleach in check if she transformed into the orange werewolf. They wouldn't let her escape if she tried to flee. They would pin her down if they could.

Or they would die trying.

—*So be it.*—

****

October Thirtieth, 7:02 p.m.

Morgan hefted the emerald Arch wand in her hand. The magic contained within the stone felt unnatural. Felt almost infinite. She couldn't imagine how she could cast magic rapidly enough to drain the thing faster than it could refill its reservoir. The whirling cyclone of magic still spun, eating up the available magic in the area, still cutting off her direct access to Fire, Earth, and Water. But it didn't bother the emerald Arch wand.

Maximum Grim, Abornazine, Mayor Fraser, and

Sheriff Jeffrey stepped out into the night. All traces of the last light from the sun had vanished. It had grown chillier. The moon was higher in the sky.

Hailey was nowhere to be found.

"She'll be here," Morgan murmured. "She won't give up this chance."

Sure enough, moments later, Hailey emerged from the woods edge, at the far side of the parking lot. But she wasn't Hailey anymore. She was something… different. Something seemed off about her appearance. Every few steps, her form would *flicker*. She snapped from human to something… unnatural. Her shape would grow skinnier and taller. Far, far taller. Her legs stretched, almost like they were becoming long, thin, tree trunks.

Her face, too, *flickered*. For half-an-instant her smooth, freckled skin and her rounded cheeks would shudder and be replaced by an elongated, antlered deer skull. As she walked closer the monstrous wendigo-like creature became more and more visible. The human witch was the illusion. The werewolf form and the human form, both were disguises.

Morgan saw the truth, as it staggered toward them.

The real witch creature was a ten-foot monster, legs gray and ghastly and elongated, arms like tree branches, fingers nine-inch-long wooden daggers. Her head, an abomination, a rotten fusion a deer skull and a vulture's face. Only her eyes remained the same between her forms. No longer emerald green.

Burning, blood-red.

Fraser trembled at Morgan's elbow. He'd kept his composure through it all, until now. Until the monster staggered toward them. Hailey knew fear was her most powerful weapon.

The pair of werewolves crouched low, snarls building in their throat. Jeffrey's set of keys began to jingle, he shook so hard.

Morgan breathed, "Don't fear her. Stick to the plan." She lifted the emerald wand above her head. "Come and get it!"

The monster snapped her form back to that of Hailey, the thick, red headed, Irish witch. "Don't be afraid, boys," she said, voice silky and playful. "When I bite, you'll like it. Just ask Max." She winked, then rushed forward, unnaturally quick.

Her whip uncoiled and flicked out first, striking the magical shimmering shield that still protected the taproom. A crack in the shield splintered outward from the impact. A blast from Hailey's wand, a direct hit on the crack in the glimmering bubble, brought the whole shield crumbling down.

Hailey's speed was abnormal, her accuracy uncanny. As her form *flickered*, she seemed to move in double-time. Morgan countered each strike from the ruby wand with her own emerald wand, but there was no confusing who was the more adept wand-wielding witch. Morgan didn't stand a chance.

Luckily, she counted on that.

She struck out, sending a spell far off course, missing Hailey by many feet.

"Haven't been practicing your aim?" Cailleach cackled, no longer disguising her reverberating, croaking voice.

The spinning tornado erupted, the magic dispersing back into the night air.

Morgan dropped the Arch wand.

She drew in the threads of power on her own, as her

grandmother taught her. Fire, Earth, Water, and Air. They were all around her now. She drew them in, flooded her veins with their power.

Morgan lashed out, at once, not waiting for Cailleach to respond. She sent a wave of Water to engulf the burning whip. Green and red and gold chains lashed around the wendigo's body, massive stakes hammered themselves into the ground, holding the monster in place.

She writhed. Her form flickered.

Orange furred werewolf.

Human.

Wendigo monster.

Human.

"Now," Morgan called between gritted teeth. It took all her concentration to keep the magic flowing through her, to keep the chains wrapped around Hailey as she attempted to slough them off.

The massive black werewolf leapt toward the creature.

She abandoned her other forms. The Wendigo Queen, Cailleach, stood before them, screeching, writhing. Her long arms slashed out; Max dodged the claws but was struck by the thick forearm. He tumbled backward. Landed on his paws. Abornazine drew next to him.

One of the chains sizzled, nearly snapping, but Morgan groaned, dumped even more magic into the chains, holding the monster's body in place. The witch shook her massive boney antlers toward Max and Abornazine, but they were undeterred.

Together this time, the werewolves charged. They dodged past her swinging claws, slipped under her stabbing antlers, and each grabbed a branch-arm at the wrist, clamping down with all their strength. They tugged and pulled and brought her down to her knees.

"Jeffrey!"

The sheriff stepped forward, key's still jangling, gun wobbling wildly. Cailleach's eyes sparkled, seeing an opportunity. Her face transformed back to Hailey's face. Back to the angelic, human disguise. Her body was still all Wendigo, dysmorphic and ghastly, and so the human face looked even more vile than the skull and antlers. But Hailey's eyes twinkled from burning, raging red back to piney green, and she smiled and her nose crinkled.

"Don't look her in the eyes!"

Jeffrey froze.

The witch spoke. "Sheriff, your soul is mine. Don't you want to help me? Shoot the beasts."

The gun wobbled, then turned ever so slightly toward the black werewolf still holding the long, clawed arm in its jaws.

Morgan shouted, "No!" but she couldn't move. It took all her power to restrain the witch in her magical chains. Morgan's body was anchored to the ground by a pillar of magic. If she moved, if she so much as flinched, the spell would be undone and the chains would evaporate.

Craig tackled Jeffrey. He'd appeared out of nowhere. The gun fired wildly into the air above Maximum Grim's head. The pistol tumbled away from the sheriff and Mayor Fraser leapt for it.

Craig punched Jeffrey in the forehead and the sheriff fell limp to the ground. "I guess I wanted to be the hero after all," Craig murmured, standing over the no-longer-hypnotized sheriff.

Mayor Fraser scooped up the gun and leaned on one

knee. Rubbed his chest. Aimed the gun level at the Wendigo and pulled the trigger.

A silver bullet smashed into Cailleach's shoulder. The hole it left behind began to belch purple smoke.

Fraser fired again, four more times.

The bullets plunged into the witch's torso, sizzling as they penetrated her elongated, bark-like, skeletal frame. Each hole in the body began emitting toxic, purple smoke.

The witch screeched.

Morgan felt the magical efforts to escape the chains weaken, and then die out completely.

"Finish her," Morgan gritted, maintaining her chains. She wouldn't put it beyond the witch to fake her death.

The bulk of the silver Morgan had brought with her to The Dugout had been magically melded into a six-inch-long dagger. The remainder was used to coat the bullets for Jeffrey's handgun.

Mayor Fraser pulled the dagger from his waist. He strode toward the witch. Abornazine and Maximum Grim kept their grip around the long arms, tugging the dangerous claws away from the vulnerable human. Morgan focused on keeping the witch restrained, ensuring she kept the flow of magic coming from the night air, into her veins, grounding her to her spot and then out into the chains.

Morgan remembered the night before, when Hailey had picked up one of the silver bullets she'd used to kill the werewolf in the parking lot and showed it to Morgan. It had sizzled and smoked in Hailey's fingers, and she claimed it was because it was still hot. But Morgan had seen the way she picked it up, the way it *began* sizzling when it touched the witch's skin. Bullets don't sizzle from the heat of being fired. Not even silver ones. No, the witch had been allergic to it, the same way the werewolves were. There was a powerful sort of magic imbued in silver.

Morgan saw fear in Cailleach's eyes as Fraser walked toward her, brandishing the dagger.

The witch form flickered again, this time the whole body shapeshifted back to human, save the vile arms that the werewolves still held in their jaws.

She was naked. Bleeding from slashes across her torso. Her makeup had run, her black eyeliner streaked down her cheeks. She looked pitiful.

"Please, mayor, don't. Please. I'll do anything if you help." Her eyes twinkled, she bit her lip pitifully. "Anything."

The mayor closed his eyes, murmured his daughter's name, and lifted the dagger into the air. He brought it crashing down into Cailleach's neck.

The silver dagger sunk into her flesh.

Sizzled. Smoked. The witch's head drooped to one side.

Hailey's form *flickered* again. The monster returned. Wendigo, lashing out with the spiked, bony antlers. She thrust them down at Fraser. He flinched back, dropped the dagger, but he was too slow. The antlers impaled him, piercing his neck and shoulder.

The blood red eyes returned, the Wendigo monster screeched in victory. She lifted her antlers up into the air, the limp corpse still impaled upon them. With a violent thrash, she flung Fraser's body at Abornazine, smashing it into the brown werewolf. Abornazine lost his grip on the arm and the witch-monster whipped it across her body in a flash, slashing the big black werewolf holding her other arm from hip to shoulder. Maximum Grim yelped as his massive body tumbled through the air.

Morgan felt a redoubling of effort against the chains she'd cast over the witch. With her long arms free, Cailleach drew the ruby wand from the ground in front of her, reached over and plucked up the emerald wand from the ground in front of Morgan.

She transformed again.

Hailey. Two Arch wands in her hands.

All human, confident, clothed in a shimmering green dress, leather bomber jacket around her shoulders. Her eyes glimmered, one emerald green, the other ruby red, both shining, sparkling jewels. Her makeup wasn't running now. She smoldered in her human form, and smirked as she approached.

She brandished both Arch wands, aimed them at Morgan. Morgan flinched backward and the chains around Hailey's body fell away. Morgan felt the press of immense magic around her.

She couldn't breathe. Let alone draw in any magic to fight back.

"You were clever enough to notice my weakness to silver. Something about it seems to affect all cursed beasts and demons of the world."

Hailey walked closer to Morgan as she spoke.

"For eons I'd been imprisoned on that small rock in the Atlantic Ocean. My island was a cage. Where The Fallen abandoned his youngest sister-daughter, never to return, never to bother seeing me again. I haunted the Irish, blighted their potatoes, sparked civil wars, consumed their broken souls. But Ireland was a fraction of the world. I wanted more. I wanted it all."

Hailey's smile widened.

"When human witches began looking for me, spouting nonsense and spells and babbling about folklore, I started to hear some commonalities. Some truth about the dark arts. Mythical tales of places of power, enchanted by the lost jewels of Gaia. They weren't lost, though. Gaia placed them there. To contain us. To contain her inbred, monstrous offspring. The jewels were our source of magic, you see, but they also were our prison.

"The sister-daughters can't escape their confinement, for the jewel traps them there, in their little region, where Gaia keeps them from harming the rest of the world… She never expected us to find our jewels, to harness them, and break them out of the ancient rocks she buried them in. Once I found the ruby and carved my Arch wand, I was free."

"You were never going to give the jewels to Vera or Ash," Morgan said.

"Of course not. They were a means to an end. Just as the false persona of Hailey was. Just as the doctorate and the years of academic research in America. When you live for millennia, a few decades of pretending to be someone else is nothing. What I really wanted was the rest of the Arch jewels. I had to hunt down my other sisters to find them. Sisters potentially just as powerful as me. When I found Pineville, I could sense Vexulta's presence. The Witch-Queen of the Blue Ridge. My elder sister. One on one, she could easily defeat me in a duel. I needed deception. I formed the coven, infiltrated the valley. Found out Vexulta embraced her confinement, had accepted some twisted savior role for the people here. She was starving herself of her true potential. And she had no knowledge of the enchanted Arch emerald.

"The werewolves were a distraction. A distraction for Vexulta and for Vlad Cosmin, who came to America, hunting me and hunting her. If he had his priorities right, he might have been able to stop me. But he was too bothered by the werewolves, and Vexulta. Who would think twice about the university professor, interested in a little magic and potion brewing, trying to help save a town? Vexulta didn't know until it was too late. Until I sprang my trap and stole her power and lo, and behold, you helped me beat her."

Morgan scowled.

The silver dagger was within ten yards. If she could gather just enough magic to bring it to her…

"You don't get it, Morgan. My Arch ruby is my prison. But it's also my shield. As long as my stone has power, I'm immortal. My jewel feeds me. The silver is painful, but it's not the killing blow you hoped it was."

Hailey lowered the wands toward Morgan.

Morgan felt the breeze blowing across the open field. She smelt the rain in the distance. Heard the autumn leaves rustling as they tumbled across the ground. The moon was beautiful, hung in the sky, no lights for miles to steal its luminous brilliance. She heard a faint buzzing, drawing closer.

"You were truly remarkable, for a mortal. But mortals can only do so much."

A snarling bark erupted from mid-air; Hailey flinched, jerked her wands away from Morgan. Joey buzzed out of the darkness, dragonfly wings a blur of speed, propelling his chubby canine body forward. He snapped, bit down onto Hailey's wrist.

The ruby wand fell from her hand. Morgan felt the

magic bonds loosen.

She reached for the silver dagger and the ruby Arch wand in her mind, summoned them to her.

She snatched the dagger in one hand, then grabbed the ruby Arch wand in the other. Gathering every drop of Air, Fire, Earth, and Water magic to give her strength, she drove the silver blade into the Arch ruby.

Cailleach blasted Joey with the emerald Arch wand from her other hand. The dog yelped just once, then crumpled to the ground.

Cailleach turned toward Morgan.

Her face grew pale.

The massive ruby stone was gone. Sparkles and shards of tiny red dust drifted downward in the static air.

Morgan's eyes flashed golden.

Cailleach snarled, "You vile girl."

Morgan whispered, glaring at the witch monster, "Mortal now, without your ruby to protect you."

Cailleach smirked. "Mortal, yes. But still, a sister-daughter of The Fallen. A demon versus a human. I'll bathe the townspeople in your blood and then burn them alive. That's the future you've made for Pineville."

Cailleach slashed a spell toward Morgan, the green earthen magic of the emerald Arch wand smashed into Morgan's outstretched hands. She absorbed the force, pulled the magic into herself.

"I may be human," Morgan said, "But I'm stronger than you ever were."

Cailleach scowled.

"We were never even," Morgan said. "You fought for yourself. I fought for them."

Magic coursed through her veins. Morgan felt the swirls of each strand, each unique in their own way. Each a tool for her use. Each a connection to Gaia. A thread through time and space to the first witch, Mother Earth herself. Morgan couldn't reach back in time to give life to those that were dead. But she could stop the life-sucking demon-witch from ever killing anyone again.

She shot a beam of light, four strands of magic strong, into Hailey's chest. The emerald wand couldn't deflect it all. Hailey screamed as the magic overwhelmed her. Her camouflage flickered and disappeared.

The Wendigo Queen Cailleach stood in front of her.

Gray and lean and tall, monstrous, deer skull head and antlers pressing forward against the magic, fangs jutting out of the beaked mouth.

The long arms slashed toward Morgan.

They melted in the heat of her magical aura.

The creature shrieked, an ear-piercing noise that sounded as if it could wake the dead.

Morgan found the silver dagger in her mind, lifted the blade into the air. She stretched it, elongated it, sharpened it into a silver arrow, sharp as a werewolf fang.

She pierced it into the black beating organ that the Wendigo Queen called a heart.

The monster shattered to purple and red dust, and the cold breeze of the night dispersed the dead ash into the mountain forest.

Morgan fell to her knees.

She crawled toward Joey's limp body.

As she drew close, she heard his tail thumping softly against the ground.

"Oh," Morgan whispered, "My good boy. You did so good." She took his head in her hands and the dog whimpered. She brought her face to Joey's and he extended a big wet tongue, very slowly, and splatted it against the tears on her cheek. "Oh, Joey, my good boy," Morgan said, crying into the fur on his neck. The dog's tail thumped a few more times, then fell still against the ground. He whined, and she saw the pain and the hurt in his eyes. He couldn't move his paws. His tail barely twitched. Morgan cried, tears rolling down her face, and whispered into his fur, "It's okay, boy. I'll be okay, now. You saved me. You can go, now. You've been such a good boy. Go find your daddy, I'm sure he's waiting for you. I love you, buddy."

Joey licked her again, gently, and then his heart stopped beating and his head dropped softly onto the ground.

Chapter 35

October Thirtieth, 7:49 p.m.

Max awoke in the field, a massive slash running from his hip to his shoulder blade. It had closed, a rough scab already forming over the wound. But it burned, throbbing with pulses of pain, echoing of a torture he'd endured once before. Remnants of a cursed wound. He might forever have a scar, like Abornazine.

Someone stood over him, holding a blanket. "You alright, man?"

Max grunted. Rubbed his head. He only had flashes of memories.

"Morgan!" he shouted, leaping up, despite the agony shooting through him.

"Easy, man, Morgan's okay. She beat the witch. She saved us. She's over there."

Max turned to go to her. A hand grabbed him on the shoulder. "Take these." The man held out a dirty pair of work jeans. "Not that, uh, you need to— uh, I just thought it might be—"

Max ripped the jeans out of the man's hands, pulled them on, and then jogged to Morgan. She was lying on the ground, collapsed over top of something.

"Oh," Max said, when he saw what she was holding in her arms. "Oh, no."

Two other men standing next to Morgan backed

away as Max approached. He knelt and put a hand on her shoulder. "Morgan, I'm so sorry."

She turned to him. Gripped his hand. Whispered, "He saved me. When everyone else was gone and beaten. I locked him in the hospital room. How'd he get out? How'd he find me here? How'd he know precisely when to show up?" Morgan sniffled.

She stroked his fur, but the dog was gone.

Max sat down in the dirt next to her. He rubbed Joey's lifeless ears. Whispered to Morgan, "Could you save him? Bring him back?"

Morgan stopped petting the dog. Whispered back, "Maybe I could."

Her fingers on Max's hand grew cold. The wind blew across the tops of the pines. The mountain forest seemed to dance in the autumn night. Morgan breathed in the cold air. Then she shook her head.

"But I won't. That's not right to do that. Joey deserves his peace. He earned his rest. He's with Alex now, somewhere far from here."

Max thought about the time he spent recovering after being struck and cursed by the werewolf in Transylvania. Thought about the serenity of the black beyond, and how Maximum Grim ripped him from that, ripped him back into the world of the living. Morgan was right. Joey shouldn't be brought back to be a shell of himself, like Victor Frank had been. Joey had earned his slumber.

"He was such a good dog," Morgan whispered.

"And when he passed, I'm sure all he was thinking was how proud he was, how happy he was he could protect his momma from that big bad witch."

Morgan nodded. "He was wagging his tail to the

very end." She rubbed Joey once more and then stood up.

Max stood with her, asked, "What are we going to do now?"

Morgan answered, gesturing toward the parking lot, "I know what you need to do."

Some of the human bodies splayed out across the ground were spasming and snarling, turning back into werewolves under the full moon. Many of them had been knocked out by Hailey, but few had died. Even a few wild wolves were limping back out from the woods, having run off when the pack broke into civil war, returning now, hearing the howls of the werewolves.

"Uh, Morgan?" Dr. Vickie Williams hollered from the taproom. "Are these things our friends now?"

Morgan looked questioningly at Max.

He sighed, told Morgan, "No, they aren't anyone's friends."

The werewolves weren't under any witch hypnotism any longer. But they were still feral, cursed beasts, hungry for flesh.

They needed a leader.

Max looked at Morgan. "I'll take them somewhere safe. Somewhere isolated, where they can learn to be their true selves. To try to make peace with the beast inside them." Max added softly, "We may end up far away from Pineville."

Morgan nodded. "I… understand."

Max reached out and brushed his thumb against her cheek. Felt the wetness of her tears, but also the heat of the magic within her. Felt her strength. His thumb ran along her jaw to her lips. He aimed her face up to him. He leaned down and pressed his lips to hers. She kissed him back, her lips parting, her tongue against his teeth. He ran his hand across the back of her neck, felt her autumn-scented hair tangling in his fingers and only then did he notice he had tears running down his face, same as she did.

A nearby werewolf tipped its nose toward the moon, desire and longing and pain reverberating out in the long howl.

Morgan pulled away from Max. "You have to go."

"I'll try to come back."

Morgan raised an eyebrow at him. "You'd damn well better."

Max turned his gaze to the moon, let go of his control, and let the lunar rays transform him. He crashed to the ground.

Maximum Grim rose from the dirt, nine-feet-tall, midnight black fur shimmering in the silvery light of the moon. He bent down, nostrils flared, and sniffed Morgan. Poked his snout against her outstretched palm.

"Thank you. For everything." Morgan stroked his fur along his wolfen jawline.

The werewolf growled, soft and deep, and then turned and ran toward his pack.

Grim snarled at the couple of big werewolves that were wandering toward the taproom. He snapped at the thighs of one, pawed another across the shoulder. He dashed in a semi-circle, turning the beasts all in toward each other. He placed Abornazine just behind him to his right, his second-in-command, and together they pulled in the rest of the beasts. They fell in, turned together, and ran behind their leader, away from the taproom, toward the tall trees and the shadowy woods beyond.

Maximum Grim paused at the foot of the dark forest.

He looked to the north, where the pine and juniper trees wound deep into the mountains.

Then he looked into the dark sky and howled at the moon, and the rest of the pack joined in, werewolves and wild wolves together. Their calls were a bestial, nocturnal chorus. A dark, mystical symphony of ancient magic all their own that rolled across the valley and dissipated out into the Virginia autumnal night.

The townspeople emerged from the taproom, watching the werewolf pack howl.

A human female voice called out, howling up at the moon, adding her call to that of the werewolves.

And then a man howled. And then another. And another.

The whole town howled. In victory, in mourning, in gratitude and sorrow.

The calls echoed across the valley, bouncing off mountains and buildings alike. In homes across the town and farmhouses miles out, survivors of the earthquake ran to their windows, throwing them open, listening to the howls. Their dogs bounded to the windows and tilted their noses to the sky and joined the cries. It seemed every dog, coyote, and wolf in the whole valley cried to the moon then, in mourning of something they couldn't quite understand, but feeling it in their hearts, nonetheless.

Morgan let her tears fall onto Joey's body, let them wet his dry fur.

Grim dropped to all fours. Slowly, the calling died away. He raced into the woods, smelling the fresh pine needles, feeling the crunch of fall leaves under his paws, sensing prey and freedom and a chance at forgiveness in the cold mountain air.

His pack chased after him, hot on his heels.

Chapter 36

October Thirty-First, 7:09 a.m.

"This is National Guard Chopper 619, we have visual on Pineville, over."

"Copy that, 619, what do you see, over?"

"Most of the town is under standing water. We have visual on, uh, looks like the wreckage from the southern bridge. It's halfway down the Shenandoah River, twisted in pieces. We're circling the mountain pass highway, uh, looks like it's also inaccessible. We'll need major crews and equipment to reach the valley via the ground, over."

"Copy that. Any place to set down, over?"

"Uh, yes sir, there is a helipad on one of the buildings. Proceed to touch down, over?"

"Yes, affirmative. Touch down chopper 619. Reinforcement crews on their way. Begin search and rescue and report back. Over and out."

The helicopter descended onto the hospital roof. Once it landed, Vickie Williams and Sheriff Jeffrey, bandage wrapped around his forehead, emerged to meet the national guard pilots.

"Bout damn time," Vickie said, as a form of greeting, reaching out her hand and shaking the pilot's. "I'm Dr. Vickie Williams. We've got plenty of wounded, we need potable water as soon as possible, and we need to roof evac at least ten different families who've been stuck above their houses for close to twenty-four hours."

The pilot seemed taken aback. He turned to Sheriff Jeffrey, then turned back to Vickie. "Doctor, who's running search and rescue? Where is the mayor?"

"The mayor is dead. It's just me and Sheriff Jeffrey. Our only other deputy is on the other side of the mountain. I'm running the show now, so get used to it. Cuz I'm not slowing down for anybody, understand?"

****

October Thirty-First, 9:23 a.m.

Morgan entered the witch's garden with the emerald Arch wand. Ash and Vera followed behind her, stepping carefully around the pumpkins and the squash and the stalks of corn.

In the daytime, with the crisp autumn sky shining brilliant blue overhead, Vexulta's enchanted glen was not nearly as eerie. It looked charming and pristine, and frankly, positively magical.

As Morgan expected, she did not find a massive pile of rubble and ruin in the garden.

The cabin was rebuilt, as if it had never been damaged, spiraling up around the massive tree that grew at the center of the glen.

Vexulta, wearing her simple black robe, appearing as an elderly lady, dug calmly at the top of a pumpkin. The only difference in the woman from the prior day was that one of her legs was purplish and scaled.

Sitting next to Vexulta, a whole row of Jack O' Lantern's. Their faces smiled and scowled, some anguished in pain, others appeared to laugh joyfully.

Vexulta did not look up when the three witches entered into view. She said, rather whimsically, "Happy

Halloween, dearies. I wondered who it would be that would reenter my garden. My immortal sister, Cailleach, or the strange, human girl with the soft green eyes."

"Are you surprised?" Morgan responded.

"I can't say either of you would have surprised me." Vexulta looked up and smiled at Morgan. "I assumed that whoever it was that made it back here with my emerald would intend to vanquish me with it. Am I correct in my guess?"

"Yes," Morgan said, just as calmly, looking down at the swirling green emerald tied to a wooden tap handle. "But the reason for your fate is different, since it is I, not she."

"Yes," Vexulta said, scooping out heaps of pumpkin guts and tossing them into the soil in front of her. "I suppose that is true. Not sure if that makes much difference to me, but it is nice for you to believe that your morality is superior to hers."

Morgan smiled softly. "In this case, I know it is."

"Perhaps you do," Vexulta said. "And you spared the two other mortals, I see."

"For now," Morgan said, a half-grin drifting across her face. "We'll see how they do under new leadership in the coven."

Vexulta groaned as she set aside her hollowed out pumpkin. "I suppose, dearie, you would understand if I attempted to… defend myself?"

"I would expect it."

Vexulta slapped her hands on her knees and stood up slowly. She stretched, cracking her back, left and right. "Oh, I'm not sure. Maybe I've had enough of the glen. Maybe it's finally someone else's turn—"

Vexulta shot out her hands toward Morgan, purple,

oozing magic blasting toward her. Morgan trapped it within the emerald Arch wand. She drew a silver dagger from her waistbelt. She channeled all four strands of magic into the blade and stabbed it into the glimmering jewel. The emerald shattered into green dust.

Vexulta leaned back and sat down into the rocking chair behind her. "Well, that does it then." She stroked her chin. "All four strains have accepted you, Morgan, and you've harnessed them all. Really remarkable for a human. Whoever taught you… well, no matter. My spell books and tomes are all yours, if you want them. I could have taught you many new things… But I may have one day betrayed you. Hard to say. Have you told the girls who your father is? Or, should I say, what your father is?"

For the first time, Morgan was thrown off-center. Vexulta had mentioned her father but hadn't mentioned she knew who he truly was.

"I've known since before I ever laid eyes on you, dearie. Benjamin visited me, from time to time. Always looking for power or some such thing. Trivial, political things to me, I never bothered with them. I knew he angled for something from this valley and would attempt to extinguish me once he got what he wanted. But I enjoyed his company. He knew he couldn't best me. He recognized something in me. We were kindred spirits, you could say. Perhaps he recognized that one day his daughter might come to odds against me."

"Surely he'd want you to win that battle," Morgan sneered.

"Oh, I don't know about that, Morgan. He's a complicated creature. He came here with Vlad Cosmin. Between you, Cailleach, and the knight of the Silver

Dawn, he stirred up enough confusion to retrieve something in all the chaos. But you ended up destroying the Arch jewels, so I'm not sure exactly what he was after. Time will tell. Immortal Benjamin Shroud, the dark prince of the undead. As quick as he came, he disappeared just as fast. Like a mist in the night. He never does anything without a reason, does he, Morgan? Like changing his name every couple of centuries? Or changing the continent where his coffin is buried?"

Ash murmured, her voice hesitant, from behind Morgan, "You mentioned him, before. Benjamin Shroud. Who is he, Morgan?"

Morgan didn't respond. She kept her eyes on Vexulta.

"Should I tell them, dearie, the name they may be more familiar with? The very first name of vampire Benjamin Shroud?"

Vera drew in a sharp breath. Whispered, "Vampire?"

"Not just any vampire," Morgan sighed.

"Oh no, not just any vampire, dearies. Vlad Dracul, blood-fiend of Transylvania, immortal lord of Castle Dracula. Benjamin Shroud is just his humble moniker he dons when he visits the new world."

Morgan took a deep breath. Her father had been here and had left. Perhaps had known she'd been in Pineville from the very beginning. He hadn't wanted her dead, but he had used her, made her his puppet.

She'd have to deal with him, one day.

Well, probably, one night, after sunset, she'd have to deal with her father, Benjamin Shroud, Count Dracula, for the final time.

But first, she had a different immortal monster to

dispense with.

Morgan locked eyes with Vexulta, sister-daughter of The Fallen, Witch-Queen of the Blue Ridge.

"Go ahead, dearie. The sky is as blue as the sea, the fall leaves have all changed colors and fallen to the soil. A cool northern wind is blowing, but for right now, it feels rather nice, sitting in the sunshine. Now, on All Hallow's Eve, I think, will be as nice a time as any for me to go to the beyond."

Morgan flicked her fingers. She felt the golden aura in the air. Felt the trees exuding the warmth of the forest magic, an intermixing, intoxicating blend of Earth and Air and a touch of Water.

Morgan envisioned a golden sword in her mind, sharp as Maximum Grim's deep brown eyes, and summoned it into her hand. She ran Fire magic along its shimmering edge. Then she slashed it through Vexulta's neck.

The witch's head fell from her body, shattered into dust and pebbles when it hit the ground. The body turned to stone, tipped out of the rocking chair, and fell like a broken statue into the garden.

Morgan turned to Ash and Vera.

"Set down the cats, please." They dropped Shadow, Lancelot, and Galahad into the sunlit garden, where they immediately began pouncing on each other and rolling in the smells of the loamy soil.

"This is humiliating," Ash mumbled.

Vera said, "I think it is very generous." She looked around.

"Yes," Morgan said, looking at the verdant garden, at the many pumpkins and gourds, and then up at the massive spiraling cabin with its many odd-shaped rooms and asymmetrical windows. "I think with a few touches, it'll make for a charming home. Since you two let Hailey burn down my first house, this'll have to do…"

Morgan lifted her necklace. She'd added Joey's bone-shaped nametag from his collar to the diamond heart pendant Alex had given her. She kissed them both then trotted toward the stairs. "Come on, girls. We've got a lot to do if we're ever going to trust you with wands again."

Ash kicked at a small stone in the garden, pulled her hood up over her pink hair, and shoved her hands in her pockets. Vera beamed, the sunshine shimmering down through the canopy of the trees, casting her tan skin in a golden glow. They followed Morgan, daughter of Dracul, the new Witch-Queen of the Blue Ridge, up into her enchanted cabin in the woods.

Epilogue

December Twenty-Fifth, 8:37 a.m.

Snow piled up against the windows. It fell heavily overnight, and it didn't look like it would be stopping anytime soon. The multi-colored Christmas lights outside the window looked so much better when covered in a blanket of snow.

Morgan grinned.

A white Christmas.

She tossed back the blankets from her bed, scattering three cats and a small white and black puppy with a single stroke.

Something smelling cinnamon-y and yeasty drifted through the floorboards. Morgan opened her bedroom door and the animals all scattered out, a cat and a puppy heading up, higher in the cabin, no doubt excited to wake grumpy aunt Ash with a dose of licks and meows. Two other cats headed down, wanting to be let out to hunt rabbits in the snow.

Morgan trotted downstairs, following the smell until she dropped into the kitchen. Vera stirred a pot of something, and another spatula stirred a pot of something else, all on its own.

"What is that?" Morgan asked.

"It's a praline peanut crunch. And it won't be ready until tonight."

"No, not what is that delicious smell. What is that?" She pointed at the spatula stirring on its own.

Vera paused. "Uh, it is a spatula, Morgan."

"What did I say about magic?"

"Well, I thought, you'd be in a good mood today, *y tal vez*—"

"Christmas or not, we agreed, even the smallest doses of magic—"

"Not because of Christmas, Morgan. Because of him." Vera turned and pointed to the corner breakfast nook.

Max sat in the far chair, leaning back on two legs, watching Morgan. "Merry Christmas." She gasped. He smiled, adding, "I see you've found even more strays, and a bigger place to keep them."

"How dare you!" Morgan said, her mouth turning downward.

"How dare me?"

"How dare you sit there silently and let me stand here, blathering with Vera."

Morgan crossed to him. Max stood up, embraced her.

"Don't be shy," Morgan said, "I've waited nearly two months for you." She tugged his chin down to her, kissed him firmly on the mouth. He pulled back, to try to say something, but she held him firm, fingers wrapped around the back of his thick neck. She opened her lips against his and he kissed her harder, and for a moment Vera thought she may need to leave the kitchen and give them some privacy.

But Morgan relented, and Max pulled away and said, "I hope you don't mind, I have a couple more strays for you."

Max crossed to the front door and threw it open. In the front garden three werewolves snarled and play fought, tumbling in the snow. One was all gray fur and long, lanky limbs, another was spotted, brown and gray and white, and seemed almost as large as Max, and the third was the small, brown werewolf, Abornazine.

Max looked back at Morgan. "These three, I don't know if they'll ever be able to incorporate themselves back into society. They've been werewolves for hundreds of years. It will take a long, long time to bring them up to speed on the world, teach them a language…"

"*O dos lenguas*?" Vera chirped in from the stovetop.

"*Si*," Max said, "*Quizás dos lenguas.* It'll be a lengthy process." Max looked at Morgan seriously. "I hope that's okay. If it's not, I totally understand."

"Please, Max, you don't have to ask. There is always room here." She took his callused hand in hers and held it. "That's what this home is for. That's why we're still here."

"By the way," Max said, "I saw Dr. Vickie Williams won the special election for mayor. And Sheriff Jeffrey finally retired."

"Yes, it's been an interesting two months in Pineville. Craig was nominated to be the new sheriff, but he swears he doesn't want it. I'm not sure if I believe him. We've been mostly staying out of it." Morgan nodded her head toward Vera, and then upstairs. "No one is ready to see these two anytime, soon."

Vera said solemnly, "We will earn our forgiveness. We don't deserve it, yet."

Morgan said, "You keep cooking like you do and you'll earn it far earlier than Ash, I'll tell you that much. Max, maybe tomorrow we can swing by The Dugout and grab a well-earned celebratory drink. Better late than never for you. Philip has brewed a bunch of new beer. I think you might like to try some of them."

"Oh yeah?"

"Werewolf's Bane. A dark chocolate imperial stout, poured through an honest-to-goodness silver tap."

Max smiled. "Seriously?"

"Or you could try Craig's new favorite, the Wendigo red ale."

"They didn't name it that!"

"They also have an Enchanted Emerald berliner weisse, complete with mystical 'witch-blood' elderflower syrup to turn the beer green."

"Really leaning into it all, huh?"

"Oh yeah, and you'll never guess their number one best-seller."

"What's that?"

"Joey's Good Boy Lager." Morgan's eyes watered slightly, and she laughed, wiping her tears away. "The town drinks the hell out of that beer."

"I bet," Max said, and he pulled her toward him again, and kissed her again, and the snow fell silently outside the window onto the werewolves in the enchanted garden below.

****

Max and Morgan will return soon…